Dark World:
Oblivion

Dark World Saga

The Alex and Jay Chronicles Book 2

A.R. Kingston

Keen Quill Press
Denver, Co

A.R. Kingston/Keen Quill Press
8547 E Arapahoe Rd
Ste. J-397
Greenwood Village, CO 80112
Arkingston.com

Publisher's Note: This is a work of fiction. Names, characters, places, and incidents are a product of the author's imagination. Locales and public names are sometimes used for atmospheric purposes. Any resemblance to actual people, living or dead, or to businesses, companies, events, institutions, or locales is completely coincidental.

Book Layout ©2017 BookDesignTemplates.com

Ordering Information:
Quantity sales. Special discounts are available on quantity purchases by corporations, associations, and others. For details, contact the "Special Sales Department" at the address above.

Dark World: Oblivion/ A.R. Kingston -- 1st ed.
ISBN 978-1-7342400-3-0

Dedicated to all the rebels, the misfits, and anyone who dares to not fit in.

Is it a sin to find beauty in the darkness?
To watch as the night sky comes alive with the eyes of the gods
To listen as the forest whispers centuries old secrets
To find solace as shadows dance the same dance they have for
eons
Powerful things lurk in the darkness and it is a sin to forget
them

−A Modern Catastrophe

Contents

CHAPTER 1

A New Beginning

Looking out the window, watching the green hills roll by as the train clanked along on its tracks, Alexandra rested her head on her hand and marveled at the view sprawling before her. They had been in Ashland for a few days, but she still could not get used to all the sights and sounds of this unfamiliar world. Fiddling with the plain silver band on her left ring finger, she re called everything that happened once they got off the boat at Clear Springs.

Once they disembarked at the docks, the dockhands ushered them into a small, red brick building with magnificent white pillars flanking the mahogany wood doors. There, they stood in line to talk to one of the Ashland officials checking people in. They must have stood there for a good hour or so as Andy was beginning to get cranky and had started to whine. Scooping the boy up in her arms, Alex soothed him as they waited for a clerk to open up, hoping it would not be much longer.

When their time came, they walked up to a small window at a wood counter and Jay handed the man in a blue uniform their paperwork. Glancing at the papers, the clerk raised an eyebrow and looked over at them with wide eyes. Returning his gaze to the papers, the man glanced over them a few more times before excusing himself. Alex was beginning to worry that something had gone wrong and that she would be on a ship bound back for Vega shortly, where Quinton would be waiting for her, sure to behead her for what she had done.

As Alex was glancing about for a way out of the building, the clerk returned with a short, portly man in tow and pointed over to the three of them standing there. This strange man had a similar blue uniform on, but it was covered in patches, so Alex knew right away he was an important official and that something was not right. Coming over to them, holding their papers in his hands, the officer smiled politely and looked at Alexandra.

"Miss. Hamilton, is it?"

"Yes." She replied rather nervously as she stole a glance towards the door, wondering if she should make a run for it.

"May I have a word with you in my office?" The officer continued smiling, paying no attention to the panicked look in her eyes.

Alarm bells went off in her head and Alex wondered how far she would make it if she was to try to escape. Glancing over at Jay, she swallowed hard, begging him with her eyes to save her, or at the very least, tell her what to do. Taking Andy from her arms into his, Jay gave her a gentle nod, and she returned her gaze to the officer in front of them. Alex still did not want to be separated from Jay or Andy, but they left her with little choice but to comply.

"I guess." She mumbled and glanced down at her feet.

"Good. Now, if you would follow me." The officer smiled at Alex before turning to Jay and giving him a tip of his hat. "Mr. Hartwood, you may sit over there with your son while Miss. Hamilton and I have a chat in my office. This shouldn't take long, I promise."

Taking Andy, Jay shuffled over to one of the worn wooden benches lining the brick walls and sat down. Having no choice left, Alexandra reluctantly followed the officer in through an imposing walnut door into the man's office. The compact square space with blank, cream walls made goosebumps creep up her arm as it appeared almost sterile and unwelcoming. Not even so much as a picture hung on the walls that swallowed up the only four pieces of furniture in the room.

She glanced at a window behind an old, tidy oak desk before trailing her eyes to a small, plush, periwinkle chair that the officer motioned for her to sit down in. Complying, Alex lowered herself on to the cushion and glanced about the enclosed space. Steadying her breath, she held her hands in her lap, fidgeting uncomfortably as she looked out at the city which lay beyond the window and across the inlet of the small island they were on.

Without saying a word, the officer moved behind his desk and plopped down in his aged, brown leather chair. Placing the paperwork in front of him, he glanced over the pages and rubbed his temples with his fingers. Rubbing his eyes, he placed his hands in front of his face and glanced up at Alex with a serious look before letting out a heavy sigh.

"Am I to understand that Mr. Hartwood is your fiancé, Miss. Hamilton?"

"Yes, sir."

"Miss." The officer frowned as he glanced at the paperwork again. Placing his hands down at the desk, he took in a deep breath and briefly closed his eyes before returning his gaze at Alex. "I don't know how to tell you this, but, are you aware that your intended is a half-blood?"

"Of course I am, what kind of question is that?"

"And you still intend to marry him?" The man raised his eyebrow as he fell back in his chair with his hand pressed against his chest.

"Yes, why wouldn't I?"

"Look, young lady, I'm not sure what it is that you are running from, but I get it. Vega is not a suitable place for a young pure-blood woman to live in, especially not one who holds the unfortunate status of being a royal." The officer pressed his lips together and leaned forward as he looked for the best way to say what he wished to say. "I just want to assure you, that whatever it is that you wish to get away from, we can help. We have people in place, and programs to set you up with a house, job, and give you a new identity. There is no need for you to go through the trouble of marrying the man out there. I'm not sure what he told you to convince you to try to pull off this stunt, but rest assured, you don't need to comply with him to be safe in Ashland."

"What?" Alex frowned. "You are the one who doesn't understand. I want to marry him. I love him."

"Ma'am do you even understand what you are getting yourself into here? Can you comprehend what you will have to endure beyond these walls with him? There has never been a record in the history of Ashland of anyone marrying a half-blood, especially not a pure-blood such as yourself. I don't even know if what you request can legally happen."

"Well, I don't care. I am not leaving here until I am free to marry Jay."

The officer looked over at Alex gravely and shook his head. The look in those green eyes of hers was stern and unwavering, making the man feel compelled to try and help the woman out. Shaking head once more, he picked up the phone receiver on his desk, and started spinning the dial with his fingers. Alex watched him sit there in silence with the brass tube pressed to his ear until she heard a click on the other end and the officer began to speak.

"Yes, hello, can you put me through to the Grand Commander right away... No, you don't understand. This is Officer Mauru over at the Livingston Island terminal. I have a rather peculiar situation on my hands, one I am not equipped to handle. I must get the Commander's insight on this right away. It is of the utmost urgency."

Silence followed his last words, and the officer looked up at Alex, attempting to give her a reassuring smile before another click beckoned him back to the receiver. "Yes, Grand Commander, Sir, thank you for speaking with me. I have a huge problem here at arrivals... Well, you see, I have a pure-blood woman from Vega, well actually, she's the missing princess of Manevia... Anyway, the problem is that she is insisting on getting married to a half-blood... yes, he is one of ours... What? Are you sure?... Yes, of course, I understand, thank you sir."

Officer Mauru smiled from ear to ear as he hung the ear tube back on the side of the phone and pushed the apparatus back to the corner of his desk. Gathering up the paperwork, he opened the corner of his desk and took out a large, round stamp, placing a red mark on all three papers. Tapping the papers on his desk to push them together, he got up from his seat and glanced over at Alex, motioning for her to stand up.

"You are in luck, my dear girl. Seems like your marriage has been approved by the East Ashland Grand Commander himself. It is with great pleasure that I welcome you to Clear Springs. Now, if you will follow me, I think we have a couple of people waiting for you outside my office."

Trailing behind the officer with a light heart, Alex thanked her lucky stars for averting what could have easily been a disaster. Whoever this Grand Commander was, she was thankful that he did not find a problem with their relationship and approved of their union. Breathing out a small sigh, Alex spotted Jay on the bench not far from her. Running over to him, she leaped into his arms, and he held on to her for dear life. Coming up behind them, Officer Mauru handed Jay the paperwork and tipped his hat.

"The ferry for the mainland leaves in about an hour, Sir. If the two of you can't wait that long to get married, we have a small chapel on site, right outside those doors. Please leave your permanent address with the officials at the Clear Springs immigration office once you get settled. Best of luck to the both of you. Gods know you're going to need it."

Nodding, Jay took the paperwork from the man and smiled politely as he too was relieved that things were not as bad as they looked at first. Giving the couple one last tip of his hat, Officer Mauru went back to his office, shaking his head at the spectacle he had been a witness to. Never in his life could he have imagined that he would be privy to such a historic event, and as he walked, he prayed that things would work out for the princess and the half-blood.

Once the man was out of sight, Jay embraced Alex in his arms, holding her tight for fear that she may slip away if he was to let go. Alex found it difficult to breathe as he continued to hug her, but she did not mind one bit. At least now she knew nothing would stand between them again.

Releasing Alex from his grasp, Jay looked at her earnestly. "So what do you say babe, will you come be my wife?"

"Absolutely, let's do this."

Taking hold of Alexandra's hand, Jay pulled her along through the door to the warmth of the outside world. Squinting her eyes, Alex spotted the small white chapel outside. Its short steeple was just tall enough to touch the great stone behemoth rising up on the other side of the shore. Not stopping to admire the view, Jay tugged her along until they walked through a set of oak doors into the chapel's modest interior. Greeting them with a warm, friendly smile was an older man, with graying hair in a long, white robe who asked them how he could be of service.

Having explained everything to the priest, he ushered the pair over to a glass display case containing bands of various sizes and styles. Jay wanted to get Alex something fancy and beautiful, but she refused, settling instead on a pair of matching plain silver bands. With their rings picked out, the chaplain quickly drew up the necessary paperwork and guided them into his chamber for a more private ceremony. Once the vows were said, all they had to do was prick their fingers and sign the papers in their blood to make it official.

By the time they were done at the chapel, the ferry had already pulled into the harbor. Not wishing to miss their chance to get off the island, they rushed to get on board before it departed. Settling down in a seat on the top deck close to the railing, the new couple, with their child and a pigrie was bound for the Clear Springs mainland a few short minutes away.

Once the boat docked on the other side, Alex stepped off into a bustling city street full of cars and streetcars chugging by, and instantly felt lost. Never in her life had she envisioned a world of self-propelled carriages and grays mingling with the pure-bloods going about their day. Not to mention she never thought she could have a life there as a free woman with a man of her own choosing.

Nudging Alex along, Jay walked with her and Andy to the nearest hotel overlooking the harbor. Having rested for a few days to recover from their journey and having explored some of the sites the city had to offer, the couple tracked down Richard's uncle, who gave them a phone number to call. Having finally learned how to use the telephone from Jay, Alex dialed the number on the paper in her hands and waited for someone to answer.

To her surprise, an elated Richard picked up the receiver on the other end after a call from his uncle. Having recalled everything that happened to her friend, Alex was told that the three of them should come and live over in Fall Harbor. Richard was working there as the secretary for the mayor of said province and would not only be able to get the new family a great place to live, but also set Jay up with a job. Eager to live some place where she had people she knew, Alex convinced Jay to move there, and he gladly obliged despite it being his old home and a place full of terrible memories. This was how they ended up where they were now, in a private car of a steam train bound for Fall Harbor.

Alex was still admiring the ever-changing scenery of rushing rivers and rolling green hills, all the while wondering what their new life would be like once they got to where they were going. Looking over at his wife's peaceful face staring out the window, Jay allowed himself to smile as his heart fluttered in his chest. He still could not believe the girl was his, and he was now praying his luck would not run out. Taking hold of her delicate hand in his, he brought it to his lips and gave it a soft kiss.

"Everything okay, sweetheart?"

"What a silly question." Alex turned away from the window to look at Jay and frowned. "Why wouldn't it be?"

"You were staring out into space, so I was beginning to worry that you were starting to have regrets over marrying me." Jay rubbed her hand and fidgeted in his seat. "We still haven't you know, made it fully official yet, so if you want to back out of it now, I'll understand."

That's right, thought Alex, as she stole a glance over at Andy who was sleeping next to her on the seat with a brown pigrie curled up on his soft, blonde hair. The two of them were yet to consummate their marriage, but how could they? It was not ex-actly easy traveling with a small child and living in hotel rooms. This was something she understood well, so she didn't push the issue, though looking at it now she could see why Jay found it concerning. Wishing to reassure him that she was not going to run, Alex squeezed his hand tightly in hers and brought it up to nuzzle it with her soft cheek.

"I would never change my mind about you love, I promise. I was simply admiring the beautiful scenery outside. I still can't get used to this land of yours that I now find myself in, and this free-dom which it granted me."

"Yes," Jay smiled, "I keep forgetting that you are like a small child when it comes to everything East Ashland has to offer."

"Why I never!" Alex pouted as she turned her head away from Jay before he had the chance to notice how embarrassed she was.

Jay just chuckled and turned her face back towards him as he peered deep into her eyes. "I did not mean it like that, darling. I think it's cute how much wonder you get out of being here, it makes me feel young again."

"You don't have to say it like that though." Alex frowned as she gazed into his deep blue eyes and melted, "I already feel child- ish enough being around you. I don't want you to think I'm too immature for you or something."

"Is that what you're worried about?" Jay snorted, waking Cosmo up from his nap, who grumped and narrowed his eyes at the man. "Silly girl, I'd never think that of you. And don't you worry love, I'll make a fully mature woman out of you yet."

Jay gave Alex a playful wink, and she felt herself starting to blush. She had always tried to picture what being with him would be like, but every time she did, she would get flustered and had to stop. As she was beginning to think of their first night together again, Alex saw a small, yellow train house with a red roof and a copper dome come into view. A small weathervane in the shape of a jackalope swayed in the breeze, and the faint light of the plat- form greeted the train which was starting to come to a crawl. Far from the white, granite behemoth that they departed from in Clear Springs, this one looked more like something you would find over in Vega, if trains were actually a thing there.

With the screeching of the wheels and a puff of steam, the train came to a halt outside a single platform swarming with peo- ple. Andy woke up and sat up, rubbing his eyes as he peered outside to the town which would serve as his new home. Taking hold of Andy's hand, Alex exited the train with the rest of the passengers and stood on the platform, glancing around the sea of people until she spotted Richard.

He looked the same as the day she watched him get on the dingy bound for the military vessel after she broke him out of prison. He had one hand in the pocket of his gray tweed pants as he glanced over at the pocket watch with his chocolate eyes. His dark brown hair swayed with the breeze, and he glanced up to look around for her in the crowd. Alex stood planted in her spot and waved her arm, calling out to him, until he finally spotted her and smiled. Swimming through the crowed, Richard ran over to her and scooped her in his arms. Embracing her tightly, he spun her around as she giggled while people around them looked on with scowls on their face.

"Goodness!" Richard beamed as he placed Alex down on the ground and looked over her. "Aren't you a sight for sore eyes."

"Hello, Richard." Alex continued to giggle, "I missed you too."

"Hey!" Scowled Jay as he tapped Richard on the shoulder. "Didn't anyone teach you it's rude to hug another man's wife?"

"I'm sorry, what was I thinking." Richard let Alex go and bowed apologetically to the two of them. "Forgive me, Mrs. Hartwood, I forgot that congratulations were in order."

"Why thank you, Richard. But I think we can forgive you under the circumstances. Can't we, Jay?"

"Yeah, I guess. Thanks, Richard." Jay said gruffly as he wrapped his arm around Alex. "Now, I was told you would have a house ready for us when we got here?"

"Yes, that is certainly the case, my friend. Come now," Richard moved forward while waving his hand, "follow me. I have a car waiting for us outside the station?"

"A car?" Alex gasped. She had seen plenty of cars in Clear Springs, but from what she understood, they were a bit on the pricey side, and far more than Richard could afford. "How fancy of you."

"Oh, it's not mine. I borrowed it from my boss, along with his chauffeur. Once he learned who the two of you were, he insisted I pull out all the stops and offer you the best hospitality our humble town has to offer. You see, the two of you are kind of a big deal around here, everyone wants to catch a glimpse of you."

"Us? Really? But why?"

"Come on, Alex. You are the first pure-blood in recent history to marry a half-blood, you can't expect people to not take notice. Not to mention, you are the former princess of Manevia, and Jay has a bit of a history around here, so you are bound to attract a lot of curiosity."

"I guess you're right." Alex frowned and peeked at Jay, who was grimacing beside her. "Perhaps after we settle in, you can introduce us to your boss? I would love to meet him and thank him personally for his hospitality."

"I plan on it. I promised the mayor that much. But for now, let's get you to your new house, all three of you look exhausted from your journey. I think you'll like this little place, it's right up Jay's alley."

"Yeah, whatever." Jay grumbled. "We'll just see about that."

Walking off the platform behind Richard, Alex stood on the polished wood floors of the small train house looking over the two ticket counters and the handful of seats containing people. Not waiting for her to finish admiring the sights, Richard guided her out the front door into the warmth of the evening air laced with the succulent scent of Wisteria blossoms coming off from the street.

Looking up, Alex saw a black automobile parked under one of the trees lining the road, with purple petals draping over its slick curves. One of the lamps glowing by the tree dropped its light onto the curved fender, bouncing up to make Alex squint. The car puffed out white steam and its round headlights shone into the distance as it waited for them to get inside.

Getting closer to their ride, Alex noted a spare tire by the passenger door and a winged, naked lady riding at the tip of the hood. She wanted to touch the polished paint of the door, but Richard swung it open and allowed his friends to climb inside. Sitting behind the passenger seat, she watched her friend climb into the front of the car, and slam his door firmly behind him.

"Lawrence," he said, turning to the man in a black bowler hat beside him. "This is my friend Alex, and her husband Jay."

Turning around, the man in the driver's seat regarded the three of them closely. He wasn't old, but his face showed signs of wear and fatigue. His pale green eyes turned to Alex and traced every square inch of her body, making her squirm in her seat. Smirking, Lawrence shot a look back at Jay before he turned to face Richard with a toothy grin.

"So, this be the fine ass lass you let slip through your fingers, eh Richard?"

"Hey!" Jay snapped. "Watch how you talk about my wife." He swung his hand at Lawrence, knocking his hat clean off. "You best apologize to her for what you said."

"Don' you be gettin' feisty with me tough guy." Lawrence turned to scowl at Jay. "Just sayin' how fine your wife be, no offense in that." He slicked back his light brown hair and placed his hat back on his head. "Though I am sorry if I offended you, lass, I meant you no harm." Turning away from the couple in the back seat, he gripped the steering wheel and glanced out into the darkness beyond the windshield. "So chief, where to?"

"The old tavern."

"What?" Lawrence jumped in his seat as he turned his head to Richard. "They be livin' in that cursed place? Have you gone mad lad, I thought they be your friends."

"They are, and it's a nice old house. Plus, Jay was a barkeep back in Winter Haven, if anyone can revive that old place it be him."

"Yeah," the driver snorted, "if they stick 'round long enough that is."

"Richard, what is he talking about?" Alex glanced over at Lawrence nervously as she tapped her friend's shoulder. "Why wouldn't we stick around?"

"Nothing, don't worry about it. Folks around these parts get awfully superstitious at times, that's all. Isn't that right, Jay?"

"Yeah..." Jay murmured as he turned to look out his window, "something like that."

Without saying another word, Richard nodded for Lawrence to get moving. Shaking his head, the driver threw the car in gear and it chugged along, bouncing as they drove down the street of pressed river rocks. Glancing out her window as they drove along the Wisteria lined streets, Alex admired the houses made of brick, wood, or stone. Everything was so different there, far from the life she had grown accustomed to in Manevia. Elated at the prospect of a clean start, she watched as they turned down a narrow street, and the name on the sign caught her eye instantly.

"Forget-me-not Lane?"

"Ah, yes." Richard piped up happily, glad to finally have something positive to talk about. "Around thirty or so years back, forget-me-nots began to bloom all along this street. No matter what anyone did, the flowers always came back as if by magic. So, instead of trying to fight it, the townsfolk agreed to let them be and remained the street to match the strange occurrence."

"How utterly fascinating." Alex murmured as she observed the clusters of blue flowers lining the streets. "And to think, I just happen to love forget-me-nots."

Nodding, Richard smiled to himself at this odd coincidence which he was already aware of and leaned to glance out his window. The car continued to rumble along for a few minutes longer before coming to an abrupt halt, causing Alex to jolt forward. Looking out Jay's window, she could see that they sat in front of a magnificent three-story brick house with a single-story tavern attached to the side. The white trim and window shutters stood out against the rust colored exterior, making the place feel more like home. At the center, a bright red door with 777 in brass numbers screwed neatly to its surface welcomed her to walk inside.

Stumbling out from the car, Alex headed through the door, and instantly felt like she belonged. Without realizing it, she knew the exact layout of the house as she glanced around the wood lined foyer. The wallpaper was navy blue, as it should have been, and a small, round table stood by the stairs with a single, cream hurricane lamp sitting lit on its surface.

Not waiting for his parents, Andy bounded up the stairs in wonder to check out how huge the place was. Standing with her arms crossed at first, Alex budged from her spot by the stairs and moseyed over into the living room across from the door to the tavern. Looking at the white stone fireplace at the heart of the room, she felt warm inside. A cream, floral sofa and a furry white rug before a crackling fire were a welcome sight, and Alex smiled at how much she thought she missed this place. In the corner of the room she spotted an old phonograph, gathering dust from years of neglect. Sauntering over to it, Alex pushed the pin into place and a record began to play a gentle melody which moved her soul.

"This place came furnished." Standing in the doorway, Richard looked over at Alex and smiled. "But we can always change out the furniture for something that better suits your tastes."

"No," Alex whirled around to look at him, "no need. It's perfect just the way it is."

"If you say so." Richard shrugged, not daring to question Alexandra's poor tastes. "Anyway, I better let the two of you settle in, you've had a long trip getting here, I will check in on you later and set up that meeting with the mayor that we talked about."

"All right." Alex nodded. "It was nice to see you again, Richard."

"You too love. See you around."

Turning on his heels, Richard walked out the door, shutting it behind him. Finally alone, Alex leaned against the wall as she continued to listen to the silky song of the piano flowing out from the phonograph, making her body sway. Coming in from the foyer, Jay wrapped her in his arms, holding her close and placed a soft kiss on her head. Melting into his arms, Alex felt the universe coming together around her. She knew she was where she belonged, and she could have stayed in his arms forever like that, if it was not for Andy coming bounding down the stairs.

"Mama! Papa! Look what I found." Andy shoved a bright red rubber ball up for his parents to see.

"Where did you get that?" Alex frowned, looking at the object she seemed to recall rather well.

"Upstairs in my new room." Andy jumped around the hall. "You should see it! It's wonderful, and big, and full of toys."

"What's wrong, sweetheart?" Jay brushed a hair from Alexandra's face. "Frowning like that doesn't suit your beautiful face."

"I'm sorry, it's nothing." Alex forced herself to smile. "It's just, there is something strange about that ball... this whole place actually, but I'm sure it's nothing, just the imagination of a woman who is exhausted from all the traveling."

"All right, if you say so." Jay furrowed his brow. "But be sure to tell me if something's wrong. I wouldn't want anything to trouble you."

"No trouble. Really." Alex smiled and looked at Andy, who glanced at her with sparking puppy eyes.

"Mama. Can I go outside and play with the ball?"

"Sorry young man, but it's far too late to be playing games. It's upstairs and straight to bed for you."

"Aww. But Mama."

"No buts, you can play with that ball tomorrow, now up you go. I'll be right behind you to tuck you and Cosmo in."

Pouting, Andy went up the stairs, still clutching the ball as Cosmo floated up beside him. Following behind them, Alex went up the wood stairs and paused to glance around the long hall lit only by the soft lights of the lanterns. Despite neither the boy, nor the pigrie being in sight, she knew exactly where they would be, and she turned to head for the room at the opposite end of the hall.

Strolling in, she glanced about Andy's room and it was precisely as she pictured it would be. The powder blue walls were still decorated with paintings of various animals, and a single bed sat situated between the two windows which looked out at the street below. Toys were sprawled out on the floor as if they were left there in a haste, while books still gathered dust on a small shelf above the bed.

Sheer yellow curtains fluttered in the breeze coming in through the open windows and Alex glance at Andy who was already laying in the wood bed with a colorful patch quilt draped over him. Walking over to give the boy a kiss on the forehead, she turned off his lamp and told him a story to help him fall asleep. Once the boy and the pigrie were snoring soundly, she left and made her way back down the stairs, trying hard to figure out why she felt as if she was returning to this place after a long absence.

CHAPTER 2

The Fury of Love

Walking through the wood arch to the living room, Alex traced her finger on the chair rail, leaving a trail of dark wood in the dust under her finger. Stopping by the old phonograph, she listened to the music for a few moments longer, allowing the melody to awaken a strange tingle in her heart. Shaking her head, she pushed the needle off the recording, and the room went silent, with nothing but a lone cricket to keep her company.

Not wishing to be alone with her thoughts any longer, Alex went to find Jay, and she knew exactly where he would be. Pushing open the door next to the stairs a crack, she peeked through to the other side, where Jay was cleaning the glasses behind the bar, with his back turned to her. Sneaking up behind him, Alex reached around his back and plucked the glass out of his hands, placing it on the counter before him.

"Hey, what gives?" Jay turned to regard Alex with a smirk. "I was cleaning that you know."

"Yes." Alex ran her slender fingers through his golden, shoulder-length locks. "And you can continue to clean it tomorrow. Tonight, you will make love to your wife."

Stunned, Jay looked at her, his deep blue eyes glistening with the pale light as his pupils dilated slightly. He felt himself getting harder, and he did not know if he should run, or surrender to the inevitable. Ignoring the look on Jay's face, Alex grabbed him by the collar and pulled him in closer, giving him a deep kiss. Wrapping his arms tightly around her, he returned her affection as he pressed himself against her, savoring her delicate lips.

Without saying a single word, Jay scooped her up in his arms. Holding her close, he continued to kiss her as he shuffled towards the door leading into the house. Pushing his back against the wooden slab, he carried her inside and headed up the stairs to their room. With every step he took, Jay's heart pounded faster in his chest, causing the blood to rush into his head, and his lungs to tighten. By the time he slipped through the bedroom door, his head was swimming with euphoria, his pants grew uncomfortably tight, and he found himself panting heavily.

Placing Alex down to her feet, Jay caressed her face before going to lock their door. With no possibility of being interrupted, he turned his attention back to her, giving her a deep, passionate kiss. Wrapping her in his arms, Jay continued to kiss her before parting from her sweet lips and trailing his kisses down, stopping only to suck on the sensitive spot on her neck. Unable to control herself, Alex let out a deep moan as her body shivered with delight, and she clung to Jay, fearing that her knees would give out beneath her.

"That's my girl." Jay said in his usual husky voice. "You know just what to do to turn me on."

Continuing to suck on her neck, Jay reached behind her, sliding the zipper of her dress down to the small of her back. Trailing his arms back up her bare skin, he placed his hand under the sleeves of the gown, slipping it off her onto the floor. The air caressed her naked skin and Alex instantly became aware of how exposed she was. Reaching her arms around herself in a tight hug, she attempted to cover as much of her exposed body as she could, not knowing why she felt so embarrassed. Glancing at her reddening face, Jay smirked and pulled her arms apart, pinning them to her side while kissing her.

"Now, now, don't hide." He leaned in to whisper in her ear. "I did not get a good look last time, so I want to savor every inch of that gorgeous body of yours now that it's mine."

Growing hot, Alex closed her eyes and allowed herself to relax as Jay kissed her neck and traced the curves of her body with his fingertips. Feeling aroused, she bit her lip and reached up to undo the buttons on his shirt, pushing it off him to land by their feet. Staring at his muscular physic in the moonlight, she felt her breathing get heavier. Hungering for his touch, Alex fumbled with his belt, until she managed to rip his pants off him, allowing them to drop unceremoniously to the floor.

Steadying her breath, Alexandra's heart raced as she traced the ripples of his body with her fingers, memorizing every part of him with her skin. She could no longer deny how much she wanted him, and she glanced up into his waiting eyes, begging him to take her. With the starvation in her eyes calling him to her, Jay picked Alex back up. Feverishly kissing her lips, he carried her to the bed and laid her down gently on its cushy peach comforter. As he climbed on top of her, Alex parted her legs to allow him closer, feeling his erection against her lace panties, right where she needed it to be.

Removing Alexandra's bustier, Jay looked over the two luscious mounds on her chest. Groaning softly, he cupped one of her breasts and it fit perfectly in the palm of his hand. Pressing a small nipple between his finger, Jay played with it, and a robust shiver ran down Alex's spine as she gasped with the delightful new sensation. Ravenous to get a taste of her nectar, Jay trailed kisses down her side, stopping at her leg.

Lifting his head to look at Alex, Jay shot her a mischievous grin before he went back up to her knee. Rubbing her silky skin with his goatee, he allowed her to giggle before kissing the inside of her leg all the way down to her sweet spot. Putting his face between her legs, he savored her sensual honeysuckle scent. Nuzzling her panties, he tugged at the lace fabric with his teeth and noticed it was soaked through with her sweet extract, which tasted like honey.

Swelling with an overwhelming desire to explore her depth, Jay kissed her other leg back up until he was gazing down on Alex who was panting on the mattress, looking up at him with her bedroom eyes. No longer able to control the scorching need inside him, Jay ripped the remainder of their clothing off, tossing it across the room. Breathlessly, he climbed back on top of her, settling between her legs as he gazed in her eyes sparkling with the light of the moon. Giving her a long, deep kiss, he stroked her hair and leaned in to whisper in her ear.

"Are you sure you want this?"

Trembling from anticipation, all Alex could do was nod while biting down on her bottom lip. Reassured, and unable to wait any longer, Jay positioned himself at her opening and stole one last glance at her before he leaned back over to lie on top of her.

"All right," he whispered in her ear, "this is going to hurt a bit, but I promise I will be as gentle as possible."

As Jay eased himself inside, Alex gasped loudly from the pain. Clinging tightly to his big, muscular arms, a searing hot sensation spread through her body, and she arched her back, trying her best to accommodate his girth. At first, she thought of asking him to stop, but at the same time she did not want him to, she needed to feel him no matter how much agony it caused her. But as Jay slid fully inside, the sharp pain gave way to a dull throb, and she allowed herself to melt into the mattress as he raised himself up to look at her.

Wiping the moist specks glistening from the corners of her eyes, Jay leaned down and kissed her. Feeling her walls tightening around him, he began to rock slowly back and forth, and Alex moved along with him. Closing his eyes, he groaned softly as her buttery-soft skin wrapped even tighter around him. Her moans were like siren calls, beckoning him to dive deeper into the ocean of her flesh, and Jay thrust harder as he tried to keep up with her bewitching song.

Gripping his broad back, Alex pulled him in closer, digging her nails into his back as he continued to drive himself deeper into her. Jay was beginning to sweat, and the musk of perspiration intermixed with his cologne to create an elixir so exotic that Alex could not help but surrender to its intoxicating effects. Drunk on the smell of his masculine perfume and the pleasure of him rubbing against her, she allowed the waves of ecstasy to come crashing through her body as she convulsed under him.

Sensing her delicate frame shudder beneath him, Jay allowed himself to release the tension building up at his core, exploding inside her with a groan. Collapsing on top of her glistening body, panting, Jay still felt the lingering of passion in his loins as he leaned over to give her an ardent kiss, before pulling away to stroke her hair.

"So, this is what it's supposed to be like." Jay whispered as he gave Alex a pained look before sliding off her and kissing her again. "I never once imagined how bad I screwed up until now. I'm so sorry, Alex."

"What for?"

"For being me. For not being able to give you what you gave to me, what you deserve. I can't believe I was foolish enough to give myself over to that woman first. She couldn't even love me for who I was. I should have just waited for you, and I feel like I failed you somehow, or broke a sacred vow. This, like the rest of my past, is something I can't change, no matter how much I want to, and it makes me feel like a failure."

"You know, Jay..." Alex rolled over onto her side to gaze at him while playing with the soft hair on his chest and let out a small sigh. "Without your past, we would not have a future."

"What are you talking about?"

"Think about it, without going to prison, you would have never met the doctor and came to Vega. And if you never had Andy, you wouldn't have stayed behind. And if you never stayed, you would have never ended up in Winter Haven. If you never owned that tavern, we would not have met. Your past, no matter how dark and painful, led you right to where you needed to be." Alex leaned over to kiss Jay's cheek before continuing to look in his eyes as she held his hand. "I know you have a hard time accepting who you were, but it's the old you who ensured that the four of us would end up together. And for that, I'm grateful, because I can't imagine my life without you."

"Did I ever tell you that you are too easy on me woman?" Shaking his head, Jay leaned over to give Alex another kiss. "I love that about you."

"And I love everything about you. Don't you forget that."

Snuggling up to Jay, Alex allowed him to hold her as he drifted off to sleep. Laying in his arms, staring up at the ceiling, she pondered at how comfortable this all felt. Their first time didn't feel like their first time, it felt like home, like they had been with one another countless times before. Everything about being with him made her feel comfortable and safe, and as she fell asleep in their bed, wrapped in Jay's arms, Alex couldn't help but think she was finally back where she belonged.

CHAPTER 3

A New Friend

The rays of the sun streamed through the window, warming her skin, as Alex was awakened by something nuzzling against her bare shoulder. Fluttering open her heavy eyelids, she smiled as she realized it was Jay's soft goatee tickling her skin. Shifting under the soft sheets, Alex realized she was not wearing any clothing and fondly recalled the events of the previous night. As the memories lingered in her mind, she felt herself blush and grew hot at her core.

"What are you doing Jay, it's still early?" Alex mumbled as she rolled over to caress his face.

"I know..." he kissed her neck before parting her lips with his tongue and tailing his hand up her side "... but we are the only ones up, and I want you."

Surrendering to his whim, Alex slipped one leg under him, bringing his body between her thighs. Inhaling her breath, Jay slid inside, getting instantly surrounded by the warmth of her cavern. Her arms were heaven, her body, the welcoming shores of his homeland, and in Alex, he felt like he was melting into eternity. It was as if he was becoming one with the universe itself, getting swallowed up by the cosmos. Closing his eyes, Jay rocked his hips slowly, savoring this moment with her for as long as he could.

Accommodating him with the motions of her body, Alex released the chains binding her soul, allowing herself to feel the unrestrained passion he granted her. Entranced by the pleasure she got from him; she ran her hands over his bare body until Jay finally released his essence inside her. With his touch still lingering on her skin, Alex looked up and brushed a wet strand of blonde hair which matted itself to his face. Leaning down to taste the sweetness of her lips, Jay entwined his body with hers, and they lay there cuddling until the clock tower outside struck seven.

Staying in bed, Alex watched him get dressed, as she recalled how every muscle of his body felt against hers. Everything about him felt native and intimate, and she found herself longing to be with him again. Glancing up to see Alex laying on her side, biting her lip as the sheet hung loosely over her, Jay couldn't keep himself from smiling at how lucky she made him feel. Stealing one last kiss, he left her to get ready for the day and made his way down the stairs.

Standing in the white clawfoot tub, Alexandra allowed the hot water from the shower nozzle to wash the remnants of Jay off her, even as she continued to lust for his touch. Having dried off, she put on her plain old dress and continued to walk down to the lower portions of the house where the savory aroma of waffles guided her to the kitchen. There, Andy was sitting at the table, watching Jay cook as Cosmo buzzed about waiting for his meal.

"Morning Mama." Andy looked up at Alex with a bright smile on his face.

"Morning love."

"You know." The boy frowned as he looked her up and down. "I think you need to go get yourself a new dress. Yours looks so boring here."

Shocked, Alex stood in the door, looking at the child who was tapping his pudgy fingers on the table. At first, she wanted to ask him why he would say something like that, but in reality, she already knew, she had thought the same thing herself. The gowns she was accustomed to wearing seemed very dated when you compared them to the dresses the women wore in East Ashland. Out in the streets, Alex stood out like a sore thumb and the stares from strangers were starting to get disheartening. But as much as Alex wished to fit in, she knew it would be unwise to spend money on a new wardrobe. After all, here, she was no longer the lady of Manevia, she was just Mrs. Hartwood, a regular woman with limited funds.

"You know what sweetie," Alex looked at Andy with a partial smile, "I think there is an old sewing machine up in the attic. Perhaps I can modify my old dresses a bit, that way I will fit in a tad better."

"Nonsense," Jay scowled as he placed food on the table. "You will go out and get yourself some new clothes. Ones which befit a woman living in this land."

"But Jay, we can't possibly be spending money on such trivial things."

"Maybe so..." he placed an arm around her, bringing her in for a kiss, and straightening the hair on her head "... but what kind of man would I be if I couldn't provide for my wife?"

"But—"

"No buts, I promised your brother that I would take good care of you. Therefore, you will go out and buy yourself some nice dresses. And take Andy with you, he could stand to get some new clothes himself."

"All right. You win." Alex planted a quick kiss on Jay's lips as she shook her head. "As soon as we are done with breakfast, Andy, Cosmo, and I will go out shopping."

"Better. Now sit down and eat your food before it gets cold."

Smiling, Alexandra joined her family at the table, laughing as Cosmo gnawed away on a waffle twice his size. True to her word, after breakfast, she finished getting ready and headed outside to find some new clothing to help her get settled into her new life. She still was not keen on spending money, but as Jay shoved a purse full of bills and coins into her hand and pushed her out the door, Alex felt as if she had no other choice.

Taking Andy and Cosmo with her, she strolled down their road as she allowed the warm summer sun to bask her skin in its hot glow. Stopping at the end of the street, she admired the for-get-me-nots opening their blue flowers to greet her. For a second, Alex wondered what the odds were of her favorite flowers growing on the street she now shared with the man she once only dared dream about. But as much as she wished to believe it was more than a coincidence, she dared not consider the possibility.

Shaking her head free of intrusive thoughts, she took hold of Andy's hand and continued their walk until they reached the capitol building of Fall Harbor. Pausing in the middle of the open square, Alex glanced up to admire the sight. Across the open plaza paved in brick were stone steps leading up to a majestic brick building, standing tall behind a blossoming fountain. The lowest floor was framed by archways spread across the building's three wings, and on top on its four stories was a clock tower that chimed every hour.

According to Jay, every province in Ashland had a capitol building much like this one. Each served as a command post for its own leader to run the territory. There was also the main capitol building for the entirety of East Ashland, which was in Wellaby, just across the river from Fall Harbor. Apparently, this was the major hub of the East, and it was there that the leaders from each province gathered to discuss political matters with the Grand Commander. Jay told her this system held each leader, and the Grand Commander accountable for their actions, and the reason they remained free for this long.

Marveling at the building before her, Alex wondered if Richard was inside working with the mayor. She wished to stop in and say hello, but instead decided it was best not to interrupt her friend, especially since she was still unsure of where their friendship stood. After all, they may have parted as friends back in Manevia, but their youthful romance still weighed heavy on her heart. She knew Richard still had feelings for her, ones she could not return, and she was not sure how to best approach him. Thinking it was best to avoid her friend for now Alex grabbed hold of Andy's hand again and stole a glance out for oncoming cars before stepping off the brick into the cobblestone street.

Once safely across, the duo, and Cosmo admired a red brick fence running along the street, capped off with white stone, concealing a small cluster of trees. Continuing their stroll for the waterfront, Alex stole a glance through the intricately cut, wood gate situated between the two white pillars. There, hidden from the outside world was a dazzling garden, welcoming them with its tranquility.

A winding, flagstone path led the eyes past the benches which were lined with trees, shrubs, and flowers to a grand, stone fountain at the center. A flower of water sprouted and spread from the top, flowing down the three tiers and splashing into the broad, quatrefoil basin. The gurgling of the water invited them to come in, and unable to resist its pull, Andy broke free of Alex and ran over to sit on the lip of the fountain.

"Woah, this is amazing." Andy squealed as he peeked at his reflection through the water lilies bobbing in the churning water.

"It is, isn't it? It almost feels magical here, if I dare say so myself."

"Come sit with me mama and look at the pretty flowers."

Surrendering to the child's whim, Alex came over and sat down on the cool stone and was instantly hit with a feeling of pure joy. A warm, loving energy radiated from the marble basin, warming Alexandra's soul. Tilting her head back, she looked up at clear blue the sky and allowed the refreshing water to mist her hair. The surrounding air smelled of cherry blossoms, gladiolus, iris, and lilacs. There was something about this whimsical oasis that gave Alex inner peace, and the fire in her heart grew a tad hotter.

Encased in the garden's mystical aura, Alex got lost in the sweet notions overtaking her until a tiny, cold brown snout bopped her forehead. Glancing at the small brown pig with green wings grumbling about reminded her that they still had things to do, and with a sigh, Alex stood up and took hold of Andy's hand. Despite her need to linger in the garden longer, Alexandra followed her pigrie's lead and walked back through the gate with the boy in tow. Strolling down the street lined with interconnected brick houses, the trio headed for the water, where Jay said a lovely little clothing store would be.

Reaching the intersection, Alex walked across the street and down to the pier since she did not get a good look as they drove by the previous night. At the dock stood a white, tri-level steamboat with a bright red paddlewheel at the back. Lawrence informed her the steamers take people from Fall Harbor to Walleby once an hour during the day. With its last passenger climbing on board, the two black towers at the top of the boat puffed out steam, and the red wheel turned, guiding Alexandra's gaze across the canal to Walleby shores.

Tracing her eyes across the deep blue waters shimmering with the late afternoon sun, the green banks of the capital city greeted Alex who stood there with her mouth hung open. There, breaking up the sea of green, stood a tall, white building with a glass pyramid on the roof. From what she knew, Alexandra surmised that was the capitol building where all the important meetings took place, and, the home of the Grand Commander himself.

She longed to take a boat across the river and visit the man who allowed her marriage to Jay and thank him personally, but she knew that for now, it was not possible. Watching the boat chug further away, Alex turned and began to walk left, heading for the clothing store. Their walk was short, and it was not long before they reached a squat white house, separated from the rest of the world by a small iron gate.

Stepping into the modest courtyard, Alexandra admired the enormous window displaying mannequins dressed in the latest Ashland fashions as they got closer to the entrance. Pulling open the door, a light jingle of a bell hanging above greeted them as they walked inside the cozy storefront crammed full of clothing, shoes, and accessories. At the center counter, a man dressed in white, with beautiful brown skin looked up to study the pair entering his store. His head shined with the sunlight reflecting off his skin and his honey-colored eyes almost sparked with the warmth of the smile coming from his dark, bushy beard.

"Welcome to the Elegant Attic Ma'am. Let me know if there is anything I can help you with."

"Thank you, I will." Alex smiled politely at the shopkeeper and nodded her head.

Giving her a wink, the man straightened out his waistcoat and went back to reading the book splayed out on the counter, allowing Alex to wonder between the racks of colorful dresses. Finding the section of gowns reserved for white mages, Alexandra attempted to sort through all the choices presented to her. Even her mother's closet was not as extensive or beautiful as what she found crammed into the tiny store.

Her eyes darted between the dresses and three-piece suits with all the sleeves and waist lines imaginable. Then there were the skirts: long skirts, knee-length skirts, and skirts so short she dared not consider them. Overwhelmed by the variety she suddenly had to choose from, her head was beginning to spin at trying to find something suitable to try on. Poor Alex had no idea where she was even going to start when a kind voice of a woman rang out from behind her.

"Why, look at you sugar, you 'bout as lost as a last year's Spring Solstice egg. Are you new 'round here?"

Alex turned around to see a woman in her late forties standing behind her, beaming from ear to ear. Her ebony skin looked lovely with the dark green, floor-length skirt, ivory top, and brown vest.

The stranger's shiny black hair was pulled up in a half twist and her molasses colored eyes studied Alexandra over carefully with a keen gaze as she continued to smile unfazed. Realizing how silly she looked trying to riffle through all her choices, Alex felt remarkably self-conscious and embarrassed. Gazing down at her feet so the woman wouldn't have to look at her reddening face, she solemnly nodded her head, and the stranger began to laugh.

"No need to be embarrassed babycakes, ain't no one judge you 'round here. So, where you from anyway Hun?"

"Vega." Alex whispered as she continued to avert the woman's gaze.

"Well butter my butt and call me a biscuit. You must be the pure-blood everyone is up in arms about." The strange woman leaned in to whisper in Alexandra's ear. "Rumor has it, that you're a princess who ran off to marry a half-blood."

"Yes, guess that's me, the former princess of Manevia and the wife of a half-blood."

"Well, it ain't no wonder you look lost love. You probably ain't seen nothin' but 'em long frumpy gowns of yours."

"That obvious, huh?" Alex's voice grew quieter as she realized how sheltered she must have seemed. "But yes, this dress that I'm wearing is all I'm used to seeing."

"No need to be ashamed of it sugar, ain't your fault the rest of the snobs in Alteria still think this be the stone age. Allow me to help you. We will get you all set up with new duds and you won't need to feel so out of place any longer." Without giving Alex a chance to reply, the strange woman started pulling dresses off the rack while eyeballing the girl to gauge her size. Spotting Andy hiding behind Alexandra's dress, the woman smiled and bent down to meet his gaze. "And who might this handsome young man be?"

"This is my son, Andy."

"Well, I'll be. Ain't he just cute as a button? I'm Gladys by the way, Gladys Carlson. How 'bout you love?"

"Alexandra Hartwood," Alex mumbled, "though most people just call me Alex."

"Sure is a pretty name you got there babycakes. It certainly is fit for a princess." Gladys placed a handful of dresses in Alex's arms and pushed the girl to the dressing room. "Let's go try all these out Sug. If old Gladys is correct, they should all fit you like a glove."

Stepping through the slatted wood door, Alex wound up in a small room lined with mirrors on three sides. Allowing her gown to drop to the floor, she paused and looked over her body in one of the mirrors. Strange she thought, she didn't look different, and she didn't feel different, but after her night with Jay, she knew she was not the same woman from last night. Pondering how she could be so transformed, and yet remain the same, Alex glanced at the white pile of material on the bench before her and decided to see how else she could improve.

Taking the first dress from the stack, she slipped it on and spun around. Looking in the mirror again, Alex let out a soft gasp at the reflection staring back at her. Now she could finally see the change which had taken place, and she was not sure how to feel about it. The dress had no sleeves to speak of, just two silk strands to go over her arms. A firm fitting bodice accentuated the curves of her body while a ruffled skirt barely covered her knees. She looked like a butterfly who emerged from her cocoon and it made her feel vulnerable with how it put her body on display.

"You all right in there Sug?" Gladys rapped softly on the door. "Everything fit all right or do you need some help getting things on?"

"Gladys, I'm not sure about this." Alex stepped out into the open while trying to cover her legs with the fabric of the skirt. "I'm just not sure I can go out looking so... indecent."

"Nonsense girl, you ain't indecent. This is the latest fashion in East Ashland and you just look spectacular in it. I bet that husband of yours will just be tickled pink to see you looking as lovely as you do in that dress."

"I don't know. I feel like there is just too much of me exposed."

"That be all that pure-blood brainwashing seeping through hun. A body as lovely as yours should not be covered up by frumpy frocks. And that bodice just makes your bosom look delightful." Watching Alex turn another shade of pink, Gladys smirked, and turned to Andy while ruffling his hair. "Tell me, young man, what do you think? Does your mama look lovely or what?"

"Yup. She look real pretty."

"Wee!" Cosmo nodded his head in approval.

"Well, all right. I guess if you all think this looks decent then I will get it."

"Of course you will punkin. And you will get the rest of 'em dresses too. Keep this one on though, I'll have ol' George check you out and get rid of that sack you came in here wearing."

Ripping the tag off the dress, Gladys gathered up the rest of the heaping mound of cloth and brought it over to the counter. Shuffling, behind her Alex glance about the store one more time while still clutching on to her old gown. She was uncertain of wearing something as skimpy as the new dress out, but Gladys had left her no choice and Alex reckoned she'd need to learn how to act as an East Ashland citizen sooner rather than later. Tossing the pile of dressed onto the counter in front of the man, Gladys ripped the gown out of Alexandra's hands and chucked it in the metal waste bucket by her feet.

"She'll be wearing that one out George."

"Excellent choice Miss. And such an improvement if I may say so myself. Why, you look just like a goddess in it."

"Thank you." Alex said blushing.

Giving her a playful wink, George happily rang up the dresses and bagged them up while Alex deposited a small sum of money on the counter to pay for them. Walking out of the store with an armful of bags, Alexandra suddenly felt as if all eyes were upon her. Resisting the urge to run back in and change into her old gown, she looked over at her new friend who was holding the gate open for her.

"Gladys. I still need to buy clothing for my son. Is there a place that sells kids clothing around here?"

"Why you want ol' Suzie's place love. It's just a bit further down the road, not far from where your friend Richard lives."

"Do you think you could take me there? I'm still unsure of being out on my own during the day."

"Sure thing Hun, but on one condition. After we're done shoppin', you and your boy come back to my place for some tea and biscuits."

"I think I could accommodate such a humble request Gladys." Alex chuckled at having found someone in the town besides Richard to talk to.

"Splendid! Now, follow me love."

Walking next to Gladys, Alex listened to the woman clamor on about the city of Fall Harbor and East Ashland in general. This was fine with her, for as much as Gladys liked to talk, Alex like to listen, and the short walk to the small brick house did not seem as bad. Entering the store behind her guide, a sort, stout woman with curly gray hair, and a man in his thirties with light brown locks pulled back into a small ponytail greeted Alex.

"What can we do you for Gladys?" asked the woman.

"My friend Alex here is new to town, and she could sure use some new clothing for her boy. Think you can help her out Sue?"

"Her boy?" remarked the man behind the counter frowning as his eyes darted between Alex and Andy. "Why the girl doesn't look a day over eighteen, and that kid must be at least three! I know them pure-bloods start up young and all, but there ain't no way someone her age can have a kid that old."

"Daniel!" Sue shouted at him. "We don't pry into other people's business like that. Have I taught you nothing boy?"

"It's all right...." Alex murmured "... I'm nineteen, and Andy is technically my stepson."

"But you love him all the same don't you sweetie?" Sue smiled at her warmly.

"Yes, I certainly do."

"So see, he is your boy, even if he is not related to you by blood. Don't mind my son dear, he could stand to relearn his manners. It's no wonder the boy is still single. I mean, who'd marry such an insensitive buffoon?" Taking hold of Alexandra's hand, Sue led her through the maze of shelves which housed random kid's items, toys, and shoes. "Come dear, let's go pick out some new clothing for that son of yours, he looks like he hasn't had a decent wardrobe in his entire life."

Nodding her head, Alex followed the woman as she handed clothing and shoes for her son. She waited for Andy to try everything on before paying for it all and acquiring three more bags in the process. Having finished with their shopping, Alex, Andy, and Cosmo followed Gladys out of the store down the street making their way to the woman's house for tea as promised. Gladys continued to give her new friend a tour of Fall Harbor as Alex turned her head and took in all the sights she was not able to admire the night before.

Walking past a row of houses, Alexandra stopped when one of them caught her eye. In the row of five brick houses squished together, the one on the corner spoke to her in the most profound way. Beyond a simple wood gate which separated the rows into sections, Alex could see a neatly trimmed lawn with a bench under a weeping willow. Hugging the brick path leading to the door, garden beds of gardenia bloomed, and under the white-trimmed picture windows, from their white window boxes, a cluster of blue tulips waved to her.

"Young Richard is at work sugar. Ain't no use dropping in now?"

"What?" Alex turned to face Gladys. "This is Richard's house?"

"Why, I thought you knew."

"No. Richard hasn't told me where he lived yet. But now that I see this place, I can see it suits him well."

Smiling, Alex looked over at Richard's humble house one more time, realizing why it felt as welcoming as the arms of her dear friend. Richard always was fond of gardening, and it was no wonder he managed to make this place look like an oasis with his hard work. Remembering the days he used to work at the palace, Alex closed her eyes while inhaling the sweet scent of flowers and the memories they carried. Shaking her head from the nostalgia, she was about to continue on with their walk when whispers of two men from behind caught her attention.

"Is that her? The princess of Manevia?"

"Yeah, that's the woman married to that miscreant, Hartwood."

"I heard he knocked up some whore over in Rexham and that she killed herself after she found out what he was."

"Oh, he did. See that kid next to her? That's his bastard son. I can't believe he had the nerve to show his face here again and bring his illegitimate spawn with him."

"What, really?"

"Yeah, I can't believe that someone of her status would go for some trash like Jay when she could have been married to a prince."

Listening to the men carry on their conversation, Alex trembled with rage as tears welled up in her eyes. Noting her young friend's discomfort, Gladys shot the two men behind them a menacing glare. Lifting her head up high, she grabbed hold of Alexandra's hand and pulled her from her spot as she spoke loud enough for the two gentlemen to hear.

"The nerve of them two flapping their gums like it's no one's business. I tell you, some people 'round here have absolutely no class. Why, where I come from, we insult a man to his face, not behind his back for his wife and son to hear."

Continuing to push Alex along, Gladys left the two men with their jaws hanging open at her boldness of telling them off. Stopping at the corner a safe distance away from any passersby, she allowed the young woman to catch her breath and wipe the tears from her eyes. Rubbing the girls back, Gladys peered into her young friend's face which was filled with pain and shook her head with a loud sigh.

"Are you okay Hun? You look like you just lost your best friend."

"Is... is that what people really think of Jay? Do the town folk here hate him that much?"

"No dear." Gladys gave Alexandra's hands a firm squeeze. "A few men may like to talk smack here and there, but I assure you sugar, most folk here don't care about a man's past, or his blood status. Now come on, let us forget about those no-good boys over some tea. I promise I won't let anyone else run their mouth while you're with me."

"All right." Alex forced a smile as the last tear fell from her face. "Let's go. I can sure use a pleasant distraction now."

Happy at having calmed her friend down, Gladys led the young woman and her child across the street. They made their way under an alleyway containing an apothecary and clinic owned by her husband which she was sure to point out to Alex in case she ever needed them. Ignoring the playground to their left which she had set up for children visiting the practice, Gladys continued to walk before stopping at the steps of a stone house hidden inside the brick alcove.

Flinging open the wood door, Gladys guided Alex and Andy into the parlor while she yelled for her husband to join them. Moments later, a tall man dressed in a black three-piece suit strolled down the stairs while holding an ivory smoking pipe. He was in his mid-fifties, with short, graying hair, a well-trimmed beard, which concealed a warm smile. Stepping down the last step, the man's soft sea-foam eyes glance over at Alex and the child hidden behind her.

"I see you brought us some company today my dear. Guess it's a good thing I got an entire pot of tea brewing and a batch of fresh biscuits in the oven." He spoke kindly as he kissed Gladys on the forehead. "Now my lovely little peach, why don't you introduce me to our lovely young guest."

"This is my new friend, Alexandra Hartwood. She came here all the way from Vega to marry the man she loved. She's the surreal beauty the entire town can't seem to stop buzzing 'bout."

"Vega? Hartwood?" The man's blue eyes went wide as he peered at Alex. "Why, dear girl, you aren't by chance married to a Jay Hartwood?"

"Why yes, I am."

"Well I'll be..." he peeked around Alex to Andy who had concealed himself behind her skirt "... that would make you little Andrew, right?" The boy leaned his head from behind and nodded. This gesture caused the man to smile and laugh as he continued to look at the child. "Why, I haven't seen you since I delivered you as a wee baby my lad. You sure have grown into a handsome young man though, much like your father."

"You... you are the doctor Jay has always spoken about so fondly. You were the one who was almost like a father to him."

"Indeed, my girl. Dr. Jackson Carlson, at your service." The man reached out his hand to shake Alexandra's. "Come in, come in. You must tell me all about how the two of you met. I have been worried sick over that boy for over three years now, wondering how he was surviving in that hostile land he insisted on staying in. But now I see he has done well for himself there. It makes me happy to know that at the very least, he found a kindred spirit in you."

Graciously accepting the Carlson's hospitality, Alex told the good doctor the story of how her and Jay met. Having moved on to the second cup of tea, she sent Andy to play on the playground with Cosmo while she finished telling the tale of how they ended up in Fall Harbor. Listening to her recount her adventure, Jack reclined in his navy, velvet chair with a smile while nodding his head. Truth be told, the doctor had missed Jay an awful lot and wished desperately to reconnect with his adopted son now that he was back in Ashland, but he didn't know where to start.

 Sitting across from him, Gladys watched the nostalgia fill her husband's eyes and knew what he wasn't saying. Realizing what the young man meant to Jackson, she decided to invite the entire family to dinner under the pretense of getting to know her new friend better. Since Alex had no other friends besides Gladys and Richard, she gladly accepted the offer and promised to drag Jay along, even if it killed him.

Having said goodbye to her new friends, Alex gathered Andy and made the fifteen-minute trip back to her house. Allowing the boy and the pigrie to go play in the yard with the ball they found, she went inside and set her shopping bags down on the floor of the living room. Having not found Jay inside the house, she pouted and looked in the tavern. There, behind the bar, her husband turned around to greet her and almost dropped the glass he was polishing as his jaw hung open and his eyes widened.

"Damn. You look ravishing darling." Jay looked over Alex with a whistle. Coming over to her, he wrapped her in his arms and brought her body closer to his. "I'm not sure how much I like you going out looking so beautiful. All the boys around town will want to steal you from me."

"Even if that was true, I wouldn't be going anywhere. I belong here, with you." She smiled and leaned up to kiss him. "By the way, you will never guess what happened to me today dear."

"Well..." Jay peered into her eyes as he arched an eyebrow trying to figure out what had his wife all excited. "You intend to tell me?"

"I met a Dr. Carlson... your Dr. Carlson. He and his wife invited us over for dinner tomorrow night."

"No way." Jay's face went grim, and he turned away from her. "I can't do that. I don't wish to ever see him again."

"But why Jay? You care for him. I know you do because of the way you always talk about him. So why wouldn't you want to see him?"

"Because of what I've done, because of Andy. You should have seen the look of disappointment on his face when I told him about my predicament with that woman, Alex. I felt like I let my father down, and then she killed herself because of what I was. I can't face him again, not after everything that happened, and the embarrassment I have caused him."

"But he misses you. In his eyes, you are his son, and he wants to see you again. He wants to reconnect. It was written all over his face today. Not to mention... Gladys is the only other friend I have here, other than Richard. So, please, come to dinner with me. It would mean the world to me, and, we all live here, so you'll have to face your demons, eventually."

"Fine." Jay sighed "But only 'cause I think you need to have more friends other than that wanker you are so fond of."

Alex swatted at him playfully, and he grabbed hold of her hand, pulling her in for a deep kiss. Letting her go, Jay allowed her to go get dinner going while he finished cleaning up the glasses at the bar. He was not keen on having to face Jackson again, and frankly, he was terrified of what the old man wanted to say to him, but for Alex, he would do just about anything. So, as he finished polishing his glasses, he contemplated on the dreaded meeting with his adopted father, and prayed it would not be anywhere near the disaster he anticipated it to be.

CHAPTER 4

The Reunion

On the way to the Carlson's house, Alex could not help noticing the stares the three of them got while walking down the street. Angry murmurs and hushed whispers broke out every time they passed by anyone. Even little Cosmo was aware of the unwanted attention his family was getting and squealed away in frustration despite no one else being able to see him.

It seemed like every person they encountered on the street turned around to glare at them and whisper whatever rumor they heard passed down the grapevine. Gossip in a small town spread faster than wildfire, and everyone seemed to know who Alex was, and who she was married to. Ignoring the stares, Alex held her head high as she looped her arm through Jay's and held on to Andy's hand as they continued to walk down the street. She figured the townsfolk were going to stare and talk one way or the other, so she might as well give them something to talk about.

Fortunately, the fifteen-minute walk was not as long as she remembered, and they arrived at the Carlson's street in no time at all. Passing under the alley connecting the clinic and the apothecary, Alex could see Gladys setting up drinks on the outside patio. Beside her, the doctor was pacing back and forth while checking his pocket watch, waiting for them to arrive. Upon seeing Jay, Jackson beamed from ear to ear and walked up to greet the three of them.

"Jay, my boy! How have you been?"

"Fine, I guess." Jay averted his adopted father's gaze while rubbing the back of his head.

"Say," Gladys put a tray of biscuits on the table, before turning to her new friend. "Why not let young Andrew go play on the playground by the clinic? This will give the four of us a chance to catch up?"

"Can I mom?"

"Of course you can." Alex placed a gentle hand on the boy's shoulder. "Just don't run off on us, I want to be able to see you."

Letting out a squeal, Andy rushed off to play on the swings situated between the house and the clinic with Cosmo flying behind to keep his eye on the lad. With the boy playing happily behind them, Alex gave Gladys a warm hug before sitting down in the chair beside her friend. Reluctantly, Jay came over to the table and sat next to his wife, all the while continuing to avoid eye contact with Jackson.

"Tell me, son," the doctor sat across from Jay, crossing his legs and lighting up his pipe, "why did you not come to see me sooner? Surely you must have known this is where I'd be."

"I'm sorry Sir. But, I was not sure you wanted to see me."

"What nonsense is this? Why would I not want to see you? I've always thought of you as a son I could not have."

"Because I'm an embarrassment to you." Jay finally looked up at his mentor. "I failed you in Vega by getting that woman pregnant. And then, she killed herself, all because of what I was. I couldn't face you after everything I've done to cause you so much grief. I'm sorry."

"No, my boy," Jackson shook his head solemnly, "it was I who failed you. I let you go out by yourself that night, knowing full well the dangers awaiting you. I knew how desperate the women of Vega were, how they would do anything to escape their oppression. I myself have encountered these dangers while traveling outside East Ashland, and yet, I sent a helpless young man into their clutches all because I was too preoccupied with my work.

"It is I who am sorry my son. I was the one who let you down that night. I should have guessed our innkeeper had her sights set on you. I have seen the way she leered at you every time we walked through the halls. I knew she was biding her time while plotting her next move. I even noticed the whole vile of Vitex missing from my bag. It was my fault she was able to trap you with a baby that night. I should have been there to stop you, or at the very least prevent you from getting drunk enough to fall for her ruse. I've always blamed myself for the predicament you found yourself in and I hated the thought of her coming back to Ashland with us given the circumstances.

"To tell you the truth, I was relieved when she killed herself. Granted, I was glad we were at least able to save the child as he was innocent in all this. I was going to suggest we turn the boy over to the orphanage, but you stepped up to be a father to him. I couldn't have been prouder of you than I was at that moment. I was just hoping you would have returned home with me. I hated the fact that I could not convince you to come back. But now I see staying in Vega was the best thing you could have done for yourself and your son. There you have found someone who loves you despite everything you have going against you. And I'm still proud of you son."

"You... you really are proud of me?"

"Certainly boy, you have accomplished so much with the odds stacked against you. You even found yourself a gorgeous wife." The doctor looked over at Alex and smiled. "She's truly amazing son, a force capable of taming the fires of chaos raging inside you, and yet, she doesn't even try because she loves the fact they are there."

"True," Gladys winked at Alex, "but isn't that what love is all about? Loving someone because of their flaws, not despite them?"

"Very true my dear, couldn't have said it better myself." Jack looked over lovingly at his wife and continued to smile. Turning his attention back to Jay and Alex, his expression grew slightly grimmer as he took a puff of his pipe. "Though, I'm afraid you couldn't have returned at the worst possible time."

"What do you mean?" Alex looked at him confused.

"There have been growing tensions between the East and the West lately. The woman in charge of the West territory is determined to rule over all of Ashland, and our leaders are struggling to keep our land free. So far in the last month there have been over fifty attacks on our soil. Citizens slain in the dead of night, women violated in their homes, and children gone missing from their yards. If this keeps up, I am not sure how much longer we can hold out."

"I see." Jay slumped in his chair. "You think the people will eventually sacrifice their freedom for the illusion of safety the West is willing to offer."

"Yes, my boy. I am afraid it is so."

"No." Sitting up in her chair Alex clenched her fists as her heart raced in her chest. "That's not going to happen. I won't let them take away what I have here, not after everything I've been through to get it."

"And what are you going to do about it sweetheart, go to war with the entire West province all by your lonesome?"

"I will if I have to." Alex turned to glare at Jay. "All I know is that I won't let them take away what's important to me. I'm willing to die protecting what it is I hold dear, are you?"

Jay glanced over at Alex with wide eyes. He always knew his wife was a bit reckless when it came to a cause she was passionate about, but he did not expect her to proclaim her willingness to die in order to be with him. Sitting in his chair, blinking in silence, Jay felt all eyes upon him, and he had little choice but to clear his throat before taking hold of Alexandra's hand.

"Darling, for you I'd venture into the fires of hell itself. But that is beside the point. We'll fight if that is what we must do, but if East Ashland falls, I want you to take Andy and run. I'd rather die knowing the two of you are safe than drag you down with me." Jay peered at Alex with enough intensity to make her shudder. "Promise me Alex. Promise me you will keep Andy safe if anything was to happen to me."

"I promise..." Alex whispered hoarsely as a single tear formed in her eye.

"Oh, enough of all this gloomy chit chat. We came here to celebrate, not ponder a war which may not happen." Gladys rose up to put the glasses and the pitcher back on the silver tray at the center. "Come now you two, let's get that son of yours and go eat. I've got a nice dragon bird in the oven, and enough wine to forget about all these unpleasantries."

Nodding her head, Alex stood up to go fetch Andy and Cosmo. As she approached the boy swinging with a pigrie in his lap, she breathed out a sigh of relief. She was glad Gladys said something to dispel the tension as she was not keen on discussing what she would really do if anything was to happen to Jay, but she knew it would not be pretty. Dark matters such as these were not something Alex wanted to think about, and as far as she was concerned, none of it would come to pass so long as she was still breathing.

Upon seeing her approach, Andy smiled and jumped off the swing. Flying through the air he landed firmly on his feet before her. Shaking her head, Alexandra took hold of the boy's hand and walked with him to the house while Cosmo rode on her shoulder. Entering the doctor's foyer, the savory aroma of Gladys' home cooking instantly greeted them. In the dining room to their left a roast bird was sitting at the center of the table, encircled by various plates of rolls and summer vegetables.

Smiling brightly across the room, Gladys waved Alex and Andy over to join everyone at the table. Shuffling over to Jay, Alexandra placed the boy between them, and sat down, tucking her chair in. Placing a periwinkle napkin in her lap, she watched Gladys pour golden wine into her glass as the food slowly made its way around the table. Placing a handful of things on her plate and placing a small portion for Cosmo in the corner, she forgot all about the possibility of war as she took in her new friend's hospitality.

At the head of the table, Dr. Carlson reclined in his blue armchair as he studied his adopted son and the family he brought into his house. He was delighted the young man he took in under his wing did so well for himself, but he still worried about the young family he was quickly becoming attached to. With everything that had happened in East Ashland over the last year, Jackson was unsure Jay could hold up to the pressure. But glancing at Alex, he found some comfort in knowing that the girl would never leave his son's side, even if the young man was foolish enough to try. Washing down the roast dragon bird breast with some wine, Jack put down his glass and gave Jay a stern look.

"Tell me, son. What are you doing these days for work?"

"I'm getting the old tavern up and running. I'm hoping to get it opened up by the end of the month."

"Slap my head and call me silly!" Gladys looked up from her plate, nearly dropping her fork in the process. "All ya'll be livin' in that cursed place?"

"What are you talking about?" Alex put down her glass scowling. "You are the second person I met who called my house cursed."

"What?" Jackson raised his eyebrow as he glanced over from Alex to Jay. "You mean to say you haven't told your wife about that house?"

"Why would I?" Jay muttered. "It's just a local legend. Stupid superstition from overly religious folk, that's all."

"I beg to differ. It's far more than that my boy. No one has been able to live in that house since the war broke out."

"Yes." Gladys lowered her voice as if she afraid some other-worldly entity would hear her. "Everyone who tried has always complained about it being haunted. Why, you got voices coming from thin air, things moving about on their own, and sounds of a woman sobbing late at night in the master bedroom."

"But I haven't seen any ghosts or heard anyone cry in my room."

"And you won't." Jay furrowed his brow as he put down his utensils and wiped his face with the napkin in his lap. "There is nothing there to see or hear. Just a bunch of scary stories retold by the townsfolk to get a rise out of one another."

"Then how do you explain that tree in your yard?" Gladys leaned back in her chair, crossing her arms and frowning at Jay. "You gonna tell me it's a story too boy?"

"Tree? What tree."

"Why the peach tree my dear that blooms in your back garden."

"We have a peach tree." Alex glanced up at Jay who was rolling his eyes as he placed his large palm over his face.

"Yes, we do. And it has a story behind it, like everything else on our property."

"What story?" Alex continued to glance at Jay as her eyes sparkled with curiosity. "Tell me, I want to know."

"Fine," Jay tossed a crumpled-up cloth on the table with a sigh, "I'll tell you. Just don't go getting any strange ideas about where we live, it's all hearsay. Thing is, we have a tree which grew in the yard while the war was still raging. And, despite the fact that no peaches grow in this part of Ashland, the tree in the yard grew fast and strong, as if planted there by magic. But this tree was odd. It was stuck in a permanent state of bloom, never producing fruit. Then, one day, it shed all its flowers and appeared to die. It was around the same time that all those forget-me-nots bloomed on our street."

"That's right," Jackson took a sip of his wine, "and the following March the tree came back to life again, blooming as it always had. Then, a few months later, in the first week of August, it shed its flowers and died again. It's been repeating the same cycle for the past twenty-nine years."

"How strange..." Alex looked down at Cosmo who seemed to be the only one unfazed by the story. "I wonder what all of it means."

"We all do punkin. But you don't want to hear about these ol' legends and superstitions, do you?" Gladys looked up at Jay's soured expression before turning back to look at Alex. "Plus, I don' wish to put any more burs in your husband's saddle and scare you off from your new home or anything. Not to mention, it seems as though whatever be livin' in there is no threat to you anyway, or at the very least, it don' wish to scare all ya'll. Instead, why don' you tell me how you keep yourself busy love?"

"I just help Jay out where I can with the tavern and take care of Andy." Alex's eyes trailed down at her lap. "I'm not exactly skilled in much of anything, being a pure-blood and all. As a former princess, I have not learned any valuable skill the women around here have, so there isn't even a lot I can do."

"I see Hun. Well, if you ever want a change of pace, you can come help me out at the clinic a few days a week. It be nice to get a helping hand occasionally, and I would be more than happy to teach you a new set of skills if you wish."

"Really?" Alex's eyes sparkled as she delighted in the prospect of getting out of the house more and learning something new. "I'd be happy to help you, Gladys. But, what exactly is it you do?"

"Why, I'm the town midwife." Gladys looked at Alex and winked. "So, perhaps I'll be seeing you in my clinic someday soon, and not as just my help."

"What? Gladys... no... I mean..." Alex turned a bright shade of red as Andy and Cosmo snickered next to her. "It's just... we—"

"What my wife means is," Jay finished coughing up his drink into his napkin, "we have not discussed such matters in detail yet."

"Oh, but you sure do want a baby with her Sug." Gladys winked as she came over to sit in Jackson's lap. "You were grinnin' like a mule eatin' briars through a bob wire fence when I mention it."

"Oh, be gentle with them my peach." Jackson chuckled as he observed Jay fidget in his seat. "My boy clearly isn't ready to have a talk with his young wife about what he wants. And if we spend too much time teasing him, he may never gather the courage to try."

"All right, all right. I won't play around with all ya'll, but you be sure to see me if you change your mind."

"Sure thing Gladys." Alex glanced down in her lap. Still a bright shade of tomato red, she dared not look up at the people staring at her. "Perhaps when the time is right."

Standing from her spot in Jackson's lap, Gladys rubbed Alexandra's back as she went into the kitchen and brought out a tray of sweet tea and honey cake. Trying to calm her nerves, Alex sipped on her drink as she stole a glance at Jay who chatted with the good doctor about their lives for the past three years. It was refreshing to enjoy the company of people who didn't find their union repulsive or unusual, but she still wondered about what Gladys said a few minutes earlier.

Was there really something Jay wasn't telling her? She delighted at the prospect of having a child with him but she wondered why he wouldn't want to discuss something like that with her. Was Jay worried about what she would say to him if he tried to bring it up this early in their marriage? Nibbling on the spongy cake, she studied her husband's face closely. It was serene, and occasionally he'd glance at her, causing her to blush. With every passing moment, Alex wanted to know where they stood and she would be sure to ask Jay when they got home, since at the very least she wanted the possibility out there.

But as the evening wore on, Alex forgot all about the conversation from earlier and settled into enjoying the company. Once the sun began to set, she promised Gladys that she'd help her out a few days a week at the clinic starting the following week. With that settled, the new friends parted ways, and the family started on their way to their house. The air was still warm and laced with the sweet scent of gladiolus as Jay and Alex walked arm in arm down the cobblestone street. Andy skipped ahead of them, carrying a tray of food which Gladys insisted they take with them while Cosmo sat perched upon his head.

The unwelcoming glares of the strangers and angry whispers continued to assault them as they made their way back and the pigrie darted his head around grumbling. His little mohawk was raised, as he barked at the rudeness these free people seemed to exhibit. Alex, on the other hand, choose to ignore them, and strolled down the street enjoying the night in the company of the man she loved, even if their presence drew ire from those around them.

CHAPTER 5

An Unexpected

Visitor

Walking past the garden hidden in the heart of town, Alex got struck with a sudden headache. Her brain throbbed as if something deep inside was trying to claw its way out. Wincing, she placed a finger over her aching temple and tried to push forward the best she could. Noticing Alex slow down, Jay glanced down at her with a hint of concern filling his deep blue eyes.

"You okay sweetheart?"

"Yes. Just a bit of a headache, that's all." Alex forced a smile as she met his scrutinizing glance. "Nothing to worry about love."

"Are you sure? We can stop if you need a break or anything."

"Really Jay, there is no need. I just had a bit too much wine at the Carlson's, that's all. You don't have to be so overprotective of me."

"Who else is gonna worry over you? At the very least, indulge me this much."

"Oh, all right. But I'm telling you, there is nothing to worry about. As a matter of fact..." Alex paused as they walked further down the street away from the garden, "... my headache seems to have gone away."

"Really? That's odd." Jay frowned as he stole a glance at his wife. "Well, let's just get home then. But if this continues, I want you to go talk to Jackson and have him check it out."

Rolling her eyes, Alex agreed to talk to the doctor, realizing she would be just as worried about Jay if their roles were switched. Continuing their stroll down the street, she noticed that something seemed off as they got closer to their house. On the street, beside the tavern, a car was parked, puffing out white smoke as two figures stood by the door, waiting for them.

Stopping a few feet ahead of his parents, Andy looked on at the strangers, frozen by fear as Cosmo barked loudly at the sight of the intruders. At first, Alexandra contemplated summoning her bow, but her fear dissipated as one of the figures jumped up and waved upon seeing them. Right away, she knew it was Richard waiting at the door for them, and he appeared to have brought a friend.

Walking briskly towards the door with Jay and Andy in town, Alex could start to make out the strange man with Richard, waiting for them in the street. He was tall, almost the same height as Jay, and he was almost as handsome too. The stranger appeared to be young, perhaps only a year or two older than Richard. He wore all white, indicative of his pure blood status. His tailored suit accentuated his muscular features and a fancy top hat sat perched on the dirty blond hair that stuck out from the sides. Leaning on his walking stick, the man adjusted his tailcoat and stole a glance at his pocket watch. Hearing the family approach, he lifted his chiseled, clean-shaven face to study the couple and the child with his baby blue eyes.

"Richard," Jay barked gruffly as they got closer to the door, "you should have called if you wished to drop by for a visit."

"I know my friend, I do apologize." Richard bowed. "But the good mayor of Fall Harbor just returned and wished to meet the both of you."

"I see..." Jay eyeballed the stranger standing behind Richard. "Still, some warning would have been nice."

"I beg your forgiveness kind sir." The mayor got closer to Jay, and Alex could see that they had a lot more in common than she originally thought. "Don't blame the boy though, this is all my fault. You see, I simply couldn't wait to meet the couple the Grand Commander couldn't stop talking about the entire week I was in Wellaby. Please, allow me to introduce myself, my name is Caleb Cox and I'm the mayor of this quaint little town." Caleb stretched a gloved hand to Jay. "And you must be Jay Hartwood."

"Yeah. That's me." Jay shook the man's hand reluctantly. "But aren't you a bit young to be a mayor?"

"Oh, one of the youngest at twenty-five my friend. I know it's unusual, but with everything going on here lately, leaders have been hard to find. Besides, I was more than happy to step up and do the job if it meant keeping my citizens safe from those ignorant cumberworlds over in the West."

"I promise you, Jay, Mayor Cox is a good man, one of the best actually. He even gave me this job when I landed on these shores. You need not worry about him."

"Thank you, Richard, for your praise, but you earned this position all on your own my friend. After all, being in the resistance was no simple task, nor was going to prison for it. It shows gumption and nerves of steel, and a man with guts and wits is a man I want by my side if anything was to happen here." Cox gave Richard a pat on the shoulder before turning his keen gaze on Alex. "But, aren't you going to introduce me to your other friend here?"

"Ah yes." Richard beamed as he motioned his hand to Alexandra. "This is Jay's wife, and my best friend, Mrs. Alexandra Hartwood, the former princess of Manevia."

"You know Mrs. Hartwood," Caleb approached Alex and took hold of her hand, "rumors of your beauty have spread as far as here. But if I may be so brazen," Cox planted a soft kiss on the back of her hand, "neither they, nor the pictures I've seen of you do you justice. You are far more lovely in person. Mr. Hartwood is either extremely lucky or an exceptional man of character to have won the heart and hand of the most beautiful woman in Alteria."

"Ruh! Ruh!"

Cosmo's mohawk went up as he darted behind Jay. There was something about the way Cox looked at Alex that displeased him. There was something else about the young man that bothered the pigrie too, but he could not say exactly what it was.

"Why, Mr. Cox, you flatter me too much." Alex blushed as she ignored her pigries cries of disdain.

"Not at all my dear lady, a woman like you needs to be flattered, and I hope your husband does a good job of that."

"I assure you, good mayor," Jay positioned himself between Alex and Caleb, coming to stand nose to nose with the man, "my wife is not lacking in attention. Now, how may we help you on this fine evening?"

Cosmo grumped in support of Jay as he eyeballed the mayor with a certain degree of suspicion. The young man seemed well-meaning enough, and under normal circumstances Cosmo would tell Jay to stop overreacting, but not here. He was not sure what about Caleb Cox made him feel uneasy, but he hated the man the moment he met him. Maybe it was the way he undressed Alex with his eyes, or perhaps it was the way he smelled of aconite and petunias, but all Cosmo knew was that this man was trouble for both Jay and his mistress.

Smirking at Jay, Cox took a step back and straightened the vest under his coat. "I just wanted to offer you the assistance of Richard and myself, and perhaps even Lawrence if you ever need it. I for one am looking forward to seeing this old place being opened up again, so anything you need to get it up and running will be at your disposal, my good man."

"Well Mr. Cox, thanks for the offer, it is very gracious of you. I will be sure to seek out Richard if I ever need any help or ask you for anything I may require. However, if you don't mind, my family and I are tired after spending the evening with our friends, and we wish to rest. I will however be more than happy to continue this conversation with you on another day."

"Of course, Mr. Hartwood, my apologies for taking up so much of your time, and for disturbing you so late in the evening. You have a good night now. And remember, my doors are open to you and your wife any time you need." Caleb's eyes sparkled as he

smiled at Jay before motioning to Richard, "Come, lad, let us return to our respected homes as well."

"Of course, sir." Richard went to follow his boss, but not before
he stopped to look at Alex. "Hey, drop by the town hall and see
me any time you want to chat. Okay?"

"All right Richard, and you drop in to see us any time you want
as well."

"Just be sure to call first." Jay scoffed with crossed arm.

"Absolutely my friend. I will be sure to phone in advance from
now on, and I do sincerely apologize for tonight, it shall never
happen again. Have a good night Alex, and you as well Jay."

Watching Richard get in the car and leave, Alex did her best
to ignore the endless string of complaints coming from Cosmo
about everything he hated about Caleb. The pigrie had sure
grown attached to Jay, and he seemed to take any action against
his new best friend personally. Coming to terms with the alliance
her pet formed with her husband, Alex took a deep breath and
went through the open door into the welcoming parlor. Putting
the food in the kitchen, she ushered Andy upstairs to bed and
turned to face Jay with a frown.

"What was that all about?" She tapped her foot on the floor as
she crossed her arms to study the man before her.

"What was what love?"

"The nasty attitude you gave Mayor Cox and Richard, it was
highly uncalled for."

"I'm sorry darling," Jay scuffed the floor with his foot as he
glanced to the floor and rubbed the back of his head, "but I really
hate when other people get too close to my wife. Especially when
they can steal you away from me with ease."

"Oh, Jay." Alex shook her head and wrapped her arms around his waist. "How many times do I have to keep telling you, you won't get rid of me this easy. There is absolutely no need for you to get jealous, I have eyes for you and only you. Not even death itself can steal me away from you."

"All right, all right," Jay leaned down and planted a kiss on Alexandra's soft lips, "but you can't get mad at me for wanting to keep you all to myself. After all, I'm still not I sure how ended up bound to you of all people."

"Maybe I chose you to be mine all along."

"Yeah right. Why would you be crazy enough to do something like that?"

"I don't know," Alex pressed her body closer against Jay's, causing him to shiver, "but how about you take me upstairs and find out?"

"Now that," Jay scooped Alex up in his arms, "I can do."

Cosmo watched as Jay brought Alex upstairs for their nightly activities before he fluttered over to the window and laid down on the familiar, wood ledge. Watching the wisteria trees sway with the gentle breeze he let out a loud snort. He could see dark shadows creeping in from the other side, and he watched a mangy black wolf observing the house with his astute, amber eyes.

He knew if Ludwig was there to keep an eye on them that terrible things were coming, and fast. The Worm was already aware of Alexandra's existence in this world, and he would follow her anywhere to see what he had missed. Observing Ludwig give him the nod of his fury head, Cosmo hoped the Amphiptere knew what he was doing when he allowed Alex to come out of the veil and help the people of Alteria.

CHAPTER 6

Voices in the Dark

Wrapped up in Jay's body, Alex woke up in a cold sweat to the sound of voices chattering about her. Sitting up in bed she felt her head throbbing, and nausea overcame her almost instantly. Dashing for the open bathroom door, she barely made it in time to lose her dinner into the porcelain bowl of the toilet. Sitting on the cold floor, shaking as the splitting headache continued to assault her, she pressed her head against the wall and the voices suddenly became clearer.

"*Alex,*" Jay's voice echoed from the distance, "*are you sure about this? Do you really wish to be with someone like me?*"

"*Of course I am, I love you. I've loved you since the moment I laid my eyes on you. There is nothing else I desire as much as you.*"

Alex could hear her own voice carry on a conversation with Jay, but she knew it was not possible, she must have been hallucinating. Noticing the pendant she wore around her neck emitting a pale blue glow, Alexandra crawled her way into the bedroom where Jay still lay sleeping soundly on their bed. Yet, despite the absurdity of the situation, she continued to hear a conversation between the two of them, as if it had been imprinted on this house a long time ago.

"Alex, I've never felt this way about anyone, and now that I've met you, I'm afraid of ever letting you go."

"Then don't let me go. Hold on to me as tight as you like, chain me in your embrace, but know this, even a fleeting moment with you feels like an eternity. I shall always cherish what we have here, even if they do tear us apart."

No, thought Alex as she stumbled to her feet, what she was hearing was not possible, and yet, their voices were clear as day. Her body continued to grow hot as the pain in her head overwhelmed her. She needed to get out of the house, escape these voices, and clear her head. Desperate to rid herself of the phantoms plaguing her, Alex threw on her robe and staggered down the stairs as the whispers continued to resonate around her.

By the time she reached the bottom of the landing, her vision was starting to blur, and she could not stop the ringing in her ears. Digging her nails into the wallpaper, she pushed herself forward towards the back door as sweat poured down her body. She managed to make it as far as the kitchen before the nausea washed over her in waves and another conversation between her and Jay filled the empty room around her.

"Don't do this Alex. Don't go. You don't have to do this. We'll figure out another way to stay together. Please, I don't want to lose you. I don't think I can survive a life without you."

"*You'll never lose me, I promise you. But this is something I have to do, and once I return, I will be yours for all eternity.*"

"*How can you be so sure? What if you never return here? What if you find and fall for someone else? What if they send me away from you while you are gone?*"

"*Don't worry love, I will never fall for anyone other than you, and I will follow you anywhere, even if it be the depth of the void itself. So even if they send you somewhere else, I'll find you, and I'll fall in love with you all over again, in any place, at any time. You're my man Jay, I chose you to be mine, and nothing will keep us apart.*"

Stifling a scream with her hand, Alex dashed forward, bursting through the kitchen door into the crisp night air of the back garden. Surrounded by the scent of the peach blossoms floating past her hair in the gentle breeze, Alex felt her consciousness fade. Collapsing onto the soft grass beneath her feet, she heard a lone wolf cry echo in the distance before darkness took over. Floating through the emptiness of space into nothingness, the last thing she remembered was the light summer drizzle beginning to kiss her skin.

Fluttering out behind his friend, Cosmo watched as drops of rain fell onto Alexandra's body splayed out on the grass. The cool water was forcing the white nightdress to hug the girl's body as her skin peeked through the translucent fabric. Flying down to the ground, the pigrie rooted at his companion's neck, trying to wake her up to no avail. But as his sea-foam wings were getting soaked by the rain something strange happened, the water stopped falling from the sky in midair and the hole in the peach tree spit out a blinding white light. Squinting at the luminous portal, Cosmo spotted just what he expected as a pink and purple butterfly fluttered towards them, leaving a trail of silver dust in its wake.

"Hoink?"

Cosmo had no idea why he even bothered asking such a stupid question, he knew exactly who was coming to see them. But, nonetheless, the butterfly began its transformation, growing and taking on a new shape until a tall man was standing before them. His long silver locks glowed under the light of the moon as they floated in waves down his back. He had his hands tucked into the pockets of his white slacks, pushing up the untucked dusty rose collared shirt as he strolled forward. At night, the man's soft, jade eyes shimmered as he gazed down on Alex and regarded Cosmo with a friendly smile.

"Groink."

"You know me too well by now my little friend." The stranger knelt to give the pigrie a gentle pat on the head before he leaned down to brush a strand of wet hair from Alexandra's face. "I felt her pain all the way from the veil and had to come check on her."

"Roink?"

"Seems like our little girl has gotten too powerful even for me. Even while her soul sleeps, she is undoing the spell I placed on her before she came here. I just hope it doesn't destroy this mortal body of hers before she has the chance to fuse with it."

"Oink, oink?"

"I can certainly try my friend, but with her powers the way they are, anything I do will only be temporary." Bending down, the stranger exhaled a mist of silver dust into Alexandra's face and as the vapor flowed into her mouth, her sweating stopped instantaneously. Stroking the girl's cheek, the man placed a hand over her body to dry her gown and warm her up. "You see Cosmo, memories are a funny thing, even for us. You can suppress them indefinitely, but once they start trickling in, there is no stopping the flood from happening."

"Hoink?"

"There is not much you can do either, other than allow it to happen. I know you have grown very attached to your friend, but she's a strong young woman Cosmo, I know she can handle it."

"Wee, rhee."

"Oh, well, I wouldn't worry about my brother. He may know where she is, but he has no idea of the beast he is trying to awaken. If she can surpass my magic, he stands no chance against her once she unlocks her full potential. Now," scooping Alex up in his arms, the man rose up from the ground, "why don't we bring her inside before that young man she is so fond of awakes to find her gone."

"Roink."

Walking behind the pigrie, the man carried Alex into the house and up the stairs into the room he was all too familiar with. It's been a long time since he had seen the two of them together like this, and it brought back memories of when Jay discovered what the girl truly was. Placing Alex back into Jay's waiting arms, he brushed the hair from her face and placed the covers over her now icy body to warm her up. Continuing to stroke her hair, the stranger leaned down and placed a soft kiss on Alexandra's forehead, making her smile in her sleep.

"Don't worry my dear girl, everything will be all right. I promise. Fatima and Bastian assure me that you have been doing exactly what you need to do. Bare through the pain a little while longer, and soon, you and Jay will no longer need to suffer."

"Hoink, oink."

"True," the man stood up and stole one last glance at Alex, "while I do love them both, this one has always been my favorite."

"Roink?"

"No Cosmo, there is no need for me to protect her any longer." The man turned and started to walk out of the room. "I think you have the protection part covered well my little friend, and Ludwig is out there if you need him."

"Rhee."

"Don't worry, more help is coming soon, just keep her out of trouble for a few more days if you can."

The man smiled and gave Cosmo a wink before he vanished into the darkness. Turning his attention back to Alex, the pigrie grunted and floated to inspect her closer. Her pain seems to have subsided, and she rolled over to drape an arm around Jay as if nothing happened. Still, Cosmo was worried about his friend, and he decided it was best for him to sleep on her dresser, so he can keep a closer eye on her.

Tucking his legs under his body, he listened to the rain drumming on the roof, and he pondered what the master knew about Alex that the rest of them didn't. The Amphiptere had never fully revealed his knowledge of the future, but he was always confident in Alex and the role she had to play. So, for now, despite his reservations about putting his friends at risk, Cosmo decided that he would just have to trust in the Amphiptere and his master plan, not only for the universe, but for his friends as well.

CHAPTER 7

A Damsel in Distress

Almost a week passed since the Amphiptere came to pay Alex a visit and whatever he did to her seems to have worked. The voices and memories which had assaulted her earlier have let her be, and she was feeling better after the night she collapsed in the garden. Happy to forget the strange events of that night, Alex and Jay were picking up the tavern after a successful opening night which lasted well until midnight. The rain came down in sheets and there was nothing but silence amongst the overturned chairs of the room as the water rapped on the windows.

Jay went out back to sort through the various bottles of liquor and beer they had acquired, leaving Alex alone in the tavern.

Sweeping the floors, humming to herself, she was lost to the rhythm of the water pounding outside when a scream pierced the silence of the deserted tavern. Pausing what she was doing, Alexandra listened closely as the screams got closer to her house. They sounded like those of a woman, and the closer she got the clearer her distress became.

"No," the screams stopped outside the tavern, "leave me alone. Please..." the woman continued to scream, "someone help! Please, someone... help me!"

Gladios

Dropping the broom, a glowing blue longsword appeared in Alex's clenched fist. Not giving it a second thought, she rushed out the door and turned to look at where the cries for help were coming from. There, a few feet before her was a woman lying on the ground, desperately trying to crawl away from a large man straddling over her. The top portion of the woman's dress was torn open to reveal one of her breasts and her curly red hair was draped over her face like a wet mop. Grabbing hold of her hair, the attacker pulled the woman back as she dug her nails into the cobblestone in a feeble attempt to hold on. Alex could see the fear in the woman's soft gray eyes as she let out another scream.

"Leave her be." Alex yelled through the rain obscuring the man's face as she raised her sword up high, ready to fight.

"And what do we have here?" The man's gruff voice broke through the desolate street. "All I see is a little girl trying to be a hero. Why not go back to your dwelling skirt and forget you ever saw my face?"

"I'll do that once the void spills over." Alex took a fighting stance, ready to strike the man down if need be. "Now I will tell you this one more time, back away from the lady."

"Lady..." the man chuckled, "what lady? All I have here is a dirty, worthless whore." Smirking, he dropped the woman to the ground and took a step over her. "But fine, have it your ways totsy."

Axium

A crimson double-headed ax appeared in the stranger's hand as he stepped closer to Alex. "I will have my way with you first, and then I will finish off the wagtail and collect my prize."

"Threatening women is one thing," Jay's voice resonated from behind Alex as he stepped out of the shadows clutching his red broadsword in his hands. "But, do you wish to try your luck with me?"

The stranger glanced at the man in black standing behind the petite girl in white. The blonde hair on his head was sticking closely to his chiseled face with the water pouring off him, and his blue eyes had an ice-cold sheen to them. Glancing between the odd pair in front of him, the attacker's eyes grew wide, and the color drained out of his face. This was the couple the entire town couldn't stop gossiping about. The man threatening him had to be none other than Jay Hartwood, a man so steeped in infamy that few even dared to mention his name. That would mean the woman next to him was his pure-blooded wife, the former princess of Manevia herself.

Swallowing hard, the man glanced behind his shoulder at the streetwalker he was hired to murder, and then back at the half-blood who had the reputation of being the toughest guy in town, and the woman who probably knew how to fight better than he did. Unclenching his fists, the man released his weapon and slowly backed away from the tavern door. A safer distance away, he turned on his heels, and ran back swiftly to where he came from. It no longer mattered what that guy paid him for the job, fighting the half-blood and the princess of Manevia was not worth a single pence.

Watching the attacker high tail it away from the tavern as the water continued to cling to her hair and dress, Alex dropped her weapon, shaking her head at the man's sudden departure. Running over to the woman, she pulled the fabric of her dress back up and helped her off the ground. Wrapping her arms around the stranger's shoulders, Alexandra felt her trembling, half from fear, and half from the rain dousing them in ice-cold water. Wiping the wet hair from the lady's face, she could see the cuts on her pasty face from where she hit the ground.

"Come with me." Alex guided the woman to the tavern while continuing to hold up the remains of the powder blue dress she wore. "We'll get you warmed up and I'll heal the cuts on your face."

"Why?" the woman glanced up at Alex with blood-shot eyes while continuing to shake from the close call she had. "Why are you doing this?"

"Because..." Alex paused as Jay held the door open for them, "you asked for help. Surely you did not expect me to ignore your plea."

The woman shook her head as Alex walked her into the tavern and guided her to the nearest table. Sitting her down in a wood chair, Alexandra began to heal the damage done to her face. As she ran her fingers over the woman's face, Alex could see that she was in her mid-thirties, but she was aged well beyond her years. Still, despite the wrinkles and age spots on her face, the stranger was pretty and not suited for the life she was forced to live. The prostitute's gray eyes studied the strange girl who decided to help her out closer before they trailed to the man who approached the two of them from the bar.

"So," Jay walked over with a glass of whiskey in his hand, "care to tell us your name?"

"Fiona." The woman turned her face away from Jay's scrutiny. "Fiona Walsh."

"All right, Fiona. Here," Jay placed the glass before her, "drink up, it will steady your nerves and get you warmed up."

"Thank you."

"Now, you want to tell me what a working girl was doing in this part of town?"

"I was with a client," Fiona grasped her glass in her shaking hands, "I got attacked when I left." Gulping down her drink in one go, Fiona placed the glass on the table and studied Jay with a piercing glance. "And what would you know of working girls, eh? Your little treasure here is far too innocent to have ever been a whore, and you sure don't seem like the cheatin' sort, 'cause trust me, I'd know if you were. Why, the whole time my tit has been flopped over you ain't even dared to take a look like so many other men would have. So, what are you, and how do you know what I am?"

Jay let out a loud snort as he crossed his arms. "That is none of your business, woman."

"Fine, suit yourself." Fiona grinned as she leaned back in her seat and readjusted her torn dress. "But I have to say, your dove here is something else. No one else would run to the aid of a fallen woman, let alone bring one inside their respectable establishment. So, tell me lambkin," she turned to face Alex as a soft smile played on her smudged ruby lips, "what's your story? Why are you so nice?"

"Lady Alexandra knows not how to be needlessly cruel. Which is precisely what makes her so special in this dark world of ours."

"Rupert?" Alex turned to see a familiar man with graying brown hair pulled into a neat ponytail standing in their doorway, dripping water with two suitcases in his hands. "What are you doing here?"

Running over to the man who was like a father to her, Alex flung her arms around the old butler's neck, and he happily reciprocated her embrace. It's been weeks since he'd seen his charge, and he had missed her immensely as he waited for the right time to join her. Holding on to his adopted daughter, the old man let out a sigh, relieved she managed to keep out of trouble for as long as she had.

"I told you, my dear girl, you wouldn't have to be without old Rupert for too long, and I meant that."

"But, how did you get here? Surely father would not have let you go without a reason."

"Your grandmother gave me a full release to go take care of... family matters, and your dear brother made sure I got on a boat headed out your way. Took me a while to find any information on you in Clear Springs, but once I found the man who knew your whereabouts, I caught the first train to Fall Harbor and the locals pointed me to this tavern. Seems like the townsfolk here love their gossip."

"Oh Rupert, I'm so glad you found me. You will have to catch me up on what happened at the palace after I left."

"Yeah, bout that..." Jay muttered from the corner, "not to interrupt your happy reunion or anything, but we don't really have a use for a butler, now do we?"

"Jay!" Alex turned to her husband with a scowl. "We can't possibly put old Rupert out on the streets. After all, we do have a spare servant's room downstairs we can give him." Glancing at Jay's eyes, Alex batted her long lashes and watched him wince. "Surely you can find something for him to do around here. He's like family to me, I can't let him be alone and it's not like it would cost us much to house him."

"Oh fine," Jay grumbled, rolling his eyes in surrender. "But only 'cause I love you baby, and I sure can use a helping hand around here."

"Not to worry Master Hartwood. I think you will find me very useful in helping keep house, working the tavern, and helping with a certain young lad who also inhabits this house. But first, I think we need to take care of the lady seeking refuge at your establishment." With his hands behind his back, Rupert turned to Fiona and smiled, crinkling the fine lines of his face. "Tell me, dear woman, do you live far from here? I can grab an umbrella and escort you home safely. Or, if you wish, we could always call a cab for you."

"No need for either one. If I could call my brother to pick me up, he could be here in a few minutes."

"Telephones are over there by the restrooms." Jay pointed behind him. "Just make it quick, it's getting late and I want to go to bed."

Without saying a word, Fiona got up from her chair and glided to the copper phone situated by the restrooms. Rotating the dial on the old machine, Fiona relayed to her brother what happened before hanging up and returning to sit in the company she found herself in. In the streets, she didn't realize who these two were, not until the strange man with hazel eyes in a servant's garb walked into the room. However, she now understood why the at-tacker ran from them as far he could, and why the barkeep knew of her profession right away.

The half-blooded son of a prostitute was far from the volatile man the rumors made him out to be. On the contrary, Jay was nothing like what she pictured him as when she heard the gossip about town. He was rugged and handsome, a man much like the one she fancied. As for his wife, well, Fiona had seen her portrait before, but it did not do the girl justice. The pictures of the prin-cess, while beautiful, lacked a certain aura the girl seemed to ra-diate when she was near. In person, she looked more like a heavenly being not meant for this horrid planet she found herself on rather than an average woman.

Right away, Fiona knew why all the men, including her brother, lusted for the girl so much, and even she found herself being drawn to her charms. The princess reminded Fiona of her first love, Catrin, the woman who took her under her wing, gave her a new name, and showed her how to use her talents to earn a living. Like the woman who showed her how gentle and pleasur-able physical love could be, Alex was a kind soul who wouldn't hesitate to do the right thing, even if she was to pay for it with her life. It was no wonder the barkeep was so protective over the girl, for it was this gentle nature that caused Catrin to lose her life.

But Alex also had something about her which made Fiona shudder with delight, the girl had a hint of darkness that was as seductive as the mermaids in the harbor luring foolish men to their death. It had been a long time since Fiona felt the soft, del-icate touch of another woman, and sometimes she still missed it. But, in her job, relationships were hard to maintain, and after the tragic death of Catrin, Fiona dared not give her heart to another woman. Not to mention that neither a man nor a woman would have stuck around long enough to make her an honest woman. Well, until now she thought.

Fiona was not entirely honest with Jay about why she was in their neck of the woods. Truth be told, the man she was with that night was more than her client, he was her lover, and possibly her escape from this dreadful life of hers. But now that she knew who they were, Fiona wished she was upfront with the pair. After all, if anyone would understand her situation it be them, especially the young princess.

Admiring the petite, porcelain girl with emerald eyes and chestnut hair made Fiona ache for the touch only a woman could give. The princess reminded her so much of Catrin, that she was picturing running her hands over Alex's small breasts and kissing her rosy lips when the door swung open, hitting the wall with a bang. Letting out a sigh, Fiona turned her head to glance at her brother, annoyed he had interrupted such a pleasant fantasy. But as mad as she may have been, she couldn't help but soften at the worry reflecting in his pastel green eyes.

"Hey, Lawrence." Fiona stood up from her chair and held the torn blue fabric over her breast. "Took you long enough."

"Fi!" Lawrence rushed in and hugged his sister. "I came as fast as I could. I was so scared when you told me what happened. But I'm glad you're all right."

"Lawrence is your brother?" Alex gasped at the revelation. "Do... do you live together?"

"Yeah, unfortunately. The moppet can't seem to hold a good woman down, so I'm stuck caring for him like I have his entire life."

"Fi... don't say that in front of the Hartwoods."

"I'm just razing you Lawrie." Fiona ruffled her brother's long brown hair as he tried to duck away. "But it is shameful that a half-blood can secure a gorgeous wife, and you can't even get the local milkmaid to bed you for more than a fortnight."

"What can I say Fi, I get my promiscuous nature from you. Besides, not my fault that they find me lacking in the sack, and in looks... and in personality... and probably finance as well."

"Guess some people just don't got what it takes." Fiona smiled as she let out a laugh at her brother's unfortunate luck with the ladies. "Now come on you buffoon, take us home so we can let these good folks be." Shoving Lawrence to the door, she glanced over her shoulder to steal one last glance at the lady of the house. "Thanks again for saving me dove, no one else would have stuck their neck out like that, you sure are one hell of a woman. You take good care of her now, half-blood."

"Will we see you again?"

"Doubtful lambkin, but you never know, Fatima is a fickle woman, who knows what lady fate has planned for any of us."

Walking out the door with Lawrence in tow, Fiona left the room oddly silent again as the raindrops pelted the roof, filling the tavern with a dull roar. Peeking out the window, Rupert watched the black car drive off into the dead of night and vanish into the blanket of water. Turning around, he looked over the man Alexandra had chosen and smiled. It was funny how in only three years Jay had forgotten all about Rupert and the conversation they had on that night not so long ago.

"So, my dear," Rupert turned to Alex, "this is the man who caused such a commotion at the palace?"

"Commotion?"

"Indeed my dear girl. Your father was livid to find out you were missing, and once rumors spread of a peasant going missing that same night..." Rupert chortled glancing at the couple, "well, you can imagine the castle hasn't stopped hearing of it since. Why, your mother has not left her room since. She says the embarrassment is too much for her to bear, and Master Quinton has vowed to hunt down the man who stole the princess and make him pay. As you can imagine, the only people who found all this amusing beside myself, were your grandmother and Master Thomas."

"Do they know where she went?"

"No need to worry Master Hartwood, young Thomas made sure to point them in the wrong direction. Although, as far as everyone is concerned, you, my dear boy, are a kidnapper who convinced the princess to murder a man on his behest."

"How much do they know?" Jay put his arm around Alex and brought her into his chest. "What do they know about me?"

"Not much at all. They know you were barkeep with a child, but they still think of you as an insignificant gray, and not a half-blood. And as I said, there is nothing to worry about, Master Thomas is making sure they do not find you. As of a few days ago, the king and Quinton are sailing to the shores of the Emerdine countryside to tear it apart in hopes of finding Alex."

"Speaking of Tom, how is he, Rupert? Is he doing well?"

"Better than well my dear. He and Master Henry have been working closely together on pushing the land in the right direction. They even have young Master Phillip on board with their plan, and rumor has it, your father is considering skipping Quinton in favor of him."

"You have no idea how happy I am to hear that, or how happy I am to see you."

"But of course, my dear. Old Rupert would never abandon the daughter he never had. Now, why don't you and Master Hartwood show me to my room?" Rupert picked up his bags and glanced at Alex. "Talk about town has it that you are assisting a local midwife in her job."

"Yes, Gladys is my new friend. She has me helping her around the clinic three times a week, and tomorrow is one of those days."

"Splendid dear girl. More reasons for you to get your rest. Now, let us close up this fine place you have here and go get some shut-eye."

Closing up the tavern, Alex and Jay walked Rupert to his new room off the kitchen. Allowing the old man to settle in, the pair went upstairs and collapsed on their bed. They were far too tired to do anything, so they opted to fall asleep in each other's arms instead. It took Alex a lot longer than usual to drift off to sleep as she pondered the events of the night while Jay lay snoring next to her. She couldn't wrap her head around how not one person wanted to help Fiona, and a nagging feeling of dread kept her awake until her eyelids grew heavy, and she drifted off into an uneasy sleep.

CHAPTER 8

Confessions and a Truce

The next morning, Jay gave Alex a kiss goodbye as she walked out the door to help Gladys at the clinic. He watched her walk down the street before sending his son and Cosmo to play outside while he had a chat with the old man who turned up on their doorstep the night before. Strolling into the tavern, Jay looked over at Rupert who sat reclining in one of the chairs with glasses of whiskey poured for the two of them. Sitting next to the man, Jay knew the butler was expecting him, so he decided the direct approach would be best, especially given their previous acquaintance.

"So. How long have you known?"

"About what Master Hartwood?"

"About Alex being destined to end up with me. What did you think I was talking about?"

"Ah, so you do remember me, my dear boy." Rupert smirked and took a sip from his glass. "I've known since before either of you were born. And to think, I thought you had forgotten all about me and the chat we had all those years ago."

"As if." Jay snorted and crossed his legs. "A bit hard to forget the man who gave you your power, don't you think?"

"Perhaps you're right son. But, you didn't react when I walked in last night, so I reckoned you had forgotten all about me."

"No chance old man, especially not after you neglected to tell me she would be a fuckin princess. I was merely keeping up the façade for my wife, so I didn't have to explain to her the shit storm you put me through to be with her." Jay gulped down his whiskey. Placing the empty glass on the table he leaned back in his chair and raised an eyebrow at the old man. "Now. Do you care to tell me who you really are? Cause I sure have my doubts about you being a humble butler for the royal family."

"I'm sorry Master Hartwood, but I think we both know it's not possible for me to reveal my secrets. At least, not yet."

"I figured that much. But what now? Surely we can't tell Alex we know one another, or that you were the man who gave me my totem."

"We certainly cannot, at least not until she remembers on her own." Rupert uncrossed his legs and leaned forward to smile at Jay. "For now, I think it be best if we pretend as if we know nothing about anything, especially not about one another. I'm sure you can handle that Jay... for Alexandra's sake."

"Fine," Jay grumbled under his breath, still unsatisfied with the lack of answers the old man provided him. "But if anything bad happens to her as a result of you being here, mark my words, I will hang you out to dry personally, after I skin you alive."

"I'd expect nothing less of you Master Jay, you always were deathly protective of the girl, and who can blame you."

With a nod of Jay's head, the two men continued to stare at one another in silence until Rupert excused himself to tend to some household chores. Jay watched him walk into the house and pondered how things came to be. He knew the man was not from their world, but he dared not question who, or what he really was. As long as Alex was safe, he cared about nothing else, and it would appear that Rupert cared about her as if she were his own daughter. Thinking it be best to keep the old man's secret, Jay rose from his chair and went behind the bar to prepare for the evening ahead.

CHAPTER 9
A Dose of Reality

Running a tad late due to Rupert's unexpected arrival and the commotion from the previous night, Alex rushed through the door of the small clinic in the alleyway leading to Gladys' house. Per usual, hushed whispers rang out in the waiting room with her arrival, but she ignored them and smiled at the waiting women and children even as they continued to gawk at her. Walking into the exam room where Gladys was waiting, she waved to her friend, and grabbed an apron off the wall, throwing it over her long white dress as Gladys raised an eyebrow over at her.

"I see we are back to dressing modestly Sug."

"Yes, I'm sorry Gladys, but I simply cannot expose my legs or arms as much as everyone wants me to."

"Don't worry about it dear, your modesty is part of your charm. At least you are showing some of your arms now, so that is a start." Fishing around the pocket in her smock, Gladys pulled out a small elastic band and handed it over to Alex. "Here sweat pea, put your hair up, it's bound to be a messy day with all these sick kids and babies coming in."

Taking the elastic from Gladys, Alex threw her hair up in a messy bun and went to tend to the tray on the table. While she was setting up the table for the first customer of the day, Gladys tilted her head as she caught something out of the corner of her eye. Turning to get a better look, she squinted her eyes as she attempted to see the mark behind Alexandra's ear. As she had thought, there was a small, reddish-brown shape of a rose there which was peculiar given what she knew about her young friend.

"Is that a tattoo you have there Sugah?"

"Oh... this." Alex instinctively reached up and traced the raised lines in her skin. "No. My brother branded me with our family crest when I was younger. You see, I dared to take the blame for Richard touching me in order to spare his life and this was my reward."

"What? Why?"

"He caught me with Richard when we were still a couple. We were foolishly holding hands on palace grounds, and when Quinton caught us, he was sure to bring it up to my father. Daddy was planning to behead him, but my intervention spared his life. Quin got upset that I ruined his plan of getting revenge on me, so he chose to punish me instead by leaving this mark on me. He told me it would remind me of my place in the world, and how pathetic I really was."

"Ah, I see." Gladys let out a sigh and shook her head with dismay. "I knew you and that Richard boy had history before you met Jay, I just didn't realize how complicated it was. Well, it ain't no wonder that poor boy looks at you the way he does. Guess he still feels responsible for what happened to you."

"He does. Unfortunately, Richard never did forgive himself for what happened that day, and things have never been the same with us ever since. So, I guess in a way, Quinton won."

"No, he didn't." Gladys traced the brand mark behind Alex's ear and looked at the girl's green eyes with a soft smile. "You are here, with Jay, living the life you've always dreamed of. That alone means he did not break you. He did not win. I always knew you to be a fighter, I just never guessed how tough you really are."

"Guess you're right."

"I've been known to be right on occasion." Gladys smirked. "And the way you love that man shows just how stubborn and strong you really are. Far stronger than any of them pure-bloods outside East Ashland."

"Oh come now Gladys, it's not like we can choose who we fall in love with."

"On the contrary, I think we can. At least I think we can at some point in time. And you chose well, if I may say so myself."

"Thank you, Gladys, for always lifting my spirits up when I need it. You are like the mother I never had."

"Oh, that I am not sure of. I am not the mothering type. But I'll settle for an older sister with years of wisdom to share."

"Hmm, I don't know, I still prefer to think of you as a mother. Especially since Jackson is like a father to Jay. So, if you really think about it, we are like a strange adopted family." Alex snickered and handed Gladys the tray even as the woman shook her head smiling. "But, enough with the joking, shall we get started? The waiting room was full when I came in. Looks like we are in for a busy day."

"Oh, I guess. Go open up the door then my dear daughter and let the first one in."

Opening the door, Alex called in the first patient and checked off the name as a heavily pregnant woman waddled through the clinic door. Resting her hand on the white fabric covering her pronounced belly, the woman narrowed her russet colored eyes as she looked Alex up and down. Letting out a snort, the woman's lips pursed as she turned to Gladys, nearly knocking the tray out of the midwife's hands.

"Are we just letting in any old trash off the streets to work here now Gladys? I thought of this as a respectable establishment, so what is she doing here?"

"Did you get a burr in your saddle Olivia? Alexandra is my friend, and an upstanding member of our society."

"Upstanding? Don't kid yourself, you can't possibly be called upstanding when you are sharing your bed with a rowdy boot-licker and raising his illegitimate little ragamuffin as your own."

"I'm sorry," Alex clenched her fists, "but there is no need to insult my husband, or my son. If you have a problem with me, I'll be happy to leave, but don't drag them into this."

"Stowe it, princess, and spare me your outrage." Olivia flicked her hair as she turned to glare at Alex. "You don't have a son. Your poor excuse for a husband does. The little ratbag living with you didn't come from your loins, so he ain't yours, and don't try to claim him as such. As for you and this pathetic clinic," the woman turned to look back at Gladys, "you can forget about de-livering my baby. I am going across the river to Wellaby, where they don't have dirty floozies working for them. And I will be sure to tell everyone in town of the kind of practice you run here. Soon enough, you won't have enough clients to sustain this place."

Olivia turned and wobbled out of the door, slamming it shut behind her hard enough to cause a picture of a barn to fall off the wall. Bending down to pick up the cracked frame, Alex felt a lump form in her throat as her heart clenched in her chest. Fighting the tears in her eyes, she was about to tell Gladys that she would leave, when her friend's warm hand squeezed her shoulder.

"Don't let Olivia get to you honeybun and don't let her words bother you. That woman could start an argument in an empty house if she wanted to."

"But she threatened to shut you down."

"Oh, don't you worry about that, she ain't got enough people to listen to her to make that happen. Now go call the next patient in and let us forget all about that uppity slag."

Nodding her head, Alex wiped the tears from her eyes and went out to call the next patient. Fortunately, no other person dared make a callous remark about Alex, or her family and the hours of the day simply melted away. Between the usual patients and the flu going around Fall Harbor, the clinic was a bustling mess up until lunch, keeping both women busy. By noon, a hungry and exhausted Alex exhaled deeply from being on her feet all day as she stole a glance at the clipboard in her hand, only one name remaining she thought.

"Next!" Alex opened the door and checked the last name off as she tucked the list behind the door. When she looked up to see the patient walk into the room, an all too familiar face greeted her with a smirk. "Fiona?!"

"Well, well. I didn't realize you worked here little dove."

"I help out once in a while. I didn't know you came here."

"Ah, I see you have met one of my more dubious customers."

"Lambkin here did a lot more than that Gladys. She saved my life last night."

"What? Why Alex, you never mention anything of the sort."

"Fiona was attacked by the tavern last night. I ran out to help her. It's nothing really."

"Why I am not surprised you'd run out to help hedge-creeper when everyone else turns a blind eye?" Gladys shook her head. "I knew you were a good sort love, but I never expected to hear this. Still, I'm not the least bit shocked by this. Oh well, why don't you help Miss. Walsh onto the exam bed."

"Ain't no need for that, I can hop on myself." Fiona jumped up on the table and sat there looking over at Alex as she kicked her feet in the air.

"So dear. What can I do you for today?"

"I just got this rash on my lady bits, that's all, it don' look bad, but it itches something fierce. Think you can do your thing and make it go away?"

"I sure can," Gladys shook her head frowning, "but you really should consider a different profession my dear. A small rash on your vagina is one thing, but I worry this lifestyle of yours will be the death of you one of these days."

"What else would you have me do?" Flicking a curly red strand out of her face, Fiona trailed her gray eyes down to the stone floor. "Once you are in this life, you can't get out. Both you and I know that, and we both know no one will hire me because of what I am. The chance of an honest life for me has been taken ages ago."

"Then maybe it's time you let that brother of yours take care of you for once. If you ask me, that boy is as useful as a trap door on a canoe if he can't support his sister working for that snake in the grass, we call a mayor."

"Caleb Cox is a good man Gladys. I know you don' agree with him, but he ain't the type of man you seem to think him to be."

"All I'm sayin' is the way that man thinks the sun comes up just to hear him crow makes my ass itch. Now, instead of arguing politics, why not lay back and hike up your skirt, so I can take a look at that there rash?"

Rolling her eyes, Fiona rolled up her ruffled knee-length skirt and laid down as Gladys placed her legs up on stirrups and stuck her head in to look. Alex watched and pondered if this was a conversation they had many times, with it always ending the same, the two of them coming at an impasse. Shaking her head, Gladys rubbed her hands together and Alex noticed they began emitting a pale white glow as she ducked back under the copper fabric of the dress.

"Gladys, you can heal people?"

"Yes ma'am." Gladys poked her head out. "Well, to some extent at least."

"But... you're a gray. How is that even possible?"

"I learned how to control my emotions and focus them into creating magic. It was hard, but with Jackson's help, I figured it out. The two of us have even been teaching the other grays in town to use magic as well, young Richard included."

"Richard? Really?"

"Yes indeed. The young man was eager to learn, sayin' something bout never being unable to protect the people he cared about again. He be doin' well too. Won't be long till he can summon weapons as well."

"Why, that's incredible. This is exactly what the Resistance back in Manevia was trying to accomplish. If only Tom and Henry could see what you have done here, why they'd be overjoyed."

"I'm sure they be impressed, and maybe one day we'll have a chance to show 'em. But for now, I gots to heal Miss. Walsh and send her on her merry way."

Winking, Gladys ducked back under Fiona's skirt and healed up the rash the woman complained about. When she was all healed, Fiona sat up and let her skirt drop unceremoniously back to her knees and hoped off the table. Bidding the ladies at the clinic a farewell, she walked out the door without uttering another word as she shut the door behind her.

Alex watched her leave, all the while wishing to run after her. Knowing what her young friend was thinking, Gladys told her to go for it and that she would finish cleaning up by herself. She did not know what role Alexandra had to play in everything going on about town, but she knew it was an important one, and befriending the prostitute was a necessary step. Watching Alex run out the door after Fiona, Gladys prayed to the gods that nothing bad would happen to either of the women when the political unrest finally came creeping into Fall Harbor.

CHAPTER 10

A Sad Tale

Running through the clinic doors, Alex paused to glance about for signs of Fiona. Spotting the copper brown hem of the woman's dress vanish around the corner, she set off in its direction, not wishing to lose sight of her again. Rounding the corner of the stone building she spotted the woman she was curious to know more about heading slowly towards the center of town. Paying no attention at the oncoming traffic, she ran across the road waving her arm, nearly getting hit by a car in the process.

"Fiona!" Alex ducked away from the bumper of the vehicle coming to an abrupt stop. Ignoring the man behind the wheel who was making obscene gestures at her, she continued to dash across the street. "Wait!"

Freezing in her tracks at a now all too familiar, annoying voice, Fiona turned to see the young woman from the night before chasing after her. The sun illuminated her porcelain skin and her chestnut hair shined like silk causing Fiona's heart to skip a beat at seeing her. She wondered what that girl saw in her, but she reckoned it had something to do with the young thing's affinity for the lowest of the low society had to offer. Still, she could not pass up a chance to chat with Alexandra more, even if social rules forbade such a travesty. So, instead of running away as she should have, Fiona stood on the other side of the street waiting for Alex to catch up until the princess was standing in front of her, with her emerald eyes glistening with excitement.

"Thank you for waiting." Alex heaved out as she attempted to catch her breath. "I was afraid I was going to lose you."

"What can I do you for, dove? Did Gladys forget to lecture me 'bout something and sent you after me?"

"No. I..." Alex blinked her eyes. "... I was just wondering if you would care to have lunch with me?"

"You wish to have lunch with me?"

"Yes. I'll buy. What do you fancy eating?"

"Lambkin, I don't think you have noticed, but a woman of my status ain't welcome in any of these fancy establishments."

"Fine, I'll grab a bagged lunch from the café across from the town hall, and we can eat at the park across the street. What do you say?"

Fiona stood wide-eyed, staring at the dainty little thing before her as she fished around for words to speak to her. Aside from her secret lover and her brother, no one in the upper echelons of society had dared to offer her any kindness before, and frankly, she did not know how to respond to such gestures. But as she studied Alex closely, her stomach rumbled, and it reminded her that she had not eaten since the previous morning. Things had been tight for her and Lawrence lately, and she skimped the best ways she knew how. Now, as she was reminded of her hunger, she smiled at Alex and nodded her head.

"All right dove, but I sure hope you know what you are getting yourself into, my kind ain't exactly who you should be socializing with."

"Stop worrying about what others might think and let's go. I don't know about you, but I'm starving."

Grabbing Fiona's hand, Alex pulled her along down the street, heading towards the town hall. Fiona glanced at the former princess and wondered what the girl could possibly know about being hungry. Sure, she may have given up her status and became a fugitive to marry the half-blood, but she was still ranked amongst the highest members of society. Unlike her, Alex wouldn't know what it was like to go days without eating. Yet, despite how naïve this newcomer was, the prostitute could not help but delight in her innocence as it reminded her of simpler times, before the streets became her home.

As the two women approached the Luna Café, Fiona noticed at least a dozen eyes burning a hole in the back of her head, reminding her of what society now thought of her. The town center was a bustling place for the snobs and rich folk to hang out during the day, and she dared not venture there before sundown, at least until now.

Fiona did not have to guess what people were thinking, she knew these folks better than they knew themselves. But as she was put on the spot all she could do was hold her head high, pretending they did not bother her. Pulling Alex to a stop outside the short wrought-iron fence enclosing the café patio, she glanced around at the people glaring at her before turning to the princess.

"I think this be as far as I'm willing to go Lambkin. I am not exactly welcome beyond them gates." Fiona nodded her head towards the 'No Wagtails' sign hanging up on the brick wall by the entrance. "Why don' you run in and get the food. I'll wait for you here."

"Oh. All right." Alex glanced behind her at the sign frowning. "What would you like?"

"Surprise me." Fiona shook her head and smiled.

"Whatever you say, Fiona. Wait here, I'll be right back."

Running inside, Alex left Fiona alone and her gaze turned to the middle-aged woman in a long, white dress with a large, brimmed hat. The socialite was shooting daggers at her over her mug as a wicked smirk played on her lips. Fiona knew this woman well. Agatha King was one of the snobbiest women in Fall Harbor, and the talk of every prostitute on the row. Her husband had frequented the brothels and street corners almost nightly, looking to escape his wife's unbearable personality with someone who treated him like a human being.

Joining her longtime friend at the small bistro table was Eliza Jones, a spinster in a black skirt and frilly top with a bun wound so tight it may have cut off the circulation to her head. Leaning over the floral arrangement at the center of the table, Agatha whispered something in her friend's ear, causing Eliza to snicker while glaring at Fiona. Rolling her eyes, the prostitute sensed she was the topic of conversation for those two, and the only thing she could do was ignore them as she always had.

The two women continued to sit at their table, chattering their latest gossip, and shooting menacing glances her way every now and then. Fiona's skin was beginning to crawl, and she thought of running away when she spotted Alex walking out the door with

a large paper bag in hand. Suddenly, as if by magic, the two har-
ridans turned their heads toward the young woman as she walked
by them, and directed all their hatred to her instead.

"There she is." Agatha remarked loud enough for the whole
patio to hear as poor Alex turned to glance at her. "There is the
woman who gave up being a princess to shack up with that mongrel Hartwood."

"Hartwood you say? Why, that name rings a bell. I think I remember that piece of work from when he lived here a few years
prior." Eliza curled up her crimson lip into a smirk. "Why, he be
the one with the harlot of a mother, am I right dear?"

"One and the same. He's also a thief, a scoundrel, and a mur-
derous scumbag to boot."

"Well, it's no wonder she spends her time buying food for that
trollop over there. The delusional little girl seems to enjoy spending her time with the riffraff and sewer rats. I bet the poor thing
isn't right in the head."

"Indeed, perhaps she's a bit slow." Agatha hissed. "Or maybe,
no amount of money can buy you class."

Standing before the black, iron gate, Alex trembled as her free
hand clenched into a tight fist. She expected such vile, ignorant
comments about Jay and Fiona from people back home, but the
people in East Ashland were supposed to be different, they were
supposed to be civilized. She wondered how townsfolk, who were
accustomed to sharing their space with people from different
walks of life could not only spout such hatred but find delight in
it as well. Trying her best to regain her composure, Alexandra
took a deep breath and turned to face the women again, giving
them the best smile she could muster.

"And I see no amount of class can acquire you enough manners to mind your own business. But what would I know, I'm apparently not as civilized and cultured as you, ladies." Alex spoke coldly as she opened the gate to the sound of the whole patio gasping at her rebuttal. "And I do use the term ladies loosely by the way. The two of you are nothing more than snobby, no good, gossiping bitties who clearly have nothing better to do with their time than spread vicious lies.

"Now, I bid you both a good day while you continue to delight in your miserable existence, which is something you seem to do exceptionally well." Turning her head up high, Alex turned on her heals and slammed the gate shut as she stormed out. Grabbing hold of Fiona's hand, she pulled her along, leaving everyone around them to erupt into chatter. "Come on Fiona, lets really give them something to talk about."

"Dang, Lambkin. You sure ain't making friends 'round here." Fiona stole a glance behind her shoulder to the wide-eyes patrons caught off guard by Alexandra's words.

"I wouldn't want to be friends with such narrow-minded people to begin with. I much rather be friends with the likes of you and Lawrence."

"What? Me? Why ever would you want to be friends with someone like me?"

"Because," Alex pulled Fiona into the garden, headed for a bench closest to the fountain, "I like you. You are a nice person Fiona, and I want to know more about you."

"You sure are a strange one dove." Fiona sat on the metal seat and regarded the splashing fountain sparkling like a thousand diamonds with the sun. "Sure is a lovely place during the day, ain't it?"

"It most certainly is." Alex sat down beside her and sighed at the calming effect the tranquil garden had on her. "This may sound silly, but I feel oddly drawn to this place. Almost like it means something to me."

"Not silly at all dove. Perhaps this place held significant meaning to you in a past life."

"Yes. Perhaps that's what it is. Thank you for not laughing at me over this."

"I ain't one of them snobs from the café you know. I hold an open mind lambkin." Fiona straightened out her skirt as she tilted her head to the bright blue sky above. "But all right, enough of the idle chatter, what did you get us?"

"A sandwich, some pear juice, and a cookie." Alex reached in the bag and handed Fiona her food. "I hope you like it. Enjoy."

"Thank you dove. You really are too nice, you know that?" Fiona looked at Alex while shaking her head. "Now, to be fair since you are feedin' me and all, what would you like to know about me? I'll tell you anything."

"Well. As long as you don't mind telling me, I'd like to know how you ended up in the profession that you did."

"I see." Fiona glanced at Alex and smiled. "Normally, this isn't something I talk about. But, given what your husband is, I see no need to hide my past from you. So, I guess you will be the first person I will tell my story to in ages. Just promise me that if you get uncomfortable listening to anything I have to say, you tell me to stop right away."

Fiona bit into her sandwich as she glanced over at Alex who nodded her head vigorously. Rolling her eyes, she had to admire the young woman who seemed so eager to get to know her, and she was hoping she would still be around after she got done.

Swallowing her food, she took a deep breath and started her story while the girl beside her hung on her every word.

"First thing you must know about me is that I grew up in the same social circle which now shuns me. My given name isn't even Fiona Walsh, it's Aisling Flinn. My daddy was a prominent government man over in Clear Springs. He used to oversee everyone who came in and out of that port and deal with any situation which might arise. He was well regarded by everyone who knew him, and we lived in the best neighborhood the town had to offer.

"To all our friends and neighbors, he appeared like a good, generous, kindhearted man. On the outside we appeared like the perfect family with him being a devoted husband and doting father. But, as often as it is, things aren't always as they appear to the outside world. What his friends, acquaintances, and co-workers didn't see, was who he really was.

"They didn't see him beating my momma senseless after he had too much to drink, or the dirty way he looked at me. At first, it was just looking as I bathed or undressed, but after mama got pregnant with Lawrence, it turned into touching. The first time it happened I had just turned twelve and was starting to develop in more feminine ways. I was taking a bath while mama slept, and my daddy watched me from the door as he always did, rubbing his crotch and licking his lips.

"I tried to ignore him as I had on many occasions. He always made me feel self-conscious from his unwanted attention, and I hated how he made my skin crawl. I thought he would rub himself off again and go back to sleep like he had all the previous nights. But, unfortunately for me, when I got out of the tub, he moved in and grabbed me by the arm, pulling me in closer. Leaning in, he smelled my hair, and savored the water on my neck with his tongue as he grabbed hold of my buttocks.

"Rubbing my bare skin, he pressed his erection against me, pushing me against the wall. I tried to pull away, but he just sucked my neck and fondled my breasts. I kneed him in the balls, but instead of letting me go, he slapped me across the face and yanked me into my room. Throwing me on my bed, he leaped on top of me, pinning me down. I wanted to scream, but he pressed his hand over my mouth and tol' me he would kill mama and me if I dared make a peep. Petrified I stayed silent while I cried and prayed for him to not hurt me.

"Satisfied I wouldn't make a sound, he climbed on top of me, spreading my legs and continuing his assault. At first, he penetrated me with his fingers, scraping my insides. I remember crying from the pain he caused me, but he was not done. Panting heavily, he took his pants off and shoved his penis inside me, stealing my innocence away. I still remember the tremendous pain as he was tearing me apart, and the only thing I could do was cry silently as he finished with me. I cried myself to sleep that night as I continued to ache from him penetrating me, and all the while I wished he would have killed me.

"And, it didn't end there. The heavier my mama got with Lawrence, the more my father thought me out to rape me. Most nights I just laid there, staring at the ceiling, spiriting myself away from what he was doing to me and praying for it to be swift. And, once Lawrence was born three months later, things went from bad to worse. My father hated him the second he came out of my mother. You see, he wanted it to be another girl that he could love and cherish, but Lawrence denied him that perversion. That's why daddy often took his anger out on Lawrie. He like to burn him with his cigars while he wailed in pain, unable to defend himself. But he always saved the worst of himself for me at night. In no time at all, he slept in my bed more often than he did in my mama's.

"Now, mama saw what was happening to her children, and she did her best to protect us. One day, she tried to leave with us in tow and run away to live with her family down south. But, my daddy came home drunk early that night and caught us. Seeing her with her bags packed, and Lawrie in her arms, he flew into a rage. He smacked Lawrence out of her hands and the poor lad flew to the floor with a loud smack before he slid into the radiator. Lawrie began wailing from the pain, but daddy paid no attention to him as he flung himself on top of mama. He kept hitting her with his fists and slamming her head on the floor. He hollered at her between every sickening crunch his fist made against her face, calling her all sorts of names, until she was barely conscious and unable to fight back. Having turned her face into hamburger, he sat on top of her and strangled her with his bare hands as she pleaded for me to run.

"Once her lifeless body lay on the floor, staring blankly at the ceiling, my father turned to me with a sneer. He left the nine-month-old Lawrence wailing on the floor where he lay, bleeding from hitting his head on that blasted radiator as he dragged me into my room. He violently raped me three times that night as I had to listen to my brother choking on his own spit while I lay in bed, powerless to help him.

"Having satisfied himself, daddy left my room and told me that if I ever tried to leave like mama did, he'd kill Lawrence and me like he did her. By the time I had the courage and strength to get out of bed and leave my room, poor Lawrence was blue in the face and barely breathing from screaming for hours with no one to comfort him. Snot and blood covered his little face as I picked him, cleared his airway, and held him while daddy went to get rid of momma's body which he rolled up in one of our rugs. That night as I cradled my baby brother in my arms and tried to comfort him while I healed his injuries, I vowed to protect him from our father no matter what.

"For the next three years, my life was the things nightmares were made from. Many times I wanted to run away, but fear kept me by my father's side as he continued to violate me at night and beat my brother senseless during the day. Every night I prayed Lady Death would take me and spare me from the pain. But fate seemed to have a different plan for me, so I continued to suffer in silence as my father tore me apart every night. Then, one day the unthinkable happened, I learned I was carrying my daddy's baby inside me. The mere idea of it made my stomach churn. I knew this was exactly what he wanted, and I could not bear to go through with it. That was the moment I knew I had to do something to get away from him. Not only did I need to save Lawrie and myself, but I had to put an end to the abomination growing inside of me.

"For the next week I plotted my escape, perfecting the plan so he would never catch up to us. The following Monday, while at school, I snuck into the nurse's office and stole some sleeping pills they kept around on hand to deal with troublesome children who were boarded there. I took the entire bottle and snuck the whole lot of them in my daddy's drink that night and even poured him a glass when he got home while I sat in his lap and doted on him. I allowed that sick pervert to take me to bed that night and do his thing to me while I pretended to enjoy it.

"Once he got done, he lay beside me, caressing me while I waited for him to pass out. It didn't take long for the pills to kick in, and he lay there snoring with his arm draped over me. Once I knew he was asleep, I got up, got dressed, stole all the money he had in his wallet, took Lawrence, and ran out the door without looking back. I ran as fast as I could that night with a lump in my stomach and a toddler in my arms, going as far as my feet would carry me.

"We made it as far as the slums of Clear Springs. It was the part of town where the lowest class citizens lived, and it was all the way on the other side of town from where we lived. There, amongst the grimy alleyways I found a rundown inn where the innkeeper took pity on me. I told her my story and what I had done to escape, and she put us for the night at no charge. The next morning, she gave me the name of a doctor in Black Hallow who would cut that baby right out of me and sent me on my way.

"I had just enough money on me for Lawrence and me to get there and to get my problem taken care of. This left us with no place to bed down for the night, and no food in our stomach. We slept in a cardboard box in an alleyway that night as the rain doused us with icy cold water. On top of it all, I bled profusely from the procedure I had done, more so than I thought I should have. I lay there, clutching my side from the pain as sweat poured down my brow, feeling Lawrie shiver beside me. I may have even bled to death that night with Lawrence freezing by my side if a kind soul had not stumbled upon us and saved our lives.

"Her name was Catrine, a local prostitute, and at eighteen she was only a little older than I was. She took us both to her small apartment in the building beside which I lay that night and gave us some food and warm clothing. She helped stop my bleeding as she listed to my tale and told me she could relate. It was her who gave me the name Fiona. She said it suited me better than my stuffy old name, and I agreed.

"We stayed there with her for a few years, enjoying our time together. She was the one who taught me this trade. She always said it wasn't much better than what our fathers did to us, but at least this way we were getting paid. And it was Catrine who showed me what love truly was. Her and I spent our nights pleasing dirty old men, and by day, we belonged to each other. She was the first person I ever loved, and I gave myself to her freely.

"She was so beautiful with her long black hair and deep blue eyes. The way she looked at me as she lay in bed and called me over to her made me shiver. And her touch Alex, it took all the pain away and made me feel whole again. With her, there was no pain, it was only pleasure as she was the gentlest person I had known up until this point. I thought she would be my eternity until fate ripped her away from me like it did my mama.

"You see, my papa, well he don' give up so easy. He had spent a lot of time and money tracking us down, learning of what I had done to his baby. And one fateful night, he finally caught up to us. It was the night Catrine had returned home early from her corner because Lawrie was sick, and it was her turn to check in on him. Apparently, my daddy knocked on our door and demanded to see us. Knowing what he had done and why he was there, she refused.

"That's when daddy tried to force his way in, but she fought him, screaming for Lawrie to run. As my brother fled down the fire escape, daddy kicked the door in and ended Catrine's life by slitting her throat. And, if that was not bad enough, he violated her lifeless body before my brother returned with the authorities who cuffed him and dragged him away. Well, at least that was what the neighbors told me as I came home to find the police carrying her out in a body bag. With Catrine's death, my world shattered once more. Yet again, daddy stole my happiness away and left me with a numbing void deep inside.

"I knew he would get out eventually, and I knew we couldn't stay in Black Hollow any longer. Not that there was anything left for me there, anyway. That night I packed my bags, took Lawrence, and boarded a train for Fall Harbor. I was told it was a bit better here for people like me, and compared to Black Hollow, it was. I covered my tracks well so my father would never be able to find us again, and I came here.

"With my meager savings, the ones Catrine and I planned on using to leave this life of ours, I bought my tiny row house and settle down. But with the money running dry, and me not having much of anything to offer, the lifestyle called to me, pulling me back in. Not having a choice, I started working the corner again so I can feed my brother and keep a roof over our head. And here we are now, years later, sitting on a park bench with me not having escaped anything. But you know what Alex, I regret none of it, for it showed me who I was, and it helped Lawrence become a better man, far better than our father could ever hope to be."

"Oh, Fiona," Alexandra's eyes grew moist at the edges, "I am so sorry you had the life you did. No one deserves to go through such horrific things. And you shouldn't continue to suffer like this, it's just not fair. If only those people out there knew why you did what you did..."

"They wouldn't care lambkin. Like my daddy, they only care about how much of a scar people like me and Jay are on their perfect society, and they don't care as to the reasons why. Truth be told, we are nothing, not even in East Ashland. We are the lowest of the low society has to offer, and once we die, we are quickly forgotten, if anyone even cares to notice that we're gone that is. This is why I'm glad Lawrence has an honest job working for a good man who cares about him. He can easily escape this life any time he wants, be an upstanding member of the collective, maybe even marry one of them snobs at the café, but that darn fool still feels loyalty to his fallen sister. He stays by my side, defends me against the callous remarks, and takes a reputation blow when he should distance himself as far away from me as possible. And the sooner the better if you ask me."

"No, he shouldn't! How can you even talk like that? You are his family. You are the one person in his life who cared enough about him to sacrifice everything you had to save him." Alex flared her nostrils and frowned at Fiona. "Can't you see, you are his entire world, no matter what anyone thinks of you."

"And what about what society thinks of him? Is it fare to him to have a sister who's a whore?" Fiona's voice cracked. "I'm an embarrassment to him, and I know it. And what of you? What about what they think of you being married to a half-blood? What do Lawrence and you get out of staying loyal to either of us other than the wrath of the feeble-minded people of the outside world?"

"We get to be with the people we care about. Why should Lawrence or I care about what anyone thinks? Those people, they don't know you or Jay as well as we do, and they don't want to even try. But it's their loss because you are both wonderful people who'd do anything for the ones they love." Alex placed a trembling hand over Fiona's. "You of all people should know that we don't abandon the ones we love just because that's what everyone expects us do. You didn't abandon your brother and Jay didn't abandon his son. You both did so out of love, so, what makes you think Lawrence and I should be different?"

"You shouldn't be, but..." Fiona squeezed Alex's hand and shuddered at what the young woman said. "How do you do it, dove? How do you stay so sweet despite everything life throws at you?"

"Like you, I have survived worse. When the fight is all you know, the fight is all that keeps you going."

"Funny, that's exactly what Lawrence always tells me." Fiona giggled as she shook her head at how strange this newcomer was. She really was like her Catrine, and that both delighted and scared her at the same time because she knew all too well how life treated people with a tender heart. "So, I guess this mean it was not pity that invited me out to lunch today. Could it have actually been a genuine interest to get to know me?"

"Of course, silly. I already told you, I want to be your friend, even if the snobs in this town condemn me for it."

"I'd be honored to call you my friend, lambkin, and you'd be my only one. Still, I can't help but worry that someone like you is not meant for this cruel world of ours. I still fear that getting close to me will seal your fate as it did Catrine's."

Shaking her hand, Alex smiled at Fiona not knowing how to respond. As nice as her new friends in Ashland were, they all seemed to worry too much about her, and that did little to alleviate her own worries. Deciding it was best to drop the subject, she offered to walk with Fiona until she got back home, an offer the woman accepted gratefully. Strolling out together from the ivy-covered archway, Alex spotted two familiar faces approaching them, and Fiona turned a bright shade of pink as she averted their eyes.

"Richard!" Alex beamed as her friend approached the park with his boss.

"Hello, Alex." Richard nodded his head. "Miss. Walsh."

"Mr. Cadwall." Fiona continued to stare at her feet. "Mayor Cox."

Walking up behind Richard with his hands folded behind his back Caleb Cox eyeballed both women. A coy smile played on his lips as he continued to look over the strange pair before him, pondering the implications. He already suspected the princess of Manevia differed from the rest of their social class but seeing her out and about with a common street whore caused him to raise an eyebrow.

"What are you two fine ladies doing together this afternoon?"

"Alex... I mean Mrs. Hartwood," Fiona turned her head away from Cox as she continued to gaze down to the ground, "was kind enough to buy me lunch today after my appointment with Mrs. Carlson."

"Is that so?" Caleb's eyes trailed towards Alex. "And aren't you afraid of what the people will say about you spending your free time with a prostitute, my darling girl?"

"Not at all. Why should I be bothered with what the ignorant have to say about me?"

"No reason at all my good woman, no reason at all. It's just that people in our society, especially of your social class, don't dare be seen with a streetwalker. I thought you might be the same."

"Then you thought wrong Mr. Mayor. Perhaps it is our society who should be ashamed for their narrow-minded ways and how they treat other people. But I will certainly not apologize for being friends with anyone I see fit."

"Of course, you are so right Mrs. Hartwood. These people really ought to be ashamed of themselves as they know not what the rest our world is like. And I, for one, am glad we have people like you living in our humble town to keep them in check." Cox nodded his head as the corners of his lips curled to reveal a dazzling white smile. "Say now, Richard and I were just off to see George over at the boutique. Seems as if the poor chap had some vandalism problems last night and had called us over to investigate. Would you two lovely ladies like to join us? It looks like Ms. Walsh could use a new dress or two, especially after the horrible incident from last night."

"Oh, no, Mayor," Fiona shook her head as she turned a bright shade of red. "I couldn't possibly accompany you. The three of you shouldn't be seen with the likes of me, and I couldn't afford anything George carries anyhow."

"Nonsense my dear woman, any friend of Mrs. Hartwood is a friend of mine. Join us," Caleb Cox extended his hand towards Fiona's, "I will have George put anything you fancy on my tab."

"That is very kind of you sir, but I couldn't possibly accept such a generous offer."

"I'm afraid I must insist." Cox pulled Fiona closer to him, putting her arm under his. "Otherwise, I would not be able to sleep at night knowing that one of my citizens is going hungry and not able to afford necessities such as clothing. I'm already distraught as is knowing someone tried to harm you last night. Don't make me fret more over you, please."

"Oh, I don't know," Fiona gazed at her feet, "what do you think Alex, should we go? I wouldn't want to keep you away from your husband and boy. Not to mention I wouldn't want to impose on your outing with your friends."

"I think Jay will be fine without me for a while longer. Not to mention it has been a while since I got to spend time with my friend here," Alex put her arm through Richard's and smiled. "I'd love the chance to catch up while you shopped, and you certainly do need something to get your mind off of last night."

"So, it's settled then. We will go to George's and investigate, while you two pretty ladies do some shopping. Go on Richard, you go ahead with Mrs. Hartwood. I shall walk a few steps behind you with the lovely Fiona and let the two of you catch up."

Nodding his head, Richard walked forward with Alex strolling by his side. Having her so close to him, being able to smell her delicate scent, flooded Richard's head with memories, and not all of them good. As they continued to walk arm in arm, he pondered what could have been if they were both born in East Ashland instead. Could he have been the one warming her bed at night instead of Jay? Pondering the missed possibilities made Richard's heart ache as he was still very much in love with her. But, he knew it was not meant to be, so he resorted to being with her in any way he could even if he had to sit on the sidelines.

Glancing to his right side, he looked over the at sun shining on her long chestnut hair and caught the glimmer in her green eyes causing his heart to flip. Cursing himself at not being man enough to fight for the woman he loved, Richard cleared the lump in his throat and Alex turned to face him with the sweet, innocent smile she always gave him. With his heart leaping in his chest, he took a deep breath to steady his nerves, realizing he could not avoid talking to her forever.

"So, I see you're busy making friends all over town..." gazing around them, Richard noticed the stares coming from the crowd as they walked by, "and by the looks of it, some new enemies as well."

"Well, you know me and the effect I have on people. Apparently, I simply cannot help but cause a commotion wherever I go." Watching Richard laugh, Alex felt the tension from moments earlier fade away. "Also, what do you expect me to do? The one person I wish to catch up with, my oldest, dearest friend, seems to have absolutely no time for me."

Alexandra's words cut through Richard like a knife. He kept avoiding her on purpose, afraid of confronting his feelings for her which continued to linger despite his best efforts. He was also plagued by dreams of the girl since he landed in Fall Harbor. Dreams so erotic, he did not dare explore them any further. Yet, not once did he stop to think of how much he was hurting her. Remembering the night she broke him out of prison, Richard realized that while he could not erase the feeling he had for her, or control the explicit dreams he had at night about her, losing her all together was also not an option. He still needed her by his side, in whatever way she would allow him to be.

"I'm sorry love. I promise to make time for you at least once a week. I also promise to spend at least a few nights with my dear friends at their tavern."

"That's better. And I could even drop by and visit you at the town hall when you are not busy. Or, we could even enjoy a spot of tea in that lovely garden of yours when you are not working."

"You know where I live?"

"Indeed." Alex nodded her head. "Gladys showed me when I first met her."

"I swear," Richard shook his head, "people in this town have no concept of privacy. But all right, if Jay is all right with it, you can drop by my place any time you wish."

"Better." Alex giggled. "I'm sure Jay won't mind if I spend an occasional afternoon with my best friend. Plus, I wish to spend more time in that wonderful garden of yours. You always did have a way with plants."

Turning from Richard, Alex continued to study the shoreline of Wellaby in the distance as they slowly made their way to the boutique. It was a warm day, and the sun glistened off the river between the two towns as birds chirped in the trees. Feeling light-hearted, Alexandra delighted in the peace Fall Harbor offered her, until they reached the small white building that belonged to George. What she saw as they entered through the remnants of an iron gate cause Alex to gasp, as her lighthearted mood quickly changed to one of pure horror at what she saw.

CHAPTER 11

A New Threat

The once immaculate facade of white the boards was covered in black paint as a strange wet symbol still ran down to the ground. ⊕ Studying it up close, Alex pondered what it could mean as she placed a shaking hand over her mouth and stilled her breath. Coming closer to it, she touched the still dripping paint, rubbing the sticky residue on her fingers as she brought it up to her nose. She thought the paint had a peculiar odor to it, a strange scent of death clung to it, and it reeked of blood and ash.

Turning her up head to see what was creaking above, Alex noted the boutique sign dangling off a single intact chain, smacking the brick with the breeze. The window which once housed the mannequins had been covered up by several wood boards. Even the gate into the garden lay flat on the ground and the surrounding plants were blackened from a fire which still stunk of fuel. Seeing the destruction around her caused her chest to tighten as she stifled another gasp at the daunting reality that now hit her.

Even in East Ashland, the free province of Alteria, Alex could not escape the hatred which permeated the people's souls.

"What in all of Alteria happened here?" Alex ran up to Richard, her eyes begging him for answers. "What is that symbol on the wall?"

"They call themselves Militibus Puritatis."

"But who are they? And what do they want?"

"They're extremists Alex. They take this whole blood-purity nonsense to the next level. Not only do they wish to eliminate the remaining half-bloods, but they strive to wipe the gray population off the face of Alteria as well."

"But why?" Alex suddenly felt herself getting faint. "What's in it for them? And what did poor George ever do to them?"

Before Richard had a chance to respond to his friend, Caleb Cox let go of Fiona and ran up just in time to catch Alex from hitting the ground. Seems the realization of what transpired finally hit her, causing her head to spin and the blood to drain from her head. Lifting the girl back to her feet, Cox assured her he would take care of everything as he handed Alex over to Richard and ushered everyone inside the store, away from the curious eyes of the onlookers gathering in the streets.

Stepping through the cracked door barely hanging on the hinges, a familiar bell chimed to signal their presence. Glancing about the charred interior of the store, Caleb scowled as he called out to the store owner. Still holding Alex in his arms, Richard looked towards the back room where a disheveled George ran out to greet them.

"Mayor Cox! Richard!" George flung his arms in the air. "Am I glad to see you. You would not believe the night I had. But," spotting the women, the store owner raised his brow and straightened out his stained white coat, "I see you have brought some company."

"Yes George, do forgive me," Cox glanced about the establishment covered in soot and broken glass, "but I didn't think it was this bad. I just thought Miss. Walsh could use a new dress or two after her incident from last night. She was against it of course but I insisted and offered to pay. I did not realize your place was in such disarray, or else I wouldn't have brought them here. Do forgive me my man."

"Of course, sir, no need to apologize. I would expect nothing less from a man as generous as you. And what about you, love?" George turned to look at Alex and sighed. "I see you have returned to wearing long dresses again."

"Sorry George. I simply cannot be comfortable in anything less."

"You are far too modest my dear," George rolled his eyes and smiled, "but I suppose that is what makes you so lovely. I do have a gorgeous dress coming in today that would be perfectly suited for you, but with everything that has happened, I haven't had time to run up to the port and pick it up."

"Don't worry about it, George. I think I have enough dresses as is, and you seem to have bigger worries on your hands right now."

"Ridiculous. A lovely lady can never have too many dresses and picking out clothing for someone as beautiful as you Mrs. Hartwood helps keep my mind off the terrible things happening here. I'll drop it off at your place as soon as I get the chance to get it."

"You certainly will my good man," Caleb patted George on his back, "you always make sure the pretty girls are well-dressed, don't you?"

"That I do, sir. That I do."

"More reasons to love you, George." Cox laughed before stealing a glance at a headless, charred mannequin by his feet. "Now, why not allow the ladies to shop the selection you have left while you show Richard and I what happened here."

"Absolutely. Marvelous idea." George turned to the two women and pointed to the back of the room where all the remaining clothing lay piled up in the corner. "Everything that survived the vandals has been moved to the back, away from the reach of the scoundrel who dared try to violate my business. Take your time looking through it all ladies. I am in no rush."

Taking hold of Fiona's hand, Alex lead her away to get her some fresh clothe as the ones she was wearing were covered in grime from a hard night's work. As the women vanished into the backroom of the store, Caleb Cox glanced around once more at the glass scattered all over the floor and turned to George with a shake of his head.

"All right. Tell me exactly what happened here. The front of the store looks like a disaster and it's not much better in here."

"I was woken up by a loud crash coming from downstairs at around three in the morning. It sounded like an explosion happened, and I damn near fell out of my bed from shock. Unable to figure out what could have happened in my half-asleep state, I rushed downstairs in my skivvies only to find my display window shattered by a brick. The mannequins lay knocked over, their clothing torn and painted over. And, on top of that, my storefront and front lawn were on fire.

"I had no time to think as the flames were getting hotter, gobbling up everything in sight. So, I grabbed a bucket of water and start putting out the fires as the scoundrel ran off into the night.

By the time I was done, the hooligans were long gone, and so was half my business. They were kind enough to leave a note in my mailbox though, but I reckon they wanted to get their message across."

"I see." Cradling his chin in his hand, Cox nodded his head. "And what did this note say."

"Oh, well, I have it right here sir." George reached into his coat pocket and pulled out a crumpled parchment, handing it to Cox.

Caleb smoothed out the paper the best he could and looked over the letters scribble in red. The penmanship was remarkable, curvy, and neat, signifying the writer was not only a person of high status but also well-educated. Frowning, the mayor read over the text and the signature, not believing his eyes. Wrinkling his forehead, Cox narrowed his eyes and handed the letter over to Richard who also glanced at the text, his eyes growing wide.

Gray blood will cleanse our streets. Whores and half-bloods will be no more. This is the coming of a new day. This is our destiny.

Militibus Puritatis

"I see the ruthless gang from West Ashland has finally struck on my soil. This is unacceptable." Cox fumed. "I will need to report this to Commander Donahue as soon as possible. He will certainly want to hear of this travesty and prepare East Ashland the best way he can. In the meantime, I shall send my people over to fix up your place and return it to normal as soon as possible."

"Thank you, sir, but it's really too much. I can't ask you to do this."

"No, George, it is not enough. I shall not have my citizens getting attacked on my watch, and I do not take such threats kindly. I'll double the patrols at night to ensure this never happens to anyone again, and maybe these scoundrels will think twice before they cross Mayor Cox again."

"Thank you, sir. You are the best leader anyone could ask for, I hope you know that."

"He is indeed." Alex walked over with Fiona in tow. "He has certainly impressed me thus far with his generosity and willingness to protect his people."

"Why, Mrs. Hartwood, I do not deserve such kind words from a lady of your caliber, but I shall accept them graciously." Cox bowed to Alex and a grin spread across his face as he knew he had won over her approval. Lifting his head up, he looked up at Fiona with three fresh dresses in her arms and took a deep breath. "Is that all you are getting my dear? I told you that you could have anything you wish."

"This is all I need, and I already feel as if I am imposing too much."

Cox exhaled deeply and shook his head. "No imposition at all Fiona. Lawrence has been too good to me, and I could never pass up a chance to help out the woman who raised him." Scooping the dresses from her hands, Caleb handed them over to George. "Charge these to my account good man, and bag them up for the lady please."

"They are on the house, sir." George went behind the counter and grabbed a small bag. "It's the least I can do after you've insisted on helping me out with fixing this place up and all."

"I'm simply doing my job George, there is no need for you to do this. And if you need anything else, please, don't hesitate to ask."

"Of course, though I do hate to impose." George handed the small bag to Fiona and glance around the mess in his room. "Anything else I can do for any of you before I start cleaning this up?"

"Perhaps you can come to dinner at my house George." Alex piped up. "Actually, you all can."

"What's this Mrs. Hartwood, are you being serious?" Cox took as step back, eyes wide at the sudden proposition.

"Absolutely. George will be too busy cleaning up this mess. He will have no time left to cook, and I haven't spoken to Richard in a long time. Not to mention Fiona and Lawrence seem as if they could use a hearty meal and some good company. And it would simply be too rude to leave you out Mr. Cox. Plus, I would love to get to know you better and see why everyone here loves you so much."

"And what of Mr. Hartwood? Will he be all right with such an imposition? He was not keen on seeing us last time, and he appears to not be one for dinner parties, or guests."

"Jay simply prefers to know when people are coming over. He will be fine with me inviting you over to the house. I promise."

"In that case, I could not possibly refuse such a tempting offer. What about the rest of you? Will you join me at the Hartwood residence?" Cox looked over at everyone else who seemed to agree with dinner by nodding their heads. "Seems it's settled then, we shall dine over at Mrs. Hartwood's place tonight, and enjoy friendly company to help get our minds of these horrible things that have been happening all over our fine town."

"I'm happy to hear this Mayor. Come by my place at six, and Richard," Alex turned to face her friend, "would you kindly invite Gladys and Jackson over for me, I'd hate for them to feel left out."

"Absolutely. I'll do that as soon as I can."

"You will do it now my good man, right after you fetch some workers to help George out with this place. As for me, I shall escort Fiona home. I want to insure she does not run into any more trouble."

"Yes sir, thank you. I am off to do as you ask. See you at six Alex." Richard waved and dashed out the door without stopping to look back.

"I suppose I should get going as well." Alex looked at the door, getting sad at having Richard run out on her again. "Jay will be wondering where I am by now, and I should warn him about the dinner party so he can help me get ready. I'll see everyone later tonight."

Bidding everyone a farewell, Alex exited into the smoldering garden and winced at the thought of someone doing this to poor George. Choosing to put the horror of the boutique from her mind, she hurried down the street to get home. Stealing a glance at the tower clock of the town hall she picked up her pace, she only had three hours left to get ready, and Rupert would surely have to help out if she hoped to have dinner ready in time for her guests. Alex was looking forward to having dinner with all her friends for once, and as her spirits soared, she forgot all about the unsettling happenings taking place around town as she rushed to get home.

CHAPTER 12

Dinner Amongst Friends

Standing in the kitchen, leaning against the counter cross-armed, Jay pouted as he watched Alex plop a boysenberry pie into their black oven. Beside her, Rupert was stirring the stew which was bubbling away on the stove. The heat from the fire and the savory aroma of the meats and potatoes did little to alleviate his concerns of dealing with impeding house guests. Instead, it only served to remind him that in about an hour his once peaceful home would be invaded by people he did not wish to socialize with.

"Must we have guests over?" Jay whined as Alex got done tending the food. "Don't we have enough people here as is?"

"Of course. These are our friends Jay. Don't you like having friends?"

"Not really. I find them rather bothersome. I'd prefer if it was just you, me, and Andy."

"Roink!"

"All right, and Cosmo, but I'm just not what you'd call a people person."

"It's hard to accept friendship when one has spent as much time being a loner as Master Hartwood." Rupert walked out from the butler's pantry carrying a tray of fresh-cut fruit and cheese. "But fret not dear girl, with time, even the lone wolf will get used to having companions to lean on."

"Like hell I will." Jay crossed his arms again, turning his back to the old man. "There is nothing in this world that can convince me to like people, let alone lean on them."

"Oh, Jay, don't be like this." Alex wrapped her arms around his waist, bringing their bodies closer. "Can't you at least pretend to be friendly... for me?"

"Fine," Jay exhaled while rolling his eyes, "but only 'cause you asked."

As he was about to turn around and embrace his wife, a soft knock resonated through the kitchen, causing Cosmo to bark and shoot up in the air. Frowning, Jay pulled out his pocket watch and stole a glance at the time. It was only five-thirty, far too early for the guests to be showing up. But, before he had a chance to move and see who intruded upon his domicile, the pounding of tiny footsteps flying down the stairs caused Jay to grumble.

Exchanging concerned glances, both Jay and Alex scurried through the door leading from the kitchen to the parlor, but they were too late to stop Andy from flinging the door open for their visitor. Fortunately for the young lad, it was only George who greeted him from the other side with his gentle, honey-colored eyes. The man smiled a dazzling white smile as he ruffled the wispy blonde hair on the boy's head before waving to greet Alex who was standing in the doorway.

"Sorry for coming by so early my dear Mrs. Hartwood, but I just picked this beauty up," George lifted up his arm to reveal a long bag dangling off a hanger, "and I thought you should wear it during dinner. Something this exquisite would look simply splendid on you tonight, and I am sure Mr. Hartwood would enjoy seeing you in it as well."

"Oh, all right George. Come on in." Alex walked over to the man, giving him a hug, and relieving him of his package. "How much do we owe you?"

"Nothing. Mayor Cox has already paid for it as a thank you gift for taking care of Miss. Walsh earlier today. So please, why not go put it on before the other guests arrive?"

Nodding her head, Alex stole a glance at Jay's scowling face before she hurried up the stairs to put on the dress. Cosmo, who was hovering by Jay's head barked loudly in his ear to protest the injustice of this Cox fellow giving gifts to Alex without his permission. Grumbling under his breath, all Jay could do was nod silently in agreement as he knew George did not see his little friend, nor did he want to voice his displeasure at another man putting the moves on his wife. But as Alex walked back down the stairs, his jaw dropped open and all thoughts of Caleb vanished from his mind.

The delicate, silk, floor-length skirt seemed to float around Alexandra's slender frame as a fragile lace ribbon accentuated her waist. Though modest, the gown was still modern with an off the shoulder puff sleeve gathered around the elbow and a flowy ruffle which lay almost flat against her chest. Feeling himself getting aroused at the thought of taking the dress off, Jay shook his head and looked away to avoid giving away his wicked thoughts as George looked on beside him with a broad smile.

"Why, Mrs. Hartwood, that dress fits you like a glove. I mean, it's not surprising since you are such a lovely woman, but still, it's almost as if it was made just for you. Then again, I bet any old dress would look vogue on you too. You could even make a potato sack look lovely. Don't you agree, Mr. Hartwood?"

"Yeah. What he said." Jay glanced back up at Alex and felt himself grow hot. "You'd look gorgeous in anything, darling."

Alex turned a slight shade of pink at Jay's words, but as she was about to reply, another knock interrupted her trail of thought. Glancing at George, she nodded her head, and the man reached over to open the door for her. One the other side, an entire group of people was standing in the street, waiting to come in. Seemed as though Mayor Cox had Lawrence pick up Richard and Fiona before coming over to their house. Upon seeing Alex, Richard's eyes grew wider and then dropped to the ground while Cable grinned and walked inside to greet her.

"Why, my dear Mrs. Hartwood, you look ravishing if I may say so myself." Cox took hold of Alexandra's hand and brought to his lips, placing a soft kiss on the back. "Is that the new dress I had George deliver for you?"

"Ruh! Ruuuh!" Cosmo's mohawk went up as his eyes narrowed at this intruder.

"It is Mayor Cox." Alex pulled her hand away and curtsied. "It was very kind of you to buy it for me, but I think my husband is more than capable of affording clothing for me from here on out."

"My dear woman, I meant it not as an insult to Mr. Hartwood." Caleb shot a glance at Jay who was scowling in his direction. "I'm sorry if it came off that way. I simply wanted to thank you for taking such good care of my dear Fiona today. Do forgive me, my fair lady for such an indiscretion."

"My good Mayor," Jackson walked through the door with Gladys on his arm, "how does one not see buying designer clothing for another man's wife as an insult?"

"Forgive me, Dr. Carlson." Caleb sneered at the man standing behind him. "I am not as old-fashioned as you are and did not realize my faux pas. I shall be sure I will not make the mistake of thanking a woman again with anything other than my words in the future."

"There is nothing wrong with thanking a lady with a gift." Jackson closed the door behind him. "But an extravagant thank you gift, to a married woman, from the most eligible bachelor in town may become misconstrued by others as an indiscreet move on the man's part to bed said woman when her husband is not home."

"Certainly. I can see you are right dear doctor." Cox gritted his teeth with clenched fists as his icy blue eyes glared at Jackson. Regaining his composure, he straightened out his vest and glanced to look at Jay. "I sure hope you can forgive me, Mr. Hartwood. If I gave you, or your lovely wife the wrong impression, I do apologize. And I assure you that I have no intention of stealing your wife away from you."

Shooting daggers at Cox, Jay said nothing as he found the man's apology to be rather phony, and a grumbling Cosmo would surely agree. As the two men continued to stare at one another, the bustling room suddenly fell silent. The tension in the air was defending and one could have sworn you could hear jolts of electricity cracking through the air as neither man was willing to relent. Alex was starting to regret putting the dress on when a whistling butler strolled into the room with a casual, warm smile.

"Ladies. Gentleman." Rupert glanced about the room still smiling. "What are you all standing around here for? Allow me to show you to your seats."

"Rupert?" Richard sputtered. "What... what are you doing here?"

"Why, Master Cadwall, did you really think I would allow Lady Alexandra to come here unaccompanied?" Rupert side glanced at Richard as he guided the guests to the dining room. "After all, someone with a level head needs to keep an eye on her and keep her out of trouble. Don't you think?"

"Yes. Of course."

Richard stuck his finger in the collar of his shirt as the temperature in the room suddenly spiked. He recalled the lectures Rupert used to give him about spending so much time romancing the princess, and he suddenly wanted to run out of the room and vanish. But as the butler pulled a chair out for him, Richard had no choice but to sit down at the table next to Alex. Andy was sitting across from him, and as he watched his childhood friend dote on the boy, his heart ached for the things that could have been.

Observing Richard gaze at Alex, Rupert had to smirk as he did not have to wonder what thoughts were going through the young man's head. She was her mother's daughter after all, and even though she didn't realize it, she had the aura of a seductive vixen around her. He knew all too well how the single men in the room lusted after her without knowing the reason why, or how she permeated their dreams and caused them to have wicked thoughts.

She had done the same to Jay for years before they met, that's how he finally managed to find the bar keep. The only difference was, Jay had already had her, and she had chosen him for eternity.

As he made his way around the table, smiling to himself, Rupert assessed the tension of the men around him. Slowly pouring everyone's drinks, he listened as Cosmo buzzed around his ears, filling him in on who was who. And, as he got around to Mayor Cox, the butler regarded him with a raised brow as his shoulders tensed at the man's energy and the hairs on the back of his neck stood up. The little pigrie was right, there was something about the man that he too, found unsettling, even if he could not put a finger on it. Pondering what the good leader of Fall Harbor could possibly be hiding, he finished pouring everyone's drinks and turned to head back to the kitchen when a small hand wrapped around his wrist. Shaking his head, Rupert turned to look at the green puppy-eyes he had gotten to know all too well over the years and smiled.

"Is there anything you require of me, my lady?"

"Aren't you going to join us, Rupert?"

"No, Madame, I couldn't possibly impose."

"But you're part of the family now."

"I know that dear, but old Rupert prefers to dine alone in the kitchen whilst we have so much company. It's easier for me to keep an eye on things that way, and old habits are hard to break. I assure you, I shall dine with you and the Master from here on out though."

"Can't I change your mind?"

"How about I join you and your company for dessert? Would that be a suitable compromise for you my dear?"

"All right Rupert, but remember, you promised."

"No need to worry madame, you know full well that I do not break my promises."

With Alex finally releasing her grip on Rupert, he vanished into the oasis of the kitchen with Cosmo by his side as the rest of the guest chattered amongst one another. The dinner went well, even if Jay spent most of it making sure no one was trying to steal his wife away from him, and by the time dessert rolled around, everyone felt at ease. True to his word, Rupert brought out the pie and an extra chair to join in on the festivities.

Realizing they had run out of wine, Jay excused himself to go fetch another bottle from the tavern cellar. Watching him walk out of the room, Fiona asked Alex where the bathroom was and covertly followed behind him. Slinking her way into the tavern after him, she shut the door behind them and paused. From the comfort of the tables, and chairs void of life she watched and waited in the shadows for him to come out from the hidden door in the wall. When she knew the two of them were completely alone, Fiona finally spoke up, nearly startling the bottle of wine out of Jay's hands.

"Alex is a strong woman you know. You really don't need to be so protective of her. It makes you look like a fool hovering over her like you do."

"Don't I though? Do you honestly believe that she doesn't need my protection? Haven't you noticed that her greatest assets are also the biggest chinks her armor? If the world was to dig its claws into her, it would tear her apart and destroy her."

"Do you truly believe her to be so vulnerable and naïve?"

"No, but the world is dark, cruel, corrupt, and unforgiving. Someone like her has no business being here."

"True. This I know all too well. She reminds me of someone I once knew, someone who gave their life in exchange for mine. Truth is, I too worry about Alex, and I too feel as if this world doesn't deserve her." Fiona put a reassuring hand on Jay's shoulder, scrutinizing his face as waves of sorrow filled his eyes. "And yet, here she is, caring about all of us. Did you ever stop to think there is a reason she's here? Maybe she's just what this world of ours needs. Perhaps her light is strong enough to outshine and erase the ugliness and hate this realm of ours has to offer."

"You really believe that?"

"I have to. Faith is all any of us have left."

"I don't want to have faith. I don't care to believe. And mostly, I don't want to lose her, I don't think I can be without her."

"You won't, at least not to another man. I've seen the way her eyes light up when she looks at you. That girl would defy death if it meant being with you. She loves you more than anything in this forsaken world we find ourselves in, and in her eyes, even someone like Caleb Cox can't compare to you."

"I don't deserve her love. I never did. How can you expect me to believe I can stay with someone like her, when I don't think I'm worthy of what she has to offer?"

"Perhaps none of us deserve her love and kindness, but it's not for us to decide who she gives it to. All any of us can do is accept it graciously. I also know that you should hold your wife close Jay, make love to her often, and never let her go. And, don't you ever forget that to her, you and that boy of yours are her world, one which she would kill to protect. You have something the rest of us can only dream of, so you best cherish it every second you got with her."

"You're right," Jay nodded his head, "and I do. I cherish her every damn day she's here. I will never stop thanking fate for putting her in my life, so no need to lecture me. But, there is something I must ask of you, a favor really."

"What is it?"

"Keep an eye on her for me when you can. I can't help but worry when I can't be there to protect her, and she has a knack for getting into trouble. She needs someone to be by her side to pull her away from the abyss when she gets too close."

"I can certainly do that for you, half-blood." Fiona smiled as she pointed to the door. "But now I think we should return to the party before anyone notices we've been gone for far too long and comes looking for us."

"Right, you first. I don't want anyone getting the wrong idea, especially not my wife."

With a nod of her head, Fiona headed through the door into the house. Watching her leave, Jay glanced down at the dusty yellow bottle in his hands and pondered what the woman said to him. He knew her words were true, and yet, he could not help but worry as the feeling of dread continued to eat away at him. A voice from the shadows whispered in his ear almost every night. Tonight, it told him that he would lose Alex soon and there was nothing he could do to prevent it. And, despite it only being in his head, Jay could have sworn this voice was not only real, but that he heard it somewhere before. Shaking his head to drowned out the murmurs in the dark, he exhaled, and walked back out of the tavern to join their guests.

The rest of the night went seemingly uneventful, and Jay was finally starting to enjoy the company when the antique grandfather clock in the corner of the room struck ten. At the table, Andy was rubbing his eyes as his lids grew heavy with the prospect of sleep and a fat pigrie was already snoozing on the windowsill. Seeing the time, and the sleepy child, the guest excused themselves, bidding Jay and Alex a good night as they ventured into the darkened street to return to their respective homes. Scooping the boy into his arms Rupert winked at Jay and left to put the child to bed, leaving the two of them alone for the first time all night.

CHAPTER 13

The House's Secret

Finally, alone with Alex, Jay took hold of her wrist without saying a word and pulled her into the tavern, locking the door behind them. Glancing over his shoulder, he studied her closely as her emerald eyes blinked at him, silently asking what he was thinking. He studied the way her waist-long, chestnut hair flowed down her porcelain skin, and the way her dress clung to every curve of her body. His heart pounded harder in his chest at the sight of her with the moonlight hitting all her delicate features, and he briefly closed his eyes to restrain himself for a little while longer.

Alex opened her mouth to speak, but Jay silenced her by pressing his lips roughly against hers. Wrapping his arms around her tiny waist, he pulled her in closer for a deeper kiss, and she responded by entangling her slender fingers in his golden hair. Pushing her slowly towards the bar, Jay could barely contain himself as he tasted her honeysuckle skin. He felt her heart rapping against his chest as her arms clung to his back, and he felt the fabric of his pants growing tighter. Pulling away from her, he gently bit down on her lower lip before stealing another glance at her.

Her once snow-like skin had a rosy shade to it and her eyes sparkled in the dark like precious gems inside a forbidden cave. Brushing a loose strand of hair behind her ear, Jay caressed the silky soft skin on her cheek as the desire for her flooded every fiber of his being. Swiping his arm across the bar he let the glasses and bottles crash to the ground in a rain of glass and alcohol, causing his wife to gasp. Grabbing hold of Alex's bottom, Jay hoisted her up to the bar, placing her gingerly on the now empty wood top and positioning her trembling legs on either side of him.

Her eyes grew wider and darted around the room as Jay yanked her closer to him, allowing the delicate fabric of her skirt to slide between his fingers as he slid it up past her hips. Leaning in for another kiss, his fingers trailed along on the skin of her legs as he fished around for the lace panties he'd gotten her a day earlier. Hooking the floral fabric with his fingers, he snatched the garment off and allowed it to drop down by his feet as he pulled away and gave her a mischievous grin.

"Jay," Alex gasped breathlessly, "what are you doing?"

"What does it look like I'm doing?" He grinned and Alex responded by glancing down at the ground as her cheeks turned bright red. "You see baby, ever since we got here, I could think of nothing else but how wonderful it would be to make love to you right here on this bar."

"Really? That's odd." Alex looked up and glanced about the deserted tavern with nothing but darkness to keep them company. "For some reason, I get the feeling you already have at some point."

"Well, in that case, let's see if we can recreate the experience in the present."

"What? Now? But... what about Rupert?"

"Doors locked darlin', it's just the two of us. Plus, I think the old man knew my plans all along. He'll leave us be for a little while."

"But," Alex stole a nervous glance at the windows pointing to the street, "what if someone walks by and sees us?"

"So what? Let them watch." Jay gave her a deep kiss as he fiddled around with the belt of his pants, letting them drop to the ground by his ankles. "This is my house, my tavern, and I can make love to my wife anywhere I damn please."

Without giving her a chance to reply, Jay pulled her bottom closer and slipped himself inside her, causing Alex to gasp. She was warm as usual, but her discomfort of being put on display caused her to be tense. Paying no mind to the slight pain caused by her walls choking his shaft, Jay pulled out and thrust himself inside her again, causing her to lean back and moan. Her slender fingers snaked their way through his hair as he continued exploring her mouth with his tongue. Finally, giving way to him, Alexandra's body relaxed and melted into his as he continued to pull her against him.

The harder he thrust against her the wetter she became until soon enough he was covered in her sweetness. Her legs wound firmly around his waist, holding him close, not letting him go, and forcing him to plunge deeper. Drunk on ecstasy, Jay surrendered to the pleasure taking over his body and released the tension building up inside him, moaning as his seed flowed into her.

Panting, and dripping with sweat, he slid out of Alex and gave her one last kiss before draping his head over her shoulder and savoring her intoxicating aroma. Holding him close, Alex stroked his hair with her fingers until he pulled away and allowed her to hop down from the counter.

Straightening out her skirt, Alex tried to calm her heart which was still pouncing in her throat. Jay had never been so assertive with her before, and this sudden display of affection took her off guard. But as fresh memories from a moment earlier flooded her head, she felt herself grow hot at how it made her feel. Suppressing the urges to be with Jay again, she reached down for her panties, and her hand froze as she spotted something peculiar on the floor by her feet.

"Jay." She whispered as a lump formed in her throat. "Do you see this?"

"See what love?" Jay snatched the white lace undies from the ground and stuffed them in his pocket with an impish smirk as he planned on having seconds upstairs.

"One of the bottles that broke..."

"Don't worry about it, darling. I'll clean it up tomorrow morning."

"No, it's not that. Look closer to where it fell."

Frowning, Jay kneeled to glanced at what had his wife so concerned. At first, nothing seemed amiss, but as his eyes traced the lines of Alexandra's finger, he spotted the anomaly that took his breath away. A broken bottle of cheap rum lay in pieces on the ground where it fell, but the dark brown liquid was nowhere to be seen. A tiny pool of pungent, woody alcohol remained on the wood floor where it spilled, but it was quickly vanishing beneath the house through a large crack in the floor.

"Well, I'll be..." Jay muttered as he stood up and turned around to light a lamp behind him. "There must be a hidden cellar beneath the house or something, probably from the days of the war when this place was used for smuggling out fugitives. Here," He handed Alex the light, "hold this."

Alex took hold of the silver house containing a red flame as Jay set about exploring the wood floor covered in sparkling beads of glass. It took Jay a while, but he finally spotted a small hole in a plank closest to the bar which was barely large enough for him to get a finger in. Telling Alex to stand back, he lifted a small door beneath their feet to the wall behind him, and an earthy breeze wafted past their faces as the wood planks revealed the darkened void hidden beneath.

Swallowing hard, Jay took Alexandra's hand in his and exchanged a glance with her before he started down the stone steps into the abyss, with nothing more than a feeble flicker of his flame to guide them. Watching their footing on the ancient wood steps, Jay and Alex descended the warped planks as their feet wobbled and the shadows seemed to consume them. Jay counted thirteen steps in all before the wood turned into solid dirt ground beneath their feet. Straining his eyes, he could not see further than his lantern for the blackness of the cellar seemed to stretch forward forever.

Tightening his fingers around Alex's wrist, Jay pushed forward through the gloom, even as the earth walls appeared to creep closer to them, suffocating them in their clutches. It seemed as if they were walking for hours when they reached a narrow doorway carved in the limestone which replaced the compact dirt. Lifting the lantern above his head, the flame behind the glass appeared to leap out on its own and float to the archway above them.

Tracing itself across the smooth stone, the fire returned to its home as letters appeared where it just was. Glowing in red as if they had always been there, two words in the ancient tongue of their people greeted them.

Quo Coeperat

"What on earth? That looks ancient." Jay mumbled as the lantern in his hand shook. "Do you know what this says Alex?"

"Yes..." Alex squinted as she reread the letters glimmering above her. "Roughly translated, it means 'Where it began.'"

"Where what began?"

"I don't know, it doesn't say, but perhaps we should go through the door and find out."

"Are you insane? What if it's a trap or something?"

"Fine," Alex snatched the lantern from Jay's hand and vanished into the blackness beyond the door, "I'll go in alone."

"To hell you are."

Rushing through the door after Alex, Jay stopped abruptly when he bumped into her standing frozen inside the room, only a scant distance from where she came in. Puzzled, he glanced around a bit before he realized what it was that had Alexandra stuck in place. They were inside a vast chamber with a brazier to the left, and a gated doorway in front of them.

A strange stone altar sat empty to their right, and like the entire chamber it appeared to be made of limestone. The fire inside the lantern escaped its confinement once more and floated towards the altar in a strange pattern which resembled a dance. Both Alex and Jay turned around in time to see it write something on the stone wall, illuminating hidden letters and a picture of a rose behind the pale gray, stone slab.

Ordo Nominus Umbra

"Order of Shadows?" Alex whispered as she handed the empty metal lantern back to Jay. "What do you suppose this is?"

"No clue." Jay frowned. "But I don't like the looks of it."

They continued to stare at the flame which appeared to have a mind of its own as it floated past Alex, tousling her hair and pushing her forward before returning to its original spot in the lantern house. Stumbling towards the altar, her hand landed on the polished cool stone causing her to gasp. Suddenly, Alexandra's head got bombarded with visions of people in cloaks gathered around it, chanting in the old tongue. Then, one vison came in crystal clear, causing her eyes to roll back into her head as if she was there living it.

Alex watched herself standing naked at the slab, bend over with Jay behind her in ecstasy. They looked almost as they did now, but slightly different. Jay appeared to be older, with shorter hair and a different goatee. As for Alex, she looked almost identical if it was not for the dark energy she was emitting. As she watched the two of them standing there, she saw they were surrounded by the cosmos as stars and planets flowed swiftly past them and nebulas enshrouded them. Letting out a soft yelp, she pulled away from the stone and stumbled backwards into Jay's waiting arms.

"What's wrong love?"

"I just had a vision. First, people in hooded cloaks were chanting, but then, I saw us standing at the altar."

"What were we doing there?"

"Well..." Alex turned a bright shade of crimson, "you know, you were making love to me."

"Oh, I see." Jay grinned and snorted. "You haven't had enough of me yet and want more. I'm up for another round if you want me that bad."

"Knock it off Jay." Alex slapped his shoulder and turned her eyes away from him as the image of the two of them at the stone table once again returned to her memory. "This isn't funny, I really did see us at that alter, and we've never been here before."

"All right, all right. Perhaps some other time then?"

"Jay!"

"Fine, I'll stop." Jay snickered as he moved to his left, studying the wrought iron brazier placed against the opposite wall.

Ignasias

Jay let a red flame shoot out from his hand to the coals gathered in the metal basin, but the flames fizzled and popped without taking hold.

"Okay, that's strange. Guess I have performance anxiety or something. Why don't you give it a try babe?"

"All right." Alex took a deep breath and got closer to the iron bucket.

Ignasias

A blue flame flowed in a steady stream from Alexandra's hand and into the brazier, but the coals inside refused to ignite once more.

"Perhaps they are just too old, or maybe they are too wet from all the moisture hanging around here." Alex pointed to the water dripping from the stone ceiling as she glanced at her husband.

Jay was about to respond, but the flame once again leaped out from his lantern and glided for the wall behind the basin. Watching the flame preform on its own again, Alex and Jay waited patiently for it to finish writing out the letters hidden from view by some ancient magic. Having revealed the invisible message concealed in stone, the fire bobbed between the two corners of the room, circling a pair of torches on each end of the chamber as the mysterious phrase twinkled in red before them.

Duo in carne una

"Oh... I see." Alex walked over to the torch closest to her.

Ignasias

The torch caught fire and began emitting a soft blue light. Taking the flame into her hand, Alex glanced at the other torch and then at Jay.

"Light that one."

Shrugging his shoulders, Jay placed the lantern on the ground and took the second torch into his hand.

Ignasias

"Now what?" Jay stood holding the bright red flame.

"We light the brazier together, with both our flames at once."

Shaking his head, Jay did not have much faith in this plan, but he placed his flame to the coals regardless and Alex joined him by placing her torch against his. At first, nothing happened. But then, to their astonishment, the flames leaped from their flares and licked the aged coals. The fire took hold as their torches sat empty, and the two flames in the brazier intertwined. A loud pop resonated through the chamber as a strange symbol formed before them, lighting up the room and the secret messages it hid.

"What is that thing?" Jay glanced at the symbol above them. "It looks like two tadpoles having a grand old time with one another."

"I don't know. I've never seen anything like it before." Alex scowled at the strange symbol in flames in front her before turning to look at the rest of the room. "Look, the gate blocking us off from the rest of the tunnel has vanished and there is more writing above the door now."

Jays eyes trailed to where Alex was pointing, and he mumbled curses under his breath as he regarded the strange message in the ancient tongue radiating above his head.

Post Tenebras lux

"From darkness, light?" Jay continued to grumble as even he was familiar with the phrase. "What in Alteria is going on here?"

"I don't know, but I think we need to find out."

Alex went to step through the newly open doorway, but Jay grabbed hold of her arm and pulled her back to him. He was shaking his head as the room around them continued to glow in shades of red and blue while sparkles of light swirled around their heads. She could see the concern in his blue eyes, and even she had to admit this was all rather strange. Still, a nagging urge to explore continued to beg her to go further. Wishing to learn more about the tunnels under their house, Alex reached up to caress Jay's face as she gave him her best pout.

"Come on Jay. Let's just have a quick look. I promise we will turn around if it doesn't look safe."

"Fine." Jay relented and let her go. "But I go first, and you stay close behind me. If anything bad happens, I want you to run and not look back."

Alex rolled her eyes at his suggestion, but nodded her head regardless, even if she did not have any plans of abandoning Jay in this place. Threading her slender fingers through his, she squeezed hiss hand as he pulled her forward through the door before them. The earthy hallway on the other side continued to glow with spirals of dancing lights which flowed into three separate directions, branching away from them. Watching streams of glowing rivers float left, right, and center, Alex pondered where all the different hallways could possibly lead, but she knew Jay would not be up for exploring them further that night.

"Perhaps we should ask our friends to help us explore them tomorrow." She glanced at her husband who stood gawking at the strange site before him. "We can split up into three groups and cover more ground that way."

"Yeah. Sure. I'm fine with that as long as Caleb Cox doesn't catch wind of this in any way. I still don't trust the guy no matter how well meaning he may seem."

"All right." Alex sighed, not understanding why her husband could not get along with the good mayor. "Guess we'll just invite George, Richard, Lawrence, and Fiona over tomorrow afternoon to help."

"Think they can keep a secret? They all seem to be pretty damn close to that Cox guy."

"They will if I ask. I'll just tell them we don't want to get the mayor involved in trivial matters as he has other problems to concern himself with at the moment. Now, what do you say we get back upstairs? I'm starting to get cold."

"I'd say, what are you waiting for? I've been waiting to get out of here as soon as we discovered this place. Come on, I'll be sure to warm you up in bed once we get there." Jay winked at Alex and pulled her back through the open door.

As the two of them exited the mysterious room with the altar, the flames fizzled out and the chamber went dark on its own. Not daring to question the sorcery behind the secret space, Jay and

Alex ran up the stairs taking two or three steps at a time before slamming the wood planks of the floor shut. Concealing the hidden basement once more they exchanged worried glances, but neither dared speak of what they found. Leaving the mess on the bar room floor behind for the morning, they locked the door to the tavern shut and scurried upstairs. Lying in bed, they stared at the ceiling and neither of them fell asleep until the sun began to crest over the harbor in the distance.

CHAPTER 14

What Lies Beyond

Ushering the last of the visitors inside the tavern, Rupert locked the door and drew the curtains shut to keep prying eyes from peeking in. The four guests stood at the center of the room exchanging glances between one another in silence as Alex leaned against the bar counter twiddling her thumbs. Jay stood behind her cross armed with a scowl on his face while silently surveying the tavern. Fluttering around the room, Cosmo begged for one of them to break the silence, but neither dared to speak. Finally, Richard, who has had enough of the secrecy decided to find out what was so urgent that it brought him there mid day on a Saturday when he should have been at home, enjoying a spot of tea and a good book.

"All right Alex, Jay. What's going on here? What's with all the secrecy, and what was so important that it couldn't wait till later?"

"Well, you see," Alex's eyes trailed slowly down to her feet as she mumbled, "last night, Jay and I... well we accidentally discovered a hidden door concealed in the floor, behind the bar."

"Accidentally you say?" Lawrence snickered as he shot Jay a knowing smile and shook his head. "You dirty old dog you, you had your wife up there on that counter, didn't you?"

"Lawrie!" Fiona smacked her brother with the back of her hand as she spotted Alex turn bright red. "Don't be so vulgar dear. Can't you see lambkin isn't as comfortable discussing her sexuality as the rest of us?"

"What's there to be embarrassed about?" Lawrence glance at Alex and shrugged. "You get down and dirty any place you like lass, ain't no one here going to judge." He gave Alex a wink and her face turned another shade of crimson. "Hell, I've had three lasses in the back of me car a few days ago. Ain't nothing wrong with where you chose to get the deed done love. Spice thing up all you like I say. Keeps the relationship fresh."

"Anyhow..." Richard reached up and put his hand over Lawrence's mouth, "you said you found a secret door. You know where it leads?"

"An ancient cellar. There was a strange chamber inside with a gate that could only be opened by the two of us." Jay muttered. "The passageway led into a second room, one which branched out in three separate directions."

"Fascinating." George strolled over behind the bar and bent over to have a look at the floorboards. "I can't see a hidden door anywhere," he ran a hand over the polished wood, "who ever put it here was an excellent craftsman. Not to mention, I've never heard of any rumors regarding secret rooms beneath this place before, though I'm not surprised given its history during the war. I gather you need our help to explore these tunnels then?"

"Yes. We trust you to keep this secret between the people in this room. At least until we know more about this place and why someone hid the basement in the first place."

"Think you can do that?" Jay glared at the people gathered around the bar.

"With the secrets I've kept for Alex over the years," Richard shook his head, "what's one more?"

The rest of the group exchanged looks, shrugged their shoulders, and nodded in agreement. This was going to be a secret they keep between them, at least until they knew more about what was going on beneath the haunted tavern. Satisfied everyone was on board, Jay stepped back and pulled up the secret door hidden beneath his feet, vanishing into the darkness of the well before anyone could say a word. Alex followed him silently with Cosmo in tow, and the rest of the party slowly stumbled their way down into the depth of the mysterious cellar after her.

Going through the motions of lighting the brazier inside the stone chamber, Alex and Jay stood back as the same symbol formed from the fire and released the balls of flames to float through the passages of the room beyond the gate. George stood to their right, studying the symbol spinning above the flames as he cradled his chin in his hand. Behind him, Fiona and Lawrence glanced up at the fresh writing lighting up the room and shimmering on the stone walls.

"So..." Fiona tilted her head back towards the couple behind her, "do we know who this Ordo Nominus Umbra is, or why they built this place?"

"No clue." Jay barked from his spot. "If we did, we wouldn't have asked anyone here."

"Then what are we waiting for? Let's get this over with." Richard walked through the gateway. "Let's see where this place goes."

Seeing no other alternative, rest of the group followed behind Richard as cold flames continued to rush past them, splitting off in three directions. The friends stood in the inky room, watching the glowing streams continue to their destinations and they exchanged uneasy look as a musty breeze wrapped them in a warm, damp hug.

"I guess this is where we split up." George whispered. "Richard and I will take the left tunnel."

"I guess Lawrie and I will go right."

"All right. That means you and I will go straight babe."

"Sure thing." Alex nodded her head as she glanced into the infinite gloom before her. "But if anyone runs into trouble, you turn around and head back to the tavern right away. We will all meet back there after we're done exploring and compare notes on what we found."

The small group agreed to her plan and split up as mentioned so they could stalk the flames in the directions which they have chosen. Taking hold of Alexandra's hand, Jay led her forward, guiding her along the slate floor down the dark, narrow tunnel which only seemed to get more constricting the further they went. Stumbling along the uneven, slick surface of the floor, she sensed the room growing colder as shadows crept along the walls, keeping their eyes on them. A sinister presence lingered in the tunnel with them, touching her as she moved along the damp corridor. Feeling invisible icy tentacles on her skin, Alexandra's hand trembled, and she tightened her grip on Jay while stealing a glance behind her.

"Do you feel that?"

"Feel what love?"

"The presence stalking us. It's dark, ancient, and angry."

"No." Jay stopped, turned around, and wrapped Alex in his arms. "I'm sure it's nothing darling, just the shadows playing tricks on you."

"No, Jay, I can feel it." Alex closed her eyes, shuddering as the invisible arms stroked her bare skin. "I can feel its pain, it's loneliness, and it's desire. It wants me, and I don't know why."

"Hoink!" Cosmo darted around the room as he too sensed the presence of the Worm in the tunnel with them. "Hoink!"

"Okay, okay, I get it." Jay released Alex from the safety of his hug while still holding her close as he walked to protect her. "Let's keep going. We'll probably be out here soon enough. This tunnel can't go on forever you know."

Jay ushered Alex to move along as he paid closer attention to the space surrounding them. Dripping down the stone walls from the ceiling, the echoes of the water sounded as if they were calling their names in the dark. Their whispering filled the tunnel and even Jay began to feel uneasy at the eerie noises it produced. He guessed they were in the city's underbelly, and the voices in the water drops were nothing more than those of people walking above. At least that's what he told himself as he pushed through the shadows surrounding them, continuing to advance forward until he finally spotted a sliver of light breaking through the gloom. Releasing Alex's wrist from his grasp, he staggered forward to see a rickety wood door standing between them and salvation.

Darting past Jay's head, Cosmo flew and snouted up a latch keeping the gate shut. Leaning his weight against the rotted wood, Jay pushed open the door and released them from the murky passageway. On the other side the bright afternoon sun caused them to squint as they stepped out into an overgrown field of yellowing grass and wildflowers. Decorated stone slabs peeked their heads from the tall weeds while some lay slumped over by their feet, broken free of their base a long time ago. Walking out from a moss-covered mound of dirt housing the tunnel, Alex and Jay glanced about their surroundings as they brought their hands up to their foreheads.

"Where are we." Alex continued to squint while trying to study the vast garden of stones which was situated a good distance from town.

"Ancient burial ground if I was to take a guess. Probably been here since before the war."

"But... why would the tunnel lead here? What's so special about this place?"

"No clue." Jay took hold of Alex's hand again. "But let's explore a bit further and try to figure it out."

"Shouldn't we close the door? We wouldn't want anyone discovering it and following it back to the tavern."

"I'm going to go out on a limb here and say there is no need to worry about that." Jay glanced at the forgotten spot they found themselves in with nothing but the chirping sounds of insects and cackling of birds to keep them company. "Something tells me no one in Fall Harbor even remembers this place is here. I'm guessing we are the first people to set foot here since the war ended."

Nodding her head, Alex looked on as a gentle breeze caused the dead grass to sway and a faint scent of gladiolus to fill the air.

Taking a step forward, the pair strolled amongst the fallen and cracked headstones as they attempted to solve the mystery of the abandoned burial ground.

Occasionally, she paused to study the stone faces, hoping to make out a name, a date, or any clue which the slabs might have offered. But there were no clues to be found, the surface of the headstones was either washed clean by years of rain and wind, or chiseled away deliberately by a vandal looking to erase the identity of the person sleeping beneath their feet. Coming no closer to solving the riddle of the lost cemetery, they continued to stroll through the sprawling field of graves until an unusual structure caught their eyes.

Before them sat a gray building constructed of marble, and as they slowly walked closer to it, they inspected its unusual appearance. Like a tiny castle it had two spires on the roof and a sturdy wood door which was housed in a stone gothic arch. Above the door was a round window of colored glass laid out in the shape of a crimson rose. This building, however, was no castle for it was no larger than Jay's cottage back in Manevia. The structure itself had a sad, ominous feel to it, one which pulled Alex closer to the mahogany door erected beyond the three stone steps leading up to it.

"What do you suppose this place is Jay? I've never seen anything like it before."

"No clue. It certainly doesn't look like it belongs here, does it?"

"No, it doesn't. But, do you suppose it could be another grave?"

"Maybe. There's no way to tell from here though."

"You're right. We need to take a closer look."

Letting go of Jay's hand, Alex staggered forward to the strange building as if being pulled to it by an otherworldly force.

Her breathing grew shallow as she got closer to the door, and by the time she was with in arms reach, her heart was pounding out of her chest. Reaching her fingers for the rusted iron door handle, Alex's left hand contacted the glazed wood and her heart suddenly felt as if it was being ripped out of her chest. Excruciating pain flowed through her as her eyes filled with tears. She felt her heart shattering as if she were losing a loved one and she suddenly got sick to her stomach.

Stumbling back from the door while clutching her chest, Alex let out a pained scream which resonated through the cemetery as she collapsed on the ground sobbing. Rushing to her side, Jay scooped her trembling body in his arms as she continued to cry hysterically and scream incomprehensibly. Holding her tighter, Jay's firm grip and the warmth of his body, washed away the unbearable pain she felt, and gently pulled Alex back to her own world. Laying in her beloved's arms, tears continued to fall down her cheeks as she gripped his shirt, scared she'd lose him forever if she was to ease her grasp.

"Alex," Jay held her head close to his broad chest while stroking her hair, "what's wrong with you? What happened?"

"I... I don't know."

"Roink?" Cosmo nuzzled Alexandra's cheek, licking the salty tears from her face. "Hoink, hoink?"

"I'm really not sure. This may sound crazy, but when I touched the door, I felt as if my entire world was ripped away from me. I know it was not my pain, but I connected with it somehow. I felt as if everything I held dear was taken from me. Like I lost the love of my life in the most horrific way possible, and in that moment, I knew wanted to die because I could not go on without him."

"But you haven't lost anything. We are all still here, and we are not going anywhere."

"I know, as I said, the pain was not mine, but it felt like a distant memory or a vision of someone I don't yet know."

"Then perhaps it be best if we get out of here." Jay lifted Alex from the ground and placed her on her feet. "I think we've seen enough, and I'd hate for you to have another episode like that. Honestly, it scared the shit out of me. Let's go home now."

"No." Alex whispered as she turned to the thicket of woods on her left. "Wait..."

"Why? What's wrong babe? Did you see a ghost, have another vision, or did you just want to do something kinky in public before we go back?"

"Hoink..." Cosmo narrowed his eyes and shook his head at Jay's odd sense of humor and horrible way of trying to make Alex feel better.

"It's those woods. I know them. I've been there before." Alex started walking to the cluster of huddled up birch trees, slowly picking up her pace as she walked. "Jay, we need to go there, there is something there for us to find."

"Okay, Okay. Slow down love and let me catch up."

"Oink."

Cosmos rolled his eyes and settled down on the nearest gravestone for a nap. The two of them would be back at some point, and Alex needed time to rediscovered familiar places. He knew hallowed ground was sacred, and that the Worm was unable to set foot inside. Jay and Alex would be safe so long as they were there and the pigrie could finally get some good shut eye while he waited for them to return.

In the distance by the woods, Jay slouched panting as he glanced over at his wife who was standing still before an opening in the trees. The branches tangled and wove together to create a circular doorway leading into the forest. There was something unusual about the way the trees leaned and knotted together to form a tunnel, but by now, Jay stopped questioning the oddities around him. He figured he'd get some answers soon enough, so instead, he watched Alex as she walked through the wooded arch and disappeared into the thicket of white and black trees.

Grumbling at how rash his wife was being, Jay dashed after her, and before long found himself standing in a room created from braided tree limbs. The branches above them were clustered so tightly together that no light was able to shine through, and he reckoned the rain couldn't penetrate the dense foliage either as the ground beneath his feet was bone dry despite the season. He was in a magical room created from the trees and Alex was standing at its center. She turned back and looked at him with eyes which still managed to shine despite being surrounded by shadows. But glancing at her face, Jay knew something had happened to her, for there was a darkness in there which he had never seen before.

CHAPTER 15

A Brief Awakening

Standing in the clearing, Jay swallowed the lump forming in his throat as he continued to drown in the twilight of Alexandra's eyes. She appeared to be suspended in time, standing on the edge of forever as a faint mist swirled around her. Observing her closer, Jay could tell she was not the same woman he walked into the woods with. She was older, more mature, a woman who knew what she wanted and was not afraid to get it. Unsure of what happened to his wife, he wanted to grab hold of her, run out of the strange clearing and never look back. But as she moved closer to him, Jay knew he was in for something he was not entirely prepared for and that the chance to leave had long passed.

"Jay," Alex spoke in a heavenly voice which resonated around the clearing, instantly calming Jay's nerves. "I know this place. I've been here before."

"When? You grew up in Manevia love, this is your first time here."

"I know." Alex bit her lip, "but I know I've been here before."

"Maybe it was a dream, or you've been to a similar place back home."

"Perhaps..." Alex trailed off in thought as she glanced around the place which screamed of home. "Say, Jay." She turned to him, and he spotted a deadly glint in her eyes as a smirk played on her lips. "You did say you wanted to make love to me in public, did you not? Would you settle for these woods instead?"

"What? Are you being serious?"

"Of course, I am." Alex tugged at the collar of Jay's shirt, pulling him in for a kiss, and sending a robust shiver down his spine. Her voice was different now, silky, and sexy, dragging him in and turning him on. "Or are you too scared now that you finally have the chance?"

"Scared? Like hell I am. Come here woman." Not daring to miss the opportunity to experience this new side of her, Jay pulled Alex in by her waist and placed his warm lips on hers.

Trailing his kissed down her neck, Jay savored the sweet taste of honey on her cool skin. He noted how different she tasted this time around, not as delicate, but more like a fine, aged mead. Getting drunk of the subtle taste of her sweat, he nibbled on her skin, causing Alex to gasp and cling to his shirt as she arched her back almost melting into his arms.

Closing his eyes, Jay exhaled, allowing himself to get aroused as her body pushed itself even closer. Reaching behind her back, he guided the hidden zipper of her dress down to the small of her back and allowed the satin gown to slip gently off her body to the dirt ground below.

The cold, refreshing air of the clearing caressed Alexandra's body, kindling the flame burning in her soul. Sucking on Jay's collar bone, she slowly undid the buttons on his shirt, and flung it open. Glancing up at him, she took the garment off, tossing it to the ground behind him. Continuing to look him in the eyes, she penetrated him with her blazing stare as she played with the soft curls of hairs on his chest and ran her fingers over the picture of the black wolf on his shoulder. Pushing her supple breasts against his bare skin, Alex wrapped her arms around Jay and savored his hardness pressing against her.

Maintained their journey on his skin, her fingers casually traced the muscles of his body as Alexandra proceed down to Jay's belt. What would have normally been an awkward moment of her playing with his buckle was replaced by an expert hand that had the thing unfastened in seconds before moving on to the button and zipper of his pants. Allowing them to drop to the ground by his ankles, she reached down and grabbed hold of his manhood. Giving it a gentle squeeze, she caused him to moan and traced the outline of her lips with her tongue. Gazing into Jay's light blue eyes with surreal hunger, she continued to stroke him, beckoning him to slide inside her.

Breathing heavily, Jay peeked into the eyes of his wife as they begged him to fill her in ways which served to torture him best. Their usual emerald sheen was filled with something he had never seen before, a fire burning deep inside them, and a lust he'd only seen in his dreams. Her slender fingers continued to grope his shaft as her eyes begged him to make love to her amongst the trees, and Jay was no longer able to resist the temptation as he laid her down gently amongst the brown leaves beneath their feet.

Laying on top of Alex, tickling her skin with his goatee, Jay continued to study her face, trying to discern what could have come over her. Glancing up at him, a devilish smile played on her lips as she nibbled on the lobe of his ear, trailing her fingernails down his back. Digging the nails gently into his flesh, she felt his erection get harder and wiggled her hips closer to it in response. Allowing him to undo the ribbons holding her panties in place, she wrapped her legs firmly around his waist and rolled over on top of him.

Pinned helplessly beneath her weight, Jay lay panting as his hands rubbed up against the skin of her bare thighs waiting for her to take him. Smirking, Alex glided her fingers across his chest, tangling them up in his chest hairs as she worked them up to slip between his golden locks. Leaning down, she brought their faces closer together, allowing him to kiss her lips as she playfully rocked her womanhood against him, delighting in the way his body quivered with her every move. Parting from his lips, she continued teasing him as she worked her way down his body, tracing patterns on his skin with her tongue as he continued to groan.

Stopping at his groin, Alex nuzzled his crotch as her fingers methodically slinked their way into the band of his underwear. Yanking off the last bit of cloth standing between them, she crawled back up to where she was and clasped his throbbing penis in her hands, watching him moan with delight as she stroked it. Giving him a gentle tug, she moved her lips down as she maintained eye contact before sliding his firm shaft partly into her mouth and clasping her lips around it.

"Alex," Jay gasped while digging his fingers into the dirt beneath his body, "what are you doing?"

"Teasing you." Alex glanced back up at Jay as her tongue swirled around his tip. "Do you not like it?"

"It's not that." Lifting his head, Jay watched Alex slide her tongue down and around his shaft as a strange glint lit up her eyes. There was something different about her, she seemed darker, more dangerous. But as she continued to suckle his manhood Jay felt as if this was something she's done countless times before and this left him puzzled. "It's just... I've never seen you like this before."

"What a shame." Alex released him from her grasp. Leaning forward, she allowed his stiff stalk to fall firmly between her breasts, enveloping it with their silky grip. "This is a lot more fun than what we always do."

Crawling back up, Alex positioned her hips on top of him and aptly slid his large penis inside her. Purring, she arched her back as she rocked her hips back and forth, allowing Jay to swell inside her, filling her core with bulging perfection. She relished in the tingling the motion of riding him gave her, and she swayed her hips faster, allowing the firm shaft to aggressively move inside her. With every thrust of him against her, the surrounding air grew thicker, slowly covering them in a swirling cloud of black fog.

Arching his back, Jay firmly grabbed hold of her hips as a guttural groan escaped his throat. His body grew tense as she quickened her pace, sliding her moist crease down his stalk with a savage force. Looking up at her, he could have sworn he saw faint outlines of wings form on her back. These did not look like angel wings, but Jay did not care, he was all hers, and he would follow her into the void if he had to.

Continuing to admire the glow she had around her, an intense, but familiarly intoxicating craving took over his body. An invisible flame began to lick him, causing him to grow hot as he felt the universe closing in on him. Surrendering to her whims, Jay closed his eyes as he relished in her current darkness as much as he did in her light.

Grinding herself faster and harder against him, Alex moaned softly as her body quivered and shuddered with delight. The earth beneath their bodies quaked, as if it too was experiencing her orgasms. The juices from her body pooled on top of Jay, saturating his pubic hairs as cracks of thunder bellowed outside and he could no longer keep the eruption from happening. Surrendering to the euphoria, he released himself with an explosion inside her, jerking as his body grew limp from the experience. Above them, the sky continued sparkle and roar as Alex accepted all of his essence before collapsing on top of him.

Exhausted and drunk from the excitement of the moment, Jay stroked her arm as she lay on top of him. Tracing the lines of her body with his free hand, he worked his way up to her face, lifting her chin to look into her eyes. The Alex who glanced back at him was the same woman he loved, but the spark of something wicked still sparkled inside her. Pulling her in for a kiss, he pondered if this was going to be the norm from now on, or if this was a temporary hint of madness that would fade after a moments time. Releasing her from his grip, he continued to admire her, even as the strange wings faded from her body.

"That was incredible." Jay stroked her cheek with one finger. "I didn't know you had it in you."

"You know," Alex gave him a quick kiss as she stood up to get dressed, "if you want it to be like this bad enough, you should take some initiative and do it."

"I didn't realize you liked it rough. I did not want to hurt or upset you."

"I like it to be steamy and passionate, and I don't mind if you play rough with me every once in a while. And, now that you know what I like," walking her fingers across Jay's chest, Alex paused to play with his goatee, "perhaps you can give it to me more often. Maybe even later tonight... at the house. Unless of course you want to have seconds now."

"As much as I would love to, I think we should save the seconds, and thirds for later tonight. If we don't get back to the tavern in time, our friends might get worried and come looking for us. And you wouldn't want them catching us as we make love, do you?"

"Well... I suppose not." Alex rolled her eyes as she yanked her dress on. "All right, I guess we can go. But, don't forget that tonight, it's your turn to tease me."

"Oh, I won't." Finishing tucking his shirt in, Jay stole a glance at the strange woman before him. She still looked like Alex, but it seemed like a dangerous succubus had taken over her body, or perhaps she was always like this, and he was only noticing it for the first time. Either way, he knew he'd have to figure out this mystery later as the light through the tunnel of trees was beginning to turn orange. "Now come on, it looks like the sun is starting to set."

Stealing a glance behind her at the sienna glaze pouring in through the trees, Alex nodded her head in agreement. Taking hold of Jay's wrist, she walked through the narrow tunnel back to the cemetery outside which now had a surreal marron glow to it. The solemn silence of graves swimming amongst the golden grass gave her soul peace as she strolled between them, looking for the one that held a sleeping pigrie. They did not have to look long, for not far from the door leading into the tunnels slept Cosmo, who shot up to greet them as soon as they came into view.

"Groink!"

Getting closer to Alex, Cosmo darted back as his mohawk stood up in the air. He could smell the old her, the scent was slowly fading, but hints of frankincense and myrrh still lingered. The familiar smell and the darkened aura surrounding her alarmed the tiny pig, and one look at Jay proved something unusual happened while they were gone. The pigrie could sense the turmoil inside his longtime friend, and he was alarmed by what this meant, Alex was waking up. This meant the Worm would be coming after her in full force soon, and his friend was blissfully unaware of the danger she now found herself in.

CHAPTER 16

Where the Roads Lead

Shutting the tunnel door behind them, Alex, Jay, and Cosmo ventured down the pitch-black corridor, guided only by the small specks of light pulling them back to the secret chamber. Extinguishing the flames of the brazier, they hustled up the steps into the tavern filled only with their small party sitting at the table by the bar, waiting for them to return. Upon seeing the two of them emerge from the hole in the floor, the group of friends shot up and exchanged looks of relief.

"Where on Earth were you?" Richard ran up to embrace Alex. "I thought something bad happened to you! Especially with that earthquake that just hit us."

"Earthquake?"

"Certainly, dear woman. The earth beneath our feet shook like no tomorrow, and it took you two long enough to get back that we thought the tunnels had caved in on you." George tapped the fingers of his right hand on the table. "Richard and I returned a few hours ago to find Fiona and Lawrence already waiting for us.

"We thought the two of you would not be far behind, but after an hour we began to worry. Richard thought you may have gotten into trouble while exploring and then the entire building started to rattle out of nowhere. I thought for sure the two of you were trapped in one of them tunnels, but Lawrence insisted you were fine. I agreed to give you both time, but, if you didn't return when you did, we would have come looking for you once we stopped bickering." Putting his hands on his hips, George looked over the couple frowning. "So, I take it that everything is all right then?"

"Oh," smirked Lawrence glancing at the pair, "I think they're better than all right Georgie. Seems as if I was right and Jay was getting the old sword polished along the way."

"Lawrie!" Fiona smacked her brother with the back of her hand. "I told you to stop teasing them."

"It's all right Fiona." Alex smirked and slinked over to Lawrence. The dark look in her eyes caused him to back up and shudder, even as she put her finger under his collar. "So what if he did? Do you want me to tell you all the dirty details, Lawrence? Would that help satisfy your curiosity, or do you just like getting a rise out of my husband?"

"Well, uhh, I didn't mean..."

"Alex," Jay gasped, "what are you doing?"

"What's wrong Jay. Are you so ashamed of what we did back there? Did you not enjoy the things I did to you?" Turning her head, Alex regarded Jay with a coy smile as he stood in the middle of the room, blinking silently. Ignoring her husband's obvious discomfort, she turned back to focus on Lawrence as she curled up her lip and pushed a finger into his chest. "And you, Lawrence, what would you like to know? Do you want to know how hard I sucked his dick before I straddled him and rode the shit out of him? Or would you rather I tell you about how I rubbed him off beforehand?"

"All right lass," Lawrence put up his hands in defeat, swallowing hard, "all right. You win, I ain't never bringing it up again, just stop with the visuals."

"Seriously man," Richard turned to Lawrence with a frown. "Can't you tone down the teasing a bit? I didn't need the mental images of Alex and Jay having sex."

"Yeah, well, if you wanted to explore her cave of mystery with your meat stick maybe you should have done it when you had the chance."

"Why I never..." Richard waved his hands in front of him as he turned a bright shade of crimson. "I mean... I never thought—"

"Sure you did, and Lawrence does have a point, Richard." Alex turned to her friend, and a shiver ran down his spine as her once gentle eyes appeared to be almost black. "But I suppose you can just fantasize about me now, like I know you do every night while you play with yourself."

"Alex," Richard swallowed hard and pulled at the collar of his shirt with one finger, "what has gotten into you all of a sudden?"

"Nothing. I'm just feeling a bit more like myself."

"Enough Alex, you have had your fun torturing them. Can we please just get back to the reason we're here?" Jay growled. "How 'bout you tell us where your tunnels led instead of concerning yourselves with my love life."

"Touchy, aren't we?" Lawrence snickered before darting his eyes to the ground as Alex whirled around to glare at him. "Sorry. Why... why don't you tell them Fi?"

"Fine, as long as you keep your vulgar mouth shut, I think you are rubbing off on the poor girl. I swear, you are the reason we don't have any friends." Fiona gave her brother a nudge with her elbow. "But anyway, we followed the tunnel down about a mile and a half until it popped out at a boiler room by the port. It was hidden inside the old barracks they now keep around as storage."

"Yeah. We must have walked right under our house to get there. What about you George?"

"At first, ours led us to an abandoned section of storeroom at the town hall."

"Yes. The entrance was hidden inside a heating vent. The whole portion was concealed behind some shelves with only a small crack one could squeeze through to access the rest of the building. I would have never noticed it was there if we didn't crawl out of it."

"You said it led to the storeroom first." Jay cradled his chin in his hand with a frown. "Where did it lead next?"

"Crazy thing this tunnel," George rubbed his bald head with his hand, "the darn thing popped out right under the train station next. It runs under and parallel to the platform. We watched the train roll by above us before we found a small door that pops out by the maintenance building a few feet down the track."

"Strange. Ours led to an old burial ground on the outskirts of the city. It looked as if it had been abandoned since the war ended. I wonder what all this means."

"Not sure." George furrowed his brow. "But if we want to figure this out, we should first learn of who this Ordo Nominus Umbra is or was. Alex, you best ask Gladys tomorrow to look into this for you. Her and Jackson know more about this town's history than anyone else. I believe they even have books in their library from before the war started. And, until we find out more, I suggest we all keep our mouth shut about it. We can't be certain of who we can trust or of why this place was hidden to begin with."

Knowing George was right, everyone agreed to keep this between them for the time being. Having a few drinks to calm their nerves, the friends speculated amongst one another what this could all mean before they parted ways and returned to their own homes. Still uncertain of what transpired in the woods, or what had suddenly come over his wife, Jay glanced at Alex and noticed she still had the same fire burning in her eyes from earlier. A mischievous smile formed on her pink lips as if to tell him she wanted more, and he saw a shadow pass over her irises as the outlines of wings formed on her back once more.

The darkness inside her still frightened him, but at the same time, it also enticed him. It was like a drug he could not get enough of, and Jay was willing to go to the ends of the universe to get another taste of it. Not wishing to lose this opportunity, he asked Rupert to lock up before he grabbed hold of her hand and dragged her upstairs. Watching Jay run up to his room, seeking the answers he so desperately craved, Rupert and Cosmo sat silently at the bar counter, not willing to discuss the obvious change in Alex with one another.

CHAPTER 17

Gathering of the Gods

Sprawled out on the bar top, Cosmo narrowed his eyes as he stared at Rupert who was leaning on the table glancing at him. Raising his mohawk, the pigrie darted his eyes to the left, curled up his lip to reveal a tiny tusk and let out a loud snort. From the taverns recessed shadows, a soft growl replied, and a raggedy black wolf slinked out to greet them. Seems like whatever was going on had even caught Ludwig's attention, and Cosmo was determined to get to the bottom of it.

"All right, Cosmo, Ludwig," Rupert sighed, "out with it. What's got you two so riled up tonight?"

"Hoink, hoink."

"Yes, I know that, I simply don't see the problem, we all knew the girl was going to awaken her power, eventually."

"Roink?"

"No, I'm afraid that I have no idea what could have sparked this change in her. And once again, I fail to see the problem with it."

"What our tiny friend is trying to say," a silky voice came from behind Rupert as a man with platinum hair walked out from the shadows, "is that the girl waking up too soon. Things are becoming more dangerous for her now. With her true nature coming to light quicker than we expected, you best believe my brother won't let it go unnoticed. He's been suspicious of her for some time now, and this power of hers will only serve to bring him here to take it."

"Sir," Rupert stuttered as he turned to blink at the man standing behind him, "what are you doing here?"

"I've sensed the energy from my favorite great-granddaughter spike and came over to check on her. It's incredible. It was so brief, but the residual energy of it still resonates in the space around us, sending chills down my spine."

"So, what shall we do about it then?"

"Nothing," said a melodic voice of a woman from behind Rupert, "there is nothing you can do. You simply have to let this run its course, even if we are not entirely prepared for it."

Turning around, Rupert frowned as a beautiful woman in her mid-twenties slinked out from within the shadows. Her long, silky black hair cascaded around the curves of her exposed golden-brown skin like waterfalls. A gold chain weaved itself through her head glistening in the dark from the candlelight dancing above her as she continued to smile. Swaying her hips as she walked gracefully on her gladiator sandals the two gold chiffon strips of fabric on her thong bikini swished on the floor while the chain mail of her gold bra clanked along rhythmically with every step she took. The light catching on the gold bands around her toned arms reflected in her cognac-colored eyes and accentuated her golden eyeshadow.

"Fatima," Rupert sighed and shook his head, "I see you are impeccably dressed as always."

"What's wrong brother? Are you telling me you are still the same old prude, even after all this time?" Fatima raise a perfectly manicured nail to her glossy espresso lips. "Guess it's no wonder that you and Desire are such a perfect fit for each other. She's just so modest... for a God that is."

"And what about your counterpart, Bastian, he hanging around here too I take it?"

"You know me too well ol' boy."

A shirtless young man with curly black hair dropped down from the ceiling and landed on his bare feet. Standing up straight, he towered over Rupert as he scuffed his foot on the floor and shoved his hands into the pocket of his loose, black leather pants. He was lean, toned, with had two identical tattoo bands around his upper arms. As he flexed his bicep, the inky waves rippled and the diamonds between them stretched and distorted. Grinning at the butler, his chocolate eyes appeared to almost disappear in his dark brown skin and the murkiness of the tavern.

"Long time no see brother."

"Indeed..." Rupert glanced at his younger sibling and frowned. "Oink..."

"You are right my friend." The Amphiptere laughed as he pulled a chair out and sat down in the middle of the room. "We do seem to have a family reunion going on here, don't we?"

"Yup." Bastian leaped up and squatted on the table next to his grandfather. "Now all we're missing is our darling little niece."

"She's upstairs with her husband." Rupert scowled as he glanced up above him. "Want me to go get her?"

"Perhaps some other time Rupert." The Amphithere laughed as he leaned back and crossed his legs. "We are here for a different reason today."

"Roink!"

"That's right, she's waking up, and even I'm unable to control her power. Why, you should have seen the commotion she caused over in the veil today, it was a site to behold."

"Does the Worm know about this?"

"He certainly does, Rupert. But don't you worry, Desire is keeping a close eye on him for me. Seems my dear brother has finally taken notice of the girl he misjudged all those millennia ago. Now he is on his way here to check her out for himself."

"So, he finally realizes what a fool he's been." Bastian sighed, "if only he knew back then that he set his sights on the wrong twin."

"I don't think it's Annabelle's power he wants darling." Fatima glided next to Bastian and played with his hair. "It's the darkness inside her he wishes to possess."

"True..." Rupert leaned against an empty table with his arms crossed. "But he did take notice of Alexandra's increasing spirit energy. Soon he will realize the light is more powerful than the dark, and then I won't be able to protect her any longer."

"When that happens my boy, you won't need to protect her." The Amphiptere leaned his face on his hand. "When that time comes, the girl will be more than capable of standing her own ground and giving my brother a run for his money."

"And what of the mortal she holds so dear?"

"What about him?" Bastian hopped down from his spot on the table and wiggled his toes to get a sense of what was going on upstairs. "Our niece chose him as her one and only. She even used Fatima's string to bind him permanently to her. And with that gift she gave him, well, he might as well be one of us."

"And I suppose you want me to tell him that his wife is a God of unconventional origin whose purpose and powers are still unknown?"

"Of course not brother. Not unless he asks. But I doubt he will, considering..." Fatima glanced up at the ceiling, watching the lamp swaying above her with a smirk, "he seems to enjoy our baby girl with a little more... spunk to her."

"Well, who doesn't enjoy a bit of good ol' cunnelingus?" Trailing his eyes to the spot above him, Bastian rubbed his toes on the wood planks of the floor and grinned even as the walls around them shook. "After all, it's not often a moral gets to taste the heavenly nectar from a God."

"And that is how I prefer to keep it. Now, can we please stop being so vulgar when referring to Alexandra?"

"Really brother," Fatima approached Rupert and reached out to play with one of the copper buttons on his green vest. "You should not act so stuck up just because you are one of the oldest. Plus," Fatima returned her gaze to the ceiling, watching the dust fall around them, "let the girl have some fun. She seems to be exceptionally good at it, like her mother."

"That's an understatement if I ever heard one." Snorting, Bastian shuffled his toes on the floor. Feeling Jay's energy though the planks he giggled at the thoughts running through the mortal's head before turning his attention to Rupert. "She is without a doubt Lilith's daughter. Why, that mortal can't seem to get enough of her, and I can't say I blame him."

"No doubt." Rupert frowned. "But Lucifer and Lilith didn't raise her. Desire, and I did. And I don't like where all this is going, especially with the Worm on her tail."

"No need to worry my boy." The Amphithere stood up and gave Rupert a pat on his shoulder. "I know it's hard to clean up your sibling's messes, but you did a fine job with that girl and she has a good head on her shoulders. Now, you simply have to trust me again when I say that nothing bad will happen to her."

"Is that what your visions tell you?"

"Yes. I see everything more clearly now. My brother will lose. The universe will stay safe. And Alexandra will join you on Sirius with her mortal when the time is right. I also know you will always be a father to her Rupert, and she will always come to you for advice. You just need to have a bit more faith in her and the master plan, that's all."

"And no harm will come to her or the mortals?"

"She's one of us Rupert, she's a god and one whose powers rival my own. Her mortal body may take a beating, she may even die, but it's nothing she can't fix. As for the mortals, they will be all right, she'd never allow anything bad to happen to them."

"Hoink?"

"Soon my pigrie friend, soon. Time is a strange thing, and despite centuries passing, this time is connected to Annabelle's. It won't be long before this is all over and we can all return home to Sirius. But, for now, it's best if the rest of us returned to the veil."

"Yes," Fatima waved her arm to create a gold, swirling portal, "Bastian and I will be meeting our niece again soon. Now, we must go prepare for her arrival."

"Yup. Sure am looking forward to seeing what that girl can do now that her powers are getting stronger."

"By the sounds coming from upstairs, and the quakes rocking the earth, apparently she can do a lot."

"Oh please, Fatima," Bastian snickered, "how often does a mortal get to have sex with a God?"

"Too often since our brother and sister decided they wanted kids of their own."

"Truer words have never been spoken." Rupert nodded his head. "Fortunately, the rest of us know how to be intimate without creating such problems."

"Oh please, ol' chap, you love that problem upstairs as if it were your own."

"She might as well be. I was the one who took on the responsibility of raising her and protect her from the Worm while her parents were off being concerned about her twin sister. Why shouldn't I also be the one to care for her?"

"All right, children, enough bickering." The elder god stepped in between the siblings to pull them apart. "Bastian, Fatima, we must go prepare for what's next. Not to mention poor Rupert has his hands full here. We shall meet again soon my boy, and under better circumstances I hope." Without another word, the Amphithere waved his hand and vanished through the portal into the veil.

"Later ol' boy. Take good care of our niece and her mortal lover for us." Bastian smiled and hopped through the swirling opening created by Fatima.

"Do take care brother. And please, try to keep her mother's temper in check if you can. We don't need any more problems associated with these girls."

"I always do..." Rupert sighed, "I always do. You take care too sister."

Smiling, Fatima winked at her brother and vanished into the veil. With her gone, the portal closed in a flash of light, leaving Rupert alone with Ludwig and Cosmo to keep him company. Shaking his head, he tilted his gaze to the ceiling and cringed. He did not sign up for any of this, but he cared about the girl enough to see it through. Whatever his niece's fate was, Rupert would be sure to keep her safe so they could go home to Sirius together. Returning his attention to the tavern, he glanced to his feet where a black wolf sat whimpering at his master.

"Yes, I smell it too," Rupert let out a sad sigh, "smelled it since they got back. It's faint, but it's growing stronger. It won't be long before the Worm will take notice too if he hasn't already."

"Groink?"

"No need to worry Cosmo, it will all be all right... I hope. Now come on, it's late, best we get some rest while we can and allow Ludwig to return to his patrol."

"Oink?"

"As master said, everything will be fine. We just need to have a little more faith."

Motioning for the pigrie to sit on his shoulder, Rupert locked up the room and vanished into his modest chamber as Ludwig returned outside to case the perimeter. Flopping on the bed, the old God glanced up to the ceiling and pondered the inevitable things yet to come. He was still angry at his sibling for creating two problems for the rest of them to deal with, but, he was secretly happy they were there, for Alexandra gave him a purpose he thought he'd lost a long time ago.

CHAPTER 18

The Bitter Truth

A week after exploring the tunnels beneath the tavern, Alex was enjoying her outing with Richard, who had the day off due to the mayor being out of town on business. Having just finished lunch at the local park which had become the favorite hangout for the group of friends, the two were slowly making their way back to her house for some afternoon tea. Ignoring the glares of the passersby, the two friends kept to themselves as they discussed the events of the previous week.

"Richard," Alex put her hand through his arm as she peered at him intently, "can you tell me more about the Militibus?"

"Do we really need to discuss those loons?" Richard tilted his head to look at her. "Aren't you content with just knowing that Mayor Cox is doing his best to take care of them?"

"No. They pose a threat to my family, and my friends. Plus, as much as I want to trust Caleb, I want to know what I'm up against."

"Oh fine," Richards rolled his eyes, "what would you like to know."

"You said they are extremists, but who exactly are they, and what do they want?"

"They are exactly that, extremists. They are an old sect of pure-blood mages that formed after the war ended, and East Ashland remained free. They were unhappy with how things have turned out, not just here, but everywhere. They thought grays were a scourge on the face of Alteria and believed they should have been eliminated with the half-bloods to keep our world clean. According to them, we should have started over and keep all blood-lines pure this time around."

"How disgusting." Alex clenched her fist while gritting her teeth. "And their symbol. What does it mean?"

"It's an arrow on a bow, shooting over the rising sun. It symbolizes fighting to see the dawn of the new age." Richard glanced at Alex who remained oddly silent as she looked to the ground. "Anything else you wish to know?"

"No," she mumbled, "I guess not."

"Okay, in that case, have you learned anything new about the order that seemed to occupy your basement?"

"Not yet. Unfortunately, Gladys hasn't been able to find anything at the library, but she's still looking."

"I see..." Richard trailed off in thought as he looked up and frowned at the sight of the small boy sitting on Alex's front porch with his head hung low. "Uh, Alex, I thought Andy was supposed to be out playing with friends today."

"He was."

Alexandra's heart dropped into her stomach as she looked up to see her son sitting by the front door, rolling his ball around with one finger. Dropping Richard's arm, she sprinted the short distance between her and Andy and kneeled down beside him. Looking closely at the boy's face, she could tell he was crying, and her heart twisted in her stomach as a hard lump formed in her throat.

"Andy, baby, what are you doing here? I thought Rupert took you to play with your friends."

"I don't have any friends," the boy croaked, "not anymore."

"What are you talking about love? You had several kids come by and visit you just last week."

"They no longer want to play with me. Their parents won't allow it." Andy looked up with his blue eyes sparkling with tears. "Molly was the only one willing to play today, but her mama ran out and dragged her away. She said she told her to not hang out with the riff raff."

"What? Why would she call you that?"

"She say daddy is a bad man, and that means I am bad too." Andy continued to look at Alex. "Is daddy a bad man, mom?"

"No, of course not. Your daddy is a good man, despite what anyone here says?"

"Then why do they say it?"

"Ignorance son," Richard put a hand on Alexandra's trembling shoulder as she looked like she was about to fall over from shock. "They are so scared of certain people because of what they've been taught, that they don't know what they're saying."

"But uncle Richard, when will they stop?"

"I reckon soon enough Master Andrew." Rupert approached the trio with a large canvas bag of produce in his arm. "Soon you will be able to play with your friends again. Until that time though, I'm afraid you will have to keep old Rupert company, and help him around the house."

"Does this mean..." Andy looked at the butler, and sniffled as he wiped the tears with his sleeve, "does this mean I can help you make tea and cookies?"

"Absolutely young man. You can be my kitchen aid starting immediately. Now, let us go in, and prepare said tea and cookies for our guest. Your mother and Master Richard look as if they could use a pleasant distraction, and I bet you could too."

Ushering everyone inside the front door, Rupert glanced over his shoulder. He did not like where this was going one bit, but he was determined to protect Alexandra and her family from whatever force threatened their happiness. Shutting the door behind him, he stepped into the family room, where Cosmo had already cheered up the boy with his playful banter. Taking the boy, and the pigrie into the kitchen, he allowed Richard to distract Alex from the events of the day while he prepared to deal with the inevitable mess in his kitchen.

CHAPTER 19

Fresh Information

Days passed since the incident, and Andy was starting to feel better about having to stay in the house. Him and Rupert had gotten into a routine they both seemed to enjoy, and the boy delighted in helping the old butler do his job. It was also precisely two weeks since Alex and Jay explored the abandoned cemetery on the outskirts of town. The spark which ignited itself deep inside Alexandra's soul had fizzled out a bit, though the flames of her true self remained. She was calmer again, back to the woman Jay had gotten to know over in Manevia, but she still had a touch of mischief to her, like grabbing hold of his behind when he was not looking.

That was how she bid him a goodbye that fine morning as she ran out the door to help Gladys at the clinic. Jay shook his head with a smile as he watched her rush out the door, and he was hoping that maybe today was the day that they would finally uncover some new information about their house. For well over a week now, the Carlsons had been helping them try and find more information on the Ordo Nominus Umbra, but they too have been coming up short.

At the clinic, the day was uneventful for Alex, as the patients who remained in Gladys' care did not seem to mind the girl who was married to the half-blood. A few of the women even chatted merrily with Alex, wishing the young woman would soon join them at the park with a baby of her own. Dismissing their wishful thinking, Alexandra simply told them that her and Jay were not ready to have more children for the townsfolk to pick on. Finishing up with the last patient of the day, Alex cleaned up the clinic as Gladys locked the door and turned to face the girl who just got done putting the linens away.

"So..." Gladys whispered as if she was afraid some eavesdropper would hear her, "I went digging in the archives of the old library the other day. It's an old, dusty place no one has dared to visit in over a century and it sure was a hassle. But I think my digging paid off, I have found some information about this Order of yours."

"Really?"

"Yes. And believe me Sug when I say I had to dig. Apparently, this group was very secret, and I only found out 'bout them by accident, when a book fell and broke a section of the wall with their diary hidden behind it."

"What did you do with the diary?"

"Why, I hid it in my smock and smuggled it on out of there. There ain't no reason for anyone else to lay their eyes upon what I found."

"So, who were they?"

"A secret order of mages who were visited by the Amphiptere himself to warn them of the dark times which were coming."

"The war..."

"Maybe, no way to be sure as the pages are not dated. But that's not the point, he also foretold of other things. Changes not only to our planet but ones to a distant star as well. He also stated that our worlds were linked together by blood. He instructed some of them to travel to this world and form the order there as well."

"But why did he visit us? What did we have to offer him?"

"I asked that question myself. Only clue I was able to find is the phrase Initium Eius Est, Omnia coeperant abhinc."

"Who is her?"

"No clue. But whoever she was, Alteria is where she belonged."

"So strange that there is no other mention of her. But what of the symbol formed from the flames then? Did you ever figure out what it was?"

"Ah, yes. Duo in carne una, I'm sure you know what that translates to."

"From two, one."

"Yes. The strange symbol you saw represents that concept, the duality of life if you wish to call it that. It's a concept of how everything in our universe, like the two creator gods, exists as inseparable and opposite forces. Male and female, light and dark, order and chaos, black and white. You and Jay seem to be the prefect representation of this concept."

"And what of the two dots?"

"All light has a bit of darkness to it, and all dark is possessed by light. It creates balance."

"So, I take it the Ordo Nominus Umbra did not believe in blood-purity then."

"I'm going to guess not."

"Is that all you learned?"

"Unfortunately, I am not great at the ancient tongue, and Jackson is doing the best he can with the free time he has. This whole Militibus Puritatis business has us running 'round void's half acre tending to folks who get injured by their shenanigans."

"I can only imagine. Someone really needs to do something about those guys." Alex shook her head. "It won't be long before someone gets seriously hurt or killed by them here, and we all know how that will work out for the rest of us."

"I'm afraid that's the end goal punkin. And I worry 'bout you, Jay, and that little boy of yours. You represent everything they hate. I worry it's you they'll be after next."

"We'll be fine Gladys, I promise. Jay and I know how to take care of ourselves, and we're no strangers to conflict." Alex smiled and unlocked the door. "But I best get going for now though. Fiona is waiting for me to have lunch. Let me know if you find out anything else."

"I will Hun, you just stay safe out there and try to keep your nose clean."

"I will Gladys, I'll see you soon,"

Walking out from the clinic, Fiona's beaming face greeted Alex as she stood up from the bench she was sitting on. The two women we accustomed to spending the afternoons together by now, and today they agreed to have lunch at the tavern. Setting off for the house, they walked peacefully down the street, when they ran into the two women who Alex upset at the café, hanging out by the town hall, waiting for them.

CHAPTER 20

An Uneasy Confrontation

Eliza and Agatha stood in the shade of a majestic oak tree, dressed in their high-neck ruffled dresses and fancy feathered hats. As Alex and Fiona walked by, the two women glared at them before exchanging smiles with one another. Looking at Alex get closer, the woman in black adjusted the feathered monstrosity on her head before turning to her friend with a nod. Nodding back, Agatha brushed her white skirt and the two of them strolled out into the street, blocking Alexandra and Fiona from progressing further.

"Oh look," the white mage hissed, "it's the scrap-muncher's lover and her bunter friend."

"Indeed, it is," Eliza smiled and batted her long lashes, "say Agatha, perhaps this half-blood loving mamsey is a dollymop herself."

"Why, Eliza darling, I think you might be right. She'd certainly have to be, to be married to that lobcock scobberlotcher, as no self-respecting woman would ever go for that delinquent."

"Ladies," Alex attempted to push her way through as her face grew visibly red, "I invite you to shut your filthy pie holes and let us through."

"Or what pinchcock?" Eliza shoved Alex away, nearly knocking her to the ground. "Are you going to run and cry to that filthy dog you share your bed with? Will he come running to your rescue, pretending to be some knight in shining armor while we all know he is nothing more than a scrub?"

"It's simply ghastly how you can allow his soiled staff to gush into your pure flower and then have the nerve to show your face in public. You are a disgrace to all the pure-bloods out there, and a black mark on our perfect society."

Gritting her teeth, Alex stood with her fists clenched looking between the two women who continued to cackle with delight. She felt a small fire ignite in her heart as she realized these two were just as vile as Quinton, if not more so. Taking a step closer to the two pure-bloods, Alex felt a tug of Fiona's hands on her skirt, begging her to not engage them further.

"Come on Alex, let's just go. I know a different way to your house. These two are not worth a spit in a bucket."

"Listen to your hedge whore friend bobtail." Agatha sneered as she fixed the small puff with a feather on her head. "You don't want to dance with us."

"Or what? You two nincompoops, who've never wielded a weapon in their life, are going to take on a princess who trained with them for a decade?"

"Princess?" Eliza screeched. "You still dare to call yourself a princess? No darling, you gave up your right to that title when you decided to marry that half-blood," she spit the last words out like venom, "now, you are nothing more than a dirty rat who belongs on the streets."

"Her and that nasty little minikin the ruffian fathered with some other scamp."

"Yes, him..." Eliza glared at Alex, "if you ask me, the tiny, scruffy slug should be put out of his misery before he grows up to be like his father."

"Why, you..."

Sheathing under her breath, Alex flared her nostril as the two women chortled and walked away. The small kindling of a flame erupted into a raging inferno inside her chest and the blood drained from her face. After recalling the heartbreak in Andy's face from days prior, Alex was no longer able to control her impulses. Balling up her left hand she allowed small speckles of blood to drip on her starch white skirt as she raised her arm in the air.

Archanium

"Alex," Fiona gasped, trying desperately to get Alex to unclench her fist, "no, don't!"

But no matter how hard Fiona tried to control Alex, she was too late as a blue arrow left Alexandra's hand and headed for its destination. No sooner had the arrow left the bow that it reached its mark on Eliza's hair, striking the puffy black hat, ripping it clean from her head, and plastering it against the brick wall of the town hall. Screaming like a banshee as she realized what had happened, Eliza flailed her hands over the top of her head, trying to see if there was any blood.

"You shot me." She continued to holler, attracting the attention of the townsfolk who began to gather around them. "Can you believe the crazy haybag shot me? You are just lucky you missed. Why you are no better than the murdering scoundrel you call a husband."

"I never miss. That was a warning shot. But threaten my family again, and you will find out just how good a marksman I really am."

"She's insane!" Agatha wailed as she pretended to feel faint. "Did everyone hear her threaten us?"

"She's unstable!" yelled a woman carrying bags from the market.

"She ought to be locked up." Hollered another man.

"I'm getting the mayor." Screamed another.

"Come on Alex." Fiona tugged at the arm of her friend. "Let's just get out of here. You can't possibly take on half the town. Let Caleb sort it out, we'll go wait this mess out at your tavern."

"Fools." Alex screamed as Fiona dragged her away. "Every last one of you. You think Jay and I are the problem when you should steal a glance at the mirror. You have grown so complacent in your ignorance that you are begging for the west to swoop in and oppress you. Is that what you want? You want your freedoms taken from you just so people like Jay and I wouldn't be able to exist? You're all idiots who deserve the death which is coming for you, but you won't see me go down without a fight when the west comes calling, even if it means standing up for the likes of you."

Fiona continued to drag Alex down the cobblestone street, wondering what had suddenly come over her meek little friend. A strange cloud darkened the once soft features of Alexandra's face, and she appeared a lot more mature for her age than she normally did. In her soft green eyes raged a storm, ancient and powerful, ready to destroy anyone who was foolish enough to get in its way, and Fiona's skin crawled at its intensity.

Pulling Alex through the tavern door, Fiona allowed the wood to slam firmly against the frame as she sat her friend down and looked over at her. The skirt of her white dress was splotched with crimson drops from the slits in her palm which continued to ooze blood. Fiona flipped Alexandra's hand over to stroke the cuts in the girl's silky soft skin, which felt like butter in her hand. Clasping her other hand over the gashes in the skin of Alex's palm, Fiona allowed herself to close up the wounds and returned the hand to her friend unharmed.

"What were you thinking lambkin?" Fiona stroked Alexandra's face. "You could get in serious trouble for what you did. Not only is using weapons in East Ashland uncommon, but you also assaulted a high-ranking member of Fall Harbor."

"I don't care. That pompous windbag deserved what she got."

"Oh, Alex." Fiona shook her head as she brought her tiny body in for a tight hug. "That I won' argue with. But you still should have kept a cool head my dear."

Savoring Alexandra's body against hers, Fiona thought the girl felt a tad warmer than usual, as if she was running a fever. The back of her dress felt moist and her skin felt like fire, but Fiona figured since it was a warm day out it was not unusual for a body's temperature to be higher, or for one to perspire more than usual. Putting her worries aside, she continued to hold

Alex's trembling frame against her bosom as a gentle rapping came on the door, and Fiona let out a deep sigh realizing what was about to transpire.

"Mrs. Hartwood." Caleb's voice came from the other side. "I think we need to talk. You're not in trouble my dear, but let's just sort this out."

"Well, that was quick." Fiona grumbled and headed for the door. "You say nothing Alex, let me take care of Cox for you." Opening the door, Fiona glanced Caleb up and down with a smile. "Mayor Cox, what can we do for you?"

"I think you know why we are here Fiona." Caleb bullied his way in, dragging Richard behind him. "Now, Alexandra, do you care to explain why Eliza and Agatha are claiming you assaulted them?"

"It was a simple misunderstanding Mayor," Fiona massaged his shoulders, "I'm sure you can't believe our sweet, little Alex could possibly assault anyone?"

"Miss. Walsh, please." Cox shoot Fiona's hands off his shoulders and continued to stare at Alex. "I wish to hear Mrs. Hartwood's side of the story. Now please, Alex, did you shoot an arrow at Eliza?"

"Yes. I did." Alex said in a cold tone without blinking. "What of it?"

"What?" Caleb fell back with wide eyes while clutching on to his chest, seemingly taken back by the way she spoke to him. "Why, dear Mrs. Hartwood, why ever would you do something like that?"

"That pigeon-livered dalcop had the audacity to threaten not only my husband but also my son. What did you expect me to do Cox, let it slide and go on my merry way?"

"Alex?" Richard mumbled as he studied his friend and noted a strange glimmer in her eyes he'd seen once before. "What has gotten into you lately?"

"Alexandra, my dear woman. I know things were different in Winter Haven for you, but here we do not resort to violence. The women were just having some fun with you, they meant you no harm."

"Fun? You call what they said to me fun?" Alex stood up and strolled over to Cox, making him shudder from fright. "I suppose it's easy for you to turn a blind eye to the hate spewing from your own townsfolk. After all, it's not your friends and family they threaten, it's mine. But rest assured mayor, I am not one to take their abuse lightly. I don't really care what these gobemouches think of me, but once they bring Jay, or Andy into it, all bets are off. I'm not going to sit idly by and let them abuse the people I care about. Do you understand that Cox?"

"I beg your pardon Mrs. Hartwood." Cox stuck a finger in his collar as he slowly backed up against the wall away from Alex. "I did not realize the women made such upsetting comments to you. I shall have a talk with them and make sure it won't happen again."

"You best see to it mayor, or else next time, Fall Harbor will be free from two bitties who do nothing more than waste oxygen."

Swallowing hard, Cox vigorously nodded his head as he noted a shadowy aura concealing Alex in its sinister shroud. Her energy seemed to almost buckle his knees as her eyes flickered with rage. Caleb would do, or say anything to escape her, and he was about to jump out the nearest window, when the door to the tavern swung open to reveal the liberating freedom beyond. Paying no attention to the commotion inside, Rupert walked in with a small, blonde boy in tow, and glanced over at the mayor's blood-drained face.

"Everything all right, Sir?"

"Yes," Cox straightened himself and headed for the door, "just a slight misunderstanding in town. I'll take care of it, nothing to worry about. You coming, Richard?"

"No, you go ahead sir," Richard frowned and looked behind him, "I want to chat with Alex more if that okay with you."

"Sure, of course," Cox stammered while slipping out the door, "take all the time you need."

Watching the mayor sprint down the cobblestone street, Rupert breathed in the darkness filling the room and smirked. He didn't need to look at Alex to know her true nature had returned, and that someone in town was unfortunate enough to warrant her wrath. But the fire was quickly weakening, as her mortal form could not sustain this much power without her soul fusing to her body. She was getting ready to crash. But before Rupert could do anything to prevent the inevitable, Andy's whimpering voice alerted him to a problem.

"Mommy? Are you feeling all right?"

"Yeah Alex," Richard glanced over his friend, still frowning at the change he witnessed in her. But as she stood before him, shaking and drenching with sweat, his concern swiftly shifted to alarm. "You look a bit more pale than usual?"

"I'm... fine." Alex whispered as the floor swayed under her feet and the walls narrowed around her. Before she could say anything else, she saw the room go black, and felt herself falling backward.

"Alex!" Richard lurched to catch Alex in his arms before she could hit the ground. Sitting on the floor with her limp body sprawled in his arms, he shot a worried glance at Rupert. "What's wrong with her?"

"You know," Fiona kneeled to place her wrist on Alexandra's forehead, "she seems to be burning up a bit. Perhaps it's a fever from the flu that's been going around. She's bound to pick up all sorts of nasty things working at that clinic."

"I bet you're right Miss Walsh. I hear this flu has been making its rounds again with a vengeance." Rupert bent down and scooped Alex up into his arms. "She simply needs a good nights sleep to get back on her feet. Miss. Fiona, Master Richard, can you watch young Master Hartwood for me while I put the mistress to rest upstairs? I promise you a good meal out of this and some dessert."

"Sure thing Rupert." Richard nodded as he watched the old man disappear through the swinging door into the house. "We'll do anything to help Alex."

Making sure he was not being followed, Rupert signaled for Cosmo by whistling, and headed up the stairs with the pigrie buzzing behind him. Laying Alex down on the bed, he felt the smoldering skin of her face, and pulled a small flask from his waistline. Pulling her mouth open, he dripped a few drops of golden liquid into her mouth and forced her to swallow.

"Groink?"

"She should be fine in an hour or so. The ambrosia should suppress her power and help her body heal a bit."

"Oink, oink?"

"I'm afraid this is all I can do. She has no control over herself right now and this fragile mortal body can't handle the full energy of a God without them being fused together, not to mention the other problem at hand draining her body. Stay here and

watch her while I take care of our company downstairs. Hopefully, she'll be awake by the time Jay gets back from the port with
his shipment. Last thing we need is to deal with that mortal and
his toxic cocktail of emotions if he sees her like this. He always
has been a tad unstable when it came to her. Not that I blame
him."

"Roink."

Cosmo sighed and settled down on the pillow beside Alex. He
watched Rupert leave and gently nuzzled her skin as she continued to sweat. But as the ambrosia took hold, his snout felt the
searing hot skin grow cooler with each passing moment, and he
breathed a sigh of relief knowing his friend would be all right, at
least for the moment.

CHAPTER 21

Militibus and the Order

Three days after the incident with the women, Alex was beginning to look better, and color seemed to return to her pale face. She did not recover in time for Jay and he continued to worry about her, refusing to let her out of the house until she was back to normal. But this was Friday, and Alex was itching to get out for a breath of fresh air, not to mention she had important business to attend to. A day prior, Richard had visited, and invited her over to his house to discuss the latest findings about the order once she got better, and Alex was determined to go right away.

Crawling out of bed, she placed a finger over her spinning head until the nausea subsided, and the room stopped wobbling. Glancing over at a grumping Cosmo on the bed beside her, Alex gave him a weak smile while attempting to get to her feet. The ground still swayed under her and the migraines were unrelenting, but Rupert's tea had always made her feel better. Shuffling over to the small round table by the window, she picked up the steaming cup and inhaled the pungent aroma of ginger before taking a sip. She allowed the sweet liquid to glide down her throat before falling into a neighboring chair to relax.

The warmth from the tea spread itself out over her as it made its way down, soothing her aching body and causing the nausea to disappear. Clasping the hot porcelain in her hands, Alex glanced out the window, allowing the steam to relieve her headache before taking a few more sips. Having finished the rest of the tea, she closed her eyes and took a deep breath feeling fully restored to normal. Exhaling with a smile, she stole a glance at the pigrie fluttering around the room.

"So, Cosmo, think Jay will let me go out tonight and see Richard?"

"Roink."

"I know he's worried about me. I don't blame him after what happened to me. But I can handle going out on my own for a bit, don't you think?"

"Groink."

"What do you mean I should rest more? I've been resting for three days now. I swear, some days you are no better than Jay, he must be rubbing off on you."

"Oink." Cosmo rolled his eyes, perplexed by her stubbornness. "Wee."

"Well, too bad, I'm telling him that I'm going to Richard's tonight whether you like it or not. Now let's go. The day is wasting!"

Sticking her tongue out at Cosmo, Alex jumped out from her seat, spun on her heals, and dashed out the door. Humming merrily to herself as she skipped down the stairs, she paid little attention to Cosmo, who was buzzing angrily in her ear. Waiting for her at the bottom of the landing was Jay's frowning face, which greeted her as he stood between her and the door with his arms crossed.

"Where do you think you're going?"

"Richard's, to talk more about the order. He did say he had some new information to share with me."

"You are in no condition to go anywhere. You are still as pale as a sheet of snow. What happens if you pass out again?"

"I'll be fine Jay. Cosmo will come with me."

"Squeee?!"

"Cosmo is the size of a peach, what is he going to do if something happens to you? And you think those town folks you pissed off are going to stop and help you? Why, they'd be quick to roll you in a ditch, or worse, finish you off so you don't cause more trouble."

"You worry too much, you know that."

"Well, you don't seem to be worried about anything, so someone has to take responsibility for your health and wellbeing. I doubt your brother would forgive me if something was to happen to you."

"Oh, so now you're concerned about what Tom would say?"

"I like all my parts attached to me, thank you. And, I love you the way you are, alive and by my side. Not to mention you still have no idea just how rough it can get out there."

"Fair enough. What if I call Lawrence and Fiona and ask them to pick me up and drop me off?"

"I guess that's better." Jay sighed and embraced Alex in his arms. "I'd still feel better if I was with you though. I can close the tavern down for the night and go with you, you know that, right?"

"I know. But that would not be fair to you or the people who want to come get a drink, few as they may be. I'll be fine. It's only a couple hours and I will be with friends who will take good care of me."

"Can you at least promise me you'll keep yourself out of trouble this time? We can't have you starting fights with the busy bodies in town again, even if they do have it coming."

"Best I can tell you is that I shall try my best. But I do not take the insults to you or Andy kindly, so I cannot be held responsible for how I react."

Groaning, Jay rolled his eyes and gave Alex a deep kiss before releasing her to go call up Fiona. He watched as she danced over to the phone humming and shook his head. She looked like her usual, carefree self again, but there was still a strange aura about her. A warm, dark, seductive, and oddly inviting energy floated about her causing him to smile and shudder. Crossing his arms, Jay heaved out a sigh and leaned a shoulder against the wall, looking at the pigrie hovering by his head.

"Keep a close eye on her, will you?"

"Groink, oink."

Snorting, both Jay and Cosmo watched Alex run around the house getting ready to go out as an invisible, ominous cloud hung over their heads. Jay did not like the strange feeling he had brewing inside him one bit, but he knew he had no control over her, and that was the way he liked her. Even if she was an untamable beast, she allowed him to get near her, gave him her trust and affection, and Jay would not trade the bond they had for anything.

It did not take long for Lawrence and Fiona to swing buy the house and pick her up. Jay let them in and watched as Alex bounced back down the stairs. Neither Lawrence, nor Fiona were keen on her going out either after the fainting incident, but they saw no point in arguing with her. Instead, they assured Jay they'd get her back to him in the same state they took her in as she pulled them out the door and into the car.

The three-minute ride to Richard's did not take long, and Alex flung the car door open before Lawrence had a chance to put the car in park outside the iron gate of Richard's brick town home. Stepping into the garden, Alex paused briefly to inhale the aroma of blooming flowers before sprinting for the door as Fiona ran after her. Grabbing hold of the shiny, cold knocker in the shape of a lily, she tapped it on the door three time as Lawrence caught up with them, leaning over to catch his breath.

Peering through the sheer cream curtains of his window, Richard waved at his friends before he opened the door and ushered them inside. The company found themselves in cozy, yellow living room with a white brick fireplace and a brown leather sofa situated in front of the sole window which looked out into the garden. A small wood table sat before the couch with paperwork from the day sprawled all over it and an empty inkwell beside it. The fire crackled like a roaring train in the compact space and Alex glanced over to the wall on left, covered in books. On the other side of the wall a small staircase lead upstairs and next to the books a small archway revealed the dining room at the back.

As Alex was admiring her friend's humble home, Richard stole a glance behind his shoulder, and waved for his friends to follow him into the next room. Sitting at small, square table amongst the blue floral wallpaper, he nodded for his friends to join him in the white chairs with plush, yellow cushions as he peered at one of the many books splayed open before him. Sitting around Richard at the table, the company exchanged glances before Alex decided to speak as she played with a musty, old book cover.

"What's with all the secrecy Richard? You are acting as if we are breaking the law by just being here."

"We might as well be. The Militibus Puritatis have been causing more havoc around town since your... incident, a few days ago. I don't want them catching me, or you, researching the order."

"Why?" Lawrence scratched his head. "What do these long dead mages have to do with the extremists running around today?"

"Well for one, it was the Militibus who drove the Order out to begin with, or at least confined them to the shadows."

"What?" Alexandra and Fiona gasped in unison. "How?"

"Here, look," Richard pushed a partially burned book of yellowed pages that contained a log of names and dates over to his friends, "these are the names of all the order members executed by the Militibus, and I am willing to bet there were more."

Pulling the remains of the book closer to her, Alex glanced over the information remaining on the page.

Name of Condemned	Crime	Date of Execution	Method of Execution
Jasper Brown	*Grand Master of Ordo Numinous Umbra*	*01/03/1034*	*Buried alive*

Giselle Davis	Harboring a half-blood	24/04/1034	Burned at the stake
Minna Lewis	*Wife to knight of Ordo Numinous Umbra*	*08/01/1035*	*Guillotined*
Selim Thomas	*Assisting the Ordo Numinous Umbra*	*26/06/1035*	*Broken on the wheel*

"Richard..." Alex frowned as she traced her finger down the browned page, studying the names of the condemned closer, "how did you find this?"

"I was tasked with cataloging the old prison logs over on the other side of the hidden cemetery. It's a shabby little place with a handful of cells hidden in the trees. Most folk don't even know it's there. Mayor Cox wanted the records to be combined, so I had to venture into the old archives and as I was gathering the old books, I stumbled amongst this in one of the portfolios. At first, I thought it odd that a handful of burned pages were tucked away between clean sheets of paper, until I noticed the crimes listed upon them. I started digging a bit further into this matter and found out that the Militibus Puritatis were once a ruling force here during the time of the war."

"Yes, that's right," Fiona nodded. "I recall my father ranting and raving about them every time he was drunk. He kept saying how the Militibus was right all along and how glorious their mission was. If I dare to remember correctly, he hoped they would one day make a comeback. I think they were almost like a religious cult from that time period, and they claimed they were striving to guide the pure-bloods into the new age."

"Exactly, the coming of the new dawn as they called it, same as the Order. And it was the Ordo Numinous Umbra who were their only opposing force. So, the Militibus took it upon themselves to exterminate as many of them as they could find. Anyone who was suspected of being part of this group, or in any way involved with them, was rounded up and executed by excruciating torture, as depicted in the remaining logs."

"That's horrible." Alex slammed her palm on the table, causing the paperwork to fly up in the air. "Is this why the order is no longer around? Are they all dead?"

"Not exactly. I did a bit more digging in the history books buried in the forgotten archives of the town hall, you know, books the leaders no longer want you to see, and I found something. Seems as if the order retaliated and fought back after an undisclosed incident. Half of them gathered as many like-minded pure-bloods, half-bloods, and grays as they could find. Using the tunnels under your house, they guided these people to the last remaining star ship and took them to a new world. The ones who stayed behind staged an uprising and drove the Militibus out of the east and established the free territory you see today. When this land's government was running smoothly, the order disbanded, fading into obscurity, and watching us from the shadows."

"But why burry the history then? The order won, isn't that a good thing?"

"Did you forget what I just told you lambkin? The Militibus did not leave the east entirely. Like me dear old dad, some stayed behind, hiding in the shadows, permeating all levels of our society, and waiting for the day they can take East Ashland back. It was in their best interest to erase the history from the memories of the people. That way, they were free to commit the same atrocities again without anyone being the wiser."

"Yeah." Lawrence leaned back in his chair. "And with them causing a ruckus now, I think it's safe to say that no one in the highest echelons of society is to be trusted."

"Come now Lawrie, we can't suspect everyone of being one of them."

"No, but why take the chance? We don't know who our enemies are, but we know their end goal. So, for now, it's best to avoid anyone this may benefit. Including our leaders."

Alex nodded her head in agreement. She was getting ready to tell Richard to hide the log, when the house was rocked by a loud explosion. Plaster rained down on their heads as the chandelier swung around violently above them. Covered in white powder with her ears ringing, Alex jumped up to her feet, knocking her chair over, and sprang for the next room. Amidst the shattered glass of the window and the scattered books which fell from the bookshelf, the small living room was bathed in a warm, amber glow as heat nipped at her exposed skin.

"What is going on." Richard muttered coughing as he made it into the smoke-filled room. "What in Alteria happened?"

Waving her hands in front of her, Alex squinted her eyes and flung open the door only to be blasted with smoldering air. Before her lay a horrifying site. The car they rode there was engulfed in flames. Its hood had been flung off across the street by the explosion, and in Richard's garden glowed two Militibus symbols as the flames twisted on their wooden surface.

"Me car!" Lawrence tried to rush past Alex, but Fiona and Richard held him back. "Them bastards blew up me car!"

Pluvia

Shouting, Alex held out her hand and with a crack of lighting and the roar of thunder, rain poured around her, dousing the flames out of existence. As the fire subsided and the smoke cleared something darting between the smoldering ambers of the car caught her attention. From the corner of her eye, she spotted a clocked figure disappear into an alleyway across the street. Waving her hand, she retracted the clouds and strained her eyes only to see another cloaked figure pop out from behind the remnants of the car holding a bright blue bow in their hands with an arrow aimed straight at her.

"Victoria aut mors" the figure shouted and lifted the bow up to Alex.

"That can be arranged."

Archanium

With a clenched fist, Alex allowed the flames surging inside her to wash over her body as a raging inferno filled her eyes. The air around her swirled, lifting dirt as she lifted her bow and aimed a steady blue arrow at the cloaked man. They both released their projectiles at the same time, and while Alexandra's found its mark at the center of the man's chest, his got deflected by the cyclone of soil and struck Alex in the shoulder.

Wincing from the burning pain spreading across her torso, Alex unclenched her fist and dropped to the ground. Clutching her wound, she felt the blood seep between her fingers as the world around her began to spin and go dim. Waves of nausea suddenly overcame her, and unable to hold back the sickness she coughed up a bit of bile as the hole she was covering continued to spray blood onto the ground.

"Dang it lambkin," Fiona rushed to Alexandra's side, folding her into her arms, "what were you thinking trying to fight back?"

"Sorry." Alex looked up at Fiona trembling as she felt the blood drain from her face and the fever return. "I just couldn't let them get away with it, and if I didn't intervene, they would have killed all of us."

"Jay is going to kill me!" Richard moaned as he clutched his head while looking at Alex in her now blood-stained dress. "What are we going to do? Should I go fetch the doctor?"

"Don't worry 'bout it so much. I can fix your girl up in no time. No need to get your knickers in a twist or fetch anyone."

Pressing her hands on Alexandra's shoulder, Fiona let her magic flow through her again, delighting in how refreshing it always felt. Waves of pleasure surged through her as her energy flowed into her friend, closing her wound up where they sat. Once more, Fiona felt a strange desire well up for Alex and she pictured herself stripping the young woman down and pleasuring her like she did to Catrine ages ago. Lost in a trance, fantasizing about kissing Alexandra's breasts, Fiona was shaken back to reality by Lawrence's sturdy hands.

"Fi. You feelin' all right? Are you done?"

"Yes. Sorry," Fiona got up, dusting her skirt off, "I was just recalling some better times, that's all."

"Oi, princess," Lawrence kneeled by Alexandra's side, lifting her into his arms, "you don't look too good lass, I think it be best if we got you home."

"I'm fine. I've had worse. You should let Jay tell you of the night we escaped Winter Haven and the wound I sustained protecting him."

"Yeah, I bet it be a good story too." Lawrence stole a glace behind his shoulder at the body lying motionless in the street. "But, what of the man you shot, think he's still alive?"

"Doubt it. Alex is an excellent shot."

Richard headed for the gate leading into the street and Alex watched him as her legs buckled beneath her. Pressing her closer to his body, Lawrence supported her weight as he helped her to the road, with Fiona trailing behind them. Standing around the hooded body, the trio watched the blood seep into the cracks of the cobble stone, flowing down the hill like rivers. Kneeling to the ground, Richard felt for a pulse, but none was to be found, so he flung the hood off to reveal the man's face.

Alex still clutched on to Lawrence as the covering fell to reveal the man's blue eyes staring up blankly at them. He was clean shaven, and not much older than Alex from the looks of it. With a sinking heart, she looked closer upon the face of the man she killed, but she didn't recognize him at all, he was not from Fall Harbor.

"He was so young." Alex mumbled.

"Yeah, but it was you or him, lass. Ain't no sense in feeling bad for defending yourself or your friends. Plus. This bastard blew up me car."

"Lawrie's right. This guy was an extremist. I say it's good riddance that he's dead."

"Sure, but he's dead outside my house. What am I supposed to do with him?"

"Call the mayor." Lawrence snorted as he looked over what was left of his prized possession which was now a heap of melted rubber and twisted metal. "I'm sure he'll want to know the Militibus struck again, at the house of his aid none the less. Not to mention, that they killed his ride."

"Fine. You three stay here though and keep Alex safe while I run into my house to make the call and hide the books."

"I ain't letting her go any time soon. Just make it quick, I want to get out of here and get the lass back to Jay before he skins us alive."

"There is no need for it my man. Your neighbors have alerted me to the commotion when the car blew up." Caleb stepped out from the shadows and stole a quick glance at the corpse by his feet. "But I see I have not managed to get here in time to prevent this."

"Mayor Cox, I can explain."

"No need Fiona. I'll give your friend a pass since she was protecting you. And," kicking the body over, the mayor smirked, "it saves me the trouble of executing him myself. Now, is anyone else hurt? Mrs. Hartwood over here looks a tad pale."

"No. We're all fine here, sir. Poor lass is just overwhelmed with the commotion, that's all. Only casualty aside from this guy is me car and Richard's house."

"Yes. Unfortunate. I'll be sure to get a new one to you tomorrow." Cox patted Lawrence on the back and turned to look at Richard. "And what about you my friend? You can't possibly stay in your house with it looking like this. Do you have a place to go while I get someone here to clean it up for you?"

"He can come stay with me. Jay and I have a few spare rooms at the house and Richard is always welcome at anytime."

"Alex, are you sure? I don't want to intrude."

"It's fine Richard. You are my friend. I'm not going to put you out on the street."

"Well. That settles it. You four return to the tavern, especially since Mrs. Harwood isn't looking too well, and I shall stay here to clean up this mess."

"Thank you, sir. I really appreciate all this. I'll just run inside and grab a few things if that's all right."

"Don't thank me Richard. Thank the lovely Mrs. Hartwood. And," Caleb peeked over his shoulder smirking, "keep the dear woman out of trouble. I'd hate for her to get hurt."

Nodding his head, Richard ran inside before running back out with a small bag he used to conceal the books in. Thanking the mayor again, he ushered his friends down the street, and into the shadows of a town which was fast asleep. Alex still had a hard time walking and Lawrence had to walk slow to support her without picking her up in his arms. But as they rounded the corner past the garden, Alex felt her world begin to swim again and could no longer feel the ground beneath her feet as sweat permeated her dress.

"Lawrence," Alex pleaded, "stop."

"What's wrong, lass?"

Stopping in the middle of the street, Lawrence glance at the woman trembling in his arms. Turning away from him, Alex doubled over clutching her stomach and threw up on the ground by the brick fence encasing the hidden oasis. There was not much left in her after the first time, and she heaved as yellow bile made its way to the ground by her feet.

"Lambkin? You sure you're all right? Maybe we should go wake the doctor."

Fiona rubbed Alexandra's back and held her hair as her friend continued to empty her stomach onto the cobblestones shaking. Supporting her weight on the stone wall with one hand, Alex heaved one more time as she gagged at the air now coming up past her throat. The darkness seemed to surround her now, creeping up to swallow her whole, and she felt her body grow cold. Shutting her eyes, she took a few deep breaths and allowed the cool air to caress her, pushing back her nausea even as the shadows continued to tighten their grip on her.

"No, I'm fine. Really." Alex coughed as the ground became solid under her feet again. "I think this was the last of it."

"What was that arrow made of, lass? I ain't ever seen a reaction this violent."

"It's nothing to be concerned about." Breathing heavily, Alex pushed herself off the wall and steadied her feet. "I'm still a bit under the weather from a few days ago. Guess that's why the arrow hurt so much more than what I'm used to."

"Whatever you say kid." Fiona placed her hand on the small of Alex's back and guided her forward. "Let's just get you home so you can lie down and rest."

Hurrying to the tavern, the group was relieved to see no more Militibus members in sight and soon the welcoming glow from the bar room windows signaled a safe heaven. As Fiona guided Alex through its wooden door, Jay looked up and dropped the glass he was holding a moment ago, letting it crack open on the floor like an egg. Rushing to his wife's side, he sat her down on a nearby chair and glared at Richard as Rupert swiftly made his way into the kitchen.

"What in all Alteria happened to her? I thought the three of you would keep her safe."

"We were. But the Militibus showed up at Richard's to trash the place and blow up me car. Your wife rushed outside to put out the flames and a member who lingered behind shot at her."

"What? I thought I told you two to keep an eye on her and keep her out of trouble! How bad did she get hurt?"

"Not bad at all," Fiona placed a reassuring hand on Jay's shoulder, "and she killed the bastard who did this."

"No harm no foul I say." Rupert walked in carrying tray with steaming cups of tea for Alex and the guests. "Mistress always had deadly aim, and after the way Master Quinton treated her, a minor flesh wound won't keep her down long. Why not have some tea," Rupert handed Alex a delicate pink cup, "it will soothe the soul and make you feel all better my dear."

"Thank you, Rupert," Alex stole a sip of peppermint and felt instantly better, "your tea is just what the doctor ordered."

"Of course. Shall I make up a few extra beds for our guests tonight?"

"Yes, please."

"Very well miss." Rupert turned and walked back into the house. "I'll get three ready to go."

"Oh, lambkin, Lawrie and I don't want to impose."

"As if we'd let you two walk home with all those lunatics running around town lately. Stay. Have a few drinks. It's not like I've been getting much business here lately anyway with the Militibus scaring everyone off."

"Why Jay," Richard snickered, "has Alex's kind nature started to wear off on you?"

"Shut it kid. I'm not so heartless as to put my friends in harm's way. And Alex would never forgive me if I did."

"I'm just teasing you old man. I appreciate being able to call both of you friends."

"Call me an old man again, I dare you."

Laughing, Richard rolled his eyes as Jay shook his head and went to the bar to fetch a bottle of whiskey for his friends. Glancing over at Alex he saw she was looking better again. The color had returned to her once pale face and aside the crimson stains on her dress, he wouldn't have guessed she was shot. Still, the Militibus activity was starting to alarm even him and he wondered if he would be able to keep his family safe if they ever did manage to take over the city, or if perhaps letting them go was a far better option.

CHAPTER 22

Discourse Between Friends

Sitting around the table closest to the bar, the friends who were still shaken by the events of the night didn't utter a word as they drank their whiskey. Jay had summoned the Carlsons to check everyone over and the sound of the bell chiming above the door signaled their arrival. Walking through the door to the tavern, Gladys stole one look at Alex and gasped. Rushing to the girl's side, she wrapped her up in a tight hug, relieved that she was not hurt more in the scuffle.

"Goodness gracious Alex," Gladys placed Alexandra's pale cheeks in her hands, "what in tarnation were you thinking taking on that thug?"

"It was nothing, really. I have taken on far tougher opponents than him. That's why he is dead and I'm sitting here talking to you."

"Don't you be so nonchalant about this child. Just look at you, stained with your own blood where he hit. Let me at least look at you and make sure you ain't gonna bleed to death."

"It's fine Gladys. Look," Alex peeled back the strap of her gown to reveal clean, healed over skin, "not even a scratch."

"Well I'll be. Who healed you?"

Glancing past Gladys, Alex stole a look at Fiona's face who was pale and wide eyed while shaking her head franticly. It appeared to Alex that she was one of the only people to know Fiona was not the gray she pretended to be. Knowing full well what it was like to want to hide one's identity, she turned to the woman frowning at her and smiled.

"Why I did." Alex shrugged, "I told you, it was nothing."

"If it were nothing, you ain't have that stain on your dress love. But I relent, you clearly know how to handle yourself," Gladys let out a sigh and shook her head, "I'm just glad it wasn't anything vital that got hit. You best be more careful next time."

"I will be. I promise."

"And how are the rest of them, Jackson dear?"

"They seem fine, albeit a bit shaken from what happen."

"I ain't blaming them. The fact that Militibus struck at Richard's and destroyed the mayor's car is rather alarming. If government workers are not safe, there ain't much hope left for the rest of us."

"I concur my love. It seems as if dark days are ahead of us."

"No, we must trust in Caleb to take care of us, he's never failed us before."

"Come on Fi. He is one man, what can he possibly do?"

"I don't know. Perhaps he can seek counsel with Tripp Donahue. Request an army to come and push them back. Anything."

"You think that buffoon over in Wellaby gives a shit 'bout us? I can almost guarantee you that he already knows, but he refuses to help us."

"That's preposterous!" Gladys slammed her hand on the table. "Tripp is a decent man, and a superb leader. If he knew what was happening here, he would intervene no questions asked."

"Oh yeah. So, what's stopping him? Why isn't he here, helping, when our houses are being vandalized and our citizens terrorized?"

"Perhaps because your so-called great mayor hasn't told him yet as to what we have to go through on a daily basis."

"And why would he do that?"

"Because, that man has a dark shroud hanging over him. You are just so loyal to him that you can't see him pulling the wool over your eyes."

"And that clown in charge of everything is any better?" Lawrence scoffed. "As if he cares about any of us expandable assets. He's only in it for the glory, he don't—"

"Enough!" Jay bellowed, causing everyone to jump. "Seems like the Militibus is winning, even in this house. Can't you see their goal is to divide us and pick us off one by one? And here you are, falling straight into their trap."

"Jay's right." Alex stood up and glanced around the room. "They are exploiting our differences, causing us to fight, that way we won't be able to rise up and stop them. But we can't fall for it. We have to do something about them, or everything is lost."

"What do you propose we do lambkin?" Fiona let out a sigh. "Even if we can get every citizen of Fall Harbor on board, they still outnumber us ten to one. And it ain't like these townsfolk will pick up their torches and pitchforks, let alone arms to do something about them, at least not until it's too late."

"I'm afraid Fiona is right." Richard shook his head. "Why, half these nitwits would see us grays killed themselves if they could. There be nothing any of us can do about them until we are past the point of no return."

"But we can't sit back and do nothing. How long can East Ashland hold out if everyone has the same attitude we have?"

"And what do you want us to do, lass?"

"We fight back. If they come after us, we come after them harder. We get a word out to Trip Donahue, and we get Caleb Cox behind us. But whatever we do, we cannot allow the East to fall."

"Jackson and I can take care of Donahue for you love. We are attending a banquet over at the grand manor later this week. We shall let him know what the West has been up to and judge his reaction. We can go from there afterwards."

"And I can have a chat with Caleb for you lambkin. I'm sure I can find a way to persuade him to take this more seriously."

"And how will you persuade the mayor," scoffed Richard, "going to bed him into compliance?"

"Why not? He is a man after all."

"That is preposterous. You can't expect Cox to go for someone like you. After all, you're just a common whore and he is the most eligible bachelor in town."

"Watch it lad, that's me sister you are talking 'bout. Just cause your girl is bedding someone else, don't mean you can insult me sis."

"It's all right Lawrie, he is right, I am just a whore. But it don't mean I can't convince Caleb to take things more seriously. He has a lot to lose too you know."

"Like what?"

"Don't worry about it lackey. That for me to know and you to find out, and if Cox hasn't told you yet, neither will I."

"Then it's settled. Jackson and Glady's will talk to Tripp, Fiona will talk to Cox, and Jay and I will do our best to keep things from escalating."

"Why us?"

"Because I have a feeling that we are their primary targets."

"Your wife is right my boy." With a solemn look, Jackson placed a firm hand on Jay's shoulder. "You two threaten everything the Militibus stands for. I would be very careful from here on out."

"Don't need to remind me pops. After tonight, I'll certainly keep a closer eye on things."

"Good. Then, since everyone is well, Gladys and I should get going."

"No." Alex screamed. "Everyone is staying here tonight. We have plenty of room, and at least this way, I know you are all safe."

"Come now Sug. Jackson and I have to open the clinic and apothecary up in the morning."

"And you can go there from here. At least wait until the sun starts to rise, and the Militibus has retreated into the shadows. You and Jackson are not exactly approved by their laws either."

"All right dumplin', but only because it will make you feel better, and I don't think you need any more stress after the night you had."

"Good. I'll get Rupert to show you to your rooms."

Dashing out of the room, Alex fetched Rupert who was more than happy to make up another bed and show their guest their accommodations for the night. After everyone had settled into their rooms, Alex lay in her bed, nestled in Jay's arms. She glanced out the window and shivered, unable to shake the strange feeling of being watched. She knew it was crazy, but while her husband and pigrie slept next to her, she could see shadows lurking just outside their window, and she heard them calling her name, begging her to join them.

CHAPTER 23

Militibus Strikes

Again

Several days passed since the incident at Richard's house, and Alex was once again starting to relax as she helped Rupert prepare dinner in the kitchen. Richard was still a house guest as his place was getting fixed up by Caleb's men, and Alex enjoyed having his company. Humming along, she placed a boysenberry pie in the oven and went over to a metal basin to wash her hands while stealing a glance out the window. Their backyard appeared deathly quiet as Andy swung on the swing surrounded by firebugs.

"Well," Rupert smiled as he put away the left over ingredients, "you seem to finally be in good spirits Miss."

"It's been quiet for almost a week now, and it seems as if the shadows have retreated too."

"Hoink?"

"Don't worry about it buddy. I simply thought the shadows were getting heavier, following me, and whispering my name through the gloom."

"Roink..." Cosmo shot Rupert a worried glance, but the man shook his head with a smile.

"I see. Nothing to worry about then, just your imagination playing tricks on you love. Say, how are the Carlsons doing? Did they leave for their trip to Wellaby yet?"

"They left last night. They should be meeting with Tripp Donohue by this time tomorrow."

"Good. Let us hope something comes out of it." Rupert set off to do the dishes, handing Alex a towel to help dry. "And what of young Lawrence and that sister of his? How have they been coping?"

"Fine, I think. Truth is, I haven't spoken to Fiona much lately. She's been very quiet since that night, not that I blame her."

"Can't say I blame her either. Poor girl has had a rough few months." Rupert handed Alex a dripping dish, "Did Master Lawrence get a new car yet?"

"He did." Alex finished drying the plate and set it aside. "Caleb made sure to replace it the next day. And it's a far nicer model than what he had before too."

"This Cox fellow comes off as quite the gentleman, doesn't he?"

"Oh, he is wonderful Rupert. And he takes care of his people like an exemplary leader should. If only more pure-bloods where like him."

"Sounds like my Mistress may have a crush on the mayor. Should Master Hartwood be worried?"

"Nonsense Rupert. You know there is only one man for me."

"I'm just making sure." Rupert stole a glance at the girl with a slight frown. "Master Hartwood certainly is something else though, can't say I've ever met anyone like him."

"You really have no idea Rupert. Jay is the most amazing man in the world, and I can't picture my life without him."

"Oh, I think I know just how unique Master Hartwood is Miss. I really think I do, at least when it comes to you."

Alex was about to reply with a joke when the door to the kitchen creaked open and Richard stepped inside the cozy kitchen. He still looked tired as he had been busy working on a way to stop the Militibus, but even through the dark circles and sunken eyes he looked radiant. His hands were stuffed in the pockets of his tweed pants and he had a weary smile on his face as he inhaled the sweet aroma of the pie baking in the oven.

"Hey Alex, Rupert."

"Sir Cadwall." Rupert nodded. "How may we help you this fine evening?"

"Jay wishes to speak to Alex. So, I figured I'd help out in the kitchen in her stead."

"Jay wishes to speak to me? Why?"

"Don't know, but it's Jay, so it could be anything."

"Fair enough." Alex put down her towel. "I'll go see what he wants. Why don't you take over the dishes for me?"

"Gladly. Anything to keep my mind off the extremists running around town and causing havoc."

Leaving Rupert and Richard in the kitchen with Cosmo, Alex wondered down the hall to the tavern door. Pushing the door open a crack she peeked inside, spotting Jay leaning over the counter, sipping on a glass of whiskey. The way the light from the lamp hit him made him appear surreal, almost as if he was a phantom of a time gone buy. Even after everything, he still caused Alexandra's heart to flutter, and she had to still her breath before forcing herself through the door.

"Hey," Alex's voice cracked, and Jay glanced from his drink to look at her, "Richard said you wished to see me."

"Yeah." Jay downed his whiskey. Walking up to Alex, he wrapped he in his arms and pulled her into his body. "Truth be told, I just wanted to get rid of him and have some alone time with you."

"Don't you get enough alone time with me?"

"Not even close." Jay pulled away and glanced at Alex. "Are you feeling all right love?"

"Yes. Why do you ask?"

"I don't know, guess it's the light, but you look a bit more pale than usual."

"I'm fine Jay. You need to worry less about me."

Alex pushed herself up on her toes to give Jay a kiss when the peaceful silence of the evening was interrupted by an explosion reverberating through the tavern. The bottles shook and fell off the self on the wall, shattering on the floor around them. Outside a child's scream could be heard crying out for his parents as the room erupted in crimson flames.

"Andy." Alex and Jay screamed in unison.

As they went to rush out of the tavern to check on their son, they were stopped dead in their tracks as the window before them burst in, sending glass shards flying everywhere and causing Alex to yelp. Hanging tightly to Jay's arm, she watched as a large brick containing a note slid to a stop by her feet. Bending over and with a trembling hand, she released the stark white parchment glaring up at her from the stone it was attached to. She was about to unfold the note and read it when the door burst in allowing Richard, Cosmo, and Rupert carrying a sobbing Andy in his arms into the tavern.

"Alex, Jay. Are you all right?"

"We're fine. How's Andy? Is he hurt?"

"He is fine Master Hartwood. The lad just got a big fright with the explosions and the fire, that's all."

"What's that in your hand?"

"Just a note that was attached to the brick that was thrown through the window."

"Well," Richard eyeballed Alex frowning, "what does it say?"

Focusing back on the parchment clutched in her hand, Alex opened it up and read the message it contained out loud.

No scrapmunchers, mongrels, or corrupt pure-bloods allowed. Get out, or you will be next.

Militibus Puritatis

Trembling with rage, Alex felt something inside her snap and a strange feeling overcame her body. A powerful, dark energy filled her to the brim, and she felt herself getting intoxicated by what it offered her. Crumpling the letter up in her hand, Alex allowed it to burst into flames without so much as an incantation and her eyes lit up with a blue blaze. Feeling the aura around his wife grow increasingly darker, Jay reached out a hand to touch her shoulder.

"Alex?" he whispered, but she did not hear him.

A fiery glimmer continued to fill Alexandra's eyes as she un-clenched her fist and allowed the ashes to rain to the floor. Reach-ing her hand out towards the door she pulled it back to her, making the wood slab rip off its hinges. A gust of wind rushed in through the opening, flinging back her chestnut hair and causing splinters to drizzle around her. A gloomy cloud shrouded her as she walked forward, out towards the flames. As she reached the opening where the door was, the sky flashed and rumbled, and as she stepped outside the clouds opened up, dousing the surround-ing flames.

Soaked by the rain, she stood in the middle of the road and studied the row of burned up Militibus symbols. As the water continued to stream down in sheets, whispers sprang up around her. At first, none of the voices registered inside her head until a middle-aged woman stepped forward and snapped Alex back to normal with a sharp slap across her face. Touching her throbbing cheek with her fingers, she finally looked up to see the crowd gathering around her.

"This is all on you." The woman shouted while shoving a finger in Alexandra's face. "All this is your fault. You and that man you dare call a husband."

"There he is," a man behind Alex shouted as Jay stepped out from the tavern, "it's that cumberworld and his bastard spawn."

"Don't call my son that." Alex spun around nearly hitting the man.

"He ain't your son, he didn't come from your loins you pathetic excuse for a pure-blood."

"That's right," the woman spun Alex around to look at her, digging her fingers into the girl's shoulders, "if you choose to lie with a fopdoodle, that's on you, but don't try to claim his filthy spawn as your own."

"Better yet," the man came over to the woman's side, "why don't you and your mongrel of a husband get out of Fall Harbor and let us decent folk be."

"That's enough from the both of you." Richard rushed over to Alex, ripping her from the woman's grasp, and blocking her off from the angry mob gathering around her. "Alexandra and Jay have just as much right to be here as the rest of you."

"No, Marvin is right, they should get out." Stepped out another man from the crowd. "None of this would be happening if they didn't move here. Their mare presence in our town is causing all these attacks."

"You're being irrational. Alex and Jay have nothing to do with this."

"No, lap dog," scoffed Marvin, "you are just blinded by your lust for the girl. Everything was fine until the so-called princess moved here married to that half-blooded son of a whore. Their union disrupts the natural order of things, even a fool can see it. Maybe the Militibus is right. Maybe we should drown people like him at birth to spare the rest of us from their tainted presence."

"Shame on all of you," George's voice rang out in the street as he pushed his way through the angry mob, "you are letting your fears control you. You are turning on your neighbors, and that is exactly what the Militibus wants. This is exactly how the first war started."

"I didn't ask for a scrapmuncher to be my neighbor." The woman turned and glared at George. "And the fact that the half-blooded scumbag has a pure-blood wife is simply outrageous. Why, it's no wonder the Militibus is targeting us."

"What Helen said." Shouted the second man. "No one asked them to move into our neighborhood. They should go live on the row with the rest of the riff raff."

"It's true that no one asked them to live here. But, who else would move into that haunted house and turn into a functioning establishment?"

"Fools that's who," screeched Helen, "or worst, those who have a pact with the Worm himself."

"More proof they are evil and should move out." Marvin threatened Alex with a fist before retreating as Jay stepped forward to challenge him.

"No one is moving these folks out, not while I'm alive." George came over to Richard's side, helping shield Alex from her neighbor's wrath. "Alex and Jay are wonderful people, and I am happy to call them my friends. Now the rest of you go home, lest you want to stay behind and help us clean up this mess."

Grumbling, the crowd of onlookers dispersed, leaving the small group of friends huddled together in the rain. The cinders of the Militibus pyres still smoldered, casting eerie shadows around them. In Rupert's arms a small boy sobbed as he looked over at his father who was trembling with clenched fists.

"Daddy," Andy finally mustered up the courage to speak, "why do these people hate you so much? What did you ever do to them?"

"Because," Jay turned his head away from his son, "I am nothing here, just a thing to be hated and feared. I'm an abomination that shouldn't exist, and you would be better off living with Alex, far away from here."

"No," Alex wrapped her arms around Jay's waist, pressing her head on his back, "don't you dare speak like that. These people are fools. They don't know what they are saying, and you have just as much right to be here as the rest of us."

"Alex is right you know." Richard put his hand on Jay's shoulder. "As George said, they are letting their fears get the best of them, don't take it personally buddy."

"It's true Master Hartwood. Lady Alexandra and Master Andrew would not be better off without you. They need you as much as you need them."

"Hoink, Groink."

"I guess you're right, I do need you." Jay turned to put his arm around Alex. "But, I don't suppose we will see any business here any time soon. At least not until these extremists dissipate and the fear from the public subsides."

"We don't need business. We have enough to get by for now, and we have each other, which is more than I could ever ask for."

"Alex is right. You two have each other, Andy, and the rest of us." George looked at everyone who gathered around Jay. "Together we can beat these lunatics at their own game. Now, what do you all say we clean up this mess they left behind and really give them something to be angry about?"

"Thank you, George, for sticking up for us, and staying to help clean up." Alex smiled at him. "But, how did you know to come here?"

"I heard the explosion all the way from my house. Figured you'd be the next likely target and came over to help. I knew your neighbors would blame you for all of this, much like they always have."

"Thanks man." Jay kicked the post next to him and it crumbled into dust. "I appreciate that we still have friends here, few as they may be."

"Dumbass," Richard laughed as he pushed the pole next to him over, "you've always had friends, as far back as Winter Haven, and we are not about to abandon you."

"Right. You have always had people who'd stand by your side Master Hartwood, even if you didn't notice. Now, if you excuse me, I shall go put the young master to bed as he obviously had a rough night already. I shall leave the cleaning up to the rest of you."

Leaving the quartet to knock over the remaining poles and sweep up the mess, Rupert and Cosmo vanished into the house, taking the boy with them. They were both concerned about the powers Alex had displayed out of her anger, but there was nothing else left for them to do but wait it out. Rupert knew harder times were coming, and he only hoped that he would be able to keep Alexandra's mortal body stable long enough for her to come into her own.

CHAPTER 24

An Unexpected

Surprise

Once the smoke cleared, and the sun began to crest over the horizon all that was left to do was the cleanup in the tavern. An exhausted Alex swept up the glass while Jay and Richard boarded up the broken window. Rupert managed to get the door back onto its hinges while Andy stayed upstairs all day with Cosmo, not daring to come down. As predicted, in a few days' time, no soul, other than their close friends came into the tavern. Seeing this as an opportunity to get out of the house, Alex put on her cloak and got ready to leave.

"Where are you going?" Jay leaned against the door frame of the tavern watching his wife reach for the door handle.

"I'm just going to go see Fiona. We haven't seen her in a few days and I just want to know how things are going on her end?"

"Why don't you take Richard or Rupert with you? It be safer if you are not alone."

"I'll be fine Jay. I can handle myself if need be. Plus, I have Cosmo with me."

"Rhee!" Cosmos somersaulted in the air.

"And what's he gonna do?"

"Come get you so you can rush to my rescue if need be." Alex rolled her eyes. "Seriously Jay, I can take care of myself, you know this."

"Fine." Jay grumbled. "But, stay safe, that's all I ask."

"I promise I'll keep out of trouble the best I can." Alex turned to give Jay a kiss on his cheek. "You worry too much."

"I can't help it."

"I know, but I'll see you in a few hours."

Giving Jay one last kiss, Alex stepped out into the brisk evening air, and fastened the cloak tighter around herself. The change in seasons was becoming more evident, and she shivered as she walked down the desolate street. A crisp breeze came from the harbor as she continued down to the alley, swirling dead leaves around her and carrying on it the whispers of the people who dared not get near her. Even in the poor part of town, citizens rushed into their home, shutting their windows, and not daring to look at the face of the woman they thought to be the cause of all their problems.

Turning her head to the ground, Alex did her best to ignore the hatred in their words and the actions that stung deep inside. On her shoulder, Cosmo snooted at her rosy cheek, sensing the distress building inside her even as she stifled her tears. Walking down the row of shabby brick houses, even the hookers turned a blind eye to her, as if the stain she carried with her would transfer on to them. Fortunately for her, a worn, marron door came into sight as a beacon in the dark, and she rushed for the safe harbor it offered.

Knocking on the door, she concealed her face in her hood, hoping to block out the glares as she waited for someone to answer. After what seemed like an eternity the door finally creaked open and Lawrence looked over at Alex while raising his eyebrow slowly. His hair was disheveled, his shirt was untucked, and she could smell the alcohol on his breath as he swayed in the doorway.

"Well I'll be. What can I do you for princess?"

"I wanted to talk to Fiona. Can I come in?"

"Who do you take me for," Lawrence smirked and stepped aside, "the idiots who think you're the new plague? You're always be welcome at our house lass, come on in."

Stepping into the small parlor of the modest house, Alex waited for the door to shut before removing the hood from her head and breathing a sigh of relief. The smell of smoke and tea welcomed her into their comforting embrace, and she felt herself relaxing by the minute. Walking out from the small living space lit only by the ambers of the fireplace, Fiona regarded her young friend with a welcoming smile.

"Lambkin, what in Alteria brings you to this part of town?"

"I just needed to get away from the tavern and be someplace else, even if it was only for a little while."

"Yeah, we heard of the incident at your place a few nights ago lass. Damn shame. These extremist thugs are really getting out of control."

"Yes, and a ballsy move attacking you, sweets. Caleb won't stand by and watch that happen to you again, I can tell you that much."

"How can you be so sure?"

"Come sit down by the fire and I'll tell you love." Fiona took hold of Alex and guided her into the cozy room, sitting her down on an old, faded, floral wingback sofa. "Not to mention you look like death herself. We need to warm you up love, it must be freezin' out there." Handing Alex a cup of steaming hot tea, Fiona sat down beside her friend and observed her paling appearance. "You sure you're all right lambkin?"

"Yes." Nodding her head, Alex mustered up her best smile. "It's been a long couple of nights, that's all. Now, why don't you tell me about Caleb? Any news from him?"

"Him and I had a long talk last night when I stopped by to pay him a visit. He was angry when he got news of the incident at your place, and I wanted to ask him if he was planning to do anything about all this. I was unsure of what to expect but he told me he's sick and tired of this happening to his citizens, especially those he considers his friends."

"So, what's he going to do?"

"I don't know yet, but he promised me that he would work something out. You just hang in there dear, I'm sure this will all be sorted out soon enough."

"I sure hope so. I don't know how much longer I can hold out."

"Yeah." Lawrence flopped down in a chair opposite of the women and took a sip of clear alcohol as he stared blankly at the fire. "Can't imagine people talking shit about you is easy to stomach. And I know that when it comes to trashing your loved one, it's almost impossible to not punch them in their filthy mouth."

"I don't care what these people think of me." Alex's eyes shot up, filled to the brim with tears. "But the way they talk about Jay and Andy breaks my heart. I don't think I can stand by and watch them treat my family like dirt and not do anything. I don't know how you put up with this Lawrence, but I swear I've reached my breaking point."

"No need to be rash sweetness. I'm sure this will all be over before you know it. Caleb promised me it won't be much longer."

Nodding her head, Alex went to sip on her tea all the while not being reassured by Mayor Cox being able to fix this. Sure, he could stop the Militibus, but he couldn't control the way the people hated them, nor prevent them from slinging insults at her in the streets. Finishing her drink, an ominous feeling gnawed away at her core. Alex knew something sinister was coming, and she didn't think she could stop it. Putting down her cup, she went to stand up, but dizziness and nausea overcame her instantly and she collapsed into Fiona's arms.

"Lambkin," Fiona cried out holding on to Alex, "what's wrong?"

"I... I just felt dizzy and nauseas all of a sudden. I think staying up all these nights really did me in."

"Oh, sweetness," Fiona shook her head with a pained expression on her face, "I don't think that's your problem."

"Then what else could it be? Do you think I've come down with something?"

"No love. I think you might be with child. I've thought so ever since the incident at Richard's place."

"No." Alex shook her head with wide eyes. "No. That's not possible."

From his chair, Lawrence put down his drink, looked over at Alex, and let out a loud snort. "Sweet tits, if Jay is even half the man, I think him to be, it's not only possible, but highly likely. I mean shit, I'd have knocked you up ages ago if I was your man."

"Lawrie," Fiona snapped, "how can ya be so rude? Can't ya see the poor thing is scared half way to death at the prospect?"

"What's there to be scared of? You do the deed long enough, you get a kid, that's how it works, everyone knows this. And it's not like they don't already have a rugrat at home, so what's one more? Plus, if she wants to be sure, why not give her one of them tests you got lying around? Not even sure why you got so many, you're as barren as the desert."

"Why do I let you live with me again?" Fiona frowned at her brother.

"Cause, I'm your baby brother and you love me, even if I am an arse."

Fiona shook her head at Lawrence before turning her attention back to the ashen girl in her arms. "What do you say lambkin? It's just a prick of your finger and we can know for sure if Jay will have another wean to keep him on his toes?"

"All right. I guess..."

"Good. Now sit down and I will be right back. I promise this won't hurt."

Placing Alex back into the chair, Fiona vanished upstairs and came back in minutes carrying a vial of clear liquid and a needle. Taking hold of Alexandra's shaking hand, Fiona pricked her finger and allowed a drop of blood to fall into the glass. The liquid inside turned and swirled in shades of pink and blue before settling down in a soft violet color.

"Well look at that," Fiona smiled, "looks like Andy is getting himself a little sibling."

A gripping panic took hold of Alex as she stared blankly at the vial of purple liquid staring up at her from the table. The hairs on the back of her neck stood up as an unnatural chill permeated her core. She felt her lungs tighten as the blood slowly drained out of her face and her heart rate accelerated. Trembling, she looked at Fiona's beaming face but there was nothing she could offer her friend other than the tears coming from her face.

"Oh no, lambkin," Fiona rubbed Alex's back, "it's all right. This is a good thing, ain't it?"

"I..." Alex sobbed, "I don't know. Jay and I never talked about it, and I... well I thought we had more time."

"Ehh, so what?" Lawrence got up from his chair and came over to kneel beside Alex. Taking hold of her shaking hand, he rubbed it in his palms while giving her an earnest look. "I'm sure Jay will be thrilled to have another babe, especially since it's with you lass."

"Yes... you're right." Alex nodded, knowing her friends would never understand the darkness surrounding her heart. She doubted anyone would. Rising to her feet she gave them a nod and her best smile. "But I think I should go. I stayed here long enough, and I guess I should go have a talk with Jay about this."

"You want me to come with you lambkin? For moral support, you know."

"No. I'll be fine. I promise."

"All right love. But be sure to call me when you get home, so I know you are safe. Plus, I want you to tell me what Jay's reaction is when he finds out."

"I will. I promise."

In a daze, Alex stumbled out of the room and headed for the door. Not stopping to put on her cloak, she rushed outside and bumped into a woman with warm brown skin. The stranger's golden-brown eyes studded Alex and a coy smile played on her soft chocolate lips. The woman was wearing a golden corset and silk skirt just past her knees, appearing to be one of the many working girls living there. Glancing Alex up and down, she continued to smile as she placed a gentle finger under the girl's chin and raised it to meet her gaze.

"Well, look at you darling." Fatima said smiling. "You look absolutely radiant, almost like you're glowing."

"Um." Alex stiffened as she backed away from the goddess. "Thank you."

"Best bundle up dear. You shouldn't be getting chilled in your condition."

Smirking, Fatima winked at Cosmo before she turned and head up the steps to Fiona's door, leaving Alex stupefied in the streets. Shaking the feeling of having met this strange woman before, Alex draped the cloak over her shoulders and stumbled down the street in silence. Shuffling down the cobblestone path, she places a trembling hand over her stomach. She thought of the life growing inside her and instantly, dread filled her heart. It's not that she did not want Jay's child, actually, she wanted it for a while now, ever since Gladys brough up the subject. But there was a daunting air around her that she could not shake, and she could not be happy about this, no matter how hard she tried.

Walking down the street, her head suddenly ached as more disembodied voices filled her ears. The whispers snickered and chattered all around her. Then, one in particular called out to her.

It was a voice she knew well, and the sound of it frightened her, as the things he said caused waves of panic to wash over her.

Alex felt the shadows close in around her, grabbing hold of her, pulling her in. Petrified and alone, she picked up her pace to escape the darkness, but the shades just grabbed at her harder. Even Cosmo felt the evil presence around them get more oppressing as it permeated everything in their quaint town. He sensed the dark master looming on the horizon, coming to claim what he thought was his, and the little pig trembled at the thought of what he would do to Alex.

CHAPTER 25

The Feud and Some Meddling Gods

By the time Alex reached the door of her house, the voices were deafening, and her head throbbed with every step she took. They kept telling her they wanted her, wanted her baby, and she did not think she would be able to stand up to them. Feeling herself getting sick to her stomach from the pain, Alex stopped to take a deep breath, pushing the vomit deeper inside. Standing in front of the door, she thought she spotted someone from the corner of her eye, but when she turned her head, the figure had vanished into the shadows.

Standing in the dead of night staring into the darkness, Alex stilled her racing heart and listened for any sound from the alleyways, but none came. Unable to shake the uneasy feeling she got from being outside, she pushed open the doors and bolted into the welcoming interior of her home. Still not sure of what she was going to do next, Alex was given no time to think as Jay came strolling in from the tavern, almost as if he were waiting for her return. The look on his brow was serene, and she felt herself grow ashen from the calmness he projected and the news which she still needed to break to him.

"You all right, sweetheart? You look pale again."

"Yes... I'm fine... I guess."

"What's wrong love? Did something happen at Fiona's?"

"No, it's just..."

"What is it? Come on, you can tell me."

"Jay..." Alex mumbled while turning her face to the ground, "... I'm pregnant."

"What? Really?" Jay's face lit up with an infectious glow as he rushed up to embrace Alex in his arms, spinning her around the room. He'd been waiting for this moment since their time on the ship, and finally it was becoming a reality. "That's great..." Pulling away to look at the soured expression in her eyes the smile quickly faded from his face, "... isn't it?"

"Jay..." Alex felt herself stiffen as a tear creeped up into the corner of her eye, "... it's just..."

"You don't want it, do you?" Shoving Alex away from him, Jay glared at her with his nostrils flaring.

"No, that's not—"

"I see how it is. It's all fun and games to be with a half-blood, until it comes time to starting a family, then you turn tail and run, like everyone else."

"No, Jay. Please... listen—"

"No, you listen," Jay bellowed, "screw you!"

"Jay, please—"

"No. I don't want to hear any more from you. Get lost Alex. Go back to your family, or to Richard, or wherever else you want, just get out of my sight." Jay turned to head back for the tavern. "I never want to see you again."

Watching Jay storm out of the room and slam the door shut behind him caused Alexandra's heart to crumple into a million pieces. A hard lump formed in her throat and she could barely breathe. She suddenly felt numb, and the tears began pouring out of her face uncontrollably. Distraught, she didn't bother to put her cloak back on as she ran out of the house, leaving poor Cosmo behind where he sat on the table glancing from door to door. The pigrie sat honking and wondered what horrible thing just transpired between his friends as this was not the outcome he expected.

In the tavern, Richard sat at a table sipping his warm beer as Jay stormed in, slamming the door so hard that the dust rained into his stein from the ceiling. Looking up from his drink with a frown, Richard noticed Jay's face was bright red, and his eyes were as ice cold as the day he first met the barkeep. Watching his friend walk behind the bar and slam a whiskey glass down on the counter, he knew something bad had happened. He waited for Jay to fill his glass with his favorite poison and chug it down before he spoke up.

"What's wrong? Did something happen?"

"Did you know," Jay tilted his head to look at the lad with a scowl, "that Alex is pregnant?"

"No... but," Richard paused, wondering how such news was cause for alarm, "that's a good thing... isn't it?"

"That's what I thought. But apparently your little princess felt otherwise."

"Perhaps, you misunderstood the Missus barkeep."

A tall, black man with a soft afro walked out from the shadows holding a stein of his own. In his mortal form, Bastian appeared fully dressed, wearing a black satin suit with fine leather shoes and a red ascot. Plopping down on the chair beside Richard, the God of Chance regarded Jay with a mischievous smirk, knowing full well what was coming next. From behind the bar, Jay glared at the newcomer, gritting his teeth, and clenching his fists until his knuckles turned white.

"And who are you to come butting in like this?"

"Just a concerned citizen, half-blood," Bastian leaned back in his chair, grinning, "and apparently one of your only patrons."

"Well," Jay took another swig of his newly poured whiskey, "if you wish to remain a patron, you'll mind your own damn business, or I won't hesitate to throw you out on your ass."

"A bit testy, aren't we?"

"And how would you feel if your wife didn't want to have your child?"

"Jay..." Richard stammered, "I think this man is right. I think you did misunderstand her. I know for a fact Alex wanted a baby with you, so perhaps it's something else that's been bothering her. Let's go clear this all up, where is Alex now?"

"Dammed if I know." Jay poured himself another drink and gulped it down. "I told her to get lost."

"You did what?" Richard screamed as he nearly dropped his beer glass when he shot up from his chair. "Why would you do that?"

"What did you want me to say to the woman who doesn't want my kid?"

"Where is she supposed to go?"

"Who knows? Who cares?" Jay shrugged and went back to drinking without looking at him. "Maybe you can take her in and have another go at it. All I know is, she ain't my problem any longer."

Anger boiled over in Richard as he watched Jay sip his drink without a care and wondered how this man could possibly be so cold to the only person who cared about him. Beside him, Bastian leaned back over in his chair and flipped a coin on his thumb, catching it as it fell from the air. It was finally time to play his part, and unfortunately, he had to wear shoes, so he was unable to feel the vibrations the mortals were putting out. Glancing between the two men standing in the deserted bar, he smirked as he knew these two would be all too easy to sway, and he leaned over to whisper in Richards ear.

"Seems like your friends had a bit of a falling out. Perhaps this is a chance for you to step in and fix this?"

"What can I possibly do?"

"Well, the way I see it, you can either go after the girl and comfort her in her time of need until her husband comes around, which he inevitably will. Or," Bastian shot a glance at the barkeep, "you can try your luck at convincing the loose cannon over there of his folly before he is ready to admit his fault. The choice is yours."

Sitting in his chair, Richard glanced over at Jay. He knew talking to him would be pointless as he needed time to calm his rage and realize what he had done. On the other hand, Alex needed him the most right now, and it was his turn to be there for her. Knowing exactly where he would find his friend, Richard nodded his head and put some change on the table before her got up and left without saying a word. From his chair, Bastian watched him leave with a smile. Even with his restrictive footwear, the lad was all too easy to predict.

"Good choice my boy." Bastian whispered to himself. "Looks like my work here is done."

Standing up, the God tossed some coins onto the table and walked out into the brisk autumn night. Stealing one last glance at Jay through the window, he snorted before snapping his fingers to open the door into the veil. The barkeep was as volatile as he remembered, but that was exactly what made him so perfect for his niece. Vanishing into the night, Bastian headed for the Amphiptere's hideout to see if Fatima did her job like she was supposed to, and to see how the rest of the night would play out from the safety of his grandfather's domain.

CHAPTER 26

The Reassurance of a Friend

Stumbling down the street as she ran, Alex ignored the bitter chill in the air even as the tears stung her face from the cold. She didn't know where she was going until she reached the gates of the secluded garden in the middle of town. Running inside the welcoming sanctuary, she collapsed on the nearest bench amongst the leafless trees. Bringing her knees up to her chest, she buried her face in her dress and continued to sob as she trembled from the air which seemed to be getting colder with each passing second.

Not too far behind, Richard had caught up to her a few minutes later and stood at the iron gate, catching his breath as he watched her weep under the naked maple tree. Seeing Alex this broken and distraught made his skin grow hot and his heart sting. It's been a while since he was reminded of how vulnerable and fragile she could be, or how much she always needed him.

Unfastening his cloak from his neck, he walked up to her, and draped the warm, gray wool around her shaking shoulders. Sitting down beside his lifelong friend, Richard didn't say a word. Instead, he pulled her into his arms and warmed her with his body as her sobs continued. Stroking her hair, he felt her body quiver and rubbed her back to reassure her that everything would be fine. When she had calmed down a bit, he lifted her face up and wiped away her tears before her spoke.

"Normally," he leaned back with a sigh while he continued to hold her, "I'd say congratulations are in order. But it seems the occasion isn't as happy as one might like."

"Not you too Richard."

Alex looked up into his face with a pout. Her emerald eyes dazzled with the tears reflecting the moon shining above their heads and Richard almost drowned in their depth. As a chill blew between them causing her small frame to shudder under his arm, he felt himself melting from how she always made him feel. Averting her eyes, he gazed up at the blackened sky and tried his best to calm the thoughts ripping through his head.

"What's wrong Alex? I thought you wanted to have kids with Jay. I clearly recall you mentioning it to me a few times during out tea gatherings."

"I do. And I should be happy, but I..." Alex started sobbing again, "it's just... I'm not sure now is a good time, especially with everything going on around here."

"You know," Richard press Alex tighter against his chest and rubbed her shoulder, "I'm going to tell you what Izzie always said to me when I asked if she regretted having to raise me. She said there is never a good time to have kids, it's a commitment you're never truly ready for, even if you think you are. She also said that you just have to make the best of it and know it will all work out at the end. So all you need to do is have faith Alex. I think this whole thing will work itself out in the end and you should just celebrate this occasion while you have the chance."

"Really?" Alex pulled away to look at him. "But... how can I be happy when I know this whole cursed world wants my baby dead?"

"Not the whole word love." Richard looked at her pained face and gave her a soft smile. "And even if they did, you really think Jay wouldn't rip everyone's head off to protect you and his kids?"

"No," Alex sniffled, "I know that's exactly what he would do, and... I don't want him to. I don't want to see him get hurt all because of me. He's already suffered so much in his life. I just can't see myself being yet another cause for him misery."

"See darling, that's your problem. You are the protector. You always have been. Under fire, you are the first to put your life on the line for those you love. And yet, you can't seem to accept that occasionally, you are the one who needs to be protected. Stop being so tough Alex. You aren't infallible, and you need to learn to rely on the people who love you as well. After all, what would any of us do in a world without you in it."

"I... I don't know. I've never stopped to think about it."

"See. I knew it. I figured such thoughts would not cross your mind. But you know what? We would all be lost without you, and that's the truth. So you have to promise me that you will allow the rest of us to protect you when you need it the most. Allow your friends and family to be there for you once in a while, and remember, we need you."

"All right, all right. I promise. Not like it matters much anymore anyway. Jay hates me now, and he never wants to see me again. Guess this means I will have to raise this baby on my own or go back home and suffer for what I've done."

"Oh, don't say that. First off, Jay doesn't hate you at all. He is just a tad hot headed and impulsive. He needs some time to cool off and think about his actions. After all, your reaction is not how he pictured this situation unfolding in his head the entire time he's dreamed about it. I mean, it surprised even me, so I can only imagine what a shock it was to him. He will come around eventually though, even if it takes some time.

"Second of all, you'll never have to return to Manevia, I would never allow it. I would also never allow you to raise your baby by yourself. And, I'm not the only person here you can rely on to help. You have Rupert, George, Jackson, Gladys, Fiona, and Lawrence. We will always be there to help you out and get you what you need. And for now, you can come stay with me for as long as it takes that husband of yours to get his head out of his ass and realize what he did."

"Thank you, Richard, for always being there to catch me when I fall."

"What are friends for if not for that very purpose?"

"You're right, thank you again." Alex snuggled up into his chest and wrapped her arms around his waist. "But, as long as you don't mind, think we can stay here like this a while longer? At least until the tears stop coming."

"Whatever you want love. Your wish is my command."

Leaning his head back against the wood back of the bench, Richard gazed up at the moon as he continued to caress the shoulder of the woman crying on his chest. He pondered what he would do if Jay didn't regain his sanity, or if that man really was serious about never wanting to see Alex again. What he said to her was true, he wouldn't allow her to have this baby on her own. He would gladly marry her and raise the child as his own. But, he knew that was not what she wanted, he knew she belonged with Jay. So, despite how much he wanted to be with her, Richard knew he needed to figure out how to fix things between his friends, even if doing so killed him a little on the inside.

CHAPTER 27

The Voice of Reason

Back at the house, Fiona walked into the tavern through the adjacent door with Cosmo grumbling behind her. Having received no call from Alex in over an hour, she worried about her friend making it home alive and went to check up on her. Having not found the girl at the house, she was hoping to spot her at the bar celebrating with her husband. However, to her astonishment, the establishment was deserted, and the only thing she spotted amongst the chirping of crickets was Jay, leaning against the bar top, half a bottle of whiskey deep.

"Hey, Jay."

The barkeep did not answer her as he continued to nurse his bottle of booze and Fiona frowned at the unusual sight. Normally, she'd expect him to be attached to Alexandra's hip, or smothering her with affection, especially after learning such good news. But now, with no response from the man and no girl in sight, she was beginning to worry that something terrible had happened to her friend in route. With no other explanation as to the man's aloofness, Fiona swallowed hard as she decided to get to the bottom of this mystery.

"Jay... have you seen Alex?"

"Yeah, what about her?"

"Well, where is she?"

"Don't know. Don't care." Jay took a swig of his whiskey before putting the glass down. "She ain't my problem anymore. She's probably bedding Richard as we speak."

"What are you talking about Jay?" Fiona rushed up to the bar and tilted her head to peer into the man's face. "What happened here?"

"Did you know she was pregnant?"

"Yes. I just gave her the test an hour ago. She left my place soon after to tell you."

"Well," Jay straightened up to glare at her, "did you know she doesn't want it?"

"What? No..." Fiona's stomach churned as she realized what must have transpired at the house. "She's just scared right now, that's all. Can you blame her with everything that's been going on 'round here lately?"

"This is what she signed up for." Jay roared. "She should have known better before she decided to share a bed with me."

"She's only nineteen you stupid arse!" Fiona's eye twitched as she ripped the glass out of Jay's hand and slammed it on the table. "She's been through so much already in her short life, much more than you know. I doubt you can comprehend all the pure-blood rules she had to abide by, or all the abuse they inflicted upon her. And what of their horrible treatment of women? Alex survived it all, and she had the strength to leave it all behind just for you. Now here you are, expecting her to bear the weight of the world on her shoulders with a smile on her face just because it makes you happy. Is she not allowed to be scared even once?"

"Stop making excuses for her. We all had it rough!" Jay glared at Fiona as his hands balled up into fists. "If she didn't want kids with me, she should have stayed locked up at that cushy castle of hers and became a breeding stock for the man she was intended for."

"You're either blind, or an eejit." Fiona shook her head. "I get it, she hurt your ego, and wounded your pride, which wasn't hard to do given the life you had. I sympathize with you, believe me, I do. But don't you see what that girl goes through for you on a daily basis? Can't you see the brave face she puts on every time she goes out, even as those fools sling insults at her all day long? Don't you notice how she keeps smiling even as she is shunned by almost everyone around her. Can't you see her heart break every time someone says something about you or Andy. And yet, despite it all, she still gets up in the morning with a smile and she tries to make the best of things because she loves you.

"If only you could see what I see. The way she looks at you, how she talks about you. You are her world Jay. You and Andy are her reasons for living. She'd gladly move mountains and take on all the armies of Alteria to protect you. So forgive her for being scared of bringing another child into this harsh world. For her, it's another person for her heart to bleed over, and maybe, she just can't take it anymore. Yes, she knew exactly what she was in for when she married you. The people at Clear Spring warned her about this, they tried to talk her out of it, and yet, she still chose you over everything, including her own safety and reputation.

"And do you know why she did it? She did it because she's madly in love with you. To her, nothing else matters, not even her own image in this damned society of ours. And you know what Hartwood," Fiona turned on her heals, "if you can't see any of this, then perhaps you don't deserve her. So, I suggest you pull your head out of that arse of yours and see what you are trying to give up, and why. Because if you don't act now, you may actually lose her forever, and I somehow doubt that is what you want."

Storming out of the tavern, Fiona slammed the door shut behind her, leaving Jay to stand alone at the bar with his jaw hanging open. He thought about everything that Alex did for him, and for Andy, and his heart dropped into his stomach. Sobering up a bit, Jay realized how foolish he had been, and wondered if it was too late to get her back. Glancing at Cosmo sitting on the bar top beside him, he dropped his head in his hands and ran his finger through his hair with a groan.

"I really screwed up this time little guy, didn't I?"

"Oink..." Cosmo narrowed his eyes and snorted. "Roink."

"I don't suppose I can fix this."

"Hoink." The pigrie rolled his eyes and flew up to come closer to Jay's face, bopping his nose with his snout. "Groink."

"In that case, do you know where she is?"

"Roink, Oink!"

"All right little friend. I'll follow you. Lead the way."

Running out the tavern with Cosmo in tow, Jay locked up the door and headed for the direction of the garden, following the pigries lead. Cosmo knew exactly where Alex would be. She's be in the one place that kept calling out to her, the place where it all began. As he flew, he was a bit uncertain if this relationship could be salvaged. After all, he knew Alexandra's true nature better than anyone and it could be rather volatile. But, if the Amphiptere was right, nothing could stand between them, not even a little spat. And it was with that hope that the little pig flew as fast as he could towards his mistress, with Jay sprinting behind him, and he hoped beyond hope that this wasn't all for naught.

CHAPTER 28

Reconciliation

Rushing up to the garden gate, Jay peered through the opening and spotted Alex curled up on a bench beneath a tree, with Richard's arms firmly around her. Seeing his wife enveloped in the arms of another man caused Jay to feel a tinge of jealousy, and for a moment he wanted to rip the young man's head clean off. But mad as he was, he knew all too well that he had no one to be angry at but himself for pushing her to it and for sending the young man after her. Still, he needed to break this up right away, before Richard managed to steal her away from him. Walking up to the seat, Jay towered over them, but they didn't seem to notice his presence as Richard continued to rub Alexandra's arm.

"Hey." Jay continued to stand before them, arms crossed and frowning.

"Jay!" Richard looked up startled. "What are you doing here?"

"I want to have a word with my wife. Alone. If that's okay with you."

"Come to your senses already I see." Richard scowled at Jay. "It's all well and good with me, but, is that all right with you Alex?"

Richard looked down on the girl in his arms who stiffened at having heard Jay's voice. Finally, she looked up at him teary eyed and nodded her head silently. Letting out a deep sigh, Richard let her go and stood up to glare at Jay.

"All right. But my offer still stands. I have a bedroom with your name on it if you need. You can live with me as long as you like Alex."

"Thank you, Richard. But I think I'll be fine." Alex curled up on the corner of the bench, not yet daring to look up.

Walking over to Jay, Richard puffed out his chest, titled up his head the best he could, and frowned as he peered into the man's face. He had always found the barkeep to be intimidating, and he used to avoid confrontation with him at all costs out of the fear of what Jay could do to him. But tonight, he found his resolve, and he was willing to get punched in the face so long as Alex would not get hurt again.

"You can talk to her all you want. I can't stop you. But, if you hurt her any more than you already have, I swear Jay, I'll kill you myself."

"Yeah right." Jay huffed. "Like you stand a chance against me. Scram. My wife and I will be fine."

"I mean it Jay. You don't scare me like you used to. Not to mention, I'll do anything to protect Alex, even from you. So, don't you dare do anything you'll regret. You hear me?"

"I won't hurt her. I promise."

"Good. See to it that you won't, or your wife will be living with me."

Turning around, Richard headed through the gate in the direction of his house, leaving Alex alone with Jay. Finally gathering her courage, she looked up at him from her spot on the bench. Through puffy eyes still filled with tears she could see the way the moonlight hit his face, making his harsh features appear soft and gentle. The way he stood there, silently, with his hands in his pockets, caused Alex's bottom lip to quiver and she stifled more tears threatening to make their escape as she pressed her knees tighter against her.

Sitting down beside her, Jay hung his head between his legs without looking at her. Seeing her as she was, caused his heart to twist in his chest, and a hard lump to form at his throat. Knowing he was the cause of her pain made him hate himself even more than he already did, and for a split second, he entertained the idea of setting her free to be with Richard. But unable to bear the thought of being without her, he wiped the crazy idea from his subconscious and cursed himself under his breath. Exhaling deeply, he turned and looked at her tear-stained face as her hot torn lip continued to quiver. A glisten of tears formed in the corner of her eyes, shining a pale blue with the light of the moon and the invisible knife dug itself deeper into his chest.

"I'm sorry darling," he spoke softly, "for what I said to you earlier. I didn't mean any of it, and I was as ass for going off on you like that. Do you think you can ever forgive me?"

"Oh, Jay," Alex flung her arms around him, buried her face in his chest, and sobbed uncontrollably. "I'm the one who's sorry for hurting you the way I did."

"No love." Jay pulled Alex into his lap and cradled her in his arms as he continued to stroke her hair. "You have nothing to be sorry for. I understand why you reacted the way you did. I was just so excited at having a baby with you that I didn't take the time to consider the situation you found yourself in, or why you were so upset. And I want you to know that you don't have to have this baby if you don't want to. I'll understand, and we can always try some other time."

"But Jay, that's what I was trying to tell you back at the house, I do want it. I wanted it for such a long time. And I really do want to be happy about this, I promise you, I do."

"Then what's wrong honey? Why are you so dismayed? Are you afraid of what those narrowminded fools in town will say about us, about our child?"

"No." Alex shook her head and glanced up at Jay. "I don't care what they think of our children or of us. They are not the ones that scare me."

"Then what is it? What has got you so upset over this?"

"Can't you see them? Don't you feel it?"

"Who am I supposed to see and feel love?"

"Not who, what. Don't you notice the shadows in the dark, closing in all around us, grabbing hold of our very core? Can you not feel the darkness encroaching with each passing day? Whatever it is, it wants this baby. It keeps telling me it does. I hear hushed whispers in the night that tell me both I and my child belong to it. I'm not sure what I'm up against here, but whatever it is, I don't think there is anything I can do to stop it. And if I can't stop it, I can protect my baby from whatever it wants to do to it."

"Oh, sweetheart, don't worry about any of it. I can take care of anything out there that wants to hurt my family."

"You can't take care of this." Alex turned her head to the dark mist forming in the corner of the park, slinking closer to them. "It's too ancient, and too powerful."

"Then we will do it together, all right?" Jay cupped her face and wiped the tears from her eyes. "No matter what happens, we will protect our children together. Understood?"

Alex nodded her head knowing full well that Jay did not understand the gravity of the situation. He did not seem feel the mysterious presence or hear its voice as it lulled her to sleep. And he certainly did not see the shadowy serpent slithering its way up her leg at that moment, trying to grab hold. All Alex knew was that Jay did not need to know any of it, the job of protecting this baby was not his, it was hers and hers alone. So, instead of trying to explain to him the imminent danger surrounding them, she simply nodded and stopped the tears from coming so he would not worry about either of them.

"All right. But let's go home Jay. I'm cold and I want to get out of this darkness."

"Sound like a plan love. You do look frozen solid. I'll be sure to warm you up in bed as soon as we get back."

Giving Alex a deep kiss, Jay scooped her up in his arms and carried her out of the garden with ease. Cosmo flew beside them as they headed home, but he was now on edge as well. Glancing around the area, he gave out light barks as his speckled nose twitched in the air. He smelled the distinctly comforting aroma of dragon's blood, intermixed with clove, oak moss, and Moroccan rose permeating the night. The white wolf and her handler were on the prowl. This could only mean one thing, that something terrible was about to happen.

CHAPTER 29

Stranger in the Shadows

Unable to sleep, Alex stood at the window with her hand placed protectively over her baby as she looked out into the alleyway below. From the shadows, she could see a strange man leaning against the wall and pondered why he was there. The stranger seemed to have noticed her staring as he looked up to meet her gaze with his striking Prussian blue eyes before he smirked, turned, and vanished into the darkness. Standing in her spot, Alex suppressed a shiver as the eyes reminded her of the catacombs, and the beast which assaulted her there.

Stirring in the bed at the opposite end of the room, Jay felt around the empty spot on the mattress next to him. Propping himself on an elbow, he glanced about the chamber and spotted

Alex standing by the window, looking out into the night. The way moon light poured in through the glass gave her an ethereal blue glow and flames appeared to spiral around her. Sitting up on the edge of the mattress, Jay admired her silhouette for a moment as she continued to light up the darkness with her otherworldly glimmer.

"You all right sweetheart?" He finally mumbled. "You aren't still upset with me, are you?"

"No." Alex turned to face him with a dazzling smile. "I just couldn't sleep, that's all."

With a sigh, Jay stood up and walked over to her, enveloping her in his arms from behind. She leaned her head back against his broad, hairy chest and closed her eyes, relishing in the safety his body provided her. Tickling her forehead with his goatee as he kissed her, Jay placed a large hand over her stomach and pressed her closer, afraid that he would lose her and their baby if he let go for even a minute.

"You're not still worried about the darkness and the unknown, are you?"

"A little, but I trust you to protect us."

"Good."

Turning her around, Jay cupped her face, bringing her closer, and kissing her deeply as her body fused into his. He felt himself stiffen as he parted his lips from hers and gazed into the emeralds that were her eyes as they sparked in a sea of black. She regarded him with the same soft expression which caused him to go wild every time, and once again Jay felt as if he was losing all control. Stroking her cheek, he leaned in for another kiss as he thrust himself against her leg, causing her to moan.

"Come to bed sweetie, I'll help you take your mind off of things."

"Will you now?" Alex spoke in a dark, silky voice as a mischievous shadow glazed over her eyes. With a wicked smirk, she grabbed hold of his manhood, stroking it with her hand, and not letting him go. "What if I don't want to be in bed?"

"Then where baby? I'll do anything you ask."

Pulling Jay's pants down, Alex undid the laces on her white satin nightdress, exposing her breasts. Liking her lips, she played with her nipples as she regarded his naked body in the moonlight.

"Anywhere you want darling but make it interesting."

"Damn you woman. You really have no idea what you do to me, do you?"

Walking up to Alex, Jay backed her up against the wall before hiking up the bottom of her gown. Grabbing hold of her buttocks, he hoisted her up, placing her firmly on his shaft and pressing her harder against the wall. Wrapping her arms around his neck and her legs around his waist, Alex allowed his thrusts to penetrate her as she moaned and played with his silky hair. Once again Jay found himself immersed in her dark, dangerous energy, but he was not afraid of it. For some reason, its familiarity soothed him and made him feel whole, especially as shadowy wings cloaked him in their embrace.

Down below, in the alley, the strange man in black watched them as they made love. His Prussian blue eyes gleamed with an otherworldly sheen and his long, curly black hair swayed with the crisp midnight air. He played with his handlebar mustache and watched them for a while longer, delighting in the earthquakes she caused. Her energy was familiar now and as intoxicating as it was back in the veil when he first encountered her. Delighting in her darkness, the man inhaled her mystery before he smirked and turned to go back to his domain.

From inside the house, Rupert kept an eye on the stranger with a frown and clenched fists. He watched him looking up at the window while licking his lips and waited for him to leave. Then, without turning around, he finally regarded the other person standing in the room with him.

"You know why he's here, don't you?"

"Of course," The Amphiptere walked out from the shadows, his silver hairs lighting up the space around him. "The first ever demigod is something to behold, even for my brother."

"And how long have you known about it?"

"Probably for as long as he has. Since the moment she was conceived. As I said, Alexandra caused quite a commotion in the veil that day. Why a whole typhoon ripped through the spot she was in on this plane when she decided to make that mortal a part of her."

"I see." Rupert turned around to look at his grandfather. "So, I take it the Worm wishes to possess their child the same way he wishes to conquer the girl?"

"No. He wished to destroy it before it becomes a problem for him."

"Will he succeed?"

"I don't think our dear girl will let him, do you? But, I suppose, it will certainly be a test of her powers."

"What do you wish me to do?"

"Nothing. Just keep an eye on her and let things play out as they should." The Amphiptere smirked. "Bastian was right, you really have become rather attached to Alexandra, haven't you?"

"She's like a daughter to me. I'd do anything to protect her."

"Well, don't worry my boy, the girl is more than capable of protecting herself and her child. You just keep that man and the mortal boy safe, for if the Worm can't have her, he'll try to have them instead."

"I understand, sir."

"Good. Good."

Nodding, the God of Time waved his hand, forming a portal in the unlit space behind him, and Rupert watched as the Amphiptere disappeared into the shadows. Satisfied he was alone, he plopped down in the nearest chair with a groan. Sinking into the soft floral cushions, he hung his head in his hands and hoped the master was right. As much as he trusted the master plan, he could not face the thought of anything bad happening to his adopted daughter, or the child which she now carried.

CHAPTER 30

A Town Meeting

As the sun poured in through the window, Jay stirred in the tangled-up sheets with Alex still nestled in his arms. He leaned in to inhale her sweetness, delighting in the strange scent of frankincense and myrrh she now had while he caressed her bare curves with his hands. The way the sun hit her skin made her appear out of this world with her entire body taking on a soft, pale blue glow. Looking at her chestnut locks flowing over her porcelain skin, Jay thought she appeared almost normal again, not like the seductive creature she turned into at night.

He thought about waking her up and making love to her again, but the pounding on the downstairs door caused him to grumble and he begrudgingly got out of bed. Rupert would surely welcome this unwelcome intrusion into his home, but Jay still wished to see who was stupid enough to disturb his peaceful morning and the chance to be intimate with his wife again. He was willing to bet it was Richard, coming in to check up on him and make sure Alex was with him. Throwing his clothing on, he made a mental note to chew the lad out as he stumbled down the stair with a soured look on his face. But as soon as he opened the door, he was surprised to find Lawrence, of all people, stepping inside his parlor.

"Rough night Hartwood, or did you and the Missus have a good make-up session?"

"What do you want Lawrence?" Jay grumbled under his breath.

"Mayor Cox has called a town meeting at the commons. Seems like our town hall was vandalized last night. I've come to escort you all there. Safety in numbers and all."

"Why you?"

"Cause, Fi still wants to claw yer eyes out, and Richard was asked to not leave."

Groaning, Jay rolled his eyes. He was not looking forward to talking to either Richard or Fiona after the way he acted last night. Both of them were right of course, and he was out of line with his reaction, but he did not wish for them to remind him of it, not after everything that happened. Jay was still mauling over whether or not he should go wake Alex up or not when she glided down the stairs to his side, putting her delicate hand around his waist.

"Good morning Lawrence. What can we do for you this fine morning?"

"Why Alex, don't you look radiant today. Much better than you did last night." Lawrence tipped his hat to the lady and smiled. "Did the old man give you a good work out last night or was it the other way around?"

"Have you ever thought of not saying something perverted," Jay snorted, "or is this just your default setting."

"I'm afraid it's just how I am you ol' dog. Not that I blame you. I mean... I'd be working her over too every night if I could." Lawrence winked at Jay before pointing to the door. "Shall we go? The town meeting will start soon."

"Can I come too?" a small voice piped up from behind.

Turning around, Alex spotted Andy standing in the hallways with his hands behind his back. He was rocking on the balls of his bare feet as his eyes studied her and his dimpled cheeks were pink from running around in the cold. Cosmo was fluttering behind him and Alex knew she could not ruin their innocence by having them worry about the Militibus business or the ignorant townsfolk of all things.

"No love. Daddy and I will go alone. I think it's best you stay here with Rupert."

"Awww. Really?"

"Yes, Master Andrew. Your mother is right. Town meetings are no place for young lads to go gallivanting about. We shall stay here and make pie instead."

"Apple pie?"

"Absolutely my boy. Why don't you go and pick the best ones out of the pantry?"

"All right. Come on Cosmo, you can help me pick out the sweetest ones! Bye mom, bye dad." Andy waved at his parents and ran into the kitchen with the pigrie buzzing behind him.

"You take care of yourself Miss., you hear me? I wouldn't want those ignorant townsfolk to get to you and Master Hartwood with their vile words and hateful stares."

"I think I can handle them Rupert."

"That is precisely what I am afraid of. You of all people should keep yourself out of conflict, and it's best not to stir the hornet's nest any further."

"I'll keep an eye out on the both of them ol' man. Besides, no one but us and the Carlsons know that Alex is expecting, so the townsfolk should at the very least be less nasty."

"See to it that you do Master Lawrence. See to it that you do." Rupert furrowed his brow as he looked over at the mayor's chauffeur. "Now, if you all shall excuse me, I have a young lad to tend to. I'm sure we shall have plenty of pie waiting for you upon your return."

"Thank you, Rupert, for keeping an eye on him."

"No need to thank me Miss. That is what I am here for. Now go on. I shall have tea and pie waiting for you on your return."

Without another word, Rupert turned and vanished into the hallway, humming away as he walked. Grabbing her cloak off the rack, Alex draped the soft wool over her shoulders and stole a glance at Lawrence standing by the door. Smiling, she took hold of Jay's hand, and looked up to give him a nod.

"Shall we go?"

"I guess..." Jay grumbled. "Lead the way Lawrence."

Walking out of the house behind Lawrence, Jay and Alex glanced about the streets with a few people walking by. Not to many passersby dared to look in their direction, and those who did were sure to scuttle to the opposite side of the street. Alex felt as though the three of them had contracted the plague, but she knew the people's apprehension could not be helped. Keeping her head down to avoid the stares, she continued to trail by Jay's side until she spotted the rest of the group waiting for them at the very back of the crowd gathered around the steps of the town hall.

Huddled together in a tight circle, their friends stood in the empty space the townsfolk had granted the people they deemed responsible for their troubles. They chatted amongst themselves, seemingly ignoring the hushed whispers and menacing glares coming their way. Upon seeing her brother, Fiona smiled and waved for the three of them to join their party. Breaking away from her two companions, Alex ran over to grab hold of her friend's arms and tell her everything that happened.

"Lambkin." Fiona smiled. "I'm so glad to see you. Richard filled me in on the events of last night. I'm glad it all worked out for you. Does this mean we can all celebrate now?"

"Yes," Gladys peered over her husband's shoulder. "I hear congratulations are in order hun."

"Indeed, they are my peach. What say you, everyone over to our place for some celebrations after this? We'll crack open a fine bottle of wine and Gladys can make her award-winning nut and jackalope casserole."

"Sorry doc." Lawrence strolled over with his hands in his pockets. "But I think we are all going over to their place for some pie."

"It wouldn't happen to be Rupert's famous pie, would it?"

"Yeah, it would." Jay came up beside Alex while glaring at Richard. "Apple pie that is."

"Nice, my favorite. In that case, I look forward to joining you."

Looking at Alex, Richard gave her a warm smile, and she suddenly felt oddly self-conscious about the whole situation. She didn't think anyone knew, but with Jay's arms around her waist she thought she sensed the eyes of every citizen upon her. Fearing the repercussions this could have on them, she continued to dart her eyes around the crowd and as the whispers broke out around them, she began to tremble and sweat. She felt her heart drop to her stomach as she caught glimpses of people looking in her direction, and she had to put her head down as she was too frightened to meet their gaze.

"Do they know?" she whispered.

"Know what Sug?"

"About... you know..."

"Oh, that, no babycakes, we are the only ones, I promise."

"How can you be sure?"

"Lambkin, it ain't like they can smell it on you or anything. They won't notice for a few more months, and by then this whole thing should be over."

"But you seemed to know."

"Oh, love, that was just a lucky guess on my part. Believe me. These eejits don't know shit, and none of us are spillin' the beans either."

"But they keep staring at us."

"So, let them stare. And let us give them something to talk about."

Jay wrapped one his arms around Alexandra's shoulder while keeping the other one over her stomach. Bringing her in closer to his body, he glanced up at the crowed and planted a warm kiss on her head. With that, the crowd broke into a chatter chock full of frowns and scowls as they mumbled angrily amongst themselves. Feeling helpless, Alex turned around, pressed her head into Jay's chest and wrapped her arms around his torso. Sheltering his wife from the mob of onlookers, Jay glared at anyone who dared sneak a peek at them, and by the time Cox got up to his podium, the crowd seemed to settle down as no one dared say anything to the half-blood with a bad reputation.

"Citizens of Fall Harbor." Cox began in his dynamic voice and the crowd gathered around him, forgetting all about Alex for the time being. "It seems that an extremist group has infiltrated our once peaceful community. They have been attacking our neighbors, vandalizing our businesses, and even went as far as to deface our town hall last night with their vile symbol. Well, I am here to tell you that I shall not stand by and allow this to continue."

"What you going to do about it mayor." Shouted a voice from the crowd.

"Will you get rid of the problem?"

"Yes! The half-blood and his floozy must go, will you get rid of them?"

Jay's arms tightened around Alex as she shuddered in his embrace form the hatred in their words. She dared not look up from his chest, but she knew her friends were gathered around her, sheltering her from anything the mob might wish to do to her. At the podium, Cox was waving his arms to calm the crowd down and protect the girl from any more harm.

"Citizens. Citizens." Cox roared over the shouting of his constituents. "You are allowing your fear to control you, Jay and Alex are not our enemy, they are our friends, our neighbors, and we will stand behind them as if they were our own family."

"And how long before someone dies here because of them?"

"No one will die." George shouted as he came up behind the mayor. "The Militibus are cowards, they don't have it in them to actually kill anyone, they rely on people like you to do it for them."

"Yes. Well said George." Caleb smiled at him as he shot a glance at the small group gathered at the back. "There is no need for fear. We are all safe here, I will make sure of it. And so long as I'm around, no child will have to grow up in Fall Harbor with such hate running amuck around them. Now go back to your homes, band together, and let us show these extremists that we will not be pushed around. Let us tell them that we will not comply with their fear tactics by embracing our neighbors instead of shunning them as these thugs want. Remember, as long as we stand united the Militibus can never win."

Mumbling at the mayor's speech, the crowd dispersed and streamed around the group of friends as if they were contagious. An occasional person dared to shoot a hateful look towards Alex, but Jay blocked them by holding her close to his chest. When everyone had finally gone back to their house, Caleb strolled over to the small group of friends still gathered at the back. As he walked, Cox radiated an air of authority that kept the stray citizens at bay and George was beside him to keep anyone away if need be.

"I'm glad to see you all came." Caleb placed his arms behind his back while analyzing the scowl on Jay's face. "I sure hope these folks are not putting you off our little town. It be a real shame if they made you want to leave."

"No need to worry mayor. I have already explained to Alex that they are only acting out of fear. They know these folks hold nothing against the two of them personally." Fiona looked up and smiled at Caleb with a light pink sheen in her cheeks.

"Of course, I would expect nothing less from you my dear. It's just," Caleb looked at Alex and Jay smiling, "I want everyone to know that half-blooded children have nothing to fear in my town. Everyone is welcome here, and I will not allow some Western bullies to scare them off."

"Then my dear mayor," Fiona straightened the collar on Caleb's white jacket, "I sure hope you can rein in this problem before it's too late."

"Don't you worry about it my dear. Soon enough, the Militibus won't be a problem for you." Cox smiled as he planted a gentle kiss on Fiona's hand, causing her to turn a brighter shade of pink. "Now, if you shall excuse me, I still have business to attend to over in Chester. I will return in two days' time and then I shall start working on a permanent solution to this problem."

"Of course, sir. I shall stay here with my friends if you don't mind."

"Not at all George, not at all."

Bidding the group a farewell, Cox walked away towards the town hall as they watch him leave. Waiting for him to get out of ear shot, Alex glanced up at her friend and smiled timidly while still clinging to her husband's arm.

"What were you doing with the Mayor, George?" Alex asked as she moved away from Jay.

"I was tailoring a suit for him in preparations for his meeting with Trip Donahue in a few weeks. I hear he is going there alone to discuss the matters plaguing our town."

"Yeah, you sure heard right. Richard and I volunteered to go with him, but he refused."

"Interesting..." George rubbed his beard, "wonder why that is."

"I figured it was something important that he need to do alone. Perhaps they will even discuss going to war with the West if it means stopping the Militibus. I'm sure it's matters that need to be kept secret, and unlike Lawrence, I'm happy to have some time off."

"I see. Makes sense I guess." George shrugged his shoulders. "So, what will you two do in the meantime?"

"No clue. But right now, we're going over to Jay and Alex's house for a little celebration. Rupert is making his famous apple pie, and I bet there will be tea as well."

"Oh? That sounds delightful. And what exactly are we all celebrating?"

"The newest addition to our family." Alex glanced at the ground as she mumbled. "And you are more than welcome to join us. We'd love to have you,"

"Why Mrs. Hartwood, it can't be?" George looked at Alex and smiled as she nodded her head. "Well I'll be. I have to say, this is the best news I've heard all day my friends. I would be delighted to join you in celebrating this joyous occasion."

"Then what are we waiting for?" Richard glanced about the group. "Let's go. We wouldn't want the pie to get cold, now would we?"

Laughing at Richard's remark, everyone shook their heads and went over to Alex and Jay's tavern for a celebration. As promised, Rupert had tea and warm apple pie waiting for them in the dining room upon their arrival. Sitting at the table with a fireplace roaring beside them, the friends dug into the delectably sweet concoction and sipped on their hot tea. As they chatted and celebrated together, they slowly forget all about the dark cloud looming over their heads and the danger hiding in plain sight.

CHAPTER 31

Tragedy at the Row

A week after the town meeting, Alex began to calm down and enjoy herself more. The Militibus had not been active since the attack on the town hall, and the townsfolk had returned to silently avoiding her. Ever since the incident on their street and the confrontation with their neighbors, the bar had become eerily empty. Aside from their friends, no one dared go inside the establishment owned by the half-blood. This lack of interaction was causing Alex to get bored, and she hated being cooped up inside the house all day. Sitting in her usual chair by the fireplace, reading a book, she let out a sigh, glanced over at Jay, and got up to her feet.

"Going somewhere love?"

"I was just going to go over and visit Fiona." Alex closed her book and placed it on the table beside her. "I'm bored and I want to get out of the house for a bit."

"Hoink?"

"I'll be fine Cosmo. It's going to get dark soon, and you know no one is out on the streets when it's dark." Alex walked into the hallway and reached for her cloak. "Besides. It's not like the townsfolk dare even look at me anymore, so I doubt they would try to do anything."

"All right. But don't take too long getting back. I'd feel better if you were close to me and I could protect you."

"Roink, oink."

"The two of you really do worry too much. But fine. How about I'll go grab Fiona and bring her here, will that make you feel better?"

"Sure will, and it be better for Fiona too, she could keep an eye on that brother of hers when he gets here."

"All right, then I shall be right back with Fiona. Why don't you go get the bar ready while I'm gone?"

Waving at Jay and Cosmo, Alex stepped out into the crisp chill of the evening air. Fresh powder had fallen on the ground, covering the streets in a sheet of white. It was unusual for snow to fall this early in the season, but everyone reckoned it was just an anomaly that happened from time to time, the wet season they called it. Glancing about the desolate space, Alex saw the sun starting to set, and as predicted, the streets were bare as a result. Smiling to herself, she tightened the cloak around her neck and set off north for Fiona's house on the Row.

Walking down the street in silence, she listened as the snow crinkled under her feet and enjoyed the otherwise peaceful night. Occasionally, a bell from a passing ship would sound in the distance, but for the most part, Alex was left alone with her thoughts. Lost in idle reflection, she approached Fiona's house and got ready to go up to the door. But as she got near the steps, a dark figure in a black cloak rushed past, and bumped into her, sending her toppling to the ground.

Hitting the walkway hard, Alex protected herself the best she could by placing her hands in front of her. Turning on her side she attempted to look at the figure who knocked her down, but only caught a glimpse of the cloak vanishing into the night. Her hands and hip ached from where she landed on the hard cobblestone and the snow stung at the fresh scrapes on her bare skin. Cursing the careless stranger, Alex stood up to her feet and dusted the snow off her dress before she caught sight of something alarming.

A few feet away, right where Fiona lived, a warm light streamed out onto the street from the door which was left wide open. Wondering why her friend would have her door ajar during an early bout of winter, Alex shuffled forward, wondering if perhaps Fiona was currently entertaining a client. Peering through the doorway she saw no movement inside and began to worry. Suddenly, dark thoughts crossed her mind and Alex thought that perhaps the figure she saw was there to ransack the place, or maybe it was a Militibus vandal who was there to leave his mark. Creeping up the stone stairs one step at a time, Alex pushed through the door and was greeted with a horrifying sight which only seemed to affirm her fears.

The inside of the house sat eerily silent. Only the gramophone in the parlor croaked out a melancholy song she knew all too well, it was a well know love song from centuries ago that Jay occasionally sang to her. Directly in front of her, a red strip of lace fabric was sprawled on the stairs, floating down to the first floor like a river. To the side of the stairwell lay a broke hurricane lamp, and the table it was on lay splintered against the ground with its legs buckled beneath it.

Swallowing hard, Alex felt the hairs on the back of her neck stand up and she turned her head to investigate the next room, wondering what could have transpired at the house. In the living room she could see more furniture skewed out all over the place. The tiffany floor lamp lay on the floor, spilling its colored glass into the parlor. Further in, Fiona's favorite tufted blue chair lay on its side, and Alex spotted drops of crimson on the velvet fabric. Stepping over fragments of the powder blue lamp by her feet, she inched into the next room and her heart instantly sank to the ground.

On the other side of the crackling fireplace, in a burgundy pool, lay Fiona, illuminated only by the amber glow of the flames. She was barely moving as she held on to her abdomen, trying to keep her insides from spilling out further onto the floor. Her once green smock was torn and stained red as the ambers from the fireplace cast haunting shadows by her side. Turning her head to the doorway, Fiona spotted Alex and mouthed something to the girl, but the words failed to escape her. Regaining her composure, Alex rushed to her friend's side and scooped her into her arms.

"Oh, Fiona. Who did this to you?"

Alex looked over the intestines pouring out from her friend as if she was a broken bowl of spaghetti. For once, she did not know what to do, or if there was even anything she could do. With trembling hands, she moved Fiona's hand aside and watched more blood come rushing out from the open cavity. Gathering the tangled mess of entrail in her hand, Alex attempted to stuff them back inside the abdomen and attempted to heal the wounds, but the fleshy tubes just slipped between her fingers.

"Hang in there, please. I'll heal you... just... stay with me a bit longer."

"No..." Fiona coughed up her words, covering Alex's white dress in splotches of red as she weakly took hold of the young woman's hand, "... it's too late for me. I'm so... sorry..."

"Fiona, no" tears welled up in Alex's eyes and Fiona reached a bloody hand to wipe them away and brush the hair out of her face, "please, don't say that."

"I'm... sorry... promise me... take care of... them."

"Who? Who do you want me to take care of?"

"All... of... them..." Fiona gasped for breath. She felt her body growing cold, and she knew her time had come, but she still needed to get a few more words out to her friend. "They... need... you... they... don't know... what's coming."

Inhaling one last time, Fiona closed her eyes and let out her last breath. Surrendering to the melodic cries of the wolf outside, she floated away from her body and it grew limp in Alexandra's arms. Not wishing to believe her friend was gone, Alex, with shaking hands kept attempting to put Fiona's bowls back in before finally giving up.

Leaning her head down on Fiona's chest, she sobbed as she cradled her friend's lifeless body while the blood continued to pool in her lap. After a few moments of silence, Alex surrendered to the inevitable as she felt part of herself die with her friend. Tilting her head back she let out a loud scream which echoed through the deserted halls of the house and out into the empty street.

Sitting in the dim living room, she knew she could not stay there. The house was not safe, and she needed to get to someone to report the crime which transpired. Staggering to her feet, Alex stumbled through the ramshackle house until she was standing outside on the bottom landing of the stone steps. Lifting her shaking hands to her face, she saw they were covered in Fiona's blood and she could not take it any longer. Overcome by a dizzying feeling, she bent over, clutching her chest, and allowed the contents of her stomach to leave her before she aimlessly staggered down the streets away from the crime scene.

Alex continued to wobble and sway down snow-covered path until the frost-etched windows of the tavern caught her eye. She desperately wished to run inside the warm interior and forget about everything that happened, but she could barely walk since she had forgotten her cloak at Fiona's house. With nothing to keep her warm, her body felt weak and frozen. Barely able to move, let alone stand, she leaned her shoulder into the wood door and forced it open as she lumbered inside. Once she was safely in the warm tavern, Alex glanced about the room in tears before allowing herself to collapse to the floor as Richard shot up from his seat at a nearby table to catch her.

"Alex." Richard screamed as he lifted her pale, frozen face up to look at him.

Across from them, Jay leaped over the bar counter and rushed to push Richard aside. Scooping her up into his arms, he noticed how frigid her body felt and was amazed she made it this long instead of falling over in the streets halfway to the house. Holding her shaking body close to his, he looked over her blood-stained dress and his chest tightened. Jay did not know what happened, but her assumed the worst as he barked at Richard to get her a blanket. Rushing into the house the young man returned moments later with a cream Sherpa throw and draped it over Alexandra's shoulders.

"Alex." Jay continued to rock her body, "what happened? Are you hurt? Is... is the baby all right?"

"Oh... Jay..." Alex pressed her head against his chest and began to sob uncontrollably. "The blood... it's not... it's not mine."

"Whose is it Alex?" Richard rubbed her back. "Talk to us. Tell us what happened."

"They... they got her... they got Fiona."

"What? Fi!"

Next to Alex a glass shattered on the floor as Lawrence jumped up off the chair and rushed for the door, slamming it against the wall as he ran.

"Shit." Muttered Richard. "That wanker is going to get himself killed."

"Then go after him." Jay barked. "Take the doctor and George with you for back up. Seems to me like there is a crime which needs to be investigated and you wouldn't want that moron to be your only ally if they come back for more blood."

"What about Alex?"

"Don't worry 'bout her Sug, I'll help Jay and Rupert take care of her." Gladys kneeled beside the girl she had come to think of as a daughter and assessed her paling appearance. Taking Alex's wrist in her hand, she felt the pulse getting weaker and frowned. "You go with Jackson and see what happened at the Row and stop that boy from doing something stupid. If he gets himself into trouble, well... I doubt our girl can handle losing another friend."

Nodding, Richard gathered the men and went after Lawrence. Watching him run out the door with the doctor and George in tow, Jay scooped Alex up into his arms and carried her upstairs. Gladys followed behind and went to fill up the tub with warm water, instructing Jay to put her in and leave them be. Washing the girl clean of blood as the water warmed up her shivering body, the midwife rubbed her back, trying to calm her down. As soon as Alex was well enough to stand and dry off, Gladys helped her get dressed in her nightgown and held her in bed, stroking her hair as she sobbed.

Downstairs, Jay and Rupert were boarding up the house to keep the Militibus away, all the while wondering what they should do if they come. Jay had always been worried something like this would happen, but he did not predict Fiona would be the first one to fall victim to their hate. Knowing this was only the beginning, and that darker times were ahead, Rupert kept an eye on the man he'd grown to hold in high regard and hoped he could weather the storm on the horizon.

CHAPTER 32

The God of Life and the Goddess of Death

Up in the upstairs bedroom, Gladys held Alex in her arms until she was sure the girl was fast asleep. Laying the young woman down on the pillow, she looked over her with a shake of her head as the goosebumps crept up along her arm. She could not imagine the trauma Alex had gone through from finding her friend murdered, or how hard it was on such a sweet girl to watch someone she cared about die in her arms. But she was sure of one thing, her dear friend was at her breaking point and another incident could end her life. Leaving the girl to sleep, Gladys tiptoed downstairs and into the tavern where Jay and Rupert were sitting at the bar, having a drink.

"How is she?" Jay looked up from his glass.

"She's all right Sug. As all right as one can be under the circumstances. But I do worry about her and the baby. Such stress can't be good for them, and I don't think your poor wife can handle any more upset."

"Indeed. We are entering some dark times Master, and I too worry for you and Alexandra."

"We'll be all right old man. At least... I hope we will be."

"Hope is what any of us have got left hun."

Jay glanced back over at Gladys and gave her a halfhearted smile when a noise from behind caused him to leap up off his seat and summon his sword. Whirling around to the door which was swinging open, Jay unclenched his fist once he saw it was only the doctor entering the tavern. The man wore a grim expression on his face as he stepped inside and removed his hat. The wrinkles on his face appeared more prominent, and his eyes looked sullen as he got closer to the bar.

"Where are the other three?"

"Taking Lawrence back to Richard's place. I'm afraid I had to sedate the lad after her saw what remained of his sister." Jackson shook his head frowning. "I'm not sure if he will ever recover after that. And I think it be best if he never returns to that place they shared together."

"That bad?" Jay reeled back while thinking about Alex walking in on something so horrific. "What they do to her anyhow?"

"The authorities are still investigating the scene, and I won't get the body to autopsy until tomorrow morning. But from what I can tell, she knew the attacker well, and she was foolish enough to trust them. I'm not sure if this was a lover or a client, but there appeared to have been a quarrel between them starting in the bedroom and it continued down the stairs.

"At some point, the attacker pushed her over the railing, and she landed on the table, fracturing her leg. She must have tried her best to get away, but they caught up with her and tossed her into the next room, knocking over a lamp and chair in the process. The girl fought hard, even gouged them with her nails at some point, but they overpowered her. They sat on top of her, beat her until she couldn't fight back, then they cut her open and ripped out her uterus."

"Goodness me," Gladys gasped, "why would anyone do that?"

"It seems as though Fiona was hiding something from the rest of us. She was apparently in the family way, and her killer wanted the child disposed of. If I was to take a gander, I'd say it was the child's father."

"What? No. She couldn't have been. She told me she couldn't have children after the abortion she got from some butcher years prior. And I saw her regularly, I would have know if she was, I'm sure of it."

"Don't feel bad for missing it peach. No one knew, not even her brother. She hid it well with proper undergarments, and from what I can tell, for a long time as well. I found the remains of a six-month-old male fetus in the fireplace. He looked like he was still alive when he went in. The poor thing must have suffered for a few moments before the flames consumed him."

"What kind of monster would do such a thing? And to a helpless baby none the less." Gladys put a hand over her mouth as she felt herself get sick to her stomach.

"One who values blood purity over anything else. Which means, Alexandra is not safe here, Master Hartwood, and neither are you and the boy."

"I know that." Jay growled. "But I'll be dammed if I let them force my family out of our home. I'm not taking my pregnant wife and son on the run. It's just not feasible and we'll have no place to hide, anyway. No matter where we go, they'll find us and you know that."

"What shall we do then Sir?"

"I don't know yet. All I know is that we can't say a word of this to Alex. She already has enough to worry about. She can't know that someone murdered Fiona over a baby, or she'll never stop looking over her shoulder."

"I agree. The poor dumplin' has had enough stress for a lifetime. We have to keep this between us, for her sake, and her baby's."

"All right, I concur with all of this. I will try to find out more once the investigation is done, and I get the body for an autopsy. Maybe the corpse will reveal more clues that I missed on first glance. For now though, keep your heads low, and stay out of the streets unless you have to go out. None of us are safe living here anymore, at least not for the time being."

"Understood." Jay nodded his head. "I'll figure out how to deal with the Militibus. We'll find a way to stop these thugs once and for all."

"We certainly will Sir, we certainly will. Now, why don't you go upstairs to your wife, she needs your comfort now more than ever. I shall escort the Carlsons back to their house and return promptly."

Nodding, Jay bid the doctor and Gladys a farewell before he headed upstairs to where Alex was pretending to sleep. Having heard their conversation, she lay petrified in the dark as a cold serpent slithered up her leg and took hold of her heart. Even as Jay lay next to her, holding her close, she felt numb, and alone with no one there to save her. As the ice formed around her heart, and the voices in the shadows got louder, Alex allowed an uneasy sleep to take hold of her and darkness to permeate her dreams.

On the other side of town, having escorted the doctor and Gladys to their home, Rupert strolled down the street with his hands behind his back. As a god, he had nothing to fear, but as he made his way home, a glimmer of a silver gown sparking in the light of the moon caught his eye. He froze in his tracks and smiled as her intoxicating perfume of dragon's blood and Moroccan rose hit him long before her words did. Relishing in her sensual aroma he closed his eyes and remembered how much he had missed her company.

"Awfully brave of you love. You are walking these streets alone, while a murderer and an extremist group are on the loose."

Opening his eyes, Rupert spotted a stunning woman in her late twenties with glimmering, purple eyes as she walked out from the shadows. Her waist long, white hair floated behind her as she glided to him on her two silver angel wings which spanned from one end of the street to the other. It has been a long time since he had seen her, and he waited for her to come gliding to stop before him.

"You know, no other soul dares venture out alone here, especially after the events of tonight."

"Desire, darling, it's good to finally see you again after all these years."

"Like wise my love. But," she reached out and brushed the wrinkles on his face with the tips of her fingers, "why don't you shed this mortal husk of yours for the time being and allow me to see you in your full glory?"

"Very well darling. Anything for you."

With a snap of his fingers a flash of light consumed the darkness and Rupert stepped out from the blaze transformed into his true form. In his god state he appeared to be a man in his early thirties wearing a golden suit with matching leather shoes. His brown hair cascaded past his shoulders and he stretched out his long, bronze wings to ruffle their feathers. It's been far too long since he exercised his wings and he smiled as he allowed himself to lift off the ground before landing next to his wife and caressing her cheek with the back of his finger.

"I'm thrilled to finally see you my shining star, but," Rupert studied the woman before him with his glistening golden eyes, "what do I owe this pleasure to? The goddess of death rarely ventures into the kingdom of the living, and two mortal souls should be of no consequence to you."

"You still know me so well my love." Desire brushed Rupert's hair and tucked it behind his shoulders. "But you're right as always, my wolves could have easily taken care of two mortal souls, except, the Master wished to put these ones in the judgement chamber right away. Therefore, I had to come get them myself. And now, I need to retrieve a certain soul of a delightful young woman from the chasms of the veil as well."

"I see." Rupert kissed Desires hand. "No surprise there, given what Fiona did for our little girl. I'm guessing the master will rule in a manner his favorite great-granddaughter would approve of and grant them immortality on Sirius. Otherwise I doubt he would have sent you."

"He certainly will." Desire let out a laugh. "I think he even has a home all picked out for them."

"Of course he does." Rupert rolled his eyes. "So, where are they now?"

"Ludwig and Rose are escorting them though the veil as we speak, their judgement will be in the morning. Still, I'm afraid my job here is far from over."

"I know. There is one crucial soul left to collect. I spotted the string on him the moment I met him and knew he was not long for this world. But you do realize how much it will hurt our dear girl to lose another one, right?"

"I know," Desire let out a melancholy sigh, "I hate hurting our daughter like this, but it can't be helped. I just take solace in knowing that they will all be together soon enough."

"Indeed, I sure hope that's the case as I tire of being in this mortal realm."

"I have no doubt, but rest assured that this will soon be over. Now, I must speak to you of the real reason I'm seeing you. I needed to discuss the more pressing matters concerning Alexandra." Desire peered into Rupert's eyes with a grave expression on her face. "Did you know the Worm has a hold on her now?"

"Yes. I knew before I left the house. I could smell him up in her chamber and I could see one of his tentacles grabbing hold of her."

"Then you also know he staged this so he could bring her into the veil. He's trying to kill the child she carries."

"I'm aware that is why he is here. But, what can I do?"

"Promise me that when the time comes, you'll talk to her. Let her know that she has to fight him. She has to release her power if she wants to stop him and keep this baby. I need you to make sure it happens. You're the first father she's ever known, and she has always loved you, more so than Lucifer, so she'll listen to you. And, once she unleashes her darkness, I will take care of the rest from the veil."

"All right, I promise, and I'll give her a sip of ambrosia too, just in case." Rupert smiled as Desire turned to fly away. "Will I be seeing you again soon?"

"I'll be back in a few days' time my love if you wish to catch me. For now, though, you just take care of Alex for me."

"You know I will, I always do."

"I know, you've been a great father to her for all these years." Desire winked at him and few up to the sky. "I'll see you around my love."

Still smiling, Rupert watched as Desire soared towards the clouds and vanished into the distance. He knew she was going to the veil to pick up her other cargo and that tomorrow she'd have to escort them to their destination. He also knew that she would be meeting Alex again soon, and he hoped their reunion would not end in tragedy for the mortal. With nothing else for him to do, he turned back into his human form, and set off again, walking down the street to the tavern.

Stepping over a black tentacle pocking its way under the door as he approached the house, Rupert frowned and shook his head at the unwanted presence. If everything worked out the way

Master had envisioned, there was nothing for him to worry about, and he realized his concern was irrational as he pushed open the door. Shuffling inside the parlor, he knew full well the Amphiptere would never allow Alex to get hurt, but he still did not appreciate the presence of the Worm near his girl, even if the old god was no match for her.

CHAPTER 33

The Power of the Worm

A few days passed since the murder and Fiona's funeral was held three days later. Only the small group of friends attended her services, as not even the prostitutes cared to pay their respect to her. For days after, Alex had been holed up in her room, not daring to face anyone who might come visit them at the house. Stirring in her bed as she did every other morning, she noticed something was different. She felt as if a knife was digging itself into her side, and a sharp pain radiated all the way down her legs. Her body had waves of stabbing pain flowing through it and she felt unusually cold despite the wood stove putting out a great deal of heat.

Not even the sun pouring in through the window could warm up the ice forming on Alexandra's heart and she lay in bed shivering as she curled up in a ball. Thinking she heard rustling in the corner of her room, she strained her eyes to see through the splitting headache but there was nothing to be found. The room was empty except for the voice coming from the shadows, telling her to join him. Unwilling to surrender to him, Alex stumbled to her feet and tried to run away. But, as she moved, she felt weak and dizzy as pain radiated throughout her core, making it hard to walk. Clutching her stomach to still the unbearable pain, she knew she needed to get away from the voice that refused to let her be.

Staggering out the bedroom door, Alex wobbled slowly for the stairs, steadying herself on the wall. She did not notice her crisp white gown was stained bright red, nor did she see the trail of blood she was leaving behind her. Barely able to walk, all she knew was that she needed to get away from the voice for it was trying to claim her soul and that of her child. Reaching the stairs, she gripped the banister and shuffled down one step at a time towards the bottom landing, desperate to make her escape.

Just as she was about to step down the last step, Richard walked in through the front door and looked up at her as he shut the door behind him. Instantly his eyes widened, and he felt the blood drain from his face upon seeing her. Alex looked white as a sheet and the front of her gown had a large, dark crimson splotch on it. Her hands were barely gripping the banister and Richard spotted a stream of blood steadily flowing down her leg to form a small puddle beneath her feet.

"Alex!"

"Richard I—"

Alex did not get to finish her sentence as her eyes rolled into the back of her head and darkness took hold of her. Her knees buckled under her weight and she went falling to the ground in front of her. Fast on his feet, Richard dashed to grab her before she hit the floor and wrapped her limp body in his arms. Holding her close, he felt her skin, which was cold and clammy. He knew he was losing her, and in that moment, he had never felt so helpless in his entire life.

"Jay!" Richard shouted through the tears in his eyes. "Rupert! Someone! Help! I need help in here."

"What is with all the shouting?"

Jay walked through the tavern door, trying to figure out what all the noise was about. He was getting ready to chew the young man out for making such a ruckus, but upon seeing Alex laying in Richards arms, covered in blood, his scowl turned to an expression of shock. He dropped to the ground on his knees trying to scream but nothing came out.

Reaching his trembling hand to cover his mouth, he sat down and slammed his back against the wall. His eyes filled with tears as his chest tightened, making difficult to breathe. Jay suddenly felt lost and unable to move until Rupert yanked him up to his feet and gave him a firm shake.

"Master Hartwood." The butler gave him another hard shake by the shoulders. "Snap out of it. You must go and get the doctor or Glady, perhaps even both. Your wife needs you. You must go, before it's too late."

Giving Alex one final glace, Jay nodded his head and stumbled out the door in a stupor. His lungs burned, and the tears stung his face as he turned and ran as fast as he could for the doctor's place. Barely able to remember where he was going, he pushed the citizens aside as he picked up his pace, plowing through crowds in the sidewalks. He heard them whispering as he staggered his way past them, but he did not care what they thought of him, or what they said, his only concern was saving Alex, if that was even possible.

Back at the house, Rupert watched Jay leave and kneeled beside Richard to look over at Alex. Knowing what had transpired, he scooped her limp body into his arms and held her close as he stood up. She hung like a lifeless rag doll against his chest and he could feel her energy growing weaker with her every breath. He needed to get her upstairs, but he worried about the child still playing outside, blissfully unaware of what was happening. Stealing a look back at Richard who was shaking by the stairs still covered in blood, he took a deep breath and cleared his throat.

"Master Richard, can I ask a favor of you?"

"Yes. Anything."

"Master Andrew is out back playing. I don't think he needs to see this mess, or his mother like this. Could you kindly take him to your place for now and keep him entertained while we take care of the Missus?"

"Yes, of course. But, is Alex going to be all right? I'm not sure I can break such bad news to a child."

"There won't be a need for it. She's a tough girl. She will pull through. Now, go clean yourself up and get the lad out of here before he comes in and sees all this blood."

"Yes. All right. Just let me know when I should bring him back."

"Of course, Master Richard."

Bobbing his head, Richard left the parlor and vanished into the kitchen to wash the blood off his clothe. Satisfied they would be alone for a bit, Rupert pressed Alex closer and headed upstairs two steps at a time. The god was hoping he'd be able to give the girl some more ambrosia before the Worm overcame her, but it appears that he was too late. It was up to his daughter now to stop the ancient beast, and he only hoped she could wake up enough of her powers before she was sucked into the veil for good.

Laying the girl down on the covers of her bed, Rupert held her hand to his lips as Cosmo fluttered about the room squealing and grunting. Her pale skin had grown more pallid in the time it took him to get upstairs and it felt almost like ice in his hand. He could see the tentacle under her skirt, wiggling about, while another one wrapped itself firmly around her throat. Remembering what Desire told him, Rupert leaned over to whisper into Alexandra's ear.

"Don't let him get you my dear. You are far stronger than him, you always were. You must fight him if you don't want him to claim your child. You have to wake up." Rupert pleaded. "Remember what Jay means to you daughter, what Andy means to you. You can't leave them here like this, you need to fight."

"Oink... oink?"

"I wish I knew my friend, but I cannot say for sure. I'm afraid she must face him alone now. All we can do is wait and hope for the best."

"Wee..."

Pressing his ears to his head, Cosmo flowed down and settled by Alexandra's head and rooted her cheek with his nose. He licked her clammy skin, and hoped to remind her of who she was, but his friend didn't respond. Refusing to leave his companion's side, the pigrie laid loyally by her side, even as Gladys came in wearing a solemn expression on her face. Leaving the three of them be,

Rupert walked out of the room and headed downstairs with his head hung low. There was nothing more that he could do for her, so instead, he shifted his focus to the man downstairs. He was not sure what state he would find the mortal in, but he knew the man would certainly need his guidance now more than ever.

Up in her room, suspended between life and death, Alex felt as if she was floating and drowning in a sea of black ink. She felt something take hold of her body in the murky water and pull her down, deeper into the abyss. The further she fell, the less pain she felt, and eventually she surrendered to the gravitation pull of the veil and the solace it offered. Closing her eyes, she allowed her body to grow limp and for the tentacles to pull her into their chasm, freeing her from her agony.

CHAPTER 34

A Glimpse of the Veil

Lost in a dense white fog, Alex strained to open her eyes. When she did manage to force them open, she found herself hovering above a field of gray with her limbs being stretched out by dark tentacles. Their suckers suckled on her flesh as a long, black appendage wound its way up her leg, making its way inside her. She could feel it penetrating her, trying to scrape her insides clean and she attempted to pull away from it as she felt pain radiating through her core again.

"No." She struggled against the tentacles holding her hands and feet. "Let go of me."

"Stay still..." a harsh, disembodied voice whispered from the darkness, "this won't take long."

"Stop." Alex thrashed in her assailant's grasp. "Leave my baby alone."

"This won't hurt much longer, I promise. After I get done here, you shall be free once more."

Alex felt a pinch, followed by a sharp pain on the inside that radiated throughout her body, causing her fingers and toes to tingle. She knew what was coming next, what this creature wanted, and she struggled to break free. But no matter how much she twisted her arms or yanked her legs, the tentacles refused to let her go, holding her down harder. She felt a small trickle of liquid running down her leg, and she grew angry at what it meant. No matter what, she was not going to give this thing what it wanted, she'd never allow it to steal the child she shared with Jay, not after how long she had wanted it.

"I said," Alex closed her eyes and tensed up her body, "leave me be."

Unclenching her fists, she allowed a surge of energy to rip through her body, ripping her attacker's limbs clean off. A screech erupted through the bleak space and Alex fell to the ground, landing on her hands and knees. Looking down on her trembling hands, panting, she noticed that her nails were longer, sharper, and that she glowed a brilliant shade of blue. Seeing this change caused her breathing to get heavier and her eyes to widen as her heart thumped rapidly in her chest.

"Calm down dear." Spoke a familiar soft voice. "You need to breathe now."

Turning around to see who was speaking to her, Alex was astonished to find a pale woman with white wavy hair and glowing violet eyes looking down on her. The woman smiled and glided over to Alex on silver wings with her silver gown floating behind her. Landing by her side, the familiar woman kneeled to help the girl up off the ground, and her touch made Alexandra feel better.

"Who are you?"

"Someone you once knew very well, but that is of no consequence now. Right now, you need to calm down and regain control. Close your eyes and take a few deep breaths with me."

"But what's wrong with me?"

"Nothing child, it's just your darkness coming to light."

"But... I don't want it to come to light. It's scaring me."

"You need not fear your darkness, it's part of who you are. Embrace it, kindle it, and use it to fight the evil surrounding you, only then will you be free."

"But... how... how am I to do that?"

"You will learn soon enough. But right now you need to return to your world, so close your eyes, and breathe."

With the woman holding on to her hands, Alex closed her eyes and inhaled until her lungs could expand no more. Letting the air slowly out, she felt the flames quelling on the inside. A few more deep breaths, and she was able to open her eyes and see that she was back to being completely normal. Smiling softly, the woman nodded her head and let go of her hands, brushing a stray strand of chestnut hair behind her ear.

"There. Good as new."

"What about my baby? Is my baby all right?"

"Your child is fine dear. Stubborn, wild, and strong like her mother. Even without the gift of sight I can see her giving her father some trouble later on, especially if she's anything like you."

Desire smiled at the girl she once raised and recalled how her relationship with the mortal started. "Now let's get you out of here sweetheart, before it's too late."

"Where exactly is here?"

"Somewhere you once called home. Now, you don't belong here anymore, so come on, before the door closes."

"I... I don't understand. Too late for what? What door? Where are we going?"

"You are going to go in through the fog before the passageway connecting our world closes and causes you to be stuck here forever. Now off you go." Desire nudged Alex into the thick cloud. "Once you're in the heart of the mist, you'll have to find a way out on your own."

"How am I supposed to do that?"

"Listen to your heart and listen to him calling out for you. You will find a way. Believe me, you will. Now in you go."

Without giving Alex another chance to reply, Desire shoved her through the fog just as the hole closed, leaving Alex trapped between worlds. Lost in the gloom, surrounded by a shroud of mist, she stumbled around, looking for where to go. But no matter where she turned, emptiness and fog followed as far as the eye could see. Feeling hopeless, she was about to give up hope when she heard Jay's voice calling her name, pleading for her to wake up.

She could not make out much of anything else he was saying, but his voice pulled her along, guiding her through the dense vapor. Walking aimlessly towards him, she felt something tug on her left ring finger and stopped. Glancing down at her hand, she spotted a red thread attached to her finger, leading the way through the darkness. Grabbing hold of the string, Alex ran in its general direction, pulling herself along until a bright light in the distance assaulted her eyes. Blinded by a flash of white, she covered her face and leaped through the opening, waking up in Jay's waiting arms.

CHAPTER 35

Waking from the Fog

As Alex was fighting the Worm in the veil, back in the world of the living, Gladys stood beside the bed of the girl she came to tend to and she didn't think there was anything she would be able to do for her. Taking Alexandra's wrist into her hand, she felt a weak pulse and noted the young woman's pale appearance and the blood-soaked bed she lay on. Closing her eyes, the midwife waited for the throbbing of the heart to fade out under her finger, and she knew the girl was gone.

Collapsing beside the bed, she buried her face in her hands and sobbed. She did not know how she would break the news to Jay, the young man would be devastated to learn he just lost his wife and child, but there was nothing she could do to bring either of them back to life. Feeling hopeless, Gladys was about to go down stair to give the barkeep the bad news when she thought she heard a faint sound of a breath escaping Alexandra's lips.

Shooting up to her feet and wiping the tears off her face, Gladys looked at the body in disbelief, thinking it was just her hope getting the best of her. But her eyes seemed to deceive her too, for she thought she saw the girl's chest rise and fall very slowly. Grabbing the limp wrist in her hand again, she felt the faint semblance of a pulse returning and it kept getting stronger with every beat.

Not believing her luck, Gladys dashed for her medicine bag and pulled out a twisted glass tube to see if by some miracle the baby had survived as well. Placing the tube over Alex's womb, she watched in disappointment until a flicker of energy caused the tube to pulsate before it began to glow a steady green. Despite all the blood on the stairs, and all over the bed, both Alex and her child were alive, and they were recovering on their own. Unable to contain her shock, Gladys made her way for the stair to let Jay know his family would be all right.

Leaving Gladys to tend to Alex, Rupert walked down the stairs, being careful to step over the shadowy tentacles littering the house. He knew he would find the mortal in a terrible shape when he got downstairs, but he was not prepared for the sight that greeted him. In the living room, he spotted Jay sitting in a chair with his head hung low between his knees as the doctor rubbed his back to comfort him.

"This is all my fault." Jay mumbled as he pulled at his hair. "She's going to die because of me."

"Don't say that son. None of this is your fault. How can you even think that?"

"Really doc?" Jay lifted his face to regard his old friend with bloodshot eyes. "First, Florence commits suicide to spare herself from having Andy and living with me, and now Alex is bleeding to death because I got her pregnant. I should have known better, done things to prevent it, but I was just being selfish."

"Wanting a child with the woman you love isn't selfish son, it's only natural."

"That maybe so, but I'm cursed, and I know it. That's the only explanation I got for why my life keeps spiraling out of control no matter what I do to fix it."

"You are not cursed my boy, even if you can't see that now. You are just given more obstacles to overcome by the gods because they know you can handle them,"

"Whatever you say, doc. Guess I'm just doomed to end up alone then. Probably better that way anyhow."

Hanging his head between his legs again, Jay hid his face from his friend, not wishing to let him see him at his weakest. Feeling unusually bad for the mortal, Rupert walked up to his side and placed a reassuring hand on the man's shoulder. He knew how much Jay loved Alex since way back when, but he never expected him to get this attached to the girl, and seeing him so broken down at the prospect of losing her again tugged at the god's heartstrings.

"I'm sure Alexandra will pull through Master Hartwood. Tough as nails that girl is. And I know she'd never allow you to end up alone. Nor would she abandon Master Andrew."

As Jay looked up at Rupert with tear-filled eyes, the old man felt an electrifying pulse of energy go through the house. The hairs on his arms stood up as the shadows vanished almost instantly, and he could finally breathe easy with all the oppressive energy gone. Impressive, thought Rupert, the girl was not even fully awake, and yet she sent the Worm packing back into his domain. If she was this powerful now, the dark master wouldn't stand a chance against her when the time to confront him finally came.

Still beaming with pride at his daughter's abilities, Rupert looked up in time to see Gladys shuffle into the room with a horrified look on her face. Her eyes were wide, and her face was streaked with tears as she held her hands close to her chest and fiddled with her fingers. Following Rupert's gaze, Jay spotted her too, and instantly went pale.

"No." Jay placed a trembling hand over his mouth. "Don't tell me. Is she..." Jay did not dare to finish the sentence for he was not ready to lose her.

"She's all right Hun, and she seems to be recovering rapidly."

"And what about the baby? Is my baby okay?"

"I don't know how to say this..."

"Oh no," Jay hung his head down again, "no. I knew it."

"No, your baby is fine Sug." Gladys ran up to kneel beside Jay, wrapping his hand up in hers and rubbing his skin. "But the thing is Hun, neither one of them should be. All this blood. Why, it's more than a body can hold. And I even watched her die, I felt her heart stop beating. Don't get me wrong sugar, I'm thrilled both Alex and the baby are fine, but it's simply not possible."

"It's a miracle then." Jackson shrugged and leaned back in his chair.

"I don't believe in miracles." Jay lifted his head and looked aimlessly at the stairs.

"Then perhaps Master, it was the gods who intervened and saved your family."

"Yeah right. If the gods are real, why would they waste time on us mortals?"

"Master Jay, the gods you so vehemently forsake are closer to you than you think. They are watching over you because you, and your family are part of their master plan." Rupert put his hands behind his back and smirked. "But instead of arguing with me, why not go upstairs and spend time with your wife while I clean up this mess? Once all the blood is mopped up, I'll tell Master Richard to bring your son back and get dinner going."

Nodding, Jay walked Gladys and Jackson out the door and headed upstairs while Rupert set about to clean the blood from the wood floors and stairs. It was true that this amount of blood was more than a mortal body could hold, but Alex was a god, and gods regenerated at a faster rate. Jay, however, was still unaware of this fact, and as he opened the door to their room, his heart sank to his stomach.

Sprawled out on a blood-soaked bed lay Alex with her eyes still closed. Her skin was deathly pale, but she had a serene look on her face. She looked almost like his mother did when she passed, and Jay nervously crawled into bed beside her. Wrapping her in his arms he felt her pulse and held her tighter, fearing that she could slip away from him at any moment. Continuing to count the beats of her heart, he buried his face in her hair and whispered in her ear.

"You scared the shit out of me darling." Jay kissed her temple as he gently stroked her hair. "I thought I had lost you and our baby. Do you know what that did to me, Alex? It broke my heart, that's what. What would I even do without you? I'm nothing if you are not with me. So, could you please stop making me worry and just wake up... please?"

"Jay?" After a moment Alex fluttered open her eyes and wrapped her arms around his neck smiling.

"I'm sorry." Jay brought her close and kissed her lips. "I'm so sorry."

"For what?"

"Everything."

"Don't be silly." Alex ran her fingers through Jay's dirty blonde hair. "You have nothing to be sorry for."

"Of course I do. I almost lost you."

"Not even close." Alex smirked. "I told you before, I won't let you off this easy."

"But I was told that you actually died."

"Even if I did, I found my way back to you, didn't I?"

"Yeah, but I'm still not sure how."

"Can't you see. No matter where my soul wonders, no matter the distance between us, I will always find my way back to you, because the only place I feel at home is with you."

"I don't deserve you. You know that, right?" Jay hugged her tight as he shuddered at the thought of her being dead.

"No, it is I who doesn't deserve you."

"Whatever you say crazy woman. Now, would you like to go clean up? I can draw you a hot bath."

"Only if you come in with me."

"Sweetie. I'll go to the void with you if you asked."

Finally smiling, Jay lifted Alex off the bed and carried her into the bathroom. Drawing up a warm bath, he crawled in the tub with her, and hold her close to his body as she washed away the blood. With the water removing the stains from earlier, she appeared to regain her color, and with Rupert changing the sheets, Jay was able to escort her into a warm bed where she was ordered to rest by the doctor.

Curing up by her side after dinner, Jay watched her sleeping. As her chest rose and fell rhythmically, he pondered if she was truly recovered, and if there was any truth in what she said to him. Would she always find her way back to him no matter what, or would the darkness claim her like the voice in his head liked to proclaim? He was still filled with doubt over their future, but as he watched her eyelids twitch and her skin glow a pale blue, he knew the old man was right, the gods did smile upon them, at least for now.

CHAPTER 36

Visitors

Dawn started to break by the time Jay finally gave up on trying to get some sleep and crawled out of bed. He spent all night watching over Alex, fearful that she would slip away if he was to close his eyes. But, much to his relief, nothing happened, and aside the blood-stained mattress, there was no evidence anything was wrong.

Sitting on the edge of the bed, watching her sleep, he noticed the color had returned to her cheeks, and she looked serene snuggled up in bed. Covering her up with the cream comforter, Jay placed a soft kiss on her forehead before heading down the stairs where Cosmo greeted him with playful bark. Giving the pigrie a pat, he slumped over in the wingback chair and began to dose off when a pounding on the front door startled him to his feet.

"Rhu?!"

"Good question buddy," Jay frowned as he glances at the ornate wood clock sitting on the mantel of the roaring fireplace, "it's far too early for anyone to be awake."

At first, Jay inched towards the window. Pulling the curtain to one side he hoped to steal a peek at their visitor, but the pounding on the door got harder and more determined. The louder the thumps echoed through the hall the more Jay worried that it would wake up Alex. Gladys instructed him to keep her in bed for as long as he could, and if he did not answer the door, he knew she would come down to investigate. Continuing to frown, he stormed to the door and flung it open only to find Caleb Cox standing on his doorstep. The man wore his annoyingly friendly smile and Jay could not help but grumble at having to deal with him so early in the morning, especially after the ordeal he had last night.

"What can I do you for mayor?" Jay snapped at the man standing before him. "A tad early to be pounding on people's doors, don't you think?"

"I do apologize for my early intrusion Mr. Hartwood." Cox straightened out the cream-colored cravat around his neck and smiled. "I simply dropped by here to check on you and Mrs. Hartwood. Rumor has it that the poor dear was not feeling well yesterday. I wanted to make sure she was all right, and that it was nothing serious."

"She's fine mayor, thanks for asking." Jay forced himself to smile as he tightened his grip around the doorframe. "She just fainted after having to deal with all the trauma of finding her friend murdered and watching her die in her arms. I'm sure you can understand how traumatic it was for her."

"Yes, I can understand that my friend, I too have lost people I cared about. It is rather unfortunate indeed how poor Mrs. Hartwood had to walk in on such a ghastly scene, it makes my stomach churn just thinking about what your poor wife went though." Cox placed his ivory walking cane on the ground and leaned on the shiny blue top with a deep sigh. "I still can't believe what happened to our dear Fiona. How can one even begin to comprehend the loss of a life as young as hers? Such shame."

Picking up his cane, Cox took a step forward and tried to push his way inside the parlor where he could assess what had transpired inside the house. He was still unsatisfied with what the barkeep was telling him, and the rumors did say there was a lot of blood involved in the incident. Unwilling to entertain the man and his need to intrude on his life, Jay placed his other hand on the door frame and blocked the mayor with his large frame. Gritting his teeth, Caleb smoothed out the vest of his jacked and glared at him with his nostril flaring.

"Tell me friend, are you feeling safe here at the tavern, with everything going on that is? I mean, if for any reason you feel even the least bit threatened, you and your family are welcome to stay at my estate for as long as you like."

"Thank you for such a kind offer mayor, but we're fine right where we are. Plus, I wouldn't want to impose by bringing my entire family to your peaceful place. Children can be quite a handful you know."

"It wouldn't be an imposition at all my dear man. On the contrary, and I'd sleep better at night knowing none of my other constituents will be attacked in their homes. Why, I have come to think of you and Mrs. Hartwood as family. I would be delighted to see you safe behind the gates of my estate, protected by my guards until this whole Militibus business is sorted out."

"Once again mayor, thank you, but we can take care of ourselves. Plus, I don't need guards to keep my family safe, I can take on the extremists on my own. Now, if you excuse me Sir, it's far too early to be up and the rest of the house is still asleep. I would hate to wake them before the rooster crows with all this chatter, wouldn't you?"

"Of course, I completely understand. I once again apologize for my rudeness of waking you up so early in the morning. You see, I was just in the area for my morning stroll and I thought I would drop by to make sure everyone was all right after the horrific rumors I heard. And, if you do change your mind about staying holed up in this cursed place, my doors are always open to you and your family. I would be happy to have all of you."

"Whatever you say Cox, I will keep your generous offer in mind." Jay snorted. "You have a good day now and don't worry too much about us."

Without giving Cox a chance to reply, Jay shut the door in the mayor's face with a deep sigh. Standing in the hall with his back pressed against the door, he unclenched his fists as he gritted his teeth at having to deal with him. Jay did not like the mayor one bit, and the more the man tried to insert his way into Jay's life, the more he questioned his intentions. Taking a deep breath, he attempted to put the strange visit behind him and went back to the living room where Cosmo was waiting for him by the warm fire.

"Roink. Oink."

"Yeah. I don't like him much either." Jay flopped into his chair and rubbed his forehead with his fingers. "I don't know what it is either. I think it's the air of arrogance around him that he wears like a fine cologne."

"Hoink, hoink, hoink."

"You're right. It can also be the way he always finds himself in my neck of the woods every chance he gets. He seems to be here constantly, checking up on me and taking every chance he gets to ogle my wife."

"Groink, roink."

"Don't worry little buddy, I would not let him get anywhere near Alex." Jay leaned his head back and closed his eyes. "And I will certainly keep a close eye on him since I am still not convinced he is as good a man as everyone claims."

Cosmo nodded in agreement and fluttered down to sit on the windowsill. Through the glass, he watched Cox stare at their door before scowling and walking off. Perhaps Jay was right thought the pigrie, maybe it was the man's arrogance he did not like, or perhaps it was the way he looked at Alex as if she was a piece of meat to be fought over. But whatever it was, he couldn't help feeling there had to be more to it.

The way the man smelled had put off Cosmo right away, but now he noticed a dark shroud surrounding him, and he did not like its presence one bit. The tiny brown pig was about to go relay his concerns to Jay, but he found the man passed out in the chair, snoring. Knowing his old friend had a rough night, Cosmo decided to let him sleep, and instead of waking him, he settled down in the safety of the barkeeps lap and dozed off himself.

When Jay finally came to a few hours later, he found George sitting in the yellow chair across from him, smiling as he drank a cup of mint tea. The tailor had come by only a few minutes ago to chat with Jay, and Rupert had let him in, informing him that the master of the house had been asleep after staying up with Alex all night. George had already figured that Jay had a rough night with everything that happen at the house the day before, and so, he decided it was best to accept the butler's offer of tea and wait for the man to wake up as the matter he needed to discuss with him was of the utmost urgency.

"Good afternoon Jay." George sipped his tea from a delicate, black porcelain cup as he studied the weary look on his friend's face. "Did you have a pleasant nap?"

"Not really. This chair is uncomfortable and now my neck hurts." Jay rubbed his eyes and looked over at the man across from him more closely. "Did you come by to bring something for Alex, or did you drop in to check up on her too?"

"Neither, unfortunately. Though I am glad the Missus is doing well after what happened to her yesterday." George crossed his legs, set his cup down on the table between them, and leaned over closer to the barkeep. "I'm afraid I have come to speak to you on a matter of grave concern."

"What's this about George?" Alexandra's voice came from the doorway causing both men to jump to their feet. "What matter of grave concern?"

"Alex." Jay rushed to her side noticing how pale she still looked and guided her to sit on the sofa. "What are you doing up? Gladys and the doctor told you to stay off your feet for a while. You should still be in bed, resting."

"I'm fine Jay." Alex placed her icy hand on his cheek and smiled. "Stop worrying so much."

"I think your husband is right Miss. Alex." George walked over and placed his hand on her warm forehead. "You don't look to well at all my dear, and you feel a tad warm. Maybe we should get you back up to bed where you can rest and recover from yesterday."

"No way. I've been in bed all day, and I still want to know what this matter of grave concern is."

"I really don't wish to worry you my dear Mrs. Hartwood. After what you went through last night, it wouldn't be wise to stress you out further. I think it be best if Jay and I discussed this on our own. He can give you the rundown of everything when you are feeling better."

"Don't bother man." Jay sighed. "My wife is as stubborn as they come. She's not going to budge knowing there is something important to be learned. You might as well say what you need to say, it's not like she won't find out eventually, anyway."

"All right. Well then," George sat back down in his chair and glanced over at Alex who still looked as pale as a ghost. "I think whoever is behind the Militibus, the rumors about the both of you, and Fiona's murder is high up in the social circle. I suspect this person may even be involved in our government."

"What makes you think that?" Alex gasped and Jay placed a reassuring hand on her shoulder, giving it a tight squeeze.

"Well ma'am, from what I gather from Lawrence, and some other prostitutes in town, Miss. Fiona was supposedly seeing a gentleman of some importance in this area of town. She refused to tell anyone who the man was, or what he did for a living, but she did say that their life of poverty would soon be over. She claimed this man was going to marry her and take care of them."

"And you think he was the one to kill her, huh?" Jay scuffed the floor with his foot as he looked at George with a sullen look. "Makes sense, I guess. If he is the Militibus leader, he wouldn't want a half-blooded child to carry his name, nor would he want to be associated with a working girl. I'm guessing he was using her for something, and the pregnancy was an unfortunate setback he needed to deal with. I bet he was the one that hired the thug who assaulted her outside our tavern, and when that plan failed, he murdered her himself to keep her quiet."

"Yes, I'm willing to bet Fiona pushed too hard for him to come out about their relationship and the child. Or perhaps she said something about this Militibus business to tip him off. But whatever it was that was said up in that bedroom caused this man to take matters into his own hands."

"Do you have any idea as to who this man could be?"

"Unfortunately, no. At least not yet my friend. Though I assure you it's not for my lack of trying. This character seems to be exceptionally good at covering his tracks and staying hidden. But fear not Jay, I will find out who he is. I have my sources. I will learn his identity and then we will make him pay for all the trouble he's caused. That's why I came here. I was hoping either of you could shed some light on the subject as you were the closest friends she had."

"Actually..." Alex paused for a moment remembering all the times she spent with Fiona, "I know she was close to Caleb Cox, and he always seemed rather fond of her and Lawrence. I'm not sure Caleb knows much about her personal life, but if anyone can help you figure out who her paramour was, it would probably be him. After all, out of all of us, he is the most familiar with that social circle. Even if he doesn't know who this person is, I'm sure he has at least heard some rumors which would be of help."

"That is a valid assumption my dear Mrs. Hartwood. I have completely forgotten that our beloved mayor was close to the girl and her brother. Surely, he will know something which will be of help. I shall go snoop around some more and see what I can find out from him. I will be sure to contact the both of you as soon as I know something."

"Be sure to it that you do." Jay nodded his head at George and cracked his knuckles. "I sure look forward to getting my hands on this bastard's throat and strangling the life out of him for the heartache he has caused my wife."

"I know you do my friend. Believe me, I know. And I certainly don't blame you. We will both deal with this Militibus threat once and for all so we can have our peaceful town back and not have to worry about the west taking over."

"You really think we can stop them George?"

"Absolutely my dear. We have you and Jay on our side. We can do anything."

Smiling at Alex, George finished his tea, and sat the cup back down on the table as got up to leave. Bidding the couple a farewell, he left and headed for the town hall to have a talk with the mayor, leaving Alex to ponder what he said. Once again, an inkling of dread gnawed away at her and she felt her stomach drop to her feet, making her sick in the process. Swallowing the bit of bile that came up, she looked at Jay with tear-filled eyes as her lip started to quiver.

"Do you think we can stop them?"

"Of course, sweetheart, without a doubt. I told you, I wouldn't let anything happen to you or our baby. I promise you, the Militibus will not be a threat to us much longer, and as soon as they are gone the townsfolk will stop treating you and Andy like dirt."

Kneeling down beside her, Jay wrapped her trembling hand in his and placed it against his lips, calming her with his touch. Alex wanted to believe him, she wanted to think this horrible ordeal would soon be over, but she still felt dread welling up inside her. The shadows which assaulted her and tried to kill her child still lingered, she could feel their oppressive presence even now, and she knew something far darker was behind all this. She wondered if the two of them would ever be able to fight something so ancient and clearly not of their world, but she also felt it was best to keep quiet. At least this way, she wouldn't have to worry about anyone else getting hurt, and that was the only way she knew she could protect Jay.

CHAPTER 37

The Threat

Intensifies

After a few days of rest, Alex was feeling like her old self again and the incident with the Worm was put far behind her. The doctor had checked her over thoroughly and given her the go ahead to get out of bed so long as she took it easy. Not wishing to stay cooped up any longer, Alex was quick to start helping Rupert around the house and assisting Jay at the bar as usual.

Sweeping up the floor, while Jay put the bottles away in the cellar like they did every evening, she was drawn away into the house by an urgent pounding on the front door. Wondering who it could be, she dropped the broom and rushed to open the door before anyone else could get to it. Spotting Richard bent over on their doorstep, out of breath and panting, caused Alex to swallow hard as goosebumps crept along her skin.

"Richard... what's wrong?"

"Alex," he heaved out as he stood up and leaned on the doorframe, "I'm glad you're here. Where is Jay?"

"Right here. What do you need? Did something happen?"

"George called." Richard continued to wheeze as he glanced between his two friends. "We must get to him fast. He said he was in danger. He knows who the leader of the Militibus is and he wants us there to confront him."

"What?" Alexandra's eyes widened. "No, that's so foolish of him. He's going to get himself killed."

"What's wrong mama?" Alex turned to see Andy standing at the bottom of the stairs glancing up at her with his soft blue eyes. "Is everything okay with Uncle Richard?"

"Yes love. Everything is fine. Why don't you go be with Rupert while daddy and I go talk to another friend of ours? He just needs help, that's all."

"Okay, whatever you say mom."

Shrugging, Andy hopped into the kitchen without questioning her further. Knowing the boy would be safe with Rupert, Alex turned around and without thinking, she pushed past Richard, knocking him to the ground as she ran out the door heading for George's house as fast as she could. A sickening feeling lingered in the pit of her stomach, she knew what she would find, but she hoped she wrong. She prayed that she could get there in time to save him. Her hope, however, was shattered by a blood-curdling scream of a woman coming from George's house, and Alex picked up her pace until a horrifying sight greeted her eyes.

In front of George's white house stood an erected Militibus symbol with something hanging off it. Slowly getting closer to it, Alex could see it was George, strapped into the wheel by his hands and feet. He was slumped over with a burgundy puddle forming below him, and she knew there was nothing she could do for him. Stumbling closer to observe her friend's body she felt like she was reliving a bad dream. His white suit was stained in a sheet of red, as blood dripped steadily from his slit throat. She reached out to touch him, but as she felt his icy skin, her worst fears were reaffirmed, she had come too late.

"Oh no, no, no." Alex whispered with tears in her eyes and a lump in her throat. "I'm sorry George. I'm too late."

"This is all your fault. Yours and that cursed husband of yours."

George's angry neighbor came out from her house, shouting at Alex. The woman was shaking and sobbing after having discovered the corpse, and her frock still had some of his blood on it from when she tried to get him down. Alex wished to comfort the woman, but her shaking fist and redden face prevented the girl from getting closer. Frightened of what the neighbor would do to her, she wanted to run, but the woman got closer, pinning her against her friend's lifeless body.

"He'd still be alive if he didn't get involved with the likes of you. When will you get out of our town and let us decent folk be?"

"Stop it mum." A small redheaded girl peeked out from behind her mother's dusty rose dress and looked up at Alex. "They didn't do anything wrong. They never have."

"Molly is right Alice. These folks did nothing wrong." A tall man with gray hair and a graying black beard came out from the house and placed both hands on the little girl's shoulders. "We can't keep blaming them for things that are beyond their control, and we can't keep holding Hartwood's past against him. He's a changed man now, even a fool can see that."

"How can you say that Elliot?" Alice whirled around to face her husband. "Have you completely lost your senses?"

"No dear, I've finally come to find them. It's true that at first, I was not keen on them living here, but I've seen the way Hartwood cares for this woman. He is far from the delinquent who used to get in trouble all over town years ago. I've also seen the way she fights to protect everyone she cares about.

"She would not hesitate to leave if she knew she was the actual cause of her friends' suffering. Until now, I've been blind. I've let my fear control me for far too long. I even shunned my neighbors and tried to drive them out of town. I forbid Molly from play with that boy of theirs, but no more. It wasn't her hand, nor Jay's that killed George, it was the hand of evil which seeks to destroy us all."

"They may not have killed him, but they are responsible for the people who did being here. The Militibus left us be until they arrived."

"The Militibus was here all along Alice. They've just been waiting for an excuse to strike, and these poor folks gave it to them."

"Daddy is right mommy. The man in black who killed Mr. George has been living here a long time, I just know it."

"The man in black?" Alex frowned and kneeled to look at the child as Jay, Richard, and Cosmo finally caught up to her. "Did you see this man? Can you tell me what he looked like?"

"Not really. But I can tell you what I saw."

"All right sweetheart, go on."

"Well, I was playing hopscotch outside my house when I heard Mr. George arguing with someone." The girl pointed to the squares on the sidewalk as she came out from behind her mother to look at Alex. "Mr. George was screaming at someone, like he was really mad. He said, 'I know what you really are, you can't fool me any longer.' Then he said, 'I'm going to tell Donahue all about you, and your family.' And then Mr. George told the man he was going to expose him to the entire town and let them decide his fate.

"Then the man said, 'no you won't.' His voice sounded awfully familiar, so that's when I came closer and peeked through the window. Mr. George pointed a finger at the face of a man in a black cloak and said, 'just try to stop me.' That was when the man in black summoned a red dagger. I wanted to run and get daddy, but my feet wouldn't move. I watched as the bad man grabbed Mr. George by the shoulders and stabbed him in the belly. Then he moved behind Mr. George and slash his throat before making the dagger disappear.

"Mr. George was grasping his throat and trying to get to the door, but he collapsed on the floor instead. Then the man in the cloak stepped over him and headed for the door himself. That's when I got real scared he would see me, and hurt me too, so I ducked and hid in the bush there." The girl pointed at one of George's prized purple Goldenglow bushes. "I stayed real quiet and watched the man run out the door in the direction of the bridge. I was still too scared to move and a few minutes later more men came. They dragged Mr. George's body out of the house and strung him up on the wood circle before they followed the bad man. I waited a few minutes longer before going to get mum, and you got here a few minutes later."

"The bridge?" gasped Richard. "Did you mean that bridge love?" Richard pointed behind Alex to the ornate black bridge which spanned the Peaceful Brook River between Fall Harbor and Wellaby. "Is that the one the bad man crossed?"

"Yes Mr. Richard. That one."

"Oh no. Anything but that?"

"What's wrong?" Alex stood to face him. "Do you know what they are up to?"

"Alex, can't you see." Richard was pulling at his dark brown hair. "Tonight, is the big yearly meeting over in Wellaby, everyone will be there. That means they are going after Trip and the congressional which is gathered over at the capitol building as we speak. They are going to kill everyone so they can overthrow East Ashland and make it part of the west."

"Then we have to go stop them."

"You are stopping nothing." Growled Jay. "You are going to go home and stay where it's safe."

"You can't possibly expect me to do that when everything we hold dear is hanging on the line."

"And you can't expect me to allow my pregnant wife to go gallivanting into battle." Jay glared at Alex with his arms crossed across his chest. "I'll go and hold them off for as long as I can. Richard, you take Alex home and make sure Rupert keeps a close eye on her. Then you go bring me as many people as you can find. Anyone who is willing to stand up and fight, you bring them. Got that?"

"Right on mate." Richard took hold of Alexandra's arm and brought her in close. "You can count on me. I'll grab Lawrence and the Doc and have them help me rally the troops."

"No, Jay." Alex scream. "You'll get yourself killed. There is no way you can hold off an army all on your own."

Breaking free from Richard's grasp, Alex ran up and grabbed hold of Jay's waist, pressing her body close to his back, not willing to let him go. With a sigh, he turned and took her by her shoulders, peering into her green, tear-filled eyes that pierced him to his core as they begged him to stay. Placing a soft kiss on her forehead, Jay pulled away and handed Alex back over to Richard.

He knew full well his chances of survival were slim, but if anything was to happen to him, at least her and his kids would be taken care of. Rupert loved her like a daughter, he would be sure to hide their real identity and move them far away from Fall Harbor and the extremists. Jay also knew Richard would step in and care for them as if they were his own, and that would mean his death would not be in vain. Resolved to go fight the Militibus on his own, Jay turned into a black wolf and without stealing a look back at the woman he was leaving behind, he set off for the bridge, heading for the other side of the river.

"No!" Alex screamed as Richard held on tight and pulled her into his embrace. "Let go." She thrashed against her friend, but he held on to her tighter. "Let go of me Richard. I have to go help Jay."

"Come on Alex." Richard hugged her tight as she wept softly in his arms. "Jay is right love. You can't go into battle now. You have to think of your child, it's not safe for either of you."

"I am thinking of my child, and Andy." Alex turned around and hit his chest with her fists, trying to get him to let go as he brought them to sit on the ground. "I'm thinking of how I want my children to have a father and not have to worry about their blood status. If the Militibus wins, none of us will be safe with people knowing as to who we are, and there is no way Jay can stop them on his own."

"Hey, cheer up girl." Elliot kneeled and rubbed Alex's back, trying to help Richard calm her down. "I've known Hartwood since he was a young lad, and he is a lot more capable of taking on a crowd than you think. Why, when he got that murder charge, he was assaulted by thirty men, most a lot bigger than him. And you know what? He took every single one of them on, including killing their leader. The Militibus stands no chance against him, especially when he has something he wants to protect."

"You see," Richard hugged Alex closer, "Elliot is right. Jay is a tough old dog who can hold his own, probably a lot better than you. He'll be fine until I get there with back up, and there is no way he would leave you a widow, it's just not his style."

"Yeah. Especially with you preparing to step in and take his place the second he's gone."

"What? I am intending to do no such thing."

"Don't lie Cadwall, I've seen the way you look at her. You regret ever letting her go."

"I do. But I'd never steal her from Jay, he's my friend. That's why I am going to make sure he stays alive, at least long enough to see his child. Now come on Alex, let's go home. The faster I drop you off, the faster I can get back to help Jay."

"All right. I guess you both have a point." Alex sighed and stopped struggling. "Jay would never leave me or his children alone, and he is a skillful fighter, he'll be fine until help arrives."

"Exactly love." Richard let her go as Cosmo fluttered above him and watched. "There you go, finally talking some sense. Let me take you home to Rupert and Andy. As soon as you're safe, I can go and get an army going to fight these thugs off once and for all."

"All right. But, tell me something first Richard," Alex stood up, dusted off her dress and looked at him while biting her lower lip. "Do you trust me?"

"Of course, with my life. Why? Where is this coming from all of a sudden?"

"Then, please forgive me, Richard."

"For what? What are you going to do? Alex—"

Somnus

Placing a hand over Richard's shoulder, Alex muttered her spell, and he crumpled to the ground by her feet.

"What did you do?" Screamed the woman. "Did you kill him?"

"No, relax, I'd never hurt one of my friends. I just put him to sleep temporarily. He'll come to in a few minutes with no side effects."

"Where are you going to go?" Elliot looked at her while twisting his hat in his hand. "Don't tell me you are still planning to go after Jay in your condition."

"Of course, I am. He might be a good fighter, but it's foolish for anyone to go into battle alone. That's the first rule of war that one learns as a pure-blood."

"Are you just doing this because you love Hartwood, or do you have other reasons for disobeying your husband's wishes and putting your life at risk?"

"A little of both. While I do love Jay, more so than you can ever know, I also have to save Trip and stop a war. If I fail, we will all be doomed to the life I am all too familiar with. And trust me, you don't want this life here, especially not for your daughter."

"Aren't you worried about your baby?" The little girl looked at Alex with bright azure eyes.

"Of course, I am. Not only am I worried about my baby but Andy, and you, and everyone else here as well. If the Militibus wins, life as you know it will be over, and many of the grays will not survive the oppression of the pure-blood cleansing. That's why I must go and fight. I have to make sure East Ashland doesn't fall. I need to ensure everyone here stays safe, and free, like it was always intended."

"Will you be back?"

"I plan on it. It's not my time to die yet." Alex turned her back to the girl. "You just keep an eye on Richard for me until he wakes up, all right?"

"I will, I promise."

"And you," Alex turned to Elliot, "as soon as he is up, you help him get as many people as you can to go stop the Militibus."

"You got it princess. You just be sure to stay safe and bring Jay back here alive."

"Oh, I intend to."

Smiling, Alex watched Elliot nod his head before she shifted down to the ground until she was covered in white fur. Shaking the soft coat on her back, she tilted her head to the sky and let out a fearsome howl which floated through the streets and echoed through the alleyways. With Cosmo grabbing hold of her mane with his teeth, she set off down the street into the direction of the bridge. Pushing her paws harder against the stone, she continued picking up speed to cover more ground. Jay might have had a head start, but as a wolf, she'd hopefully be able to catch up to him before he got himself killed.

CHAPTER 38

The Battle to the Capitol

Approaching the bridge that spanned the wild river separating the two towns, Alex could see the capitol building on the other side. She'd seen it many times before, but tonight the white beam of light shooting up to the stars from the glass pyramid perched at the top of the cream-colored building sent an ominous signal across the murky waters. Alex knew what was going to go down behind the citadel's walls, and she knew what was at stake, not only for her, but for the rest of East Ashland as well. With everything to lose, and nowhere else to run, she pressed on harder, running as fast as her wolf paws would allow, until she reached the black metal behemoth she'd have to cross to get to Wellaby.

When the bridge was built three-centuries ago, it was not done so with pedestrian traffic in mind, and those on foot were required to find another way. Through the center of the bridge, ran the railroad tracks that brought her family to Fall Harbor. To either side of the rails was a paved road meant for cars, leaving little room on either side. If Alex wanted to make it across the river, she'd have to risk running with the cars and on the tracks. She hated the idea of dodging traffic, but, seeing no alternative, she pressed on. Fortunately, with everyone huddled up in their homes due to the Militibus threat the roads were empty, and not a single headlight greeted her as she ran.

In the distance, just on the other side, she could hear the screams of men and sounds of swords clamoring and clashing. By the sounds of the voices ringing out through the darkness, Alex knew Jay was in trouble, and she ran harder despite the lump forming in her side causing her pain. Over halfway across, she finally had to stop and catch her breath as she panted and licked her jowls. Every fiber of her body ached, her throat was parched, and she did her best to still the bile threatening to come out. She wished to have more time to regain some of her stamina, but upon hearing Jay's pained scream, she forgot all about her discomfort and ran as fast as she could to make it across.

Nearing the edge of the bridge, Alex could see Jay fighting off a large group of men armed with swords, daggers, and spears. She couldn't make out the exact number, but she counted at least half a dozen men dressed in black clocks swarming him. They looked like a hoard of slaterbugs attacking a piece of a pie, and she could tell Jay was having a hard time holding them off.

Realizing the darn fool wouldn't have made it much further if she hadn't shown show up, Alex let out a low growl. Transforming back to human form, she crouched down to the ground and resumed the rest of her journey by foot with Cosmo buzzing along beside her. In front of her, she could see Jay taking on three men at one time, with three more gathering behind them to take a swing.

Gladios

Summoning her blue longsword, Alex dashed forward, driving the blade clean through the closest man's back and out his chest. He let out a soft groan as he slumped back on the blade impaling him. Yanking the sword from the corpse, she allowed it to drop to the ground and looked as two more men where rushing up on her. Side stepping to her left, she thrust the tip of her blade into the man dashing at her with a spear. Once his body lay by her feet, she swung around with her sword over her head and brought it down, slashing a cloaked figure trying to assault her from the right.

Having taken care of the three men, Alex looked on to Jay, who now only had two Militibus members to contend with. He was busy fighting off a man who wielded two blue swords and did not see the other one summon a red spear and aim it at his head. As Jay decapitated his attacker a glowing spear tip was rushing for his face, but before he had the chance to react, the man's head rolled off his shoulders, covering Jay's face in a red mist. Blinking his eyes, he looked behind the body and saw his wife recalling her sword. Upon seeing here there, his eyes narrowed, his jaw clenched, and his nostrils flared.

"I thought I told you to go home."

"Why, so you can get yourself killed? Just look at how close you've come." Alex seethed as she stood on her tiptoes to get closer to his face. "If I didn't come when I did, you'd be dead, and our children would have no father."

"Better than Andy being an orphan!" Jay roared. "You have no business going off to fight an army alone."

"First of all, I'm not going in alone, now am I? I'm going in with you, you bloody idiot." Alex shouted. "And second of all, you have just as much, if not less business fighting an army. At least I've had more practice."

"Why are you so stubborn?"

"Because," Alex stood normally and crossed her arms, "only a stubborn woman would put up with your abrasive personality."

Groaning, Jay rolled his eyes and ran his hand through his hair as he looked down on Alexandra's pouting face. He knew she was right, she always was, and he also knew the reason he loved her so much was because she was impossibly stubborn. Like an un-tamed wild horse, she was a sight to behold. No one could break her, despite how hard they tried, yet she allowed herself to be vul-nerable around him, and that made Jay feel special.

Noticing Jay's eyes soften, and a slight smile form on his lips, Alex smirked, knowing full well he had surrendered. She was about to tell him they should get going when she noticed that his black shirt appeared to be wet. Scrutinizing his sleeve closer, she noticed a tear in the fabric of his shoulder and a fresh wound which was slowly seeping blood.

"Jay," she gasped, "you're hurt."

"I'm fine." Jay glanced over at his shoulder with a wince. "It's nothing, just a scratch."

"Oh, for the sake of the gods, stop downplaying everything." Alex frowned and reached over for the cut on his arm, which was a lot deeper than he made it out to be. "At least let me heal you."

"No." Jay pulled away and clutched his arm cringing. "We have no time for that right now. You can heal me after all this is over. Right now, we have to keep moving if we are to make it to the capitol building in time to stop the Militibus."

"What are you talking about? We have plenty of time, it's only a mile away, we will be there in minutes."

"Yeah, under normal circumstances we would be. But tonight, we are also facing a large number of men who have been trained to fight, and they are all waiting for us. Just look over there." Jay pointed to the lawn across from them and Alex could see two dozen men patrolling the perimeter with their weapons out. "There will probably be even more guards once we get closer to the capitol. We'll be lucky if we can make it inside in time to stop them since we'll be fighting our way in the whole time."

"Wait a minute..." Alex glance at the pond separating the park and the steps of the capitol building. "We don't have to fight our way through all of them."

"What do you mean?"

"I have an idea."

"Well, what is it?"

"Tell me love, have you ever changed into anything other than a wolf?"

"I've been a griffon once, why?"

"Good, so you know how to be other things."

"Well yeah, the black wolf did teach me his ways you know. What does this have to do with your plan?"

"Simple, we'll change into komoducks and swim across the basin. No one will suspect a common waterfowl, and the Militibus doesn't have men waiting on the water because they won't be expecting us to go that route since they don't know what we are. Once we are on the other side, we have a straight shot to the capitol."

"They'll have more men waiting for us up front you know."

"I know. But I am an expert archer, and you are great with your sword. I go long and pick off as many as I can from a distance, and you go in close to finish the ones I miss. With us working together, we should be able to get to the steps of the capitol in no time at all, and with me not seeing close combat our baby should be safe."

"I knew there was a reason I married you." Jay looked over at Alex, smiling and shaking his head. "All right, let's go."

"That's the spirit." Alex winked at Jay and began her transformation, with him not far behind her.

The two small black ducks, with shiny azure heads and white bills stood on the edge of the lawn wagging their tails and observing the patrolling guards. The smaller of the ducks, which was Alex looked over at Jay and nodded its head. He let out a quack, and they began to wobble across the grass to the pond. A pair of guards stopped and looked at the creatures smiling before scooping them up and putting them in the water. Cosmo snickered as Alex and Jay exchanged glances and paddled their way to the other side of the pond.

Having made it across, the pair transformed back to their human forms, and crouched behind a bush as they watched armies of men shuffling about. Nodding her head, Alex summoned her bow and aimed three arrows at the men patrolling the road.

Standing up in her spot, she released her fingers and three of men crumpled silently to the ground. Hearing the bodies drop, three more guards ran up from the tree line to see what happen. Summoning his greatsword, Jay leaped out from his hiding spot and dispatched them with ease as Alex covered him from behind.

They pulled off the same routine three more times as they crept up to the steps of the cream-colored behemoth which rose before them. As Alexandra looked up to take in what she saw, her jaw dropped at never having witnessed anything as spectacular. The square, marble structure towered over them, topped by a sloping roof with a glass pyramid at its top. A beam of light shone from the glass to signify hope for all the citizen of Alteria still living under pure-blood oppression. At the base of the roof, on every corner of the building, was perched a stone dragon with spread wings spewing out fire to the sky.

Between the two floors, sixteen-foot spiral columns rose from the balcony to the roof, making their way around the structure. At the center of the balcony, facing out to the pond, was a set of great, iron doors trimmed in studs of gold. To each side of the doorframe was a mural cast out of gold and molded by a skilled craftsman. The one on the left depicted the battle between the Worm and the Amphiptere before the universe was formed, while the one on the right showed East Ashland's battle for independence. Above the doors was a glass window with a rising sun made of gold embedded in the glass diamond panels. On a perch at the top of the door was a gold statue of a naked woman with spread arms and dragon-like wings standing before the rising sun, welcoming the coming of the new dawn.

Below, on the main floor was an iron door, with great bronze torches on either side. A blue and a red flame glowed in each lantern to symbolize the union of their people despite their blood status. On the top landing of the steps were two rectangular rooms protruding from the main structure, and from what Jay and Richard told her, Alex knew these were the personal quarters of Tripp Donahue. In front of each chamber, on pedestals encasing the second set of stairs were a pair of marble griffons with their left paws raised in the air. Their beaks were open, their wings spread, and their tail raised in the air to guard the capitol from external threats.

Looking about at the two set of steps, with guards patrolling each landing, Alex thought the griffons didn't do such a good job that night. Turning to Jay she watched him give her a nod of his head and she summoned her bow. Kneeling on the ground by the steps, concealed by shadows, Alex let her arrows go, killing the first set of guards. Shouting, the men at the top of the landing came down upon them, with more running up from the other sides of the building.

Standing back to back, Alex and Jay summoned their swords, fending off their attackers until the only thing left was a heap of corpses by their feet and a waterfall of blood running down the stone stairs. Exhausted from battle, the pair quickly caught their breath before scaling the steps to the top. Standing before the iron doors, Alex admire the inscription etched in the floor: Faith is the eternal beacon of light which grants us strength. Together we will conquer all.

"Words to live by I guess." Alex mumbled.

"They sure are. Now, let's go inside. Something tells we will have to fight our way up to the second floor as well."

Pushing open the iron gates studded with gold, Alex and Jay wound up inside a vast, silent, marble chamber. The white walls were divided by tall, black columns rising to the ceiling with an iron brazier before each one. Murals on the wall depicted different gods and their purpose in the universe as described in the stories once told by their people. Above, pendulum lamps swung from the honeycombed ceiling, illuminating the floor below.

Like the walls, the floor was made from white marble, aside from the black strip of stone running down the center, leading the wondering eye to the stairs. On either side of the steps was a pedestal with a black marble statue of a naked woman on top. The women, with spread wings greeted the visitors to the capitol with outstretched arms. They looked similar, almost like twins, except one had angel wings, and the other had the dragon wings, both spread out in all their glory.

In front of the stairs, at the center of the room, was a large marble alter with a pair of Wellaby guards laid out of the smooth surface. The blood from their wounds dripped steadily from the top, pooling on the floor below and echoing through the silent chamber with every plop. Both Alex and Jay glanced around the room and thought it was oddly empty. Surely the Militibus would have men posted inside, and yet, the eerie silence was telling them otherwise.

Alex could hear her heart thumping inside her chest, and the heavy breathing coming from Jay as she turned to Cosmo who had his little snout raised in the air. He might not have been able to see the cloaks stirring behind the doorways, but he could smell their putrid aroma, which was exactly what he told his friends. Clenching her fists, Alex felt the flames surround her body once more, like they did back in her dream when she met the woman who encouraged her to embrace the darkness. And this time, she did not fight them, she allowed them to engulf her. As she opened her eyes, which were now glowing like lanterns, she glanced around the room and saw the aura of men hiding behind the walls.

The earth beneath her feet started to shake, causing walls to crack and pendulums to sway as cloaked men ran out from their hiding spots like insects. There was at least fifty of them, gathered around them with their weapons drawn. Smirking as she glanced at them approaching, Alex took in a deep breath. Flinging her arms behind her, she floated up into the air, rising high above the men's heads. Opening her hands, she flung her head back, allowing the flames to come up from the floor and swallow the Militibus members whole.

With the men wriggling on the floor like earthworms, Alexandra pulled the fire back inside her soul and dropped back down to the ground. With the threat eliminated, her eyes returned to normal, and she turned to look at Jay who had his chin cupped in his hand as he stared at her with an open mouth and his eyebrow raised.

"What?"

"Nothing darling." Jay snorted with a smile. "You just keep surprising me, that's all."

"Keeps thing interesting, don't it?"

"Sure does. But," Jay grabbed hold of her hand, "let's go end this now, that way you can surprise me later... in bed."

Not paying attention to the rouge spreading across Alexandra's cheeks, Jay pulled her along behind him as he headed up the stairs. Rounding the corner, he paused to admire the quote by the first grand commander before heading up the marble steps to the top alcove where two black columns framed another iron door. The bronzed gate was encased in an ornate ebony frame, decorated in a motif of gold suns, stars, and moons. To each side of the column, were carvings in gold of a phoenix and a dragon engaged in a permanent, circular dance.

Above the door, standing in front of another diamond pane window was the same gold woman. She was still naked, with her dragon wings spread, her arms out, and her head tilted to the sky. Up close, one could see that she had a set of spiraling horn coming out from above her temples, and a tail wrapping around her legs. Standing beside Jay, admired the figurine, Alex suddenly felt her husband's body go rigid and turned to see what had caused him to tense up. Before them, sitting slumped over in his ceremonial marble chair was the grand commanders first knight, looking up at them through his glazed over eyes as his throat oozed fresh blood. Fearing it was too late, Alex stayed her breath and pushed through the doors into the ceremonial chamber, interrupting the ritual that was about to take place inside.

CHAPTER 39

The Militibus

Uncloaked

Behind the door lay a vast, green chamber made of marble, with empty benches to each side, and three chairs for Tripp and his two advisors at the front. Tripp's chair stood inside an alcove draped with an eggplant curtain made from crushed velvet which bore the Donahue family crest at the center in gold embroidery. In front of the three commanding chairs, at the heart of the room stood a green marble alter with a man sprawled out across it, his hands tied to the corners.

Tripp Donahue was a hefty man in his late fifties with a healthy tan and wispy white hair draped over his forehead. He did not appear to be severely injured, and he struggled against the ropes, staining them red as he thrashed. To his side stood a much older man, one in his late sixties if Alex was to hazard a guess, dressed in a black suit similar to the one worn by Donahue. He had the hood of his cape flung back and his deep blue eyes glared at his victim with a red dagger poised above his white head of hair. Having heard the door fling open, the man froze and glanced over at Jay and Alex, standing arm in arm, glaring at him.

"Oh no you don't." Jay shouted while rushing the man to the ground. "Not on my watch."

"Jay?" The man looked up in bewilderment, and the expression on his face softened. "Is... is that really you my boy?"

"Yeah, pops, it's me." Jay curled up his lip in disgust at having to see his father again. "And I have been looking forward to paying you back for what you did to my mother for a long, long time."

"Pops?"

"Roink, oink?"

Alex and Cosmo exchanged confused glanced as they observed Jay sitting on top of the man, he claimed was his father. The stranger was raising his hands over his face as Jay kneeled above him. Flaring his nostrils, he placed one hand on the man's shoulder and with a reddening face raised the other one above his head.

Gladium

"Jay, please, you don't understand..."

"No father, it's you who doesn't understand. You have no idea what I've been through because of what I am, because of my blood status. You have no idea of how much I've struggled, and what I have lost. And now, that I finally have the tides of luck turning in my favor, you show up, and try to take it away from me again." Raising his dagger over his head, Jay got ready to cut his father down. "Well guess what pops, I won't let that happen. I won't let you take it all away from me. I'll kill you so you can't ruin my life any more than you already have, and I'll end the Militibus once and for all."

"Tisk, tisk. Such anger." A woman's voice came from behind Jay and he felt a sharp object poke into his back. "I wouldn't do it that I were you boy."

Turning around, Jay spotted a short woman in a black and gold caftan, holding on to his shoulder and jabbing a red dagger into his side. Between her disheveled short blonde hair, her wide-open blue eyes, and the wicked smile on her thin lips, she had the appearance of a mad woman who had just escaped from an asylum. Glaring up at Jay, who towered over with a frown on his face, she continued to poke her weapon into his side causing the blood to drip down his shirt and down her hand.

"Why, if it isn't Hailey Rosenburg, the wicked witch of the west." Jay snorted and pressed his large palm into her frail shoulder. "And what's stopping me from killing you first, you decrepit old bag of bones?"

"I am."

Caleb Cox's voice rang from behind a velvet curtain as he exited his hiding spot and wrapped his arms around Alexandra's waist, pulling her body against his. Looking over at the young woman with a smirk, he dug his fingers into her side and pressed a red dagger against her throat.

"Well, me and your weakness for your beautiful young wife, who I know means the world to you. It be a darn shame if I was to slit her pretty little throat, don't you think?"

"Cox?" Jay frowned as he felt his knees wobble. "Why are you doing this? I thought you liked Alex, why would you want to hurt her?"

"Oh, you poor, misguided fool, you. You still haven't figured it out, have you?" Cox chuckled and presses the dagger deeper into Alex's neck, causing a small steam of warm blood to trickle down her skin. "Haven't you questioned my striking resemblance to you? Haven't you wondered why I have taken such an interest in your life, and your family, or why I've been trying to steal your wife right out from under your nose?"

"No..." Jay swallowed hard as his eyes widened, "it can't be."

"Oh, but it is, Jay, it is. As you have already guessed, Cox isn't my real name, it's Rosenburg. As in your younger half-brother, barkeep. I only took on the Cox persona so I could fool that moron on the alter into letting me run Fall Harbor."

"But why?" Jay let go of Hailey and frowned. "Why would you do all this?"

"Can't you see brother, it's because of you. It's always been about you. Ever since I found out about your putrid existence, I have wanted nothing else but to destroy you. I was heartbroken when I found out of my father's affair with some gray whore. But I was even more livid when I learned his infidelity resulted in a child. I couldn't believe my ears when I heard the servants discussing how that disgusting woman kept her illegitimate spawn, or how much father cared about him. Imagine me learning, that I, a pure-blood with a crown had a half-blood for a brother. Why I couldn't stomach it. So, as I grew up, I decided to do the only sensible thing a man in my position could do. I decided to hunt you down and kill you like the dog you are.

"It was no simple task by any means. Took me years of questioning the filthy peasants who knew my father's dirty secrets before I learned of your name and last known location. Then, I spent months learning all about your escapades, your murder charges, and how a certain young doctor adopted you as his own son. Finally, I knew where to find you. Unfortunately, by the time I tracked you down to Fall Harbor, you were gone, living with your little bastard child over in Rexham. But I knew it would not be long until you had to come crawling back here. After all, you can run all you want, but you can't hide from your past, and you definitely can't hide from what you really are.

"With that knowledge in mind, I waited, and I hatched a plan on how I would take you down. I took on a new name, disguised myself as a white mage, and convinced that idiot Donahue to install me as mayor of Fall Harbor. As you can imagine, with my good looks and charismatic nature, none of those fools dared contest me. And while those disgusting peasants worshiped the ground I walked on, I worked silently to destroy their lives and purge Alteria of their presence. For two whole years I've waited in silence for you, plotting, and bidding my time. I was starting to lose hope I'd ever get to exact my revenge on you, thought that perhaps you were already dead. But then, by some stroke of luck, I finally got word that a half-blood had arrived in Clear Springs from Vega of all places.

"I knew it was you, it had to be, it couldn't be anyone else. And now, imagine my shock when I also learned that you took on a pure-blood as a wife. And not just any pure-blood, but the princess of Manevia herself. I couldn't believe my ears that a woman like her chose to end up with you. And then, I saw her." Caleb closed his eyes and nuzzled his face into Alexandra's hair, inhaling her sweet aroma, and causing her to wince. "And let me tell you something brother.

"Boy, oh boy do the rumors of her beauty not do her justice. Even that simpleton I took under my wing couldn't prepare me for what I saw that night we first met." Cox trailed his face down Alexandra's skin and licked her chin as she recoiled from his touch. "I still can't for the life of me fathom how someone like her would settle for the likes of you. Not only were you a single-father and a peasant when she met you, but you were also a disgusting half-blood. The mare thought of her sleeping next to you, pressing her delicate body against yours, copulating with you, it all made me physically ill. I knew I had to put a stop to it right away. That was when I took on the role of the Militibus leader like my mother always wanted and started to terrorize that pathetic little town.

"I was hoping the threat of the Militibus would be enough to tear the two of you apart. I was hoping you'd divorce her for her safety, or that she would wake up and realize you are not worth the trouble, and that she made a terrible mistake by being with you. I thought that once she saw you for what you really are, she would come running into my arms, and that I could have her. But that's not what happened at all. Instead, this foolish girl stuck even closer to you, going as far as defending you at the cost of her own reputation. I couldn't believe she still loved you after everything she'd seen and heard about you. That's when I knew I had to destroy East Ashland and put an end to your union once and for all."

"You are insane." Jay shouted, trying to lunge at Caleb, but a blade sticking its way deeper into his side stopped him. "You did all this to punish me for something our father did? And now you are trying to punish Alex, and for what? For associating with me?"

"Oh, no dear brother. I am punishing you for existing. Abominations like you and your children should be wiped off the face of Alteria. As for the lovely Mrs. Hartwood," Cox grabbed hold of her neck and cut off her airways, "well, she needs to be reminded of who she is and what her duty is in this world."

"Don't you dare hurt her!"

"Why not?" Grabbing hold of Alexandra's waist, Cox yanked her closer against him, as the dagger cut deeper into the skin of her neck. "She made her bed when she decided to lie with you brother, now she can pay the price for her indiscretion."

"Let go of me you lunatic." Alex struggled against Caleb's grip, but her just pressed her tighter against him as the blood from her wound stained her gown. "Jay has as much right to be here as you do. You can't go around killing people simply because you don't like their blood status."

"Oh, but I can my dear. And I will. And after I kill the both of you, I'll go collect my reward that your dear father has promised."

"Son please." Bramwell Rosenburg put his arms up in front of his face as he stepped closer to Caleb. "You don't have to do this."

"Don't I, father?"

"Of course you don't. Stop letting your hate consume you. Jay is no threat to you or the crown, he never was. You are my only legitimate heir, you know that. Don't listen to your mother, she never was able to forgive me for what I did, and I don't blame her. But you, you don't need to be like her, you can still let go. Forget about East Ashland, let them lead their province like they always have. Let's just go home and take care of our own people. Leave your brother and his wife be. There is nothing they can do to hurt us."

"Really now? Is that what you really think, father? Well, let me tell you something. While it's true your bastard son here has no claim to the crown, did you know that the lovely princess here is carrying your grandchild?" Placing a hand over Alex's neck, Caleb trailed his dagger down to her stomach, jabbing it in just above the pubic bone and causing a small crimson flower to bloom on her dress. "That's right father, your favorite son has sown his seeds again, and this time, in a pure-blood woman of all places. So, do forgive me pops but, I think I will eliminate my brother and his family despite your objections. And I shall start with this little monstrosity growing inside her."

"Let her go!" Jay dashed for Alex but was stopped by Hailey crossing her sword in front of his chest, pushing him back into an armed guard while Bramwell looked on in bewilderment. Gritting his teeth, Jay clenched his fists and scowled at his brother even as a dagger stuck itself into his ribs. "Please, just let Alex go Caleb. Forget she even exists, and you can kill me, I won't put up a fight, I promise."

"Sorry brother, but that's not how this is going to work. As I said, I simply cannot allow for more of your kind to exist. And the child of a half-blood and pure-blood, well," Caleb smirked as his eyes shone with delight at seeing Jay's distraught face, "it's an abomination which has been unheard of for centuries. Gods only know what such a child could do to the delicate fabric of our society, and I for one, don't wish to find out. So, I shall do Alteria a favor by doing what our father was too weak to do. I'll cut your filthy little spawn right out of her and end her life, just like I did to that red headed vixen."

"Fiona..." Alex whispered "... so it was you who killed her. You were her secret lover, and that was your child you burned up in the fireplace. And all because you couldn't come to terms with the fact that she was pregnant with your son."

"That wasn't my son, it was a disease which needed to be stopped before it became a stain on everything I believe. It was a freak of nature which shouldn't have even existed, so don't you dare refer to that thing as anything worthy of holding my title, you dirty wench." Caleb jabbed the dagger deeper into Alex causing her to squeal as blood started to run down her skirt. "Did you know your whore friend told me she was sterile before she dropped that bombshell on me? I pretended to be happy, but I knew that thing needed to be disposed of, just as my father should have disposed of Jay when he had the chance. After all, gray whores are not meant to carry the children of the pure-bloods."

"You idiot," Alex chuckled, "you had no idea, did you?"

"Had an idea of what? What was I supposed to know?" Caleb took a step back. "Why... why are you laughing, you stupid whore? You should be reeling in fear at the thought of me cutting you open like I did your friend."

"Of course you didn't know, why would you?" Alex continued to chuckle. "I should have known she wouldn't tell you. She had no reason to. She thought you loved her for who she was, so she didn't tell you because she probably thought it would not matter. Too bad she was wrong, or she might still be alive."

"Tell me what?" Cox screeched. "What do you know that I don't, wench?"

"You poor, hateful fool, you." Alex snorted. "Fiona was a pure-blood black mage, just like you. In your narrow-minded igno-rance, and your desperate attempt to not be anything like your father, you killed a legitimate heir."

"No, that's impossible."

"Oh, but it is Caleb, it is possible." Alex continued to laugh. "Fiona wasn't her real name, she was born as Aisling Flinn in

Clear Springs. She was the only daughter a prominent government official who you have probably heard of judging by the sound of your teeth grinding. When she escaped his abuse with Lawrence, she ditched her family name and kept her blood status a secret."

"No. You're lying you filthy trollop. What you say can't possibly be true. Nolan Flinn's children were kidnapped by his wife. He never stopped looking for them until the day he died."

"Oh, is that what he said to cover up the fact that he murdered his wife after she tried to run away from him? Or maybe he was covering up the fact that he raped his daughter repeatedly and mercilessly beat his infant son. Did he also mention how he impregnated Fiona, and that she ran away from him to get an abortion because she couldn't stomach the thought of having her father's child? I'm willing to bet he omitted all of this when talking to the authorities after he killed Fiona's girlfriend when she refused to let him see Lawrence. It still amazes me how some of you pure-bloods seem to be cut from the same cloth. Far too many of you are just vile and ignorant, and there is no need for it."

"Quit telling me lies." Cox howled at the top of his lungs. "I am done listening to you! I won't allow you to defile an exemplary man like Nolan. Now, I'm going to shut you up the same way I did your dear friend."

Alex didn't reply, she simply shook her head in dismay, not knowing what else she could say or do next. She thought she would be able to reason with him, convince him to see the error of his ways, but Cox didn't seem to care about his son, or anyone else for that matter. Revenge had consumed him whole and there was nothing left inside him to salvage. Thinking she could strike down Hailey and give Jay a fighting chance if she could only break free, she tried to wiggle away, but Caleb had too tight a grip on her and she could not move. Letting out a deep sigh, Alex was starting to feel hopeless when she caught a glimpse of something from the corner of her eye.

Across from her, Alex spotted movement from behind the velvet curtains hanging above the commander's chair and looked up to see what it was. There, on the ledge behind the three thrones, were Richard and Lawrence, crouching down next to one another. The two men had quietly crawled in through the ornate, stained glass window behind them when Cox was busy giving his speech and were now kneeling behind the eggplant panel. Giving Alex a wink, Richard placed a finger on his lips, signaling for her to keep quiet. Glancing to his side, she saw that Lawrence was holding a red bow, with an arrow pointed straight at Cox. Tilting his head to the side a few times, Lawrence motioned for her to get out of the way if she could and she nodded her head, silently telling him she could.

"You killed your own son you bastard, now you will pay for your sins."

Gladios

Alex summoned her sword while simultaneously whacking Caleb in the crotch with the back of her hand. Doubling over from the sharp pain, Cox released his firm grip on her and she was able to twist away without a problem. With her safely away from his grasp, Lawrence got a clear shot he had been waiting for and he released a red arrow which found its mark, piercing the mayor's left shoulder. Watching him fall to the ground screaming, Alex made a dashed straight for Hailey, knocking the sword out from her hands. Take off guard, the mad woman stumbled over her caftan and fell on her back as the young woman placed the tip of her sword against her neck.

"Don't move." Hissed Alex.

Taking the opportunity the commotion presented him, Jay summoned his sword and whirled around to knock the head of the guard behind him. Outside the walls, he could hear the citizens of Fall Harbor storming the citadel. Screams and sounds of swords clashing told him that the sheer numbers of people willing to fight for their freedom were overwhelming the few members the Militibus had left. With all the people of Fall Harbor on their side, he knew the remaining capitol guard would able to start reclaiming the building.

"Now for you." Jay roared as he dashed for his father, pressing the blade of his sword against the old man's throat. "I'm going to get rid of you once and for all."

"Please, son, it's not like this. I never wanted for anything bad to happen to your mother or to you. None of this was my idea. I loved your mother, and you, you have to believe me. I mourned for her when I learned she had died, and the only reason I asked her to get rid of you was because I knew of what Hailey would do to you if she found out."

"That's a lie." Jay raise his sword, getting ready to cut his father's head of. "You just didn't want me to be born, admit it."

"Stop it Jay." Alex shouted from her spot. "This isn't like you. The man I love wouldn't kill someone in cold blood, and he wouldn't take revenge on his father, no matter how much he deserved it."

"My wife's right pops." Jay, unclenched his hand, making his red blade disappear. "The old me would have cut your head off without question. But I'm a changed man now, and I have no reason to kill you. Whether or not you're telling the truth, I don't really care. All I know is that you're better off rotting in a Wellaby prison, where you will have a long time to repent for the pain you have cause my mother, and myself."

Placing his father's hands behind his back, Jay restrained the man and watched his friends slide down the velvet curtains. Richard summoned a small, white stiletto knife and ran to the alter to release Tripp Donahue from his restraints. On the floor, Caleb stood up from his spot while clutching his injured shoulder. Scowling at the woman who brought him so much misery, he summoned a shortsword and got ready to cut her down and save his mother.

Taking a few steps towards Alex with his arm raised, he was getting ready to take a swing when a red cutlass sliding across his wrist stopped him in his tracks. Releasing his blade, he clutched his bleeding arm as he looked on horrified at the man next to him. Smirking, Lawrence jabbed the hilt of his weapon into Caleb's stomach, causing him to collapse on his knees. Placing his boot on the mayor's chest, he pushed him to the ground and glared down at the man he once looked up to while he restrained him with his foot.

"That arrow was for what you did to me sister, you ignorant prick. I can't believe we trusted you, you vile pile of dung you. Oh, and this," Lawrence spit in Caleb's face as he stomped on his throat, "is for what you were about to do to me friends. Prison is too good a place for you, but I'll be content knowing that it gives you time to think about your punishment in the void."

"Guards." Tripp shouted for his man to assist him as he ran up the group with Richard close on his heels. "Arrest these people and throw them in jail for treason. Tomorrow we shall start our liberation of the west, now that their leaders have been de-throned. Oh and," he turned to regard Alex and Jay with a nod, "make sure these two stay put. I want to have a talk with them once I check on my wife and the rest of my leaders."

Frozen in fear by his words, Alex stood still and glanced up at Jay while the guards gathered the Rosenburg family and dragged them away to the holding cells below the capitol. Walking over to her, Jay placed his hands around her back, and she allowed her body to crumple into his arms. On the other side of the room, they observed Tripp open the door hidden behind a velvet panel and release everyone who managed to get inside while the building was being stormed. Paying no attention to the stream of people filtering into the room, Jay looked down at his wife and place a soft kiss on the top of her head.

"Thank you." He whispered as he pressed her closer.

"For what?"

"For seeing the good in me and reminding me that it was there. If it wasn't for you, I might have done something I would later regret. You always keep my temper in check, and for that, I'm grateful."

"Oh Jay, you really don't need me to remind you of the kind of man you really are."

"Groink... Roink."

"He's right, you know. I am a pig head scoundrel, and I do need you to keep me sane."

Giggling, Alex looked up at Jay before the smile faded off her face. She watched as the room erupted in whispers and cheers and remembered what Tripp said before he went to release the other mayors. Once more, fear gripped her heart as she did not know what the grand commander wanted to talk to them about, and she was too scared to ask. Turning her gaze to the door, she spotted Tripp talking to a woman with long golden hair, wearing a white gown. The woman turned to glance at the two of them with a smile, and Alex felt herself shudder in Jay's arms as she approached them.

CHAPTER 40

Forward to a New Dawn

Standing in the middle of the room, Alex trembled as she continued to wonder what the commander needed to talk with them about. But she would not have to wonder long as the man in the black suit and the woman in white approached the two of them smiling. Stopping in front of Jay and Alex, the commander studied each of them closely before turning to the woman beside him with a smirk. The lady gave him a playful wink, and he turned once more to regard the couple in front of him.

"So..." Tripp put his hands behind his back grinning. "You must be the pure-blood princess and the half-blood knight I keep hearing so much about."

Frowning, Jay put an arm across Alex's chest and pushed her behind his back. As he thrust out his chest and clenched his fist, he caused the old commander to laugh. Bewildered by the man's response Jay's eyes darted around the room, looking for the nearest exit.

"Relax son." Donahue waved his hands. "I have nothing against your union. In fact, I think East Ashland owes you a big thanks for saving us and stopping the Militibus."

"Yes." The woman in the white gown bowed to the two of them. "Not to mention your union give us hope for our son's future."

"You..." Alex stepped out from behind Jay, "you have a son together?"

"Yes, Magdalene and I do have a son, Christopher. But as you can imagine with him being of mixed bloodlines, we have to keep his existence a secret."

"That's right, most people don't even know we have a child. They assume Christopher is the son of one of our advisors and a pure-blood. I can't imagine what the people would say if they learned he is half black mage and half white. We were not even sure what would happen to him once he grew up. But we always had hope that he wouldn't have to keep his blood status hidden long. And then, you came along, and we saw an opportunity to make it happen, to make everyone see that being of mixed blood was no big deal."

"I see." Jay relaxed and stepped closer to his wife's side. "I had no idea that's why you approved of our marriage, but I guess it all makes sense now. Sorry for being defensive just now. I guess society puts you on edge like that, especially when you're a half-blood like me."

"No need to apologize son, I understand perfectly well what you have been through." Tripp patted Jay's back. "And please, don't hesitate to ask me for anything, it's the least I can do. Why I'll give you half the land in East Ashland if that is what you wish for."

"We don't need land Sir. Donahue, we are happy with what we've got. Although," Alex spoke meekly, "there is something I do wish to ask. I have something I've been wondering about since we got to this building, and I was hoping you'd be able to tell me."

"What is it my dear? Ask me anything you like."

"I... I just want to know what's with the statues of the naked woman that I keep seeing all over this place."

"Oh," Tripp looked at her blinking his eyes, "you've never heard the story of the winged goddess?"

"No," Alex shook her head, "in Manevia, legends of old were forbidden."

"Oh well, listen here my dear, I'll be more than happy to teach you. Centuries ago, when our world was on the brink of destruction, a young lad found himself on the wrong side of the oppressor's sword. Just as the blade was about to cut the child down, a woman swooped in and stayed the man's hand, and reduced him to ash. She was a beautiful young woman not of our world, and she had shadows of dragon wings on her back blocking out the sun. The woman told the boy to get out of there and keep his head down if he wished to live. He took this opportunity to run home to safety where he told his friends what had happened to him. He thought that was the end of it, but later that night, he was visited by the God of Time himself.

"The ancient god told the lad that the woman he met was a sleeping goddess and that she will come to rescue this world in the future and set our people free. He said she was the mother of dawn, and that her blood will save the universe from destruction. The boy listened to what the Amphiptere had to tell him and re-layed it to anyone who would listen. As he grew up, he gained more power and became the first leader of the resistance. At twenty-one he went on to slay the Militibus and became the first grand commander of East Ashland. He is the one who built this building, and he was sure to include the winged goddess every-where, standing before the rising sun. He said this was so that every leader after him would be reminded of a new dawn that was approaching, and to always have faith. So, she is here to show us that we should never lose hope, and we should never stop fighting for our freedom."

"Oh my, I had no idea. But it is such an incredible story though, and a great reminder as well."

"It is, isn't it? It's always been my favorite, and I have insured the goddess always looks her best because of it." Magdalene ap-proached Alex and lifted her face to look the young woman in the eyes. "But enough of that. Tell me something darling, did your father raise you as a proper princess?"

"Yes," Alex trailed her eyes down as her cheeks turned bright pink, "I'm afraid he did."

"So then, as a former princess I bet you have a lot of political experience, coupled with war strategies, and years of combat training, don't you?"

"Yes, I'm an exceptional marksman and I'm a skilled fighter with my sword as well. But... what does my upbringing have to do with anything?"

"Oh, that is not my place to tell you dear. But I am sure my husband will be more than happy to discuss my idea with you. Won't you Tripp?"

"Yes, absolutely Mag. Now come on kids, follow me." Tripp positioned himself between the pair and put his hands on their shoulders. "Seems as if the three of us have a lot to discuss, so let us do so somewhere more private."

"Can Lawrence and I come too?" Richard spoke up from where he stopped to observe the conversation. "You know, since we helped too."

"Of course, lads," Tripped chucked, "of course, follow me."

With his hands still on the pair's shoulders, Tripp strolled to the stained-glass door framed by the eggplant curtains. The guards to each side, nodded their heads in unison as the commander approached. Stepping in, they opened the doors so that their leader could escort his guests onto the balcony overlooking the city.

As the door shut behind them, the friends could see fires raging below them on the capitol lawn. Gray smoke filled the horizon and blanketed the sky, snuffing out the stars above them. Paying no attention to the chaos of the ground, Tripp approached the balcony with the small group and a fat pigrie in tow. Letting Jay and Alex go, Donahue silently strolled to the railing, and leaned over to look at the battle which still raged on outside. Taking in a deep breath, he heaved out a sigh as he glanced one last time at the bodies littering his steps and turned his attention back to the Alexandra.

"It seems my dear that Cox's betrayal and subsequent trip to the dungeon has left me with an untimely mayoral position opening in Fall Harbor. Personally, I was not sure what I was going to do on such short notice, but Mag suggested I offer the position to you Mrs. Hartwood." Tripp looked at the young woman's face and smiled. "I don't suppose you'd be willing to take me up on that offer and help an old man out?"

"What, me?" Alex frowned. "I couldn't possibly take on such an important role. I don't think I'm qualified."

"Sure you are Alex." Richard put his hand around his friend. "You were born for this role. Why, there is not a mayor in East Ashland who is as qualified as you. Not to mention, you'd get to work with me every day. If you wish to retain my services, that is."

"He's right lass. Plus, I'm still the mayoral chauffeur, and if I'm going to cart someone around town, it might as well be someone I know I can trust."

"No way." Jay scoffed. "My wife's pregnant. You can't expect a woman in her condition to be a mayor at a time when you decide to go liberate the West. A battlefield is no place for a pregnant woman."

"Don't you worry son. The mayors will not be going into battle, if there even is one. I need them to stay in their towns and keep the morale of our people up while my army takes care of the rest. I assure you, your wife will be safe, and," Tripp shot Jay a huge smirk, "I'm sure if anything does happen on our soil, you will be more than capable of protecting her."

"But, the people of Fall Harbor hate us." Alex shook her head as she glanced at the Grand Commander. "They'll never accept me as their mayor. They'll be contesting my position on the first day."

"No, they won't Alex. Just look around you. Look at how many men came to your aid when you needed them. Almost every single person Lawrence and I asked was willing to pick up arms and come fight with you. And once they learn of what Cox has done to their town, and what you did to stop him, why, they'll welcome you with open arms."

"What about those who didn't come? And what about people like Eliza, and Agatha?"

"All right, so maybe a few will contest you, but there won't be enough to unseat you. And, with some time, they too will get over their prejudice towards you. At least I hope."

"Yeah, and if they don't," Lawrence cracked his knuckles, "I'll be sure to put 'em in their place."

"Oink, Oink!"

"All right, all right. You talked me into it." Alex looked at her friends, and at Jay. "And I guess as long as I have all of you there beside me, I'll do all right."

"Does this mean I have a new mayor to announce this morning?"

"You sure do Mr. Donahue. After all, someone needs to make sure our kids have a safe place to live, and that blood status won't determine one's place in society. And who better than me I guess."

"Excellent. I'll go with you to Fall Harbor and announce your position to the town once dawn finally breaks."

"You sure you're up for this sweetheart?"

"If I wasn't, I wouldn't have married you."

A soft smile spread on Jay's face and he brought Alex in for a tight hug, pressing her close and kissing her forehead. Standing on the balcony they continued to embrace as they looked over the smoke-filled sky and the lights of Fall Harbor twinkling on the horizon. The commotion had finally died down. It seems the battle was over and even Lawrence strolled over to steal a glance at the changed landscape. Looking down at the crowd gathering below, he let out a whistle, and looked over at his friends who were still entangled in each other's arms.

"I'm glad everything worked out for you guys. You two sure did a hell of a job." Lawrence slipped his hand in his pockets and stole another glance at the crowd of onlookers swarming the stairs. "I only see one problem with this celebration?"

"Oh yeah," Jay scoffed, "what's that? No liquor to wet your pallet?"

"Ah, if only it was that."

Lawrence approached the couple and put his hands on their shoulders to guided them closer to the railing. Following the finger pointing at the crowd down below caused Alexandra's heart to stop for a moment. There, standing at the front were reporters, with flashing cameras taking pictures of the two of them. Knowing the gravity of the situation had finally hit her, Lawrence took a step back, and gave her a pat on the back. Nodding his head as the sky continued to light up with the popping of bulbs he turned and looked at Jay.

"Yeah... news of your wife's new job, and her marriage to a half-blood will soon spread all over Alteria. I can't help but think that her family won't remain oblivious as to what she has been up to for much longer. And once they learn where you two are, well..."

"Crap." Jay muttered. "How many of them do you think we can stop?"

"Not enough I'm afraid." Tripp snapped his finger, signaling for his guards to run downstairs and put an end to the news crews. "But fear not, all of East Ashland will be ready to back you up when the time comes. Manevia will stand no chance against all our armies combined."

"I sure hope you're right old man. I sure hope you're right."

With his arms firmly around Alexandra's shoulder, Jay brought her in close as they watched the reporters scatter the second the guards rushed out to grab their cameras. They knew there was nothing they could do to keep the news of the two of them from getting out, and they wondered how long it would take for Lord Hamilton to come storming their shores. Huddled together with their friends on the balcony of the capitol building, they watched the sun crest over the murky waters of the river as they looked on to an uncertain future together.

If you enjoyed this book, please take a few moments to write a review of it on the site of your choice.

Thank you

ABOUT THE AUTHOR

A.R Kingston is an indie fantasy author with a small independent press. Her book Dark World: Genesis has earned praise from Self-Publishing reviews who gave it four stars. She enjoys blending the traditional fantasy genre she grew up reading with modern literature the readers can easily relate to.

Kingston holds a bachelor's degree in psychology and is passionate about helping people. When she is not working on her books, you can find her reading a book, playing video games, or enjoying a hot cup of tea.

She lives in Colorado Springs with her family, which includes two potbelly pigs who she considers her second children.